AF431687

LONG LIVE THE *Rebel*

Long Live the Rebel

By E.L. Irwin

All rights reserved. This is a work of fiction. Names, places, characters, and events are fictitious in every regard. Any similarities to actual places, events, or persons, living or dead, are purely coincidental. Any trademarks, service marks, product names, or named features are assumed to be the property of their respective owner(s), and are used for reference only. Endorsement is not implied should any of the terms be used. Except for review purposes, the reproduction of this book in whole or in part, electronically, or mechanically, shall be constituted as a copyright infringement.

Copyright © 2026 E.L. Irwin

ISBN: 979-8-9911671-7-8

Cover Design by Jena Brignola

For everyone who bravely stands in the gap for our safety.
For everyone who wears a uniform or pins on a badge.
Wade, we love you and are so thankful for you.
For everyone who thought they'd never measure up or be enough.
This ones for you.

Greater love hath no man than this,
that a man lay down his life for his friends.
John 15: 13

The Blues Avenue Series:

Out of the Blue

Written in the Deep

Beauty from Ashes Series:

The Lost and Found

Standalones:

Long Live the Rebel

Contents

PROLOGUE

Ryler Dean swallowed as he paused at the door, hovering, preparing himself, his throat tight against the strong odor of decay and disinfectant. The withered and wasted man lying in the hospital bed drew his gaze. His own heart clenched at the slow and labored rise and fall of the man's chest, at the breath rattling loudly in his worn-out lungs. The only other sounds in the room were the beeping machines as they monitored the slow and steady process of death.

Against the weight of the inevitable, Ryler shrugged his shoulders, gritting his teeth as he stepped into the room. Silently, he shifted a chair closer to the bed, careful not to disturb any of the various tubes and wires flowing in all directions. As quiet as Ryler had been, dark greenish-blue eyes met his own deep blue-greys and despite the pain and the drugs the old man had to be experiencing, those green eyes were alert. Of course, they'd be. Jake wanted to know if Ryler had been successful.

Jacob T. Daniels had been like a father to him for a good portion of his life. Jake had taught him almost everything there was to being a man and there was so much Ryler wanted, *needed* to say to him. He simply didn't have the words. They'd never come easy to Ryler. He was more a man of action; quiet, but observant, always looking out for those around him. He'd done his best to care for Jake these last two years that he'd been battling this disease. Forced to watch as the cancer slowly worked its way through the older man's body, deteriorating it, wasting and tearing it down until Jake was little more than a skeleton in sagging skin.

It'd been one of the hardest things Ryler had ever had to go through. To watch as this robust, confident man was reduced to no more than a shell of who he'd been. Gut wrenching was putting it mildly.

"How'd it go?" Jake wheezed, coughing and choking to get the words out. "Were we successful? Did they get it?"

Ryler ground his teeth, refusing for the old man to see his tears, not because he was ashamed to cry in front of Jake. But rather because it would make Jake uncomfortable to be cried over. Before Jake could continue, Ryler gave him a smile. "Yeah, Jake. She got it. And, before you ask, yes, I got confirmation from her agent, Leslie Simeon, that it was received, and Simeon verified she'd be in contact with her within the week. I'll hear definitively one way or the other what the outcome will be. So, you have nothing to worry about."

Jake nodded, his eyes watering with his emotion. "Thanks, Rye." His voice was weak, raspy.

"Sure, no problem." Ryler laid a comforting hand over Jake's. "Everything's taken care of. There isn't anything else for you to worry over. All you need to do is rest."

"I'm thankful." Jake gave an affirmative nod. "I've made a provision for you in the will—I told you that, right?"

"Yeah, you did. Don't worry about me. Don't even worry about her; she doesn't deserve you."

"She doesn't—" Jake coughed, wincing as he did, his entire body jerking with the efforts. "Doesn't even know about me." Ryler did his best to hide his agitation, but Jake saw through his smokescreen. "Don't blame her, Rye. She doesn't...she just doesn't know. Promise me. Prom—" He coughed again, needing a drink to clear his throat.

Unable to watch him suffer, Ryler quickly got him a glass of water, then gently took Jake's bruised, frail hand in his and held it. "I promise, Jake. I promise to make her feel welcome—if she even comes. And to watch over her and help out any way I can. I promise."

Jake nodded as he sighed, his body relaxing. He gave Ryler's hand a mild squeeze, hardly any pressure in it at all, then he smiled and closed his eyes.

CHAPTER ONE
What the French Toast

AJ

"No way," I breathed, trying to calm my thundering heart. But that organ was having no such thing as it raced away. "I mean...*shut the front door*." Standing in the large foyer of the comfortable, beach-view home I lived in on Ocean Drive, I shook the letter in my hand and brought it nearer to my face. Thinking *illogically,* if I looked closer it might not say what I thought it said. A second reading only confirmed what I'd read the first time. Which was shocking the ever-loving crap out of me, to the point I almost felt dizzy. I mean, what the French toast was this? Blood pumped swiftly through my veins, adrenaline surging, making the room sway. *Focus.* Calm down and just breathe.

My eyes traveled around the foyer, taking in the large cream-colored tiles, the milky blue walls, the tall windows, and settled myself. *This* was known. Comforting. My body followed my gaze, turning slowly where I stood. Far out, across the street, past the dunes, the surf crashed on the beach. This view, the ocean, was always comforting to me.

It had been sheer good fortune when I'd found this place nearly four years ago. It wasn't easy finding living accommodations on Coronado Island near San Diego. But the elderly woman who owned the place hadn't liked living alone, and as she had plenty of room, she'd decided to rent out a few of the bedrooms. I was one of five lucky tenants living here with her. First, was the quiet, oftentimes awkward middle-aged man who smelled faintly of those clove cigarettes he favored. Paul was his name—nice guy, just socially reserved. I was never quite able to shake the uncomfortable feeling I'd get whenever he was around. Though, I did try to be kind, not wanting to hurt his feelings. Thankfully, he kept to himself for the most part. He was a freelance photographer for a travel magazine here in the US called, *American Roadtrip*. His job kept him on the road a lot as he traveled around the country taking pictures and highlighting any interesting details. He did good work. I know because I've read several of his articles. Then there was the younger—just slightly older than my twenty-three years of age—newlywed couple who seemed to fight and make up a lot. Like, *a lot*. Tessa and Matt were their names. They were really nice, just passionate...and vocal.

Then there was the cougar. Kat, she called herself. She had to be in her sixties, though she seemed to believe she was barely in her thirties. Bleach-blond hair, darkly tanned skin, fit, and she favored leopard print everything: spandex, blouses, bags, bathing suits, and shoes. She must have had something working for her, because she brought home a new sailor nearly every week. Her tramp-stamp might have had something to do with it—*Tiger* it read at the base of her spine. I kept promising myself that one day soon I'd interview her, for research purposes only, of course.

And then there's me. AJ McAdams, author. I was first published at the age of nineteen and currently have nine novels under my belt. All military themed romances, one of which is being made into a miniseries for A&E. Living near the North Island Naval Air Station definitely has its perks. My last book, *Falling for a Seabee*, hit the New York Times number one spot within the first forty-eight hours of its release. I was on tour with that one for almost two weeks, having an incredible time due in part to being invited as a guest for a Military Appreciation event at Miramar. *Queue the Top Gun theme song now.* I've been home from that trip for just over a month. In addition to writing novels, I blog about life here on the island—Barefoot in Blue Jeans, the blog is called.

Being an author who values her privacy and space, I rarely make time for a social life, despite the efforts of my agent, Leslie Simeon, to the contrary.

Leslie frequently threw cover models my way and sent me texts reminding me to get out more. I mean, I get out. I need coffee and food after all. But I haven't seriously dated anyone for close to three years. My last relationship had been a heartbreak of a disaster, enough that I'd sworn off any personal romances for the time being. Plus, I'm a workaholic, and haven't decided yet if that's a curse or a blessing. Either way, I'm almost always writing no matter where I am, because there's almost always a story in my head. And it's a little strange, even though I spend most of my time in make-believe, not much catches me off-guard.

Until this letter.

From an attorney in Washington State.

With supposed information about my biological father and the will he wrote with my name as the beneficiary. The letter had gone to my agent first and she'd in turn forwarded it to me.

My heart was still pinging off my ribcage. "*Shut the front door!*"

Mrs. Carson, my landlady, popped her head out from the study. "What was that, AJ? What's wrong with the front door?" Her aged blue eyes looked to the door in question, then back to me.

"Oh." I closed my eyes briefly, willing myself to calm down. "It's nothing, Mrs. Carson. The door is fine. Sorry. I was...just...shocked about something."

"Hmmm..." Mrs. Carson responded. She wasn't sure what to make of me. And never had been. To her way of thinking I didn't act the way a young woman ought to. She'd expected me to have a parade of boys traipsing through at all hours, or at least a steady boyfriend, or lover, or something. And no, I'm not speculating or assuming this was her thinking—she'd told me this to my face. Nicely, but still.

I waved to her as I headed up the doublewide staircase to the second floor and my room, where it overlooked the ocean just yards away. As I opened the door to my room, taking in the sand-colored walls, and the light blue-tinted floorboards, my cat, Josephine, crawled out from under the bed where she'd been sleeping. Josephine wound herself around my leg a time or two, happy to see me. Bending to pick her up, I held her in my arms for a moment, scratching behind her ears, stroking her long calico coat, listening to her soft purr. Then a bird fluttered onto the balcony and she wanted down.

Sitting at my little writing table where my laptop was set up, I reread the letter from Kerry Wahler, Attorney at Law. Mr. Wahler had been retained by a man named Ryler Dean, for one Jacob T. Daniels, who, according to this letter claimed to be my biological father. He had left me all his possessions, including his house and some land near Sequim, Washington. At least that's what this letter was saying, and that I needed to be in touch with Mr. Wahler soon to make arrangements to settle the estate.

What in the actual heck? Saying I was shocked put it mildly. First, because I'd been told by my mother that my father had *died* before I was born. And that his name had been Hank, not Jacob. And second, because my mother and I do not have an easy relationship. We never have, really. Ours had been rife with many stops and starts along the way. And reading this, taking in all the ramifications of it…my stomach was in knots.

Setting the letter down on the table, I let my eyes wander, not really seeing anything, just trying to think past the haze clouding my vision. My gaze landed on my answering machine—yes, I was one of those old-fashioned types who still used a landline and answering machine. The blinking light indicated a waiting message.

A quick scroll through the caller ID showed it was from Leslie, and considering the letter I had in my procession, I assumed it had to do with this. Pressing the button, I listened to the message. "Hey beautiful," Leslie's low, almost sultry voice said in her mild southern-twang. "I received an important letter that pertains to you: I need you to give me a call, sweetie."

Needing answers, needing to speak with Leslie before I called my mom, I quickly dialed her number.

"Lez," I said as she answered. "What the *heck* is this letter?"

"AJ, hon, I got the letter yesterday and overnighted it to you. It was addressed to me, with a note attached explaining the circumstances, mainly that your address is private, and this needed to reach you ASAP. I took the time to verify what I could about the details. Kerry Wahler *is* a legitimate attorney in Washington State. I even verified the death of Jacob Daniels...I'm sorry. I spoke with the attorney, Mr. Wahler; I called him. He has a county certified paternity test proving Mr. Daniels is, *was*, your father. He won't let me know what is in the will, only assures me you are named the beneficiary. He also says he has information explaining all these circumstances and more to you."

My mind was a whirlwind of thought. Closing my eyes, I rubbed my forehead and tried to calm down. "Lez, I just...I...just don't even know what to say, what to think. Mom told me my dad had died before I was *born*. If he was alive all this time, why was he never in touch? Why did he let my *entire* life go by without any contact, until his death...?"

"I don't know, sweetie. I really don't...." Her voice, laced with compassion, rang with sincerity.

I nodded to myself, decision made. "Okay. I'm going to give my mom a call and see what she has to say. Then I'll try to be in touch with Mr. Wahler. Thank you, Lez. You're the best."

"Sounds like a solid plan; let me know how things go."

"Will do." I promised.

Coffee. Coffee is what I needed if I was going to be in touch with my mother. It was too early for wine. Rising from the table, I grabbed my purse, told Josephine to hold down the fort, and headed back out my door.

Sun and Surf Café, on Orange Avenue, wasn't too crowded when I arrived; the large clock on the wall showed it was just after three. I only waited about five minutes or so to place my order. Kevin, my favorite barista smiled as I approached the counter. "What's up, shorty?" *Shorty.* I snorted under my breath as my lips curled. That was what he'd called me the first time we'd met four years ago. I'm not *short* per se, however, compared to him, I suppose I am. My frame is just shy of five feet four and half inches. Kevin has to be somewhere in the ballpark of six feet four, or maybe five. All I know is I come to just about his chest. And I know this because

Kevin's a hugger. He means it in a completely platonic manner, nothing inappropriate, more like a big, cuddly teddy bear, or older brother. With swoon-worthy chiseled features that did nothing for me, sadly. "Nothing much, tall man."

Kevin studied me closely, eyebrow rising in disbelief. "You sure about that?"

"Yeah, Kev. Just have a lot on my mind."

"Book stuff?" He dipped his chin. "You're looking for a hot model for your next cover, aren't you? I told you...I volunteer."

That made me grin. "If I am ever in need of a hot guy for my cover, you know you're my man."

Kevin handed over my coffee. "I made you smile at least; means I've done my job. You take it easy, shorty."

"You too, Kev. And thanks."

I'd ridden my bike. It isn't far, only about a mile or so from the house. And I liked to bike. Or walk. I just liked it *here*. Coronado was about as ideal and beautiful a place as you could want. Temperatures were almost always perfect, and the white gold beaches, the sunsets, sunrises, the swaying palm trees...they're all just beautiful. But seeing as how I now had my coffee, I decided to walk my bike back to the house, rather than ride.

Orange Avenue was one of the main business streets on the island, but I was able to maneuver through the traffic fairly easily. As I neared Alameda Blvd, I spied Sandy, a local man, whom I'm almost positive makes his living panhandling and lives on the beach. We've enjoyed a cup of coffee, or bowl of soup together a couple times. Sandy was across the street and as I wasn't in the mood for company, I simply waved to him and continued on my way. I ended up on a rock about fifty yards from the house. From my perch, I gazed at the beach and the waves beyond as I sipped my coffee. When nearly finished, I pulled out my cell phone and dialed my mother.

Complicated. That was the best way to describe our relationship. Everything with her was complicated. My heart beat slow and heavy in my chest as I waited for her to pick up, not looking forward to this conversation. "Hi sweetie." Her voice was bright and cheerful as she answered.

"Hi." I tried keeping my tone mild. "Hey, I need to ask you something."

"Sure, what's up?" The sounds of water running, and some mild clanging noise came from the background, and I figured she was out in her garden.

"Mom, who is Jacob T. Daniels?" The sudden silence on the line was deafening. Several long moments passed. "Mom?"

She cleared her throat. "Where, uh...where did you hear that name?"

"Why, Mom?" I fought to keep my voice level. "Who is he?"

"Answer the question, AJ!" she snapped.

"No, Mom." My control snapped as I fairly growled at her. "*You* answer the question. Who is he?"

"I'm hanging up." I heard panic in her voice, the tremble. "I'll talk with you when you're willing to be an adult about this."

"His attorney sent me a letter. His *attorney*, Mom. It seems Mr. Jacob T. Daniels died about a month ago." She inhaled sharply, shuddering as she exhaled. "It also seems he's claiming to be my father. And that up until a month ago, he'd been alive all this time. Which is odd...because *you* told me my dad died before I was born. So, I'll ask you again, Mom; *who* is Jacob T. Daniels?"

"We shouldn't talk about this over the phone, AJ." Her voice wavered. "Why don't you come home, we can talk then."

"I am home. *This* is my home. And I don't have time to come to Florida right now. I need to know, though, so I'd appreciate the truth from you."

"I'll talk with you when you come here, not over the phone."

"Fine." I knew she'd act like this. I knew, and yet it still hurt.

"Good, I'm glad you're willing to be reasonable. When do you think you'll be able to come?"

"You misunderstood. You refuse to tell me your side of this story. Fine. I'll just see what the attorney has to say."

"*No!* AJ, no!"

"You had your chance." My voice came out in a whisper even as a hollowness settled in my chest. Swallowing, I firmed my voice. "I gotta go." Even anticipating her response, it still hit deep. This was just one of the many reasons our relationship was always strained. I hit end before she could respond and headed back to my room. Ignoring her repeated attempts to call, I settled onto my bed, where Josephine climbed onto my lap. Then, I dialed the number for one, Kerry Wahler, Attorney at Law.

The phone rang four times. "Law Office, Wahler Speaking." The voice was average, the tone mild, not giving any clues as to age, ethnicity, or anything.

"Mr. Wahler? Mr. Kerry Wahler?"

"Yes, this is Kerry. How may I help you?"

"Mr. Wahler...this is AJ McAdams." I paused, then continued. "You sent me a letter...about Jacob Daniels."

"Ms. McAdams." He drew in a long slow breath. "Yes, thank you for being in touch. We have a lot to talk about. I'm sure you have questions for me, and there are some things I need from you as well—"

"Mr. Wahler," I interrupted. "Everything about this is confusing to me. I was under the impression my dad had died before I was even born. And now you're claiming that this man is, or was, my father. I don't understand any of it."

"I understand, Ms. McAdams. Have you spoken with your mother yet?"

"I did, yes." I exhaled, trying for patience.

"And was she able to shed any light on this?"

"She was not." I admitted. "She refused."

"Based upon what I know, I anticipated that and am sorry."

"And just what is it that you know, Mr. Wahler?"

"Due to the legal ramifications of this situation, I can only tell you so much over the phone. The rest will need to be said and done in person. What I can tell you is that your parents came to an...agreement...after you'd been born. I have a copy of that document and can give that to you when I see you in person. I think, once you read this, and some other documents and letters Jake left for you, I think things will make more sense. I am sorry for your loss. Jake'll be missed. A lot."

His last comment gave me pause and took me a moment to gather my thoughts. "You knew him well?"

"I did. He was a fine man. A fine man."

"And yet, he just left me, ignored me my whole life. That fine of a man?" The emotion began to clog my throat, and I silently tried to clear it.

Mr. Wahler was quiet for a moment, no doubt acknowledging my pain and confusion, before proceeding cautiously. "I know this is difficult, Ms. McAdams, but I truly do believe things will be clearer once you come here and can see for yourself."

"So, I'm just supposed to head off to Washington State? To deal with the estate of a man I've never met, or known?"

"Again, Ms. McAdams, things will make much more sense, when you come here. I promise."

Fighting for patience, I inhaled long and deep. "All right. If that's the best that you can do. I'll have to get back with you."

"I know this is a lot. I know it is. I can only assure you things will make sense after you're here and are able to look through all the documents I have for you. At least come and hear the will and decide what you want to do then."

"I'll think about it. I'll give you a call before the weekend. Thank you for your time, Mr. Wahler."

"Call me Kerry. And I'll wait to hear from you. You take care."

"Thank you." My head was spinning as I hung up. Five minutes later found me still seated in the same spot, my mind still nothing but turmoil. When the phone rang, I jumped, startled. It was Leslie. "Hey, Lez."

"Did you call?"

"Yeah."

"And?"

"He wants me to come to Washington."

"And are you going?" she drew the question out.

"I don't know. I have a lot going on here. I'm in the middle of *Midnight Marine*...."

"You can take that with you," she encouraged.

"So, you think I should go?"

Leslie paused for a moment, then said, "I think it might be a good idea. Just go. See what all this is about. Then come back. No commitments. No worries."

"Yeah, I...guess."

"It'll be fine. You want me to check on airline tickets?"

"No. Not yet. I need to check my calendar and see what's coming up."

"The next thing I have for you is in June. On the 20th. You have that speaking engagement at the Book Warehouse in Anaheim. Then after that, you're doing a signing for Author's Unlimited in L.A. in July. Then you're clear until September for your release of *Friendly Fire*."

I chuckled. "This is why I love you, Lez."

"So, should I book that flight?"

"No, actually, not yet. If I go, I think I'm going to make a road trip of it. Take my time, just let my mind relax and mentally prepare for whatever I might learn there."

I heard the amused grin in her voice. "Sounds like a plan. You need me to make any arrangements for you?"

"I'll let you know if I do."

Deciding a shower before dinner would be nice; I slid Josephine off my lap and headed for the bathroom. The phone was ringing when I stepped from the cloud of steam. Looking at the caller ID, I saw it was Mom. Again. Still not wanting to speak with her, I ignored it. Then my cellphone began to ring. *Wow, she's being persistent.* I ignored the cellphone, too. Then the room phone began ringing again.

"What, Mom?" I fumed as I answered.

"AJ! Look, hon, don't call that attorney. Wait until you can speak with me. There is nothing to gain by heading down that road. Trust me."

"*Trust* you? Mom, you *lied* to me. And you won't tell me the truth about it. Why should I trust you?"

"What I did was for the best. To protect you."

"To protect me from what?" What was she even talking about?

"From *him*, sweetie."

"What does that mean? Is, *was* he dangerous?"

Mom was quiet for a moment. "At the time, yes."

"Well, he's dead now—for real this time—so I don't think I'm in much danger from him."

"Please don't...don't pursue this any longer." She sniffed, emotion strong in her voice. "Just let it go."

"I've already spoken with the attorney. I leave this Friday."

"*Dangit*, AJ! I asked you not to!"

"I know you did." I shook my head. "And *I* asked you for the truth, but you wouldn't give me that. So, I guess we're even."

"You're going to regret this, AJ. All this is going to do is bring you pain and misery. But you won't listen to me. You *never* listen to me!"

"What are you afraid of?" I whispered over my pounding heart.

"I'm only trying to save you from being hurt!"

"Hurt by whom, Mom?"

She inhaled sharply. "That's not fair. You're taking a perfect stranger's word over mine, your mother's!"

"I'm not taking anyone's word on anything." I tried to remain calm. "But I am going. So, I can find answers."

"This is a mistake, AJ." Her tone held bitterness now.

"You said that already. I gotta go."

"I love you." She shifted emotional gears again, as her voice quivered. "I hope you know that."

"I love you, too, Mom. But I'm still going." Not giving her a chance to respond, I ended the call and fell backward onto the bed. *Why are things always so difficult with her!* Josephine crept close, meowing softly as she nudged my hand, wanting to be scratched. Smiling, I pulled her close, soothed by her purring.

Glancing at the clock, I saw it was almost dinner time. Still needing to dress, I rolled off the bed, making for my closet. Normally I'd just throw on jeans, go down to eat, then head back upstairs to write. But tonight, thanks to recent events and conversations with my mother, I wasn't in the mood to sit in my room. Reaching for my cell, I dialed Harley. Harley and I have been best friends ever since we'd met working at a pizza joint our senior year. We even moved from Florida to Coronado together. I was the brake to her accelerator, our friendship the perfect balance.

Harley works for the *Hotel del Coronado* in Guest Services, and I've used several of her more *fun* experiences in my books over the years. She's my wingman, and I know I can always count on her to have my back no matter the situation. And right now, I needed her.

"Hey doll!" Harley answered on the second ring, sounding like she was busy.

I knew her job kept her hopping so didn't want to stay on the phone too long. "You have plans tonight?"

"I've got a meeting with upper management in about twenty minutes; some big client is coming in, and they want to prep us for the occasion. That should last about an hour. Then I'm free. What's up?"

"Wanna head to CBC and get a drink?" CBC is short for *Coronado Brewing Company*. They'd opened some twenty years ago; a couple of brothers, getting a jump on the craft-brew craze, and are now well-established, offering a brew with a coastal tone.

"*Yes*. Definitely. Can I meet you there?"

"Yeah, see you in an hour or so."

We hung up and I quickly stepped into my jeans, threw on a T-shirt, and headed down for one of Mrs. Carson's awesome home-cooked meals before heading out to meet Harley, and hopefully relieve some of this awful stress.

CHAPTER TWO
A Time for Every Season

AJ

The *Coronado Brewing Company* was moderately crowded when we arrived, but we'd found a table easily enough. Wading through those gathered around the bar, we skirted several large and boisterous groups as we followed the hostess.

Harley had been as shocked as I was when I'd told her my news. And even now, some thirty minutes later, concern was still clearly stamped across her face. "What are you going to do?" she asked between bites of carne asada fries, smearing each one in guacamole and sour cream. "What did your mom say?"

Harley was well aware of the relationship I had with my mom. She'd been witness to numerous attempts Mom had made over the years trying to manipulate me to her way of thinking. The way she critiqued everything from my chosen profession to the friends I kept, the men I dated—or didn't date—my hair style, my tattoos, and my decision to move to California. I exhaled in a rush. "My mother was...my mother." I shook my head. "Completely unhelpful. I spoke with Leslie, though, and I'm going."

"You are?"

"Yeah," I nodded. "I am."

"You think that's smart? I mean, yeah, he left you property and all, but he *ignored* you for your entire life."

"I know...it's just... It's just, I feel like I *need* to do this. I feel it in my gut, Harley."

Harley nodded thoughtfully, then took another bite of fries. "Well, I guess there's a time for every season, or something like that. That's a literary quote, I'll have you know."

I chuckled. "Of a sort. It's from the Bible. From the book of Ecclesiastes. Third chapter. First verse. King Solomon wrote it."

Harley laughed now. "This is why I love you. You're a walking knowledge bank, AJ. How in the world do you even know that?"

"I've read the Bible—you should try it. Valuable stuff in there."

"Yeah, I'll have to see about that." Harley sipped her drink, tucking a wavy brown strand behind her ear. "How long will you be gone? Like a week or so?"

"I'm anticipating at least two weeks. Probably longer, though. I guess there are a lot of extenuating circumstances in play here."

"Wow. That's a long time." Harley kept her eyes down as she finished her beer, then looked up at me, worry in her gaze. "What am I going to do without you, AJ?"

I chuckled. "What you always do—*shine.*"

"Yeah, but I shine best when I'm with you. You know that. *I* need *you*. I mean, come on, just tonight we've each had three phone numbers handed to us. I need you here, AJ."

I couldn't contain my eye roll. Harley is tall, with chocolate-brown wavy hair and blue green eyes. She's stunning in her own right and people have often wondered if we're sisters. My hair is longer and darker, and my eyes tend to be greener. I'm far shorter than she is, still we look similar enough, they ask. And despite her insistence that she needed me, the truth was she didn't. Harley was fully capable of being on her own and making a success of everything she attempted. "You don't need me, Harley. You do just fine flying solo. But I promise I'll be back just as soon as I'm able."

"*Promise* me."

"I just did."

"You know I won't be able to keep the cat. The apartment doesn't allow pets."

"I know. I figured I'd have to bring Josephine with me."

"On a plane?"

"No; I'm going to drive."

"All the way to Washington State? On your own?"

"Harley, please. Yes, on my own. I'll be fine. Maps will get me there and I'll keep everyone posted as to my progress. Promise." Harley nodded thoughtfully, a mischievous look suddenly in her eyes. "What?" I shook my head at her.

"Well...I was just thinking...you'll be in Washington, right?"

"Yep."

"Just watch out for those sparkling ones. I mean, don't get bit or anything." I stared at her in silent disbelief. "What?" she shrugged. "It could happen. Odder things have happened, AJ."

"Harley, your teen is showing. Besides, *Twilight* is based in Forks, Washington. Not Sequim, Washington."

"Pssht, close enough. All I'm saying is to watch out."

Rolling my eyes at her warning, I assured her I would be safe, and even promised her if I was bitten, I'd come see her and return the favor.

We finished eating; I paid the tab, as I'd been the one to ask Harley to join me. Then we said our goodbyes and I headed back to the house. Checking my phone as I parked in the driveway, I saw it was closing in on ten. Lights were still on in the house, so I figured now was a good time to let Mrs. Carson know I would be gone for a while.

Mrs. Carson was in her study. It was cozy, almost reminiscent of an old Victorian sitting room where ladies sat and gossiped. A cup of tea sat beside her on the little table. A fire crackled in the marble fireplace, despite the fact that we lived in sunny, southern California. "Mrs. Carson?" I asked as I entered the room.

"Yes, AJ?" she replied, laying down her book. Glancing at the cover I saw it was a Courtney Walsh novel. She seemed to really enjoy those ones.

"I just wanted to let you know I'd be leaving for a while. I have some personal things I need to take care of. I'll be gone for at least two weeks, possibly longer. And I'll be taking Josephine with me. I'm paid up for the next six months, aren't I?"

"Oh, yes, dear. You are. You're taking your cat? Is everything all right? You never take your kitty with you on your jaunts."

"Yeah, I know. But I'm taking her this time; I have to go to Washington State. Like I said, it's for personal reasons. I'll let you know if my stay needs to be longer. I just wanted you to know. I'll be leaving on Friday."

"All right, AJ. Just be careful. I wish you had someone close by, that could watch over you."

Gritting my teeth, I managed to smile. "That's really sweet, Mrs. Carson, but I'll be fine. Truly. I'll talk to you later, okay?"

Mrs. Carson nodded and went back to her novel. Leaving her in the study, I was almost on the stairs before I spotted Paul standing against the wall in the shadows beside the tall window. My heart lurched in my chest before I'd recognized him, before I caught that distinct smell his cigarettes gave off. "Yeesh, Paul! Cut that out, will ya? Darn near scared the crap out of me."

Paul was probably one of the most nondescript people I'd ever met. He had plain brown hair. No variation to the color...just brown, cut in a simple, unassuming style. His eyes were brown like his hair. Just...brown. Nothing extraordinary to them. He looked at me in that quiet way of his. "I didn't mean to startle you, AJ. I just happened to be coming down for a snack when I heard your conversation. You're leaving us again?"

"Yeah, just for a bit. I've got some things to take care of." I shrugged. "Personal things."

"You'll be gone for a while, then?"

"A couple weeks or so, yeah."

Paul was quiet for a moment or two, and I almost moved on, assuming the conversation was at an end. "Were you and Harley out tonight?" he asked suddenly.

I chuckled. "Yeah, we went to CBC for a bite. Nothing fancy."

"I'll bet you still received phone numbers...didn't you? You always get male attention. And sometimes female."

Boy, this conversation took a turn for the weird quickly. "Yeah, well it was nice chatting, Paul. I need to start preparing for my trip. I'll talk with you later. You take it easy, all right?"

I was about halfway up the stairs when I glanced back. Paul was still standing where I'd left him. Leaning against the wall; his gaze on me. Speeding up slightly, I made it to my room and quickly stepped inside

AJ

Blog Post

Hey Beach Bums, it's ten at night; I just got home. Now I'm sitting on my balcony, watching the stars, listening to the waves....

I have no beach-vibe tidbit for you today, I'm sorry; because today...today has been nuts. Crazy. *Insane.* Nuts. I was hit with some news that was rather like taking a rock to the head. Not sad, or bad news, just *crazy* news. News that required a trip to CBC this evening, and knocking back a couple with my girl, Harley. It's also going to require a road trip. A really long road trip. To Washington State, no less. Northern Washington State.

Are there even beaches in Washington? Guys, what am I going to do without beaches?

And I have no idea how long I'll be gone. Could be just a couple weeks. Could be a couple months. But, have no fear, I promise to blog and stay in touch while I'm away, no matter where I have to blog from. So, I'm signing out for the evening. I'll be in touch soon!

All the best,

Your Siren of the Surf, AJ

AJ

It didn't take me long to pack. Well, it didn't take me *that* long to pack. Only three days. Mainly my packing consisted of tossing everything onto my bed, checking the weather forecast for Sequim, and my planned stopping points along the way, then throwing some things together in a duffel bag or two. *Who was I kidding?* I packed four solid bags. A girl's gotta dress. Then I sat down at my laptop and planned my drive. Made reservations at each hotel I'd stay in, locating the gas stations and coffee houses. I checked my emails, responding as needed, and checked my blog again.

Most of my followers were amazing, being kind and courteous, but there was one. Wasn't there always? She'd been following me for a little over a year now. *Ambergoldenone* was her online name. Her comments seemed to border on the aggressive and proprietary side; Leslie had suggested I block her. But I figured Amber *Whoevershewas* would just get herself a new email and be right back to seeing what she could do to get under my skin. So, I tended to simply ignore her as best I could, despite her comments indicating I was abandoning my readers all the time—I wasn't. And that I owed it to them to stay here on Coronado and supply them with the various tidbits of my life. Quite a few of my followers would chime in to defend me each time she went on the attack, and I'd have to do my best to calm ruffled feathers.

As I checked my blog, responding to several comments, I saw one from Amber. And in typical fashion, she was expressing irritation that I was once again going out of town. What I found funny was that Amber always seemed to present herself as if she knew me personally, and that my leaving was a personal affront to her. To my knowledge I didn't know an Amber.

Of course, I reminded myself, people could and did use fake names and created fake profiles; they did it all the time.

Today she seemed thoroughly annoyed, indicating I was irresponsible and inconsiderate in my actions. As I make it a policy to do my absolute best to respond to all comments, kind or unkind, I apologized and promised to find new things to blog about on my journey. Hoping my response would pacify her, I gathered my writing materials, double and triple checking to make sure I had everything I'd need for my extended leave of absence.

I'd given Harley a key to my room years ago, when I'd first moved in, in case she needed to borrow something. I knew if I'd forgotten anything, and was desperate enough, I could always ask her to UPS it to me.

I took my time on the trip, only driving about six hours each day. On the first night, I made it just north of Santa Clarita before stopping. The next night Josephine and I made it to Stockton. On the third night we made it to Redding. By this time, the landscape was noticeably different. Pine trees dotted the ever-increasingly rugged landscape. By about noon on the fourth day, we'd crossed into Oregon and pushed on for Roseburg. The terrain continued getting rougher, more beautiful, lush. On the fifth day, before arriving in Sequim, we stopped in Olympia and Josephine was glad to be out of her crate. I'd blogged about each travel stop, taking pictures of the scenery, posting them to my page, and stayed in touch with Harley and Leslie. After dinner, I put a call in to Mr. Wahler, letting him know where I was and about what time to expect me. Then I ordered a glass of wine and ran the bath water, simply needing to relax and mentally prepare for tomorrow.

The long drive had allowed me ample time to think through a lot of things. For instance, it occurred to me that I should have called my stepdad to see what he knew. Even though Dave and Mom had divorced when I was in fifth grade, he and I had still stayed in touch. I wondered if he'd known that Mom had lied to me about my dad. *Had he known the truth all along?* And now, just thinking that Dave may have been a party to Mom's deception, I was a tad nauseous.

This line of thinking was doing me no good—I needed to change gears—and fast. Instead of thinking about what may, or may not have happened in my past, I began to imagine what the next day would bring. What new information I'd learn. My bath water was rather tepid by the time I was done. So, after finishing the wine, I brushed my teeth, set my alarm, and headed to bed.

Ryler

Ryler heard the music long before he saw the car. It was a sleek, milk-blue M4 convertible. A pricey number. The car came to an abrupt stop in the middle of the road, tires squealing mildly on the damp pavement. The stereo was instantly silenced, then the car quickly backed up, before shooting forward again, pulling into Kerry's parking lot, not quite on two wheels, but nearly so. Ryler had been repairing the mailbox stand—high school students had been playing mailbox baseball again. He shook his head in irritated exasperation, dropping his drill into his toolbox, taking a step in the driver's direction, before checking himself. Wanting to give the driver a piece of his mind was probably not the best idea. Instead, he held his ground and glared at the vehicle in question, hoping the driver noticed him.

Then she stepped from the car, and the heat Ryler felt quickly shifted, smoothly changing gears from irritation at her lack of courtesy to...just heat. Just your run of the mill, punch to the gut, basic, general male response to an attractive female kind of heat.

Ah, heck.

Her hair was dark brown and long. A couple strands hung down into her eyes and his fingers twitched even as she brushed those aside in an almost absentminded way. He noted the graceful curve of her neck, the way she held her head. Confident. Ready. Assessing. Her skin was deeply tanned, and even from a distance of thirty feet or so, it looked velvety smooth. She moved a step away from that blue car, wearing a faded grey dress of some kind. It looked more like an over-sized t-shirt than it did an actual dress, only it hugged her form, rather than hiding it. The neckline was wide enough that it had slipped off her nicely shaped shoulder, revealing a large, red rose tattoo. His mouth had gone dry at the sight.

The sun, shining down through the pines, caught her hair, lending it a caramel tint. It was only the second week in April; temperatures were still cool and at times, frosty. Yet here she was looking like she'd stepped right from the tropics. He could easily imagine a coconut scent coming off her skin. She was wearing a pair of strappy, toe-less heels that accented the curves in her legs. Ryler stared, unable to help himself, trying to figure out how it was possible for someone that short to have legs that long. Legs that just seemed to go on. And on.

She stood still for a minute, and he watched as she *changed*. That confidence slipped and she shifted on her feet. Now, she seemed uncertain. Silently he watched as she chewed at her lip, nerves now on display. Then she glanced behind her into the car. "Oh, hush," she muttered. Her voice was like the ocean surf somehow, calm and soothing. "I'll just be a minute or two, I promise." Then she took a deep breath, squared her shoulders, raised her chin, cocking it like she was preparing for a fight, and headed for Kerry's door.

As the woman moved away from her car, her eyes traveled the parking lot, no doubt just getting her bearings. Her eyes scanned the tall pines, the other vehicles parked here, then those eyes, like evergreens framed in thick, dark lashes, landed on him. And stopped. *She* stopped. Mid stride. Those eyes now traveled slowly over Ryler, making him tighten with tension. She started at the top, meandering all the way to his boots, before flicking back up. Touching lightly over his tall frame; noting the short-cropped hair, the tattoos, the scars, the fact that he wasn't wearing a shirt—digging the new post hole had made him sweaty, but she was producing a different kind of heat in him now. And then their eyes collided. He saw hers widen, a palpable tension in the air between them. Her tongue touched her lip, and he felt it like a kick to the gut.

She seemed to remember herself then, where she was, what she was doing, because she jerked her gaze from him, color blooming across her cheeks, before continuing to the office door.

Ryler watched her move, noting the grace and balance in each step, each swing of those hips. The play of toned muscle under her tanned skin made the breath lodge in his lungs. Then she was inside, and he suddenly remembered what *he'd* been doing. Fixing the stupid mailbox. In his gut, Ryler knew who she must be. Jake's kid. The daughter. The one Ryler really wanted nothing to do with. The one he'd promised Jake he'd look out for. And even if she wasn't Jake's long-lost daughter, he still wanted nothing to do with her, Ryler sternly reminded himself. Women were trouble. Especially women like her. And there wasn't a snowball's chance in hell that *this* woman, used to her busy, flashy California lifestyle would ever be enticed in to staying here in Sequim, Washington, or even wanting to be with a guy like him.

Ryler turned his back to the building, ripped his t-shirt off the hood of his Bronco where he'd tossed it, stuffing himself back into it in jerky movements. Then he bent and gathered his tools. He'd settle with Kerry later. He just needed to get away, to be gone before she was back outside. Ryler remembered his promise to Jake, to make her feel welcome. To help her out—if she came—while she was here. And she *was* here, and he fully intended to fulfill his promise. But not today. Not while he was this...unprepared.

AJ

The office of Kerry Wahler, Attorney at Law, was decorated rather like a man cave. The floors were tiled in shades of grey; the walls were painted in light blue-grey. Dark oak balanced the room. Mr. Wahler was a *Seahawks* fan; signed and framed jerseys were hung around the room. Along with banners, flags, and team photos.

Five chairs sat off to the side. A simple counter was against the back wall. A bell had loudly rung at my entrance, alerting whoever was through the open door behind that counter of my arrival.

"Be out in a sec!" a man's voice called out.

"Okay," I called quietly back, then turned, letting my eyes move around the room, before facing the parking lot and that stunning man as he loaded some things into an older black Bronco. My face was still warm—I could feel it. I haven't had such an intense reaction to a man, in maybe ever. Rattled, that's what I was. My pulse pounded, adrenaline surging, making me jittery. I needed to calm down, fast. He limped slightly on his right leg, seemed a little stiff in his movements. The man was tatted and scarred—*scarred from what*—and beautiful. He was sharp-edged, like a blade, and yet still beautiful.

"AJ McAdams," the voice said pleasantly from behind me. The man was tall, really tall, I noticed as I turned back around, away from that parking lot. Away from that distractingly attractive man. I focused now on the one before me. He had to be somewhere in the ballpark of six feet seven or so. His hair was sandy in color, a little thin on top, longer in the back. He held his hand out, a friendly smile on his face echoed in his hazel-green eyes. "I'd recognize you anywhere. It's a pleasure to finally make your acquaintance."

"Mr. Wahler?"

"Call me, Kerry, please. How was the drive?"

"It was all right. I think I made pretty good time, even though I took it slow."

Kerry bobbed his head in small nod, a smile playing around his lips, as he studied me, before asking, "Well, Ms. McAdams, are you ready to get down to business?"

"AJ, please." I nodded, though I wasn't sure I truly was ready.

"All right, let's go into my office."

Kerry led me into the back office; this room was a continuation of the front reception room. The *Seahawks* were again prominently displayed on the walls. Kerry sat behind a large dark oak desk, indicating the two leather chairs in front for me. In the center of Kerry's desk was a large manila envelope. My eyes were drawn to it as I took the chair on the right.

"You want some water, coffee?" Kerry nodded to the right where a coffee maker sat atop a small refrigerator.

"No, I'm good for now. Thank you. Mr. Wahler, Kerry, how long do you think this will take?"

Kerry stuck a toothpick in his teeth, mildly mouthing it. "Well...I guess that will depend on you. I'll let you read the document I have. The one your parents agreed upon concerning your dad's involvement in your life. Or I can tell you the gist of it, read you the will, explain what Jake was hoping for, then if you're up to it, take you by the house."

I took a deep breath again, willing myself to remain calm. "Let's do that, I guess."

He studied me silently for a moment longer, all the while worrying that toothpick. "From reading the document, and the accompanying letters Jake left for me, and for you, I can tell you, *assure* you, that he loved you very much. And I know that's hard for you to comprehend, however, I think you'll see the proof in time. Now, for a bit of history. Jake joined the army in '87, and about a year later was selected for the RIP/Ranger program. His first deployment came in '90 at the end of the Panama War, with Operation "Just Cause" as a part of Task Force Red-Romeo. He then went on to serve in the Gulf War. He returned home in 1991. He then redeployed in '93 to Mogadishu. Jake was shot in the shoulder during that deployment and came home. It was during that time he met your mother.

She became pregnant, and you were born in '94. Your parents never married. Donna had...issues with the military. She'd been hoping you might be the influence to keep Jake home permanently. Jake loved you, AJ.

I've got some pictures of you with him. He was so very, very proud of you. But he wanted to redeploy, and Donna was having none of that.

Jake struggled with adapting to civilian life; she threatened to move away, get a new identity, and he'd never see or hear of you again. Needless to say, that took his feet out from under him. Then Donna convinced Jake to sign over all rights of you to her, and in return she promised to send him quarterly updates on you until your eighteenth birthday. He had to agree to never be in touch with you. She'd convinced Jake it was better for you, because he'd most likely die in battle and all it would do was hurt you.

Against most everyone's opinion, and his better judgment, Jake agreed to these terms." Kerry paused a moment before continuing. "Please understand, he was really struggling. It wasn't that he didn't love you or care. It truly wasn't. He's followed you, stayed updated on your career and progresses. He's written you letters explaining things more fully and better than what I'm trying to say."

My mind was reeling with all I'd just heard. I'm pretty sure I looked rather like a fish out of water for several moments, as my mouth just opened and closed, no sound coming out. "How's about that water now?" I could only nod.

"As for the will Jake wrote up...he owns a home on fifteen acres up off of Bear Creek Road. The home is well built. Secluded. You'll have plenty of privacy. As a part of that property, on five acres toward the top of the mountain, is Ryler's place. Ryler Dean. Jake took Ryler under his wing several years back when Ryler came back from the war. Jake allowed him to build a cabin up on the hill. The way the will is written up, you are prevented from selling the property for the expanse of one year, during which time you'd be expected to live at the house. If you do, the property taxes will be paid for you; if you decline, then you'd be required to pay for them yourself. Then, if after one year, you desire to sell, Ryler Dean would have the first option to buy before it could go on the market." He paused again, no doubt letting me wrestle with what he'd shared. "Before you decide what you'd like to do, may I suggest you go to the house? See it.

Check it out. Stay there at least a couple days. Jake's done a lot to fix things up, make things right for you."

Not knowing how to respond to this new information, I let my mind focus on another question milling about in my brain. "How long was he sick?"

"Jake was diagnosed with cancer little more than two years ago. He declined treatments, not wanting to go through all that. He knew he was going to die, wasn't afraid of it."

"He wouldn't do the treatments? *Why?*"

"Jake had watched his own mother, your grandmother, go through the battle. Saw what it had done to her, what it had done to his family, and just didn't want to do the same. He wanted to be able to live whatever time he had left in relative comfort, able to enjoy life. And, he had things he was trying to get done, things that were important to him."

"More important than getting treatment? What could be more important than that? Treatment might have saved his life, might have extended it."

Kerry just looked at me quietly, expectantly.

"You mean...do you mean that he refused treatment because of me? That doesn't make any sense. *At all*. He didn't even know me."

"I think you'll understand, AJ, when you get to the house."

I inhaled deeply, held my breath, then let it out. "Let me get this straight. I will need to live at this house for an entire year, before I can do anything about it, before I can sell it?"

"That's correct."

"And if I don't live there? If I choose to just head home, and forget all about this?"

"Well, you'd still have the taxes to be paid, and regardless you'd have to wait a year to sell anyway."

"Oh, well that's just *freaking* perfect."

"Just go to the house, AJ. Stay for a few days, see what you think. All right?"

"I don't know if I'll be able to stay for an entire year. I have other commitments. And, I still have my place on Coronado...."

"Just...just go to the house, take a day or two to think it over, all right?"

"Just go to the house.... All right." I sighed. "I'll go. I'm not promising anything, but I will go."

Kerry smiled then, lighting up his entire face. "You'll want to stop at Safeway and pick up some groceries. We had the house cleaned, so there's nothing in the way of food or anything there."

"All right. Which way is Safeway?"

"Make a left from the parking lot; it's about five blocks down. How's about you get what you need and meet back here. Either Ryler or myself will take you out to the house."

"Okay." I rose from the chair.

Kerry walked me out to the front room, heading to the door to open it for me. He searched the parking lot before turning back. "Looks like Rye already took off. I'll be the one to take you out there."

"I'll see you shortly."

Driving to Safeway, I took note of several places I'd like to stop. If I stayed any longer than the original time I'd allotted for this trip. Namely coffee shops and bookstores. Because, you know, coffee. And books.

Even though it was Safeway, and Safeway was essentially the same as Von's, it was still a different store than what I was used to, so my shopping took a little longer than I'd intended. But when it was all said and done, I had enough food to last for several days. And I remembered to get supplies for Josephine, as well. Considering all that I'd just been through, I felt I'd done a fine job, so after loading the sacks into the trunk, and assuring Josephine she'd be out soon, I headed back to Kerry's.

CHAPTER THREE
In Sunshine and in Shadow

AJ

Kerry drove a newer Ford F150 extended cab with a *Seahawks* logo on the back window. I followed him for several miles, heading in a southerly direction. We turned onto an unpaved road and followed that for a couple hundred yards or so as the road meandered away into thick trees, crossing over a small wooden bridge that spanned a fast-moving creek. The elevation of the land increased slightly, then leveled out as we came to a large clearing about an acre or more in size.

The two-story house sat nestled beside a thick stand of what looked to be both white birch and aspen trees. One thing I'd noticed as I had driven north was how clear the air became the farther from California I got. And here, I noted, with the Olympic Mountains pretty much in my backyard, and being so close to the Strait, the air was exceptionally clean-smelling. Like a literal breath of fresh air. As I stepped from my car, I inhaled deeply, savoring the fragrances around me.

Jacob's house was an interesting mixture of rustic log home, and country cottage. From the base of the house, near the footings, river rock reached up the sides about three feet or so, with split logs spanning the rest, with the exception of an honest-to-goodness turret, like in a castle or something, built from large grey-stone bricks. The windows were leaded, giving it a charming cottage-like look. The roof was done in a deep green metal of some kind. And ivy grew up the north-facing wall, creeping along the eastern side as well.

The front of the house sported a flagstone path and entry way. Ferns of various kind grew along the pathway to the front door. Kerry allowed me to look my fill, seemingly understanding as best as he was able what I might have been feeling. I noted the attached garage, and the roses blooming in various tubs scattered around. Surprised was putting things mildly. Had there been a woman here? If so, who was she? Where was she? Did my...did Jacob have any other children? This just wasn't what I'd expected from a bachelor living on his own.

And, as I surveyed my surroundings, noting the way the home sat in both sunshine and shadow, I reflected how like my personal life the house was, situated in sunshine, and yet covered in shadow. Kerry unlocked the front door, stepping back to allow me inside. He offered to help me carry my belongings in, and after a quick glance around, I readily agreed. At least it gave me something to do to keep my mind off the enormity of what I was actually doing.

Once everything was inside, Josephine included, I let her out of her crate and put food and water out for her. Then I made sure to fill her litter box and place that where she could easily find it. Kerry waited patiently as I performed these few tasks. When those were finished, he showed me through the house. The foyer was welcoming, with those same flagstones from outside continuing inside, and deep cream-colored walls. The foyer led into a great room with a large rock fireplace and a patio door led out onto a covered deck. The kitchen seemed to be fairly modern; the appliances were up to date at least. Kerry assured me they all worked. Other than the foyer, the entire downstairs floor was in hardwood of a brownish-grey color, reminding me of old barn wood. Jacob had several large throw rugs around to make it feel cozy.

The staircase sat beside the foyer, and a mixed beige carpet began at the foot. We passed the staircase as Kerry pointed out the utility room, and the door connecting to the garage. Then we headed back, passing the entryway again, as we headed towards what I assumed was the turret room. It was a library. Jacob had built a library; a small fireplace sat between two tall windows, with large, oversized comfy chairs and ottomans placed perfectly. The walls had built-in shelving that were half-filled with books. Out of curiosity, I took a moment or two to peruse his collection, to see what had interested this man.

Jacob had what looked to be a complete set of Louis L'Amour books, as well as various wartime and history books. I spotted a well-worn Homer, as well as Mark Twain and Charles Dickens. And then, just as I was turning away, I saw *my* books. All of them. My heart thudded painfully, slowly in my chest. And, for some odd reason, I felt a little light-headed. With a trembling hand, I reached for one. It was a copy of *Hellfire Heroes*. And as I opened the cover, I saw it had been signed. By me. *Dear Jake,* I'd written. With the book still in my grasp, I turned to Kerry. "I don't...I don't understand."

"They're all signed. You did a signing in Seattle a year back or so. He went. That was just after Jake had been diagnosed. He wanted to see you in person just once before he died. You signed his books for him." Kerry shook his head. "He was so proud of you—talked about it nearly nonstop for months."

My eyes welled, and I spun away, trying to control my emotions. Trying to comprehend. I remembered that event. He'd come to my signing. He'd been there. And had never said anything. Never given any indication as to who he might have been. Kerry retreated from the room, leaving me alone for a moment, no doubt recognizing my need to regroup. He returned a moment later, his large hand appearing beside me holding several tissues. Sniffing a laugh, I accepted them with a nod.

"It's a lot to take in," Kerry quietly stated. Nodding again, I finished cleaning myself up, then placed the book back on the shelf.

Kerry led me upstairs next, showing me the master suite and two spare rooms. The view from upstairs was breathtaking with the Olympic Mountains looking close enough to touch. The upper portion of the turret resided in the Master Suite. This was situated as an office, complete with a large desk and writing surface. The windows offered an inspiring view of those amazing mountains. And just to the right of the window, I glimpsed wisteria winding its way upward.

The bedroom also sported its own balcony. Stepping to the French doors, I peered out, noting the small wrought iron café table and chairs. Taking a slow, deep breath I turned back to Kerry. "Thank you. For bringing me out here, showing me around."

"Of course. It's the least I could do for Jake." Kerry held up that thick manila envelope. "I'll leave this downstairs. When you're ready, it'll be there. Now, how's about you just take a few days to look things through, think things over...and I'll leave you to it."

"Okay." I squared my shoulders, then as we made it back downstairs, asked, "Is there Wi-Fi here? Or dialup at least?"

"There is Wi-Fi. Jake had it installed for you." We'd made it out to the driveway by then, and Kerry pointed to the road we came in on. "If you follow that road further up, you'll run into Ryler's place in about three hundred yards. He's a quiet guy, Ryler is. But he was like a son to Jake, which is why if you have no interest in the place, Ryler will have first dibs."

"Did Jake ever marry? Have any other kids?"

"Jake never married. He dated a bit, but that was it. And you're his only biological child. He had no intention of going through that again. Ryler would be the closest thing he had to a son. If you need anything, Ryler's the one to call. He's closest, and he did most of the work on this place. Your Wi-Fi info, the house key, and the remote for the garage, as well as Rye's number are inside that envelope. You have my number, so let me know if you need anything. I hope you'll be happy here, AJ, and I hope you'll find the answers you're seeking."

"Thanks, Kerry," I said. "Me, too."

Kerry drove away. And the silence hit; it was so incredibly quiet out here. Just the occasional chirp or call of some bird, or the buzzing of an insect. It was peaceful. Reaching deep into the soul. I stood there for a few minutes, just listening, taking it all in, and the longer I listened the more I became aware of the sound of whispering. A light breeze moved through the pines, spreading the rich fragrance around, intertwining with that lovely, almost musical whispering.

Turning back to the house, I couldn't help but think of how much this place reminded me of something from a fairytale. Breathing deeply once more, I headed inside to get situated and try to settle in, settle down.

Wood had been cut and neatly stacked on the back porch, so after an easy dinner of grilled cheese and tomato soup, I sat before the roaring fireplace and went through that envelope. At least, I looked through things. I wasn't quite ready to read those letters yet. Soon, but not yet. I'd sleep on them a day or two, first.

Kerry had included a county plot map of the property, highlighting the location of the house to the boundaries of the land. My eyes lit on the two creeks, Bear Creek, and Wolf Creek that ran across the land, one to the south, the other to the north. My gaze continued to a section highlighted in green. Ryler's land.

Ryler. Who was he? By the comment Kerry made back at his office, when he'd scanned the parking lot looking for someone—he'd said Ryler had taken off already, and I'd guessed at who he'd been referring to. The only person I'd seen there had been that intriguing male; the beautiful one, the one with the limp, the scars, and the tattoos. If I were a betting person, I'd bet he was this Ryler. He hadn't stuck around though, despite his rather interested gaze. And it had definitely been interested, heated and stirring. If he was Ryler, and had been like a son to Jake, then he most likely was resenting the heck out of me right now. Which was really too bad, because the pull I'd felt towards him had been strong. Stronger than I'd felt in quite some time. And a part of me wanted to respond. To give a little tug back and see what happened. Even now, heat curled in my middle at the thought of the tall, dark-haired man. He wasn't quite as tall as Kevin, but he was wider. More built. Solid. This was a man used to working with his body. Roughened and tough. And I wouldn't mind getting to know him better.

I wondered then if Jake had any other family still in the area. Siblings, nieces, or nephews. I'd call Kerry tomorrow to ask. It'd be awkward to run into them while I was here. Then again, it might be better if we were unaware of each other at all. They didn't need to know I was here; I could take care of business and leave without them being any the wiser for it. It occurred to me then that this might have been how Jake had felt when he came to my signing.

After dinner I washed my dishes and put them away, then wandered more slowly back through the house, taking things in, noting the pictures on the walls. Stopping to peruse the faces, studying each one, trying to get a feeling for the man who'd fathered me. Jake had many pictures of me. School photos, photos I'd released on my webpage, and there was one—of myself and a man—at that book signing in Seattle. From the other pictures Jake had mounted on the walls, ones of him in uniform, military type pictures, I knew the man beside me in that photo was Jake.

My heart tripped over itself as I studied his face and noted his eyes. Dark greenish-blue. Twins to mine. I'd always wondered where I'd gotten my eyes from, considering my mother's were brown. I'd always just assumed they were from my deceased father, though from the one picture Mom had given me, his eyes had appeared brown also. Never in a million years had I considered they'd been from a very much alive father. I wondered what he'd been thinking in this moment. The look on his face was one of pride and pleasure. One might have assumed it was from meeting a favored author, but now, in light of all I'd learned, I wondered if it wasn't something more.

Trying to stem the overwhelming feelings, I called Leslie, letting her know I was here and settled in, then called Harley and told her the same thing. Of course, she'd asked if I'd seen anyone that sparkled yet.

"Harley, you remember I'm in Sequim, not Forks, right?"

She assured me she did and was only teasing. For a brief moment I considered the man, the one I assumed was Ryler, and the way the sweat had glistened on him, before shaking my head and moving on. I didn't, however, tell her of the stipulation in the will that I live here for a year, before I could do anything with the property. *That* was for another con-versation.

I didn't sleep well the first night. It was too dark. Too quiet. Other than the exterior house and garage lights, it was utter darkness outside. Nothing but the stars in the sky; I'd almost felt like the last person on earth. And to someone used to the sounds and lights, the bustle of activity that was Coronado, it was somewhat disconcerting.

The next morning, I drank my coffee while answering emails. Then headed outside to take some pictures of the magnificent view to post on my blog page. I made a mental note to check out the hiking opportunities in the area and wanted to make a trip to see the Strait as well.

I worked late that night, getting my laptop set up, trying to settle back into *Midnight Marine*. The characters were being a little stubborn though. No one wanted to speak with me. I ended up doing a favored writing exercise, leaving behind contemporary romances, I started work on a regency era fantasy, complete with knights-in-shining-armor and damsels that could kick your butt as well. Josephine climbed into my lap a little after one. It had begun raining at some point while I'd worked. The sound loud yet comforting on that metal roof. Close to two, I stretched and saved my file, then headed for bed.

Ryler

Ryler stood deep in the tree line, his dog Shiv beside him, a constant presence. The large, black Irish Wolfhound mix had whined, wanting out, and Ryler had been restless. He'd been restless for the last day or so. Basically, since he'd seen Jake's daughter in Kerry's parking lot. He hadn't even spoken to her, and she was already under his skin. Like an itch he couldn't quite reach. When his phantom pain acted up, he had mental exercises he'd do to help relieve the tension and irritation. Pretending to flex and stretch each of his toes, his foot, his leg, mentally moving those muscles, feeling them in his head. The itch Jake's daughter was producing didn't seem to have a connection in his skull. He didn't know how to flex and move this irritation. Moving, walking, staying busy seemed to help the best. So, when Shiv had whined to be out, Ryler had gone with him, just for something to do. And he wasn't sure just how they'd ended up here. Looking out over the clearing, towards the house. Maybe it was because Shiv had been used to visiting with Jake and it was habit for the both of them to wander this way. Glancing at his watch he saw it was just past one in the morning. The only lights from inside the house coming from that upstairs bedroom.

Ryler saw movement inside, but he was too far away to see much of what she was doing. And besides he didn't want to intrude on her privacy. So, he whistled quietly for Shiv, who'd been meandering into the tall grasses of the clearing, and headed back to the cabin.

AJ

After the deluge from the night before, I was somewhat surprised to wake to a bright sunny day. Josephine sat at my balcony door, tail switching as she watched the goings on of a couple birds just beyond her reach. I opened the door for her, then stepped out to admire the view, which was truly impressive. That wisteria vine nearly reached the balcony, and I leaned over the railing just a little to see if I could reach one of the blooms. My height became a factor, so I stepped onto the bottom rail and tried again. I was able to reach a cluster and picked them off. As I stepped down from the rail, my slipper caught on something and pulled from my foot, slipping between the slats of the rail and falling to the pavement below.

Glaring at the slipper in annoyance, I turned from the railing and headed back inside. Josephine seemed content to stay where she'd sprawled in a patch of warm sunshine, so I left the door open behind me as I headed downstairs. The pavement was still a little damp from last night's rain, so I quickly tiptoed the six steps or so it took to reach the wayward object. As I bent, reaching for my slipper, I heard the door snick shut. Whipping around, my eyes confirmed it was closed. Huffing out a breath, I grabbed the slipper, praying I'd unlocked the door when I'd stepped out instead of simply opening it. Dread settled in my middle as I grasped the handle. *Locked*. Grinding my teeth, I tried strong arming the lock into submission. Guess I needed to work out more. Or something.

Stepping back, I eyed the balcony and open door above me. Josephine watched intently, her tail flicking back and forth. "Don't suppose you could be bothered to use those incredible feline skills to open this door for me?" The long-haired calico rolled onto her back and stretched leisurely in the sunlight. "Yeah," I muttered. "Somehow, I didn't think so."

Slowly spinning around, I searched for a way to get that door open. There was nothing. Nothing short of a rock. And I wasn't quite *that* desperate. Yet. Spinning once more, my gaze landed on the garage. Which was also locked. Of course, it was. Why wouldn't it be? Heading back to the patio, I noticed the patio furniture, and wondered if the table would be tall enough to give me the boost I needed to reach my balcony.

Several sweaty minutes later, I'd managed to maneuver the heavy wooden table as close to the balcony as I could without it slipping off the edge of the patio. The balcony was not directly over the patio beneath it, but more off-centered as steps meandered between the edge of the patio and the underside of the balcony. My best bet was to get the table as close to those steps as I could, then hopefully jump high enough to grasp the balcony railing before falling to my almost-certain death.

I mean, it wasn't *that* bad, but still. Taking a steadying breath, I studied the setup, trying to do simple physics in my head. Here goes my audition as *Indiana Jane*. What I wouldn't give for a bullwhip right now. I'd never really thought of myself as afraid of heights, however, as I climbed onto that table, reaching as high and as far as I could stretch, I felt a little wobbly. And I was still too far away. It would have to be a big jump to grasp that railing. I needed to be a little closer. Climbing back down, I looked around again, this time my eyes landed on one of the chairs. Unfortunately, it was one of those swivel-style ones, not my first choice, but my only option. Telling myself I'd be fine, nothing to worry about, and imagining all the bragging rights I'd have for Harley after this, I carefully climbed onto the chair. *Please, don't let me fall*, I whispered to Whoever might have been listening and jumped.

Ryler

Shiv had been quietly snoring when the dog suddenly jumped to his feet and scratched at the door with a throaty rumble. Ryler opened it for him, leaving it open for his return, and headed back to the kitchen where he'd been pouring his coffee. Shiv scampered off into the scrub, scouting some scent or answering the call of nature. He was gone about ten minutes or so, when suddenly he was back and rumbling under his breath. He ran down the steps of the porch again, then ran back inside, now barking loudly. Ryler headed for the door, scanning to see if anyone was approaching. The road was clear however, so he growled, "Shut it." Shiv only barked louder, more aggressively. Ryler studied him for a moment before shrugging and heading out the door after the dog. "This had better be good, mutt."

Shiv led him south, in the direction of the big house. And as Ryler reached the clearing his sharp gaze instantly saw what was bothering the dog. Her. *She*. Jake's daughter was dangling from the balcony; her feet swaying this way and that, trying to gain a purchase.

Ryler ground his teeth, even as his pulse leaped in pleasure, and instantly hopped the fence, snarling at Shiv to stay put. Moving quickly, he crossed the field, intending to aid her before she fell. As he drew closer, Ryler saw better what she'd been attempting, the chair and table on their sides just under her frantically swaying feet. He also saw what she was wearing. That stopped him short. He needed a moment to absorb the shock to his system. Those legs. Those *mouthwatering* legs. Her short bathrobe had ridden up and peeking out from beneath was her shapely backside encased in what looked to be a pair of men's blue boxer briefs. Tattooed on her upper left thigh in shades of white, yellow, orange, and black was an image of the sun. The design seemed to have a Celtic feel to it. Whatever it was, he liked it. Wanted to take his time and explore it. Ryler swallowed as he stepped closer. Then her scent hit him; coconut, and cream, and somehow like the salty sea air, like the ocean, and he felt the blow deep in his gut, turning him inside out.

AJ

My arms were shaking with the strain of trying to hold myself up. I definitely needed to work out more. I didn't know how much longer I'd be able to hang on. As gravity pulled me downward, just as my fingers slipped, large firm, warm hands grasped my legs. They gripped just below my knees, then slid upward, and were now supporting my weight. "Let go," a low voice gently ordered. "I've got you."

The scream that had been intent on erupting, lodged in my throat. I'd avoided glancing down, but at that warm touch, that low, almost growling voice, my gaze was ripped downward. Heat barreled through me again, making me dizzy. His eyes were dark blue-grey, like ice, but so much warmer, framed in thick lashes under slashing brows. His hair was dark, as dark as mine, darker maybe, cut short, military style. His mouth, ringed in stubble, was set in a grim line. I swallowed, trying to calm myself, and he spoke again, the almost growling sound playing havoc with my insides. "Let go. You won't fall; I've got you."

Something in his tone told me to trust him so, I did. Letting go of the balcony, I instantly transferred my grip to his shoulders. Thoroughly enjoying what was under my palms. The way the muscle played under his skin. And then I was sliding through his hands, my backside snagging in his grip, but before that sensation could properly register, I was on the ground, on my own two feet, and he'd moved away from me.

Somewhere in the back of my mind, I caught the sound of a near-silent squeak. Like a hinge that maybe needed adjustment, or oiling. But that wasn't the focus of my mind right then, so easily dismissed in the face of what was happening, and what had just happened.

"You like to live dangerous, AJ?" he grumbled almost angrily over his shoulder as he righted the table and chairs. "Was there something wrong with using the door on this level?"

At his sharpened tone, I felt my hackles rise. "Well, excuse the heck out of me for getting locked out and inconveniencing you. I don't recall asking for your help you know."

Ryler just snorted. He'd reached my back door with that faint whirring squeak occasionally sounding. My gaze flicked to his right leg, noting he favored it slightly, and found myself wondering what might have happened, if he was wearing a brace for support. Ryler tried the door and found it locked. He turned back towards me, and I couldn't help my arched brow, nor the cocking of my jaw.

"The spare key is here. No need to go climbing walls." Ryler bent stiffly, and angled a large, blue-colored flowerpot. He then turned back to the door and, without looking at me, held the key up for me to see before unlocking the door, and swinging it open. He then replaced the key and stepped off the patio, heading back towards the trees. That faint whir, an ever-constant sound, faded as he moved away from me.

"That's it?" Disbelief colored my tone.

He stopped and glanced over his shoulder. In rapid succession, his gaze hit me, the open door, the table and chair, then came back to me again. His jaw was tight. "What else do you need?"

"Nothing," I mumbled. "I just...you're just leaving like that? Don't you even want to come inside? We haven't been properly introduced yet." As much as his tone had irritated, the thought of his leaving irritated even more.

"You're AJ." He stabbed a finger at me, then jerked a thumb at himself. "I'm Ryler. Now we know each other." That deep voice was all snarly, causing equal measures of heat and annoyance to stir. "And I've got things to do, thanks anyway."

Flummoxed, I watched him walk away. Stomp away was more accurate, despite the fact that he favored that leg the entire way. *What the heck*? My mind and my body were currently at war with each other. Because my head said he could kiss off, but my body was chiming something entirely different. And I wasn't exactly sure who would win this battle.

Ryler

Ryler's hands were still tingling, still shaking. He could still feel her, even now, the heat coming off her, her skin.

He tightened his fists, then opened them.

Tightened.

Opened.

The entire walk back to his cabin.

Those legs. That skin. Her scent. His heart was still pounding. His mouth dry. Ryler glared at the large dog beside him. "Thanks for that. Now stay away from her, ya hear?"

Shiv responded with a cocked head and huff of breath, then whined low. Ryler made it back into the cabin, ignored the coffee pot and mug, and reached for an ice-cold bottle of Guinness. He had it half finished before he took a breath. *Dang* her anyway. Trouble. She was nothing but trouble with a capitol T.

Ryler's head echoed with the sound of his promise to Jake. He knew he was going to have to bite the bullet here soon, fulfill that promise. But not yet. Not when he had to hold himself on such a tight leash around her. Because right now, what he wanted most was to taste that skin, her mouth. To hear her raspy voice make that little sound she'd made just now when he'd gripped her legs. It was all just driving him a bit crazy. So, for the time being, he'd keep his distance. Though he knew that soon there'd have to be a reckoning.

CHAPTER FOUR

Sequim

AJ

It's been two days since I last saw Ryler. Two days since he'd, obviously unwillingly come to my rescue. Yes, I was now able to admit that he had, in fact, rescued me. Two days that I'd spent storming around the house, grumbling under my breath, imagining stomping up to his door, banging upon it, and giving him a piece of my mind. But of course, I did none of those things. No, I just stayed here and stewed, going through that envelope, looking at photos, and trying to wrap my mind around everything.

I'd read one of the letters Jake had left for me. Folded with the letter was a copy of the arrangements my mom had made with him. It made me sick to my stomach to know she'd lied to me my whole life. Telling me my father was dead, supplying me with a fake photo, fake name. All so she could have me to herself, because she was mad Jake wouldn't leave the military for her. Did she not understand how much it hurt him; how much she'd stolen from me? It was more than I could focus on and process in one, or even two or three sittings. This was going to take me a while.

In my perusing around, I found the key for the garage. Curious, still trying to learn about this man who'd been my father, I opened the garage side door and let my eyes adjust before stepping inside. It was, I supposed, a normal type of garage, not that I had gobs of experience with garages. Jake had what looked to be a Jeep of some kind, sitting in the center of the space, partially covered under a brown cloth tarp. The hood of the vehicle showed it to be black; at least, what I could see of it was black. I wondered if it still ran. But that was something to learn another day.

To one side, I spied several lawn and garden tools—rakes, shovels, and a wheelbarrow. Hammers, wrenches, and hand tools rested, untouched for some time, at least by the amount of dust covering them, on the work bench at the back of the garage. I was turning away, intending to leave, not being interested in those types of things, when I saw the tire of a bicycle hanging from the rafters towards the far left of the garage.

Upon further inspection, I found it was actually an entire bike, not just the tire. I stared at it for a moment or two in consternation, trying to figure out how to get the darn thing down. Because I sure as heck was *not* going to ask Ryler for any help. After a few minutes of searching, I found a sturdy folding stepstool tucked behind the open garage door. With minimal difficulty, I was able to lift the bike to the ground. It was white, had a wide comfy-looking seat, and everything seemed in working order. There was even a wire basket attached to the front.

Back on Coronado, I'd biked around the island quite a bit, and knew it may take me all day, but decided to ride into town, do some more looking around. Maybe get a little more familiarized with the area.

Two hours later, I was coasting into Sequim. I'd looked through the paperwork Kerry had left and found a small county map with roads highlighted, showing the route into town, as well as several spots of interest. Sequim is one those charming little towns you might see on a postcard. The lampposts were painted deep lavender, reflecting the flower the town was famous for. Baskets, both hanging and standing were everywhere, filled to overflowing with various flowers and other kinds of foliage. It was, all of it, very charming. And as I meandered around, just taking in the sights, I noticed a large commotion off to my left, down a block or so. Angling in that direction, I found a farmer's market in full swing and decided to check it out.

I parked the bike in one of the racks and locked it up, then began a slow stroll through the area. In addition to the normal fruits and vegetables one might expect to find at a farmer's market, I also found booths selling every-thing from fudge to handmade jewelry, paintings, sketches, and photos. Leather work, wood carvings, candles and soaps, jams and jellies, and fresh bread and pastries. There were vendors selling cotton candy, hotdogs and burgers, and thankfully, I found an espresso stand as well.

A local band was playing; they had an interesting sound, similar to *Ed Sheeran*. Part Blues, part Rock, part Pop, part something else entirely. I liked them, though, and after listening to several songs, bought their album. *The Jolly Roger's,* they called themselves. I continued my mean-dering, taking my time, looking through each booth, just breathing in the atmosphere that Sequim offered. After buying several items, I found a small table off to the side where I could enjoy the music and my coffee. I tried not to feel self-conscious about being here, tried to play it cool, and just be incognito, but I drew a few long looks, from multiple sources. Questioning, interested looks. I ignored them all for the most part, telling myself they weren't connecting me with Jake, just noticed that I was one among many strangers in their town.

Time went faster than I'd anticipated. When *The Jolly Roger's* broke for a while, I noticed the sun was already dipping in the sky. Not wanting to ride back to Jake's in the dark, especially on unfamiliar roads, I decided I'd better get going. I'd brought a small backpack in place of a purse, so I was able to store most of my finds and purchases in that, at least the ones that didn't fit in the basket on the bike.

I was just a little way past the edge of town proper, when I noticed my bike felt funny. Sluggish. Slowing, I looked at the tires and found the front one was flat. *Freaking just great!* Quickly climbing off, I inspected the tire and found nothing wrong, other than that it was definitely lacking in air. Unsure what to do exactly, I considered my options. Did I head back to town and try to locate a bike shop? Or just continue back to the house. After a moment or two, I decided I was tough enough and would just walk the bike back to Jake's. It wasn't that far—I could do it. I'd gone maybe a mile and half when the sound of a loud engine neared. The sun hadn't quite set yet, but it had definitely sunk well below the tree line, casting me and my surroundings in shadow. So as the vehicle came nearer, the headlights illuminating the roadway in front of me, I moved the bike over, so as not to be in danger of getting hit. Still, the driver downshifted, slowing the vehicle.

My nerves were a little frayed at this point. I'd been worrying over wild animals coming out at night, looking for their evening meal. And though I knew I was being an idiot, I couldn't help but wonder about Harley's warnings to me as well. I'd glanced around repeatedly, looking for a sparkling presence, or a huge shadowy wolf-like image stalking in my direction. Now it seemed I'd have another kind of animal to worry over. The vehicle pulled in behind me and came to a stop, the headlights dimming until just the running lights were on. Next, I heard the door open. Turning, I saw the outline of a man moving in my direction and my heart lodged in my throat.

Coronado isn't isolated. There are people around at all hours. It's busy and loud. But here? There was nothing out here. No lights; save for those from the vehicle behind me and the ever-fading sunlight. There was no one around. And it suddenly dawned on me just how alone I truly was. Apprehension left a bad taste in my mouth. I stepped around the bike to face the driver, putting the cycle between us, mentally preparing to have to defend myself if need be.

"Hi." I wanted him to know I saw him, that I wasn't afraid, even though I kind of was. My eyes took in the dark colored Bronco in the background, wondering if anyone else was inside.

"Is there something wrong with the bike?" the voice rumbled towards me from the gloom.

My heart lurched in my chest, pounding out a slow, thudding rhythm as I recognized Ryler's voice. Heat twisted, curling like a satisfied cat in my middle and I couldn't form words, needing a moment to collect myself. So many emotions flooded through me. Relief, sheer, intense, relief that I wasn't about to be murdered. Annoyance, at his tone of voice, like I'd gotten a flat just to tick him off or something. Fire, flashing, burning fire, at the rebel yell that was now sounding inside my skull, to accept the challenge he offered. Wonder, that he was affecting me so thoroughly, so undesirably. All this combined to have my tone come out a tad sarcastic. "No, Ryler, there's nothing *wrong* with the bike. I was bored and decided to let all the air out of the tire so I could push it home, you know, just for kicks. Seeing as how there's nothing else to do in this backwoods town of yours."

Ryler tensed; I saw it, felt it; heard the soft growl of warning from him, the sound of pure irritation. And I relished it. *Two can play at this game, buddy. You want to be a jerk to me, well mister, I have teeth, too.* Deciding not to give him the opportunity to respond, I turned my back on him and continued pushing the bike down the road. My steps now strong and energetic, ire coursing through me, fueling me on.

I'd gone only thirty paces or so, when I heard the slam of his vehicle door, the revving of his engine, the squeal of his tires on the pavement and in the gravel. My gloating smile was short lived as Ryler slammed the Bronco to a stop directly in my path, cutting me off. He was out of the vehicle, around the hood, and in my face faster than I'd anticipated he could move. And he was mad. Oh boy, was he mad.

"Get in," he growled.

"No thanks; I'm good." I snapped, trying to move around him. But Ryler took hold of my bike, lifting it away from me with one hand, and carrying it to the back of the Bronco. His limp was minimal today; the squeak from the other day gone. Maybe the brace, or whatever it had been, was finally off. The bike was quickly placed inside, my packages carefully placed next to it, before I could really do much of anything. Then he was right beside me, taking my arm and opening the passenger door. "Get. In."

Don't ask me why, because I really couldn't say, but Ryler's come-and-go limp had sparked my curiosity. You'd think I might have had something, anything else, on my mind in this situation, but no. No, my response to his demand was, "What happened to your leg, Ryler?"

That stopped him short, which surprised me. His nostrils flared, his lips thinned. And I saw the vein throbbing in his neck. "That's *none* of your business, AJ. Now get your butt in the Bronco and do it now."

"No *freaking* way! And get your hands off me!"

Ryler let go, stepping back some. "AJ, I'm not playing games here. Get in. Now."

"Well, that makes two of us, Ryler, as I'm not playing games either. I didn't ask you to stop, I didn't flag you down; I don't need or *want* your help. So just give me back my bike and let me go home."

"*Home*?" He snorted. "You stickin' around then?"

"That's none of *your* business. Now give me back the bike."

"Just get in, AJ. You're not walking home."

"Yeah? Watch me." I decided he could keep the bike, and as I was already walking, at least it wouldn't slow me down to have to push it. But he grabbed my arm again in a firm, yet gentle grip, pulling me around to face him. We were so close for a moment and as his gaze flicked down to my mouth and back, I'd thought he was going to kiss me. And darned if that didn't send my stomach into somersaults. The heat curling there made me shiver. And as I did, Ryler released me as if he'd been burned, seeming to realize what he'd been doing. "You really want to walk? It's nearly seven miles, and you're in shorts and sandals. The temperature is going to drop another thirty degrees tonight."

Out of sheer stubborn will, I just mutely nodded at him. Also, there was the fact that my breath was still missing from my lungs, the desire to be kissed still pulsing through me, stealing my voice. Ryler lifted his hands out to the side and took another step back. "Suit yourself." And in somewhat disappointed disbelief, I watched as he left me there; slammed the passenger door shut and climbed back into his Bronco without another word. I stared after him for a moment, before turning away to, once again, begin my trek back to Jake's place. It occurred to me as I moved forward that I couldn't remember just how far it actually was to the turnoff, nor what the name of the street was. So, I took my backpack off and dug around inside for the little map. Of course, the light was fading quickly, making it difficult for me to see clearly. In daylight the map had seemed simple and easy to follow. Now, in the quickly fading dusk, nothing seemed to make any sense at all. Not even my cellphone flashlight helped; everything still looked foreign and backwards.

Gritting my teeth, I shoved the map back inside and shot a glare over my shoulder at Ryler who was still there in his Bronco. Like he was waiting for me. Hoping I'd give up and just come with him. Well, I wouldn't. I could do this. Without his help, *darn him anyway*. He could take his heat-inducing self and just shove it. I'd walked maybe twenty feet when I heard the rev of the Bronco, and the crunch of the gravel. Glancing over my shoulder, I saw Ryler was following me. Caution lights flashing, just creeping along.

Are you freaking kidding me? Was he seriously planning to follow me all the way home like this?

Fine.

Whatever.

If the temperature hadn't indeed been dropping like he'd promised, if I hadn't been wearing shorts and sandals, I'd have crawled home on my hands and knees just to annoy him, but as I was already feeling the bite of the chill, I decided to ignore him as best I could and continue on.

I'm not sure how long I'd been walking, a half hour, maybe more, maybe less, but despite my exertions I was shivering in the cold, cursing myself for not having brought, at the very least, a sweatshirt or something. And to make matters worse, it began to drizzle.

Tears pricked my eyes at the injustice of it all. Water now ran down me in rivulets from the ever-increasing downpour I was stumbling through; my eyes stung from the mascara bleeding down my cheeks. I'd tried wiping it off as best I could, but I'm sure I looked a mess, regardless. Roadside dirt and mud were splattered up my legs, which were screaming in protest, and I was sure I had blisters on top of blisters, from my sandals. Ryler pulled up beside me once more. Stubbornly I refused to even look in his direction, even though I was so relieved, so *thankful* he hadn't left me and just continued to trudge along in my misery.

He stopped the Bronco, stepped out, and made his way to my side. "You planning to walk all the way back to California?" Stupidly I turned to him, unsure what he meant. "You missed your turnoff, about a half mile back."

Defeated, I pulled my gaze from Ryler and looked behind me, facing the roadway I'd just come from, wanting nothing more than to lie down and cry. Shoulders slumped, in limping steps, I turned back the way I'd come. He muttered something unflattering under his breath, and the next thing I knew was the strength of his grip and the heat of his hands. Ryler swung me up in his arms, cradling me like a child.

Against my will, unable to help myself, I turned into him, curving into his warmth, breathing him in. Ryler smelled of wood and pine, and something stronger, spicier. He opened the passenger door. "Get in the back, Shiv," he muttered, before depositing me gently on the seat. Ryler took the time to fasten my seatbelt before closing the door and making his way to the driver's side. A deep rumbling *humph* sounded from behind me. Something sniffed at my shoulder, whining low and concerned-like. Glancing behind, I saw a massive, furry, black shape. A part of my mind thought I should be afraid, or at the very least concerned. But the dog's golden eyes were soulful and thoughtful. His presence and demeanor comforting.

Ryler climbed inside the cab and turned the heat on high, then shifted to reverse, muttering to himself about stubborn women.

"You named your dog after a knife?" I asked once the shivering had subsided. Ryler shot me a long look, nodding sharply, before turning back to the windshield. Five minutes later we pulled up to the house. He shut the Bronco off and climbed out. Without a word, he lifted me again and carried me to the house. Unlocking it somehow without putting me down, he carried me all the way up to my room. The limp and the whirring squeak were back again. Gently he sat me on the bed, then quickly stepped back, as if touching me were somehow distasteful. I felt a curious sense of loss at the absence of his touch.

"Can you make it from here?" his voice was low, controlled.

"Yeah," I nodded. Without another word, Ryler left.

Ryler

He was going to kill her. Either that or kiss her. Maybe both. Either option would land him in hot water, though. Ryler was still fuming by the time he returned to his cabin. Her scent clung to him, his clothes, his skin, making him restless, aggravated. Not since he'd first awoken, after the explosion, after the initial surgery, once the healing had begun had he felt this wound up, this ready to erupt. His body shook with the tension, the *itch*, the irritation that AJ aroused in him.

Aroused—that was a good word. That was what he was, what his problem was. Ryler was good and aroused. The *itch* AJ generated fast becoming something he was unable to ignore. Not since he'd had to detox from all the pain meds he'd been on had he been this agitated, this trapped inside his own skin, clawing and scraping, just trying to get the tension out, relieve some of the pressure.

Ryler opted for an ice-cold shower. It helped very little. He was still a mountain of smoldering tension and desire. Especially when he reentered his bedroom and could still smell her and desire slammed into him once more. Grinding his teeth, he snatched the discarded clothes from earlier and stomped into the utility room, throwing them in the wash, slamming the lid shut. He *would* master this, because there was no way under heaven he was going down this road again. Once was enough. Ryler didn't need women, and he sure didn't need this one, no matter what his body was demanding.

AJ

After showering last night and weakly climbing into bed, I'd slept like the dead. The house could have burned down and I'd have never known. I awoke in the morning feeling rather like I'd been run over, repeatedly, by a very large truck. *Or Bronco.* Either way, I felt like crap. Literal crap. And I looked it, too.

My face was haggard, eyes still somewhat smeared with yesterday's mascara, red and puffy. My hair looked like some sort of varmint had climbed inside and made a home. And as I stood in the bathroom, just looking at the image before me in the mirror, I decided that I just didn't care. It took too much effort to care. And I simply had no energy for it.

My head was pounding and I could feel a cold coming on. My chest was tight, my throat achy. My middle was tight and cramping. Checking the calendar, I saw my cycle was due to start. Perfect. I guess that explained my crazy emotions. With coffee in hand, I climbed into the bathtub full of steaming water and fragranced Epsom salts, a groan escaping me. I soaked for a good half an hour, until the water had cooled, before climbing out and getting dressed. Now I stood at the balcony door, staring unseeing out at the sunshine in the yard, my mind still on the events of last night. With a disgruntled groan, I turned away, climbed back into bed, and slept the day away, not waking again until late in the afternoon when my cell phone began ringing.

Not wanting Harley to hear how miserable I was at the moment, I decided to forego that conversation for the time being and sent her to voicemail. Rolling out of bed, I headed back downstairs. I was sipping another cup of coffee, standing on the back patio, when I saw something big and dark move inside the tree line across the field. From this distance, I was unable to tell exactly what it was but wondered if maybe it was Ryler's dog. And I wasn't ashamed to admit that I hoped it was Ryler's dog and not some wolf, or bear, even.

I sighed. There was a conundrum if ever there was one. I wasn't sure just what to do about Ryler. For the most part he seemed to barely tolerate me. Then there were times where I'd swear the man was feeling the same heat I felt whenever he was around. I told myself it was just because he was basically *unknown* to me, something interesting and new. That it was because it had been a while since I'd last been in a relationship. Whatever it was, this ratcheting heat and tension between us would take care of itself one way or another. Either we'd take a long close look at what was possibly between us, unable to ignore it any longer, or it'd burn itself out and we'd move on, no longer interested at all.

Suddenly annoyed, I turned from the door, reaching for my cell-phone. Harley answered on the second ring. "Doll! How're you doing?"

The sound of her voice brought tears to my eyes. *Stupid hormones.* I had to swallow past the lump in my throat to answer. "I'm good," I lied. "How're you? Things going well there? You surviving all right without me?"

"Just barely. When are you coming home?"

It was on my tongue to say, *soon*, but instead I heard these words coming from my lips, "I'm not sure. There are some things I'm still working on, trying to work out. Some things I need to figure out, ya know?"

"You really all right, AJ?" I heard the hesitation. "You sound a bit...I dunno...off, I guess."

"Yeah, I just have a lot on my mind is all."

"Stuff with your dad?"

"That...and other things. Like I want to come home, but...."

She was silent a moment, then, "But you feel like you need to stay?"

"I think so." I whispered.

Harley drew in a long breath, holding it a moment before letting it out again, "Okay; I miss you, gobs and gobs, but I understand. Take all the time you need. Just, don't let it be forever, all right?"

I smiled. "Thanks, Harley. I promise." I'd also promised to call Mrs. Carson, and Leslie, when we hung up, letting them know my plans. We chatted a little bit longer, Harley filling me in on her work activities. We laughed over the antics of a younger couple with two small children, who were apparently learning to potty-train, as they continually attempted to strip down to their bare skin, regardless of where they were. Like at the table in the dining room. By the end of the evening, both parents were at their wits end, as they led two screaming toddlers upstairs for bed.

Both Leslie and Mrs. Carson understood my need to stay longer and wished me well. Leslie even offered to fly up here, to help go through papers and things. I'd been blessed when I'd landed her as my agent. Not only had she looked out for me as an author, steering me in the right direction, guiding me along the way, but she was also a true and trusted friend. I couldn't ask for better. Once I hung up the phone with Leslie, I wrote a quick blog post, talking about how beautiful it was here. Then, I decided I should go ahead and read through that envelope Jake had left for me.

CHAPTER FIVE
The Choices We Make

AJ

If I'd thought my eyes were red-rimmed and bloodshot yesterday, then today I looked like I'd contracted some sort of disease. I hadn't slept at all and had cried most of the night through. Hard, crushing sobs that stole the breath from my lungs. That made my head throb and my eyes ache. I cried until there were no more tears. Cried until there was nothing left.

I'd had a dad, a father-figure who had loved me as his own child, who loved me still. Dave, my stepdad, had been good to me. Even after he and my mom had divorced nine years ago, he and I had stayed in touch. We still talked on the phone; I still called him for advice, or to share some new triumph in my life. And I'd wanted to call him last night. Wanted to hear his voice. Wanted him to tell me everything was going to be all right, that everything would work out. To talk about all I'd learned. To ask him what he had known, if Mom had ever told him the truth.

But I was afraid. What if he *had* known and had kept the truth from me? What if he'd been part of the deception?

It wasn't that hard to imagine Mom doing what she'd done. But Dave? Just the thought of him being part of this made me want to dry-heave. So, I hadn't called him. Not when I'd first learned of Jake and not now. That was a phone call I would postpone for the time being. Talking to my mother, confronting her, was another phone call I'd be postponing for a good, long while.

I know in life we make decisions. Sometimes we're forced to make very difficult ones. Even painful ones. After spending last night reading through all, and I mean all, every last scrap of paper that Jake had left for me, I felt hollow. There was a void inside. Sounds echoed. Memories fluttered. I wasn't numb. It was almost like I was vacant. Numb indicated pain was still there, it was just buried. I wasn't numb. I was empty. Like every last part of me had been scooped out. And now, as I looked around myself, at the papers strewn all over the bed, it was like I was looking at what was left of me. Trying to decide what to put back, what to leave out. Trying to decide *who* I was now.

The choices we make in life, sometimes they're simple, other times they can be indescribably complicated. Jake had made some hard and difficult decisions. Some he'd had support for, some he hadn't. Like when he'd joined the Army, and again, when he was selected into the Ranger program. His parents had been proud of him. Worried, but proud. When, after his injury, he'd reenlisted, they hadn't been as happy. They'd felt he'd already done enough, sacrificed enough for his country. Jake had dealt with a lot when he came back. The least of it, PTSD. And at the time, PTSD wasn't something really talked about. You were simply expected to soldier on. Stay strong. Never quit. Jake had written that civilian life was difficult for him. He'd been more comfortable with his unit. There were too many variables in civilian life, too many unknowns. Slowly, he said, he'd begun to unravel.

Then after his injury, after I was born, still unraveling, still unable to adapt, he'd believed Mom. She'd convinced him I'd be better off without him. He'd never be ready to be a father. He hadn't even known how to be a man, only a soldier. Only a warrior. She'd told him he'd die in service to his country, and if he'd had any true honor, he'd want what was best for his child. And that was to let me go. To let her find and create a life and family for me that wouldn't include death. One that was safe.

So, Jake had agreed. He'd loved me enough to let me go. To let her try and create that magical life she'd told him about. Jake had loved me, loved me until the day he'd died. And I'd never known. It was hard to process. Hard to comprehend. Difficult to fathom.

I wasn't even sure just what to do with the information. What to do with this knowledge. Who was I now? What did all this make me? Was I a Daniels, after Jake? Or was I still AJ McAdams, after Dave? As my mind flickered, rather like a light bulb just before it goes out, it occurred to me that maybe I was having a hard time thinking because I hadn't eaten in over twenty-four hours. So, I headed downstairs, glancing at the clock in the hall as I moved toward the kitchen. Ten to ten. My stomach grumbled angrily. What I wouldn't give for one of Mrs. Carson's home-cooked meals. Even some of her leftovers would be great. As it was, all I found was an almost too-ripe banana, and a small jar of peanut butter. Not the meal I was hoping for, but I could make it work.

At some point today I'd need to pick up more groceries. And I guess I'd need to make a decision about what I was going to do. Stay, or go? And, if I was being honest, I'd need to talk with Ryler. Jake had also explained Ryler to me. What Ryler had gone through, who and what Ryler was to him. How Ryler had stood beside Jake through his illness, through his personal battle with cancer. Jake hadn't mentioned much about Ryler's time in the military, other than that he'd had a hard time before going, and a hard time when he came back. A real hard time.

I needed to talk with him, with Ryler, to thank him for what he'd done so far for me, what he'd done for Jake. And hopefully just get across to him that I wasn't his enemy. We didn't have to go to war with each other. That decision made, I finished that banana and peanut butter and headed up to shower.

A closed gate blocked the entrance to Ryler's property. Padlocked and chained, with a sign hung on the post to the right: "Private Property: Keep Out." I stared at that sign for a moment or two, debating my choices.

Deciding to break the rules a little, I shut the car off, got out, climbed over that gate, then hoofed it on up the drive.

Ryler's cabin sat near the top of a small peak, about a hundred and fifty yards from that locked gate. Tall pines surrounded it, covering the two-story structure in dappled shade and sunlight. A large porch extended from the front of the building, spanning the entire width. Shiv rumbled a low greeting as I neared the steps, but there was no sign of his irritating and intriguing owner. Knocking on the door produced no response either. Feeling far braver than I actually was, I tried the handle. Locked. Like the gate.

As I'd already come this far, climbing the locked gate, trying the handle, I figured I may as well go one step farther in my lawbreaking attempts, so I peered through the windows that faced the porch. Ryler's cabin was clean, orderly. Not what I'd expected from a bachelor. Even so, I saw no sign of him. On a whim, I turned and jogged back to my car, reached for my purse, and dug through it to find a pen and scrap piece of paper. Quickly I wrote my note for Ryler, grinning as I left it under a rock right in front of his door. Shiv sniffed at me, licking my face as I scratched his ears. "Make sure he gets that," I told the dog as I turned to leave. Shiv rumbled in his deep voice, and I was sure he was agreeing to my request.

The note I'd left at Ryler's door read, "I'm staying; we should talk. I'll be at The Oasis until you show up."

Ryler

Ryler stared at the rock on his doorstep. More to the point, he stared at the note tucked under it. Glancing around, he squatted carefully, studying the rock and piece of paper. Looking for anything out of the ordinary, other than the fact a note had been left in the first place.

Shiv lay there watching him, head cocked, tail thumping mildly. Picking up the rock and note, Ryler examined them briefly before tossing the rock off the porch. As he brought the note closer, he caught a faint trace of coconut and cream and growled. "The heck was she doing here?" he accused the large hound. Shiv thumped his tail harder and rolled onto his back.

Shaking his head in disgust, Ryler read the note and tried to still his pulse. But her scent had him. And her words. She was staying. No reprieve was coming for him any time soon.

Swearing under his breath, Ryler stomped into the house, needing a shower.

She was staying.

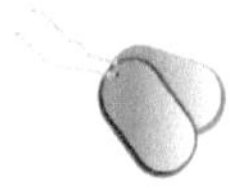

AJ

I waited close to an hour and a half, beginning to think Ryler wasn't showing up. The Oasis Bar and Grill wasn't too crowded when I'd arrived. However, as the time passed, people began filtering in. I'd chosen a table outside on the patio, out of the way, trying to remain unseen as much as possible. The server, Terri was her name, had suggested I try the *Life Jacket Citrus IPA*; it was nice, light, smooth, with just a hint of citrus—I liked it. I was still sipping on my first one, when the chair across from mine was pulled backward and soon filled with the dark mass that was Ryler.

We looked at each other silently for several moments. All thoughts of what I'd planned to say jumped ship as he took me in. Those blue-grey eyes, framed in thick dark lashes, scanned me carefully before returning to mine. The silence dragged on, until someone appeared next to us. "Hey, Ryler. Long time, no see. What can I get ya?" Terri asked, her voice friendly.

"Guinness, Terri. Thanks." His gaze stayed firmly on me.

"Bottle, or draft?"

"Build me one, thanks."

"Draft it is." Terri turned to me. "And how're you doing? Ready for another? Or you want to place an order for food?"

"I'll have another, thanks. And put Ryler's on my ticket. What does he generally order, Terri?"

"I'll get my own, thanks." Ryler interrupted Terri's reply, still holding my gaze.

"Nuh-uh, *I* invited you. That means it's on me. You want to pay, then next time *you* invite me." I turned my gaze back to Terri.

She grinned. "Ryler likes the bacon guacamole cheeseburger with onion rings and ranch."

"We'll take two, please. Though, I'd like blue cheese with mine."

Terri wrote that down then headed off to put our order in. "Thanks for coming," I told Ryler.

He nodded thoughtfully. "You're staying, then?" He asked the question like he wasn't sure if I'd meant it or not.

I nodded, taking a sip of my drink. "Look, I'm sorry we hit it off on the wrong foot. Jake...all of this...it was all just a big...a really big shock. I'd gone my whole life, at least up until almost a month ago, thinking my dad had died before I was born."

His eyes narrowed. "That what your mom told you?"

"Yeah." I nodded. "So, when I got the letter, I was pretty shocked."

"I bet."

"At any rate, I wanted to tell you that I'd be staying for a while. A few months at least. Jake mentioned several things he thought I'd like to see and do here, and I'd like to give those a shot. Also, I...wanted to thank you, for, well for coming to my assistance. What with the door, and my bike's flat tire...."

"Sure," he nodded.

"And also, to just say...thank you for staying by him. Jake, I mean. With what he went through. Thank you."

Ryler cleared his throat and just as he went to respond, Terri was back with his drink. Once she'd set that down, and left again, Ryler looked at me. "I was honored to do it."

It looked like he might have said more, but he quickly took his mug and swallowed. His answer had me wondering. It may have referred to several things. Helping Jake, or helping me, or both. I waited, wondering if he was going to expand, but he seemed to be focusing on his drink. Mentally shrugging, I turned to mine as well.

"I'm glad." Ryler said several minutes later. "That you're staying. Jake would've been pleased."

I wasn't sure how to respond, so ended up just saying, "Good."

Terri brought our food then. And as we ate, the silence seemed to have settled to an almost uncomfortable level. I caught Ryler looking at me several times. Each time those blue-grey eyes landed on me, my stomach leaped, and my pulse kicked up a notch or two, before settling down again, allowing me to eat. I searched my brain for something to say, something to talk about.

"We might look tame," Ryler said suddenly, seemingly out of the blue. "Decent, and nice, but there are...animals, and things to be cautious about." His statement caught me off guard, and I just stared at him. *Animals*? What? He must have noticed the lost look on my face, because he added, "I'm not talking about the four-legged variety. It's the two-legged ones you need to watch out for here."

"Oh." I blinked. "You mean...what do you mean exactly?" I glanced around us. There were about a half-dozen tables out here and we were the only two people on the patio. Who, and what, was he talking about? Jake had mentioned that Ryler had been injured in Afghanistan, that he'd had a long recovery time, had gone through some pretty intense PTSD, and I wondered if maybe he was experiencing flashbacks of some sort.

"Sequim. This community. It appears nice, friendly even. And for the most part we are. But don't forget we get our crime as much as any city will.

Being off on your own, on a deserted highway, after dark...that isn't smart. It's asking for trouble."

"Oh." Understanding dawned on me. "You mean the other night. I hadn't meant to be out that late. Time just got away from me. And it got darker earlier than I'd expected, and I hadn't planned on the tire going flat...and besides," I chuckled, feeling a warmth begin to build inside at the thought that he might be concerned about me. "I live on Coronado Island. We get plenty of crime. Trust me."

"That being said, you should be careful. Don't take unnecessary risks."

"Okay. Thanks for your concern, Ryler."

"I'm not trying to be a jerk, or butt into your business, AJ," he explained. "I promised Jake I'd look out for you...if you came, if you stayed. I'm just trying to follow through on that."

Feeling a little of that warm glow I'd been experiencing at the thought of Ryler's concern for me begin to deflate, like the slow leak of helium from a balloon, I nodded. I was being an idiot. Ryler had been following through on his promise to Jake, not trying to show any interest in me, or make a move. "Oh, okay. Yeah, thanks. That's...that's very nice of you. But I can look out for myself. I've been on my own since I was eighteen. Thanks for your concern, though."

Ryler just looked at me, his eyes boring into mine; a speculative glint in them. *What*, I wanted to ask him, w*hat are you thinking? And why are you thinking it*, especially if you're just following through on your promise to Jake? You shouldn't seem so interested...if you're really not. "For how long?" he finally asked.

"What?"

"You've been on your own for how long?"

"About six years now. Why?" Ryler shook his head; a dark, breathy chuckle blew from his mouth. "What?" I asked again, unsure at this point about everything.

"You seem older than twenty-three," was all he said in response.

"I'll be twenty-four in December," I offered. To which he only glanced up at me before looking back down to his plate.

We finished eating; I paid, just as I'd said I would. Then we parted ways in the parking lot. Ryler waited until I was in the car, before he climbed into his Bronco. He said he'd see me around, and to call if I needed anything. I nodded and that was that. At least for the next two weeks or so. I'd see him around town, doing this, or doing that. From what I could tell, he was some sort of handy-man type. A man-of-all-trades and talents kind of guy.

We'd wave at each other, or nod in passing, but he didn't really reach out to me, and I didn't really reach out to him. I guess you could say we were giving each other some space. Friendly space, but still, it was space. One day I saw him under the hood of a car, another day he was painting a fence, and still on another, I saw him hanging a sign and planting flowers. I couldn't help but notice him. Ryler drew attention without even trying. Maybe it was that tough, confident, he-could-handle-anything-life-tossed-his-way persona, maybe it was his hardened, rugged good looks. I really couldn't name just what it was. All I know is that despite my best efforts, and my many internal lectures, I noticed him. Thoroughly. It was annoying, really. I also couldn't help but notice, though, that Ryler's limp didn't seem to be getting any better. His injury must be of a more permanent nature. And I wondered again, against my will, what he'd done, what had caused it. If this was due to the injury he'd received in service.

In that time, those two weeks or so, I checked out several of the places Jake had mentioned in his letters. I also placed two needful and important phone calls. The first was to my mom. Letting her know that I was staying, at least for the time-being.

"AJ," she began, after I told her the news. "I'm sure you're upset with me, and maybe a little confused. But I had my reasons. He was unstable. He didn't know how to be a husband, much less a father—"

"Mom, stop," I cut her off. "I don't want to hear it. I didn't call to talk about your reasons. I'm just letting you know that I'm staying. And while I'm not cutting you completely out of my life, I do want you to back off.

I need space. You lied to me; you've hurt me, and it's going to take a while for me to work through all this. So, I'm going to go now. I'll let you know when I'm ready to talk. Okay?"

"AJ," she sniffed through her tears. "Please, don't do this."

"I've got to go, Mom; goodbye." Hurting her was not something I wanted to do. But my trust in her was shattered. And anger still simmered beneath the surface. I needed space. So, after saying goodbye again, I hung up.

My second important phone call was to my stepdad, Dave. Being too frazzled from my talk with Mom, I waited until the following day to call him.

"Hey, kitten," Dave said as he answered.

"Hi, Dave." I dreaded this conversation, what I might learn.

"Your mom called."

I swallowed, nodding. "I figured she would. She had to have known I'd be calling you next."

"Yeah." He sighed. "Go ahead. Ask me."

I inhaled, trying to calm my frazzled nerves. "Did you know?"

"No, kitten. No, I didn't know. And I'm sorry you had to find out this way. I'm sorry she never told you the truth."

"You really didn't know?" My voice trembled.

"I really didn't know."

I could hear the honesty in the timbre of his voice, and a weight lifted, or at least lessened from my shoulders. Relief flooded me, and I was so thankful. That he hadn't betrayed me as well. That would have been too painful.

Dave and I talked for a little while, twenty minutes or so. He asked about Jake. What kind of man he was, what he was like. What my plans were. So, I filled him in. Then we said our goodbyes and promised to talk again soon.

One of the places Jake had suggested was the Strait of Juan De Fuca. It quickly became a new favorite of mine. Coronado is white sands, brilliant sunsets, and warm sunshine. The Strait is rugged, beautiful, and breathtaking. Like a kid, I spent time along the Dungeness Spit, crawling over rocks, exploring the tide pools, and taking pictures. I took tons of pictures, wanting to share this place with my readers. I even spent a day at the Dungeness Lighthouse, learning its history, seeing how it was run, talking with the locals.

And then there was downtown Sequim, with its Saturday Farmer's Market, the bookstores, coffee, and candle shops. I found myself falling a little in love with it all. In love with the town, its cuteness and down-home quality, and the people—I'd met some amazing people. Like Kerry, Attorney at Law, who I stopped in to say hello to, once or twice and to update him on my intentions. And Pam, who owned Some Good Books; I'm fairly certain she recognized me, but Pam allowed me to explore her store in peace, answering questions I had, and finding titles I was looking for. There was Macy, who worked at Lavender Brownes, a darling little tea shop, where I found a tea set themed from the *Lord of the Rings* movies.

Jo's Café was my new favorite place to grab a cup of coffee and pastry. Jo herself waited on me. She's the quintessential grandmother, a little on the plump side, but not overly so. Her thick hair, though graying, still managed to show off its deep burgundy color, along with her alert, bright blue eyes and bright smile that could light up the cloudiest day. Jo's face lit up that first time I'd come in, looking to get out of the quick downpour that had hit suddenly. She'd brushed off the water running down my shoulders with a quick, yet gentle touch.

"You're a new face one isn't likely to forget." Her voice had a pleasant quality. Soothing and welcoming. "You new to the area, or just passing through?"

"A little of both, I think."

"Hm, and what brought you in this morning?"

"Well, it was suggested I give your pastries a try."

"Oh, and by whom?"

Uncertain just how to explain it, I simply said, "Someone I'm getting to know."

At that she nodded with a spark in her eye and led me to a table in the corner. Once seated, she placed a menu before me. I looked it over, noting the mixture of Irish and German offerings. That first day I tried Irish Apple Cake. On another visit I had the German Strudel.

Jo is an amazing chef, and as I complimented her talents, she'd explained that her mother had emigrated here from Ireland, and her father was a second-generation German migrant. She liked to keep the family traditions alive, so everything she cooked and baked was from a trusted family recipe, handed down for generations. I loved the history in that. The meaning. And while there seemed to be a steady stream of customers, her restaurant was never loud and boisterous. One was able to enjoy their meal without feeling rushed or interrupted.

Another person, or rather people, I met and liked were the Paiges. They were a mother and daughter team who owned and worked *Turning Paiges*, which at first glance, at least from the outside, seemed to be a simple used bookstore, but upon closer inspection, turned out to be so much more. On my first visit, as I stepped through the glass door, the bell overhead cheerfully wringing, I heard a gasp from the counter off to my left somewhere. A girl I was guessing was somewhere in her late teens stood behind a counter constructed of some kind of corrugated steel and redwood. She had pale blond hair with deep purple tips that came to her shoulders. Her eyes were green and friendly. And she was tall. *Curvy* and tall. She had the kind of figure that one might kill for. Literally. And you could tell she was comfortable in her skin.

"Hi!" she said breathily, with maybe a hint of excitement in the mix. Those green eyes of hers were flashing; a bright grin was upon her face.

"Hello." I smiled. "How're you?" Sometimes, when someone recognizes me in public, and if they're a fan, they can be a little on the star-struck side. The first few times it happened, I'm not certain who was more uncomfortable, me or them. So now, when this happens, I just try and smile through it, and smooth things over by not making a big deal about their excitement.

"Good." She grinned back. "I'm Poppy; can I help you with something?"

"Hi, Poppy—I love your name—I'm AJ...and I'm just looking around right now. But I'll let you know if I have any questions."

She chuckled a little self-deprecatingly. "Poppy is actually my nickname. My real name is Paige, like my mom. We own the store. I've been Poppy since before I can even remember. Grandma says my grandfather took one look at me and said I was as pretty as a poppy. The name just stuck; I've been Poppy ever since."

I smiled again as I began to look around. What an amazing little store. *Turning Paiges* was a pleasant and unique combination of old and new, the quirky and the serious. It wasn't a huge store but was well-spaced. It sported four support columns, and they'd decorated each making them look like a tree, complete with fake bark, branches, and leaves. I was completely enthralled by it all. They were like one of those ranch and home type stores that have literally everything in it you could imagine and some things you couldn't, only this store was more for the book lover.

There were fuzzy, bookish themed socks and blankets. Coffee mugs, literary teas, T-shirts, book bags, magnets. They had Funko Pops and Legos. Posters, signs, and various other little knickknacks—many of them handmade from everyday gadgets. I even found this amazingly detailed dragon paper weight that I had to have. The dragon's scales were what initially caught me with their greens and purples so dark they almost seemed black. Poppy informed me that it actually wasn't a dragon; as it had only two legs. Dragons have four. This two-legged one was a wyvern.

I'd also found a small stained-glass window hung with an antique looking chain. It measured about eighteen by twenty-four inches and had rugged, Moorish mountains in the background. A dark castle sat in the foreground; one small window lit in an upper turret. The words Jane Eyre were printed across the width of the glass in a deep red Old English script. I loved it instantly.

As Poppy was ringing me up, another woman entered the store. She reminded me of an older Poppy, with longer golden hair. Her figure was fabulous. Poppy introduced me to the woman, who turned out to be her mother. I guess that explained the unfairness of their fantastic body shape. She asked if I was just passing through, or if I thought I might stay in the area. Her hopeful attitude was somehow touching and made me say, "I'm not sure yet, but I'm really enjoying myself. The people here are amazing. It was very nice to meet you both."

"And you; we hope you'll stay, AJ." Poppy said; that hopeful tone in her voice had me looking up. Her green eyes stared into mine beseechingly. "I mean," she continued, "if you like it here and all."

Smiling at that, at her welcoming attitude, I nodded. "I'm seriously considering it, Poppy."

"I'll see you later hopefully."

"Definitely. I love your store."

She smiled again and handed me my packages. I waved as I left and knew I'd be back soon. They were my kind of people. I'd have to find them online and share their links on my blog page; I made a mental note to do that soon.

CHAPTER SIX
Wicked Charlie's

AJ

Blog post

Hi there, Beach Bums!

Hope you're enjoying your lovely Coronado weather. What's kicking on the beach, guys?

So, like I shared a while back, I'm out of town, and it looks like I'll be here for a while. Where is *here*, you ask? I'm in Sequim, pronounced Skwim, Washington. And guys, it's so beautiful here! I'm loving it. Below I've posted some pictures of my adventures here so far.

I've met some incredible people who I want to share with you. I'll be telling you about them over the next few days or so and posting more pictures.

So, big news is: I won't be back for a while. I'll be here at the very least through the end of summer. Maybe longer. It just depends. But have no fear, I'll be in touch. And YES, I'm writing. I promise. I've got some good stuff coming for you all, so stay tuned.

Love you all,

Your Siren of the Surf, AJ

AJ

Another place Jake had suggested I check out, if I was looking for another side of Sequim, was *Wicked Charlie's*. Jake wrote that it might shed some light on who he'd been, what he'd been like. He said to expect a saltier crowd, a rawer atmosphere, but he also said he thought I'd like it. So, I found myself packing up my laptop, my notepad, pens, and headphones one afternoon. I kissed Josephine goodbye and headed out the door.

Wicked Charlie's sat towards the north end of town, on Brown Road. It stood alone; a one-story building that, from the outside at least, looked like it had seen better days. The parking lot was worn, with a few cracks and potholes; the stripes faded. An American Flag waved proudly from a pole near the front entrance. Someone had made the attempt to spruce up the exterior, as half wine barrels stood to either side of the door, sprouting many colorful flowers. The walls were painted dark grey and the windows were glowing with neon signs advertising various beers. The front door was propped open with a heavy brick to let in the cool coastal breeze.

Like any bar, I guess, the lighting was dim, dimmer than out in the parking lot at least. So, when I stepped inside, it took a moment or two for my eyes to adjust. Several heads turned in my direction, curiosity evident on their faces. A sign stapled to a wooden post sunken in a concrete-filled bucket, read '*No one under the age of 21 allowed*' right above another sign that directed me to seat myself. Glancing around the room I chose a booth off to the left-hand side.

I'd been seated maybe three minutes or so, just enough time to get my laptop set up, and pull out my various needed items, when a waiter came to the table for my order. "You know what you're after, or you need to see a menu?" His voice was even and had a growling quality to it. He wore a faded *AC/DC* t-shirt, and a cautious, yet friendly smile. Silver threaded through his dark hair and beard and tattoos covered his arms and neck. If I were into older guys, this one would have snagged my attention hard. As it was, I simply acknowledged his good looks to myself.

"You have Pacifico?" At his nod, I said, "With lime, please."

"You got it. Anything else?"

"Mmm...I don't know; whatcha got?"

"Nuts, pretzel sticks, or chips?" He scratched at his beard, his biceps bunching as he did. "Or you want a regular meal?"

"You have salsa to go with those chips?"

"Sure do."

"All right, bring that. Thanks."

"You got it." Nodding, he moved back towards the bar. The bar was an old-fashioned kind, with lots of wood. It stretched out into the center of the room, nearly dividing it in half. Various military paraphernalia were hung around the establishment, giving it a patriotic feel. The barstools were covered in red, white, and blue vinyl, adding to the ambience. To the right side of the bar were two pool tables. One was currently occupied by a man and a woman in the middle of a game. The other was empty, waiting. A television, hung above the bar, had ESPN on. About half a dozen men were seated randomly around the bar itself.

Not quite five minutes later, the waiter was back with my drink, a small bowl of sliced lime, and another couple bowls, one with warm tortilla chips, the other with salsa. "You're new," he said. I just nodded, still trying to get a feel for this place, see what it was Jake thought I'd appreciate. After a moment, he said, "Name's Vic, but most call me Chief. I'm the owner, so holler if you need anything."

"AJ." I nodded. "And thanks, Chief; will do."

Turning to my laptop, I got to work, occasionally sipping at my drink, or munching at the chips. First, I checked my blog and replied to the comments. Amber left an especially nasty one in response to the news I'd be staying longer than I'd first anticipated, calling me a rather unkind and colorful name. Basically, I was the epitome of selfishness and didn't deserve to breathe. *That woman needs some serious help.*

After finishing with the emails, I settled into my writing rhythm. Several productive hours later, I'd added about six thousand words to my document. My characters, Reese and Darrel, were beginning to shape up nicely. Their chemistry was coming along at a good pace. And I knew Leslie would be satisfied, as would my publisher.

And what had only been intended as a one-time event soon became habit. *Wicked Charlie's*, for whatever reason, helped me focus and write. Maybe it was the military-themed atmosphere, serving as my muse that gave me the inspiration, I really couldn't say. It just worked, so I found myself there several days a week. And before I knew it three weeks had gone by. Now, when I entered *Charlie's*, it was a bit like stepping into an old episode of *Cheers*. Everyone seemed to know my name. My booth was always open and available, and Vic had my Pacifico ready.

A couple times Vic had slid into the seat across from me, asking about what I was working on. When I told him I was an author, he'd said, "Seriously?" Then he'd turned and shouted it out to the other patrons. A cheer went up. Then the questions poured in, asking what type of books I wrote, had I been published, would my books make them blush. Laughingly, I took it all in stride and tried my best to field the questions.

"So, Chief," I said one afternoon as he slipped into the booth across from me. "What's your story? Why Chief?"

Chuckling, Chief scratched his chin, eying me. "Navy. I was Chief Warrant Officer on the USS Midway."

"No kidding? I was able to tour her about a year ago. I figured it had something to do with the Navy."

"You don't say. And why were you on my ship?"

"I write military-themed romances, Chief. And I live on Coronado, and as I do a lot to support our military, I was invited to tour her."

Chief nodded, then someone called out, needing a refill. "Duty calls."

Jake had been right; I did like it here. I liked this crowd. The people, the atmosphere. All of it. It was a little scary how fast and how well I fit into life here in Sequim. I hadn't expected that. Life here is so different from life on Coronado. And yet, I was making memories. Roots were being established and I didn't know just what to make of that. Staying hadn't been on my radar at all. Now, I wasn't sure just how, when, or why to leave.

I'd seen Ryler a handful of times in these last couple of weeks. Again, just around town, in passing. And I wondered about him. A lot. More than I should. More than I wanted to certainly. But he was darn near impossible to ignore or forget. I wanted to know him better. And that was a bothersome desire, because I wasn't sure just where it was stemming from. An overactive libido, possibly. He was like a thirst demanding to be quenched.

I was staring off into the distance, my mind taking a break from the book, when the door to *Charlie's* opened. And, like he'd materialized out of my imagination, Ryler stepped inside. My heart tripped over itself as my mouth instantly dried out. That thirst suddenly close to driving me insane. For a brief instant, I considered just walking up and kissing him. I could see it, see me doing that, bringing a blush to my face and neck. This had to stop. Taking a deep breath, I fought to wrest some control over myself. A huge dark shadow had followed Ryler in, and with a deep rumbling sound, Shiv lumbered to my table.

So glad for the excuse of not having to watch Ryler walk towards me, afraid I'd like that too much, give away too much, I spent that time making a fuss over the big dog. Petting, scratching, and making a gooey voice at him. Several people hollered Ryler's name in greeting. When he'd reached my table, I forced myself to look up at him in a calm manner. And found my breath rattling around my chest. Even with me not seeing him up close these last few weeks, he was still deeply affecting me. How would he respond if I kissed him? What would he do? Where would it go? Far; I was certain it would go far. And was that a road I wanted to go down again? I'd been there twice. Two times thinking I'd found the love of my life. Twice being led to believe that, twice being let down abruptly, painfully. No, no I definitely did not want to end up in the same place again.

"Hey." I cleared my throat. Forcing myself to ignore the way my body came alive near him.

Ryler's blue-grey eyes slid over me briefly. Just a glance, a soft caress, making my breath catch again, before returning to mine. "Sorry about Shiv; he must like you."

"He's fine." I was so thankful we were talking about his dog, and not any apparent attraction he saw on my face, that I blurted, "You want to sit down?"

"I'm not interrupting you, am I?" he glanced at the laptop.

"No. My mind is stalled right now anyway. Sit—if you want to."

Ryler held my gaze a moment longer, then slid onto the seat across from me. Quickly saving my document, I closed my laptop and slid it into my backpack.

Silence crept across the table between us. And heat. Lots of heat. At least, I was warm, with those eyes of his on me. But the silence was lengthening, deepening, causing the warmth I was feeling to build. I was saved when Chief brought Ryler a tall mug of something dark and frothy. Just say that word, *frothy*. It rolls so well off the tongue. Frothy.

"Thanks." Ryler and Vic chatted for a couple moments, catching up. Thankful for the interruption, I quickly took a drink from my own bottle, and almost choked, swallowing too quickly.

"Easy there, kid." Chief chuckled, "Don't go choking on me, or I'll have Ryler perform mouth to mouth." That made me cough even more. Chief gently patted my back, "You gonna make it?" I continued to cough, trying to catch my breath. "I don't know, Rye, she might need you."

"I'm good." I wheezed, then choked again. My face was red, but at least I had the excuse of nearly choking to death.

"If she starts turning blue," he stabbed a finger at Ryler. "you'd best see to it."

"I've got her." A gleam in Ryler's eyes seemed to turn his icy-blues to liquid.

"I gotta get back behind the bar. Allen's helping himself to the tap again."

Chief headed off, and I made my eyes meet Ryler's. "You all right?" he asked quietly. Shiv lay between us under the table, warming my feet.

"Yeah. I just tried inhaling instead of swallowing."

"You know, you probably shouldn't do that."

Nodding, I, carefully this time, took another sip. Silence began creeping back in. Before it could take hold again, before I could say something I might regret, I blurted, "Talk to me, Ryler."

He cocked his head to the side, eyes gaging me. "About what?" he finally asked.

"I don't care. Anything. Just...talk with me." Help me relax around you.

"All right." He gazed at me thoughtfully for a moment or two. "Is Pacifico your favorite beer?"

That made me chuckle, the randomness of his question. "It's *a* favorite, but not my absolute favorite. And to answer that follow-up question I see coming, my favorite is the Guava Islander from Coronado Brewing."

He nodded, giving me nothing. "Your turn."

"Mmm, what's your favorite, then?"

"Guinness."

"That was easy. Very precise. Your turn."

"Coffee, or tea?"

"Depends."

"On what?"

"The mood I'm in. Sometimes I want coffee. Sometimes I want tea." I nodded at him. "Same question."

"Same answer."

We continued like that for some time, and somehow, I ended up asking the questions. So far, I'd learned his preference in music: Rock. Ice-cream: Cookie Dough. Sports: hockey. Team: Blackhawks. Season: winter. Chips:

any, just not the salt and vinegar kind. Food: all kinds. Movie: anything with John Wayne, or Clint Eastwood. He said military and war themed movies tended to irritate him, though, as they never seemed to get anything correct.

I learned that his parents had divorced when he was in the third grade. His dad had split, leaving his mom and him—mainly because he hadn't been convinced Ryler was even his. He'd been born in Northern Idaho, and after the divorce, his mother had turned to drugs and drinking to cope. It hadn't been long before the state had had to intervene, removing Ryler from their house. He'd bounced around from foster home, to foster home, never staying anywhere more than six months before the foster parents had changed their mind.

When he was fourteen, he'd been in a group home and hung with the wrong crowd, and before he knew it, the guys he was with had stolen a car and taken it for a joyride. They'd intended to return it, but they were caught beforehand. Ryler, being only fourteen, and just an accessory, had been given the option to enter a rehabilitation ranch for troubled boys, or spend time in juvenile hall. He'd chosen the ranch. The Lost and Found Ranch was located several hours northeast of where he'd lived near Boise, Idaho. And there he'd stayed until he'd joined the Army. Like Jake, he'd been selected for RASP, formerly RIP, or Ranger Training, about a year later.

Billy, the man who owned and ran the ranch, had encouraged him to enlist, to leave Idaho, and not come back. To leave behind the negative and create something new somewhere else. Something strong. So, having nothing to go back to in Idaho, Ryler had decided on Washington State as his new home. And once he'd reached Sequim, he'd taken a liking to it. Jake had seen something of himself in Ryler, so with understanding, patience, and compassion, he'd taken Ryler under his wing after he'd come back from his first tour.

The load of information I was processing right now weighed heavily. I honestly hadn't expected him to answer my questions, not the ones about where he'd come from or anything. My heart hurt a little for him now. And I desperately needed to get my mind off all that I'd learned.

So, before thinking things through clearly, I just blurted, "Boxers, or briefs?" I really can't say where that question came from...it wasn't like I'd been thinking about the possible answer or anything.

Ryler choked on his beer, coughing into his hand. "Boxers," he coughed after a moment or two, when he'd been able to breathe. And, somehow, I knew what his return question would be. I just knew. So, I wasn't surprised when his eyes flashed. "Same question."

Heat curled in my gut, swirling and tumbling about. "Boxers." My answer was barely more than a whisper.

He took a slow deep breath. "If I remember correctly, you wear boxer briefs." I could only nod at that observation. "Hm," he muttered, almost more to himself. Then said, "Is that it?"

"For the most part. They're comfortable," my shoulders lifted.

He chuckled under his breath. "That's good to know, I guess, but what I meant was, is that all the questions you have for me right now? I need to get to work."

My face flamed red. Oh. *Oh. Good gravy, I cannot believe I just said that. Somebody shut my mouth.* "Sorry. I'm so sorry. Um, yeah. Yeah, that's it. I should get going as well. Thanks...thanks for this. For talking."

"Anytime, and don't worry about it."

AJ

My face was still enflamed, my body still warm, hot even from this time with Ryler. And while I'd learned so much about him, I felt there was still much to learn. When we'd parted ways just now, we hadn't made any plans to get together again, even just to talk. The lack of it was an irritation.

Sitting in my car in *Charlie's* parking lot, I stared towards the entrance, considering going back inside, just to see him again, maybe make some plans with him.

Chickening out, I started my car and headed home. Once there, I showered, and over a relaxing cup of tea, pulled my things from the backpack. As my laptop slid out, my cell phone tumbled out with it, landing on the floor. Picking it up, I saw ten missed calls from Harley, and one from Mrs. Carson. Ten is a lot of calls—I dialed her back instantly.

"Oh, my word," Harley screeched as she answered on the first ring. "Where have you been? I've been trying to get a hold of you!"

"What's wrong, Harley? Are you all right?" Concern threaded my words.

"Mrs. Carson called. She's been trying to get hold of you, as well. Why haven't you answered your phone?"

"I'm sorry, Harley, I'd slipped it into my backpack and forgot about it. What's going on? Is Mrs. Carson all right?"

"Babe...babe, someone broke into the house. Ransacked her study. Turned the place upside down."

"*What*? Oh, my word, is she all right?"

"She's fine. She wasn't home at the time; she was at some doctor's appointment. But there's something more...the house was vandalized. Your door...they wrote...well, they...."

"What? What did they do, Harley?"

"They wrote something on your door, and the wall near your room. The police are looking into it. They're starting to think maybe it was a fan of yours or something. No one else had anything happen to them."

"What was written?"

"It's weird, AJ. They wrote the word, *selfish*. That's it. Just selfish, over and over again."

"Only on my door?"

"Yeah; that and the wall near your door."

My heart skipped. "That's...disturbing...and really weird."

"The police want to speak with you. You should be getting a call from them soon."

"All right. I guess I can call them. I'll call Mrs. Carson as well. Thanks for the heads-up, Harley."

"Yeah, of course. Hey, I gotta run. I'm at work and need to get back. Love ya."

"You, too. And thanks again."

Ryler

Ryler watched as AJ walked out of *Charlie's*. Every move she made was designed to entice, whether intentional, or unintentional. She was grace and purpose. She was undiluted desire. And she was driving him insane. AJ was a breath of fresh air—it was a bit like being unaware you've been suffocating until you're suddenly able to breathe freely.

Chief slid another Guinness towards Ryler as he neared the bar. "On the house."

"Thanks." Ryler lifted his chin as he took a sip before stepping behind the bar. Chief had called him this morning, said his icemaker was on the fritz again. It was a temperamental machine and did this every so often. When it did, Chief would call Ryler to come and take a look at it. And Ryler would get it working again, until the next time it shut down, or Chief decided to replace it.

Ryler got to work, taking the machine apart, cleaning out all the water lines that sometimes got plugged up with one thing or another. He checked the fuses and all the wiring, making sure everything was in working order. Occasionally he'd stop to take a sip from his drink. All in all, it took him just under two hours to get the crotchety machine up and running again.

As Ryler gathered his tools and cleaned up the watery mess he'd made while cleaning the machine out, Chief leaned on the counter near him. "She's a looker." Ryler looked up, brows raised in question. "AJ. She's a looker."

"Mmm," Ryler grunted in answer.

"Jake's kid, huh?"

"She tell you that?"

Chief shook his head. "It's in her eyes; they're the same as his."

"Yeah." Ryler rubbed his scalp in a show of mild irritation. "Yeah, that's her."

"She's not what I'd expected." Chief scratched his chin, a thoughtful look in his eye.

"Me neither."

"I like her, though. A guy could do a whole lot worse."

"Yeah."

When Ryler made no further move to expand on that idea, Chief just chuckled a bit knowingly. "Thanks again for coming in, Rye. You take it easy."

Ryler nodded to Chief as he downed the last bit of his drink, then gathered his tools, whistled for Shiv, and headed out. He wanted to see her. Though she'd left just a couple hours ago, he already wanted to see her again. And as he drove down the dusty road towards Jake's place he slowed, contemplating stopping. But what excuse could he give? What would he say? Shaking his head, he drove home, deciding this was a road fraught with danger around every curve. But man, those curves....

AJ

Feeling restless after my phone calls with Harley and Mrs. Carson, I stepped onto the back patio, trying to breathe in the cool, fragrant air. Trying to calm the pounding in my veins. I'd called the Coronado Police Department. The detective assigned to my case was unavailable at the time, so I left a message. Now I had to wait. And think. Think about what had happened, wondering if the blame lay on me. If this person was truly targeting me, then I'd brought this on poor Mrs. Carson, and I felt horrible about that. She was such a sweet, darling, old lady; I didn't want anything to happen to her, and I didn't want her to live in fear because of me. Now I wondered if she'd want me to move out.

Today had started off in such a great way. Time at *Charlie's* is always well spent. And the story had flowed; words had poured out of me. *Midnight Marine* was nearing completion. Then there was my time with Ryler. And now that was something else I needed to think about. As I considered Ryler and these urges and feelings I was experiencing on his behalf, I heard a series of loud popping sounds echo off the trees surrounding my backyard.

Silence followed the popping. A few minutes later, they began again. Turning, I tried to figure out just where the noise was coming from, what was causing it. It seemed to be coming from the general location of Ryler's place. *What in the heck?* I ran back inside to grab my keys off the counter and then headed out to my car. Minutes later I was parked once more in front of Ryler's locked gate.

The sounds were much louder now. And were definitely caused by gunfire from the sound of it here. *What was going on?* What was he doing? Not letting the locked gate deter me, I swiftly climbed over it and headed towards his house. The noise was coming from off to the right of Ryler's house, so I veered in that direction. Sure enough, behind a small stand of evergreens, Ryler was coolly firing a handgun toward targets set up several yards away.

I spied Shiv laying in the shade under one of the trees. His big head lifted as I approached and he climbed to his feet, coming to greet me. After a quick hello Shiv retreated to his spot under the tree, so I followed him. Then, with my fingers in my ear, I simply sat and watched. I've seen guns being shot before; I've been given demonstrations of technique and usage, as part of the tours I'd had of various bases. But watching Ryler was somehow different. He was fluid, energy in motion. His focus complete. His manner intentional. The way he held his firearm, the way it was cradled in his grip.

What Ryler was training for I wasn't sure, but he was definitely training. Or maybe he was just keeping himself in a state of readiness. Whatever the reason, he was doing drills, practicing moves, accepting nothing less than perfection from himself. Not even his bad foot held him back as he ran, ducked, rolled, jumped, firing, firing, firing. He'd eject an empty magazine, only to replace it seconds later with a full one, and was once again firing, once again moving.

I'm not sure how long I watched him; I was mesmerized by it, by him, though. Completely enthralled, at least until the silence descended. Then he turned in my direction. He didn't seem surprised to see me, like maybe he'd known I'd been there the whole time. Ryler holstered his weapon, putting it to rest on his thigh, and moved towards me. He dropped carefully to the ground near me. "Twice in one day? If I didn't know better, I'd think you might like me." I shrugged, ignoring his attempt at humor, not sure just how to answer him. He studied me carefully. "Did something happen?"

Drawing in a deep breath, I held it for a moment or two, before letting it out in a rush. "I'm not sure exactly...I...I got a call from my best friend, Harley, letting me know someone had broken into the house on Coronado Island and vandalized it. Thankfully my landlady wasn't home, but still. I think...I think it may have been my fault that it happened."

Ryler was quiet for a moment. "Why do you say that? That it might be your fault? What did it have to do with you? You weren't even there."

"Yeah, I know," I shook my head. "But they destroyed her study and targeted *my* room. Spray-painting the word *selfish* all over my bedroom door and wall. No one else was targeted."

He was quiet a moment, then said, "I'm assuming the police are involved; what do they have to say?"

"I've put a call in to them, but the detective handling the case was unavailable, so I'm not sure what they're thinking about it. I'm assuming it's a crazy fan or something, maybe someone didn't like my last book...who knows."

"Maybe...are you concerned?"

"Not for myself, but for Mrs. Carson. She's just this sweet old lady who'd never hurt a soul. I worry about her. She was gone at the time, but what if they make a second attempt? What if she's home at the time and is injured?"

"Doesn't sound like there's anything you can do about it. And it definitely doesn't sound like it was your fault."

I just nodded, noncommittedly, still feeling like I was somehow to blame. Ryler was staring at me. The weight of his gaze was like a physical touch. As I looked at him, something began to build between us; the tension mounted with each beat of my heart. Like a moth to a flame, I was drawn to him. "What's your full name, Ryler?" I asked, trying to sidetrack my brain from the direction it so desperately wanted to travel.

He chuckled, just a soft rumble of sound. "Ryler James Dean. I'm told my parents were torn over what to name me. My mother wanted Ryan and my father wanted Tyler. Eventually they settled on Ryler." He shook his head. "It's ridiculous, really." He sighed silently. "I'm told they didn't agree on much of anything."

"It's interesting." I disagreed. "Not ridiculous at all. You want to hear something ridiculous? Try my name. Anna Joanna. It sounds like Banana. *That's* ridiculous. Seriously. Sometimes I wonder what exactly my mother was thinking. About a lot of things...."

"AJ fits you. Though, now I'm tempted to call you Banana."

"Don't you even think about it."

"Too late...Banana."

"*Jerkhole.*"

"Whoa. Easy now. There's no need for swearing." Ryler smiled. Well, it was more of a grin than a smile. But all the same, it was stunning. Beautiful. His blue-grey eyes were lit from within, and I was finding it difficult to maintain my distance. Especially as that light in his eyes began to change. It warmed, heated, seemed to smolder. My mouth became dry. And I noticed the shadow growing along his jawline. The way his lip curled, flashing bright white teeth at me. My pulse picked up, ratcheting into high gear. And all thoughts of break-ins and crazed fans went out of my head. Basically, the only thing on my brain right now was Ryler.

Ryler. And his mouth. His hands. Seemingly of its own accord, my body began to lean in his direction. And I don't think I was imagining that Ryler began to lean in my direction as well. My gaze flicked up to meet his, but Ryler was focused on my mouth. Intending to speak, to say anything to remedy the incredible pressure building inside me, I drew a deep breath. But before I could say anything, my cellphone rang, causing us both to jump.

At first, I was unsure just what I was supposed to do, or who might have been calling, but then it all hit again, and I was scrambling for my phone. "Hello!" I fairly shouted.

"AJ McAdams?" the voice on the line asked.

"Yes, this is she."

"Miss McAdams, this is Detective Whitaker with the Coronado Police Department. I wonder if you might have a couple minutes to answer a few questions for me."

"Yes, of course."

"Is now a good time?"

I was about to say yes, when Ryler stood, reminding me where I was. What I'd been doing. Standing as well, I said, "Actually, I'm not at home right now. May I call you back in like ten, fifteen minutes?"

"Yeah, that works. Just call the number you did before and ask for me, Detective Whitaker."

"Okay, I will. Thanks."

Ryler had walked away a few paces while I'd spoken with the detective, but as I ended the call he looked back at me. "I gotta run," I said. "I told him ten minutes or so, so...."

Ryler nodded. "All right. See you later."

Ryler began to turn away again. "Thank you," I quickly said. "For talking with me, just now."

"Sure thing," he nodded again.

"Are you doing anything later? Tonight, I mean?" I took a deep breath. "You wanna go get a drink or something?"

Ryler studied me quietly for a moment, speculation thick in his eyes. "I'd planned to stay in this evening. I'm not in a people mood, I guess." Maybe it was because he saw the way my shoulders slumped, maybe he'd intended this all along, but as the feeling of rejection began to settle in my middle, he said, "But I could bring something over to your place, if you'd like."

Unable to contain my grin, I said, "Yeah, that'd be great. You all right with Mexican? I can make dinner."

Ryler nodded. "See you about six?"

"Six," I agreed, then quickly turned to go.

CHAPTER SEVEN
Taste of You

AJ

The Coronado Police Department were treating this as an aggravated breaking and entering. When I'd called Detective Whitaker back, he'd said they'd fingerprinted the house and interviewed everyone who lived there and that they'd all checked out. The police were in the process of interviewing neighbors and checking for security videos in the area. He asked if I'd had any issues with any fans lately. My first reaction was to say no—I have amazing fans—but then that word *selfish* began to clang in my head. The same word that had been sprayed on my door and wall. The same word Amber had used in her angry tirade against me on my blog page a couple weeks ago when I'd said I was going to stay here longer than first anticipated.

Once Detective Whitaker heard about Amber, he indicated she was now a *person of interest* in this case. He'd requested access to my blog page, which I gave, and promised if Amber contacted me again, I'd let him know. When I asked if I should block her, he said no, and to continue as I normally do, blogging and responding to my fans, and hopefully she'd respond and they could get more information on her.

Promptly after hanging up with the Detective, I wrote a quick blog post, letting my fans know how I was doing, and what I'd been up to, and offering a give-away of three of my books. As I hit *post*, I hoped Amber would read it and respond. And that the police would be able to gain information from her response. It'd be so easy and convenient if she not only was my token crazy fan—every celebrity, regardless of popularity, had at least one, right—but was also the one who'd broken into my house as well. This could all just be a bad memory real soon if they could catch her.

Once done with that, I got busy making dinner for Ryler and myself. Sour cream chicken enchiladas were a specialty of mine. It was one dish I could cook with confidence. I'd found the recipe many years ago in an issue of *Taste of Home*. I'd tweaked it some to make it my own and tried to fix it at least once a year. Typically, I made it for Harley and me. We'd stay in and watch the entire series of the BBC version of *Pride and Prejudice* and lament over our meal, that we'd yet to find our own Mr. Darcy.

The enchiladas were about ten minutes from done when there was a knock at the front door. Checking the time, I saw that it was six-o-one. Ryler was right on time. I glanced at my reflection in the window over the sink. Decent, I mentally shrugged. Then went to answer the door.

Ryler had changed clothes. He still wore his typical cargo pants and plain T-shirt, but he'd showered and changed into a clean set before coming over. He held a paper bag in his arms. I opened the door for him, offering a smile as I swung it wide to let him enter. Ryler's lip curled slightly, his eyes flashing as he came across the threshold. He knew his way around, of course he did, he'd been here many times before, and headed towards the kitchen without needing direction.

He set the bag on the counter and with his back to me began removing items from it. "Smells good."

"Thanks." I tried desperately *not* to notice the fit of his shirt across those shoulders. Or the way the fabric moved with him. Stretching and flexing. Pulling tight over the hills and valleys his muscles made.

Jerking my gaze from Ryler's back, I stepped to the sink, in need of a drink. My throat was dry. Parched even. Which was odd, because my mouth was sure watering; I wanted a taste of him. The kitchen counters were formed in the shape of a wide U, with a large island in the center. The sink sat at the apex of that U, with the cooktop and oven off to the left. Ryler was finished with whatever he'd brought and was now resting a hip against that island. Turning in his direction, I choked, spitting the water I'd tried to swallow all over the floor as I spied what he'd brought.

Bananas. He'd brought bananas. And a six pack of Guinness. *Oh, ha-ha, very funny.* Anna Joanna, like banana. Ryler was laughing, seemingly thoroughly enjoying his joke and I liked the sound of it. Even at my expense. The deep resonance of it did something to my insides. Made them tremble. Made my heart pound faster. So much so, it took me a moment to move or even get my breath back. He was still laughing as I attempted to clean up the water, still chuckling and wiping tears from his eyes. Without really thinking about what I was doing, I swung the wet towel at him. He laughed harder. Wheezing as he chortled over my actions. Stepping closer, I put both hands against his chest and shoved. Or tried to. It was like pushing against a boulder. No give. At all. Ryler placed his hands atop mine, holding me in place.

I became still, frozen in place. My fingers were splayed wide across his chest. That strength and heat I remembered from before sent a tremor from my palms up my arms, rattling my brain. My gaze focused on his mouth as his laughter continued to rumble deliciously over me. And I just held still. Afraid to move. Afraid if I did, this, whatever *this* was, would end. That things would return to awkward again.

It'd been such a long time since I'd been close to anyone like this. And maybe I just needed that closeness, or maybe I just didn't want to be his enemy any longer. Whatever the reason, I wasn't ready for space between us just yet. I'd been so caught up in analyzing my feelings that it took me a few moments to realize Ryler was no longer laughing. That he, too, had become still. His hands continued to hold mine in place, flush against him. His thumbs slowly rubbed back and forth across my skin, heating me more with each pass. My gaze focused on his throat, watching the way it moved as he swallowed, the flutter of his pulse. His breath brushed my face, smelling of mint and something darker, stronger. Like maybe he'd had some liquid courage before coming here.

I might have leaned toward him, had the oven not beeped, startling me, making us both jump. And just like that, the spell was broken. Taking a ragged breath as he released me, I turned to the oven to shut it off. Picking up the oven mitts, I glanced over my shoulder. "Bananas…of course you brought bananas."

"I told you I'd be tempted." He watched as I removed the pan from the oven.

I chuckled, sounding breathless to my own ears. "Yeah, you did."

Dinner was nice. Easy, delicious, and relaxing. We ate slowly, savoring the meal. Ryler seemed to enjoy it and that was a good feeling. Occasionally, we asked questions of each other, continuing our conversation from *Charlie's*. "First job?" I asked between bites.

"Working the ranch at the L&F," he replied after a moment's hesitation.

"What was that like?" I wondered out loud, remembering when he'd mentioned having stayed at the boys' ranch in his youth. "What kind of work did you do?"

Ryler scratched at his jaw for a moment, then a sucked in a quick breath before letting it out. "Just hard work. The L&F was meant to teach us how to work hard, as well as give us confidence in ourselves. And teach us responsibility and basic life skills. How to build and repair a house or a car. Stuff like that."

"You liked it there?" I'd have thought he'd have hated it. That he'd have bitter feelings about being forced to go there.

"I did. I guess it was one of the first places I ever felt safe."

I opened my mouth to ask Ryler another question. My mind always seemed to come up with more of them, as I tried to delve into who and what this man was. What had shaped him. But before I could, Ryler leaned across the table, and placed his finger on my lip, silencing me. Blinking, I held still; my breath rattling out in a rush.

"My turn." Ryler held my gaze a moment, before flicking his eyes down to my lips and back. And where his eyes landed, heat blossomed. I wanted to lick my lips, but Ryler's finger was still against my mouth. And I knew how things would progress if I did. Ryler seemed to remember his hand, because he quickly withdrew it, and I felt that curious sense of loss once again. Ryler cleared his throat. "Same question."

It took me a moment or two to settle my brain enough to comprehend what he'd asked and to remember how to respond. "My first job was at Regina's in Florida. It was an old-fashioned ice cream parlor in Naples, near where we lived. Which was just outside Naples."

Ryler nodded, his gaze flickering to my mouth and back again. "Worst job?" I asked, trying to get my mind to refocus.

Ryler met my gaze in a brief, yet hard look for a moment, before standing to his feet. "Pass." He carried his plate to the sink, then stood there with his back to me. His shoulders were a stiff, hard line. The sudden distance between us, both physical and emotional, was harsh, like a slap to the face. I hadn't meant to offend him. Hadn't realized my question would offend him.

"Hey..." I cleared my throat. "I'm sorry." When Ryler remained silent, when he didn't acknowledge I'd even spoken, I rose to my feet and began clearing my own dishes. "All right...I'll tell you about my worst job. After Regina's, I worked at a pizza joint where I had to clean the bathrooms. This joint, The Pizza Barn, served alcohol, so we'd get a varied, interesting crowd." I set my dishes on the counter and turned toward the stove to begin dishing the remaining enchiladas into a storage container. "At any rate, I'd have to clean the men's bathroom as well as the women's. And it never seemed to fail that I'd get hit on while working." I kept rambling, trying to eat up the silence. "In fact, one time, I had a guy come into the bathroom as I was trying to clean out the urinal—"

My little story was abruptly cut off as I was suddenly spun around, and Ryler's mouth was against mine. His hands took a firm grip on my face, thumbs under my chin, directing my mouth upward as he pulled me to him. His whiskers were a rough caress and I shivered, enjoying the feeling, straining to be closer. His mouth searched mine so carefully, thoroughly. And as suddenly as it started, the kiss ended. Ryler wrenched himself from me, stumbling back several steps. He rubbed a knuckle against his mouth as he shook his head, from disbelief, maybe, I wasn't sure. What I *was* sure of was that *I* wasn't finished. Not by a long shot. Not with him. I wanted more.

Three steps and I was against him, less than two seconds and my arms were around his neck, pulling him down to me. Like a compulsion, magnets surging together, I had to have his mouth on mine again. I wanted to drown in the sensation. Ryler rumbled an approving sound as he lifted me, our mouths dancing together. My legs wrapped around him, and for a moment he seemed indecisive. Unsure as to where to go. The counter, or the table? The counter was closer.

Not breaking contact, he walked in stumbling, shuffling steps until my backside was against the counter, then on top of it, and he was leaning into me. My fingers snarled themselves in the fabric of his t-shirt, brushing against bare skin underneath. His satisfied growl rumbled from deep in his throat; his hands now gripped my hips, tugging me closer still.

His mouth left mine, moving down my neck, across my collarbone, and I didn't think I'd ever breathe again. I wanted more of his skin, more of him, so I wrenched his shirt upward. His arms pulled free and his shirt was off. Letting it drop to the floor, I leaned back to better see what was right in front of me. Back in Kerry's parking lot, I hadn't really had the frame of mind, nor the time to truly see and appreciate all that was Ryler. But I was clearly seeing him now. My hands were warm and tingly, the need to touch him building.

My breath came fast as I lifted my fingertips. I traced his mouth, my thumb offering a feathering caress across his lips. Then gently drug my fingers through his beard, reveling in the softness, before trailing down his neck. I was trembling as I skimmed over him. His chest. His shoulders and arms. His skin was deeply tanned; that I remembered. He had tattoos. Many of them. This I remembered as well. Though now I was afforded the ability to take my time in looking them over, appreciating them. Appreciating him. Ryler was a work of art. With some brushstrokes done in angry, violent colors and motions. Others were calmer, done in melancholy hues. He had scars. Many scars. Some barely visible. Some that drew the eye, claiming attention. They crisscrossed over his chest, his stomach, his side, and his arms.

Each of his biceps were inked. One in the American Flag, the other was an Army Ranger emblem. The left side of Ryler's chest bore six tattooed slash marks, about two inches in length each. They were lined up in two rows of three, one over the other, reminding me of tally marks, though I couldn't be certain that's what they were. I wondered what they meant. What they stood for.

Ryler had become motionless under my scrutiny, barely breathing. Like he'd locked himself down, away, becoming unreachable. And now as he stepped back, his limp became more pronounced. His eyes, turned cold like ice-coated steel, were shuttered against me, and my heart thumped painfully in my chest at the sight. Turning away, he bent to retrieve his discarded shirt from the floor. The scaring and ink continued onto his back. And centered between his shoulder blades was the word, *rebel*, in big, bold, black print. Beneath that were the words, *never surrender*.

"Ryler." I was unsure how to proceed. Unsure of what to say. Unsure what had happened, what had caused his walls to go back up.

"I can't do this." He cut me off as if he hadn't heard me. He nodded in my direction as he put his shirt back on in jerky movements. "I'm sorry...AJ, dinner was great. I...I just can't do this."

"Um, okay." I held my breath a moment before exhaling in a rush. "Ryler, *I'm* sorry. I didn't mean to...upset you."

"You didn't, okay? I just...I gotta get going. Thanks again for dinner. I'll see you around, huh?"

"Yeah," I whispered as he walked out. "Yeah, I'll see you around."

I slid down from the counter on wobbly legs as I heard the front door close quietly. Reeling from what had just occurred, I made my way to one of the couches in the living room, sinking down into its cushioned softness. *What just happened?* Just when I thought I was making some headway with

Ryler, like maybe he didn't really hate me. Just when I thought there might be something there between us, he pulled away, effectively slamming the door in my face.

And it wasn't because he wasn't interested. He was more than interested. My mouth and the skin around it were still tender from his attention. Which had been anything but uninterested. Why did life have to be so complicated? Why couldn't people just say, think, and do what they really meant? I didn't know anymore. My eyes drifted shut as I considered all these thoughts and more.

"I was married." Ryler spoke quietly from behind me. "Before. And things, things didn't work out." At the sound of his voice, I'd lurched forward, spinning on the couch to face him. My heart galloped in my chest; I hadn't heard him return. "And I know you aren't her," he continued. His eyes sought mine, holding them, seemingly searching for understanding. "But you don't strike me as someone who'd be interested in a one-night-stand and that's about all I'm capable of right now. And regardless, I can't do that to Jake's kid. I just wanted you to know."

Nodding, I took a deep breath. "Thanks...I appreciate your honesty, Ryler. And you're right, I'm not a one-night-stand kind of girl. But I also think I'm a grown woman and capable of making my own decisions about what I want and don't want."

"Fair enough." He shifted on his feet. I watched as Ryler's gaze shifted to my mouth, taking in its swollen state, the evidence of his earlier attentions, and caught the flash of fire, of satisfaction and desire in his eyes, before it retreated once again.

"So, I guess this means we're at an impasse."

"Yeah, I guess it does," he rumbled.

"Are we going back to acting like we're enemies again? I'd rather not if it's all the same to you."

"I'd as soon not head down that road again, either."

"So, I guess we'll just...see what happens, then?" Ryler gave me a long look, no doubt trying to gauge my sincerity. "You see, Ryler." I stood carefully and walked towards him around the sofa. "I think you like me and I like you. So, I'll give you space, because I do have some self-respect, but something tells me that you and I are not finished, not by a long shot." I'd shocked him with my statement, that much I could tell. What he'd do about it remained to be seen. But seeing as I had the upper hand right then, I decided to keep it. "Goodnight, Ryler. Thanks for having dinner with me."

Ryler nodded. He turned towards the door again and I caught the near-silent squeak of his leg brace. As I watched him walk out my door, I decided I wanted to know just what had happened to Ryler. Both to his body and to his heart. And maybe this wasn't the wisest of decisions, but I felt I needed to know, regardless.

Ryler

Ryler stood in his living room, his thoughts in turmoil, trying to remember how he'd gotten there. His gaze roamed aimlessly, flicking from one image to the next, seeing nothing. His mind was still back at Jake's. With AJ.

He wanted her. Wanted her badly. He could still taste her, still feel her. And he wanted more. Infinitely more. But between them stood a wall. Solid. Impenetrable. Preventing him from having what he wanted. Ryler wanted to rage against the wall, beat it down, breach it, bring it into submission.

But he'd fought that battle already. Fought it and basically lost, barely survived. There was no way he was going through that again, no way he'd survive a second time.

Shiv moved to him, a rumbling whine coming from deep within. Absently Ryler scratched behind the hound's ears. That simple action, that simple touch, began to calm him. His mind settled, not relaxed, just became somewhat focused, a little less chaotic.

Taking a deep breath, Ryler turned towards his bedroom, patting the big dog on the head as he did. Shiv stayed beside him, a constant, supportive presence, to help fight the darkness back, to keep the feelings of aloneness and fear at bay. Ryler flicked the light on in his bedroom as he entered. Moving to the fireplace, he carefully knelt and added a few logs, starting it with efficient movements.

Soon the crackle and hiss of the flames, the smell of smoke and wood filled the room, lending another layer of comfort. Ryler sat heavily on his bed, like all the energy had just drained out of him. Forearms resting on his knees, he stared at the wood floor, his head hanging. Shiv sat beside him, leaning against his leg, offering acceptance and comfort. After several minutes had passed, and the fire had begun to heat the room, Ryler sat up. He slipped his shoes off, setting them aside, then stood and removed his shirt. Absentmindedly, he rubbed at his chest, then reached for his belt. He slid his pants down, then off, and stepped from them. Then he reached for the silicone suspension sleeve that held his prosthetic in place. Sliding this upward, he carefully removed the leg and laid it beside him on the bed.

Rolling the sock liner down off what was left of his limb, he laid it aside as well. Then he began a slow inspection of the area, looking for any signs of infection, or irritation. Finally, he reached for the tub of moisturizing ointment he kept near the bed, rubbing some into his leg, around the end, massaging it.

Once done, Ryler stood in his boxer shorts, balancing on his left leg. He took a deep breath, preparing for the demons. Shiv was instantly on his feet, lending his size and strength to Ryler, aiding, as he moved towards the crutch just a couple feet away. Ryler hobbled his way into his bathroom where the hound slumped to the floor beside him. In the mirror, Ryler surveyed his reflection, taking in what was left of his body after the bomb and after the surgeons had finished with him.

His eyes noted the tattoos, spending several moments on the six marks across his heart. Representations of the six men he'd lost that day. The muscles in his jaw tightened, as he blinked the moisture from his eyes. Before moving on to the scars. He touched on those briefly, just skimmed them in quick succession.

Then Ryler's eyes moved lower. He clenched his jaw, angry once more.

Lorna had loved him once.

When he'd been whole.

Before.

But after. *After* she'd been unable to love him, love what he was, love what was left of him. His head echoed with the words she'd screamed in hatred and fear, "*You're not even a man anymore! How can I be with you? Why did you let this happen? You're nothing to me!*"

Ryler closed his eyes as those words repeating endlessly in his skull. And somehow, Lorna's voice changed to AJ's. And it was AJ in his head screaming those things at him. Looking at him in fear and disgust. Dizziness struck with a swift blow and Ryler was on the floor. Shiv lunged up, worried, and whining. Ryler barely made it to the toilet before the nausea and vomiting hit.

CHAPTER EIGHT
Fight or Flight

AJ

Six vehicles were in the parking lot of *Wicked Charlie's* when I arrived the following day. Thankfully, Ryler's wasn't among them. I wasn't ready to see him yet. Chief was behind the bar when I came in. We waved to each other as I made my way to what had become known as my booth. After a couple of minutes Chief slid onto the seat opposite me, like he was prone to do.

He studied me silently for a moment or two. "This isn't a working visit, is it?" At my expression, my raised eyebrows, he added, "No bag. Or laptop."

"No." I chuckled humorlessly under my breath. "I guess it isn't."

He scratched his shadowed chin while I put my thoughts together. "You're on reconnaissance." His statement came after a moment of perusing my face. I nodded. "Well," he continued. "You go ahead with your mission. Just understand that I may not be at liberty to provide you the answers."

"Fair enough." I exhaled. "It's Ryler." Stopping, I took a moment to gather myself before continuing. "There are...there are times I've thought he's hated me. Then there are other times that I'm actually certain he's definitely *not* hating me, you know? And just when I think I'm getting somewhere with him, like things are warming up between us, he pulls away, effectively slamming the door in my face." I shrugged helplessly. "I don't know what to make of it, Chief."

He studied me carefully, taking his time as he went over what I'd just shared. Then he asked, "And just what is your question to me, kid?"

"What is it, Chief? What is it that makes him shut down and pull away?"

"Has Rye told you anything?"

"A little. Like, I know about his time in Idaho. About his home life and then the group homes. And that ranch. I know he was wounded in service. I know he was married and things didn't work out between them. But that's it."

"He tell you all that?"

"He did. Ja—uh someone, someone else uh, told me about his being wounded."

"Your daddy you mean?" At my look of consternation, he said, "Jake was one of my best friends. You think I wasn't going to recognize his eyes when you walked in? Or that he might not have mentioned you to me?"

Sighing, I shook my head, thinking I should have known, or at least suspected something like this. It was Jake that sent me here in the first place. "Yeah, Jake told me. And...I didn't know you two'd been friends, Chief."

"Jake was a private guy; he didn't want you feeling awkward with those he knew here. He wanted you to learn this place all on your own. Rye is a private guy also. So, I won't give you details, but I can tell you that he was indeed injured and that his young wife of two years was unable to handle his injuries or his recovery and she left him."

"His wife left him...because of his injury? What the heck kind of person does that? What happened to 'For better or worse, through sickness and health'?"

"A weak, self-centered kind. It took Rye a long time to recover from his injuries. And no, I won't tell you what they were. When Lorna left, that took him a long time to get past as well." He paused for a moment, thinking. "Let me guess, he started to make the moves on you, then suddenly turned that off?" At my nod he continued. "He's in *Fight or Flight* mode. And right now, flight is winning."

"So, what should I do?" A sense of helplessness was settling over me like a scratchy sweater, and I wanted it off stat.

"Let him work through it." Chief advised. "Give him room to figure himself out. You see, you've scared him is all. He's just not sure what to do with you, AJ."

I exhaled in a rush. "So, I just give him space? Let him be?"

"Yeah. Let him pull himself out of flight mode and reenter the fight. He'll come around, kid."

I nodded. "Chief?"

"Yeah?"

"How long after he returned—with his injury—how long until Lorna left?"

Vic stared hard at me, no doubt weighing whether to answer or not. I waited patiently. It took him a moment before he responded. "He was still on bedrest."

"That soon?" I breathed. "Like she didn't stick around at all?"

"That soon." He nodded. "Being married to a military man was a romantic notion, for Lorna. And all was hunky-dory until she had to prove her staying power, until she had to step in and help nurse him back. That wasn't the romantic image she'd fallen in love with."

In silence I stewed over what Chief had told me. Wondering about the woman Ryler'd been married to. What could have possessed her to turn her back on her husband.

"Let me ask you something, AJ." I nodded for him to continue. "What's your stock in all this? In Ryler? Are you planning to stay, or to go? Because unless you're planning to stay, AJ, unless you're planning to stick around for the long haul, then I'd like to ask that you not pursue this any longer. Don't put him through any more than he's already been through. Ryler is strong, but this could break him, could bring him to his knees and just leave him there. So, before you go any further, please stop and consider everything."

Nodding, I leaned back in my seat, resting against the backrest. My mind was spinning; thoughts whirled as I tried sorting through all I'd learned. Vic allowed me my thoughts in silence and after a minute, I leaned forward and nodded. "I will, Chief. I promise. And thanks for talking. I need to go; I have some things to do in town. Thanks again."

"No problem, kid. See you around."

Leaving *Charlie's*, I headed for *Turning Paiges,* wanting to get something for a giveaway and to send something to Mrs. Carson in apology over what had happened. Poppy was behind the counter when I entered the store. She waved, her beautiful face lighting up even more. "AJ! I'm so glad you came in. That you're still here."

I smiled at her warm greeting. "Hello, Poppy, what's new?"

"We just got some new plaques in, and last week we got our shipment of graphic novels. And the week before that, we got some really pretty classics in."

"Oh, nice. Thanks, I'll take a look around."

"Oh, yeah, of course. Let me know if you have questions."

I smiled at her as I began to look around. Something infinitely special, almost magical happens when perusing a bookstore. Looking at all the titles, the cover art, the various editions. Smelling the books, feeling their textures, the pages. I could spend hours inside a bookstore. Hours. In fact, I did. Two hours later, I was walking back to my car with packages under my arms. I'd found a blanket to send to Mrs. Carson, and a matched set of the Bronte sisters' novels that were leather bound for myself.

After leaving *Paiges*, I headed to UPS to mail the packages and went to the grocery store to pick up a few things I was out of. My cellphone rang as I was carrying the bags into the house. My hands were full, so I let it go to voicemail. Once inside and I was able to set the bags down, I checked to see who'd called and saw it was Harley. I dialed her back as I put away my groceries.

"AJ?" Harley's voice sounded thick, like maybe she had a cold, the poor thing.

"Yeah, what's up, babe?" I had the eggs in one hand, and the milk in the other, with the phone wedged against my shoulder.

"AJ," she sniffed. "You need to come home."

"What's going on? You sound terrible." Harley sniffed again, almost sounding like she was choking back tears. "Are you all right?"

"AJ, it's...it's Mrs. Carson. She...she's *dead*."

The eggs and my phone dropped. And my heart went with them. Slowly, I set the milk down on the counter, and bent, reaching for my phone. "What did you say, Harley?" I whispered past the knot in my throat.

"She's gone, AJ," Harley choked out. "You need to come home."

"What...what happened? When?"

"She was found this morning. She'd been...she was...murdered. Kat found her."

My body shook; tremors racked me, and I couldn't find my breath. Sliding to the floor, I wrapped my arms around myself, trying to piece together what I'd just heard. "What...what are the police saying, Harley? Was it my fan? The one who broke into the house?"

"I don't know. I haven't heard."

"I don't...I don't...this is my *fault*, Harley!" Hysteria crawled its way up my throat. "She's dead because of *me*!"

"AJ, sweetie, you don't know that. We don't know that. And even if it was the fan, that wasn't *your* fault. It wasn't, okay?"

Shaking my head, I tried to catch my breath. "I'll catch the first flight I can find. Thanks for calling, Harley." Hanging up, I sat for a moment, trying to understand. Trying to think. I needed to get to California. I needed to get a plane ticket. I needed someone to look after Josephine. Contemplating for a moment, I dialed *Wicked Charlie's*. When Chief picked up, I explained my problem, that I needed to leave town for a bit and could he please look after my cat. Chief agreed almost instantly, offering his condolences, and didn't bother to ask why I hadn't called Ryler. I told him where the spare key was kept and thanked him profusely. I quickly cleaned up the mess on the floor. Then I ran upstairs to begin packing and to call the airline. I found a redeye from Seattle to San Diego, and within the hour, was on the road.

Ryler

Ryler avoided town, avoided people, and left his phone off for three days, fully aware he was hiding out. Like a coward. Facing AJ after what had happened between them wasn't something he was keen on doing. He was torn. At a crossroad. He wanted her. And he wanted her to want him. But whether or not she was able to see past all that he was, and all that had happened, to see who he truly is, was the question. And Ryler didn't know if he was brave enough to find out. He didn't know if he was up to traveling that road any longer.

On the fourth day, Ryler turned his phone back on and found two messages. One from Jo, her new sign was in, and she needed it hung up. And one from Chief. Ryler called Jo first, making arrangements to install the sign that morning. Then he figured he'd swing in and see Chief. Most likely the ice machine was out again; he'd have lunch while he was there.

Jo's new sign was designed like an old-fashioned lamp post, with a cross section near the top dangling a hand-painted sign that read, *Jo's Café* in fancy script across the image of a steaming apple pie.

The sign didn't take long, just a couple of hours. Long enough for the concrete to set up, and for Jo to approve the way it looked. She brought him out a coffee and a piece of strudel when he was done. After Ryler finished, he told Jo he'd send a bill. Jo hugged him and sent him off.

Charlie's was amid its midday run of customers, those on lunch breaks and those just starting or finishing their day. Chief was behind the bar, building a drink for a customer. He nodded at Ryler, then began to build another; this one he slid to Ryler.

"Thanks." Ryler nodded.

"You're gonna need it."

That stopped Ryler, the glass midway to his mouth. At the look Chief was giving him, Ryler lowered the glass, setting it down on the bar. Facing Chief, bracing for impact, he said, "All right, let's have it."

Chief turned to his other patrons, stabbing a finger in their direction. "Behave yourselves; I'm just right over here." He jerked a thumb, heading to one of the booths off to the side.

Ryler stared after him for a moment or two, contemplating Chief and the words he'd spoken, the look he'd given. And for half a heartbeat, Ryler almost felt like a rebel teen once again, about to get a severe lecture. Exhaling sharply, he followed the other man.

Chief was silent for a moment after Ryler'd sat down. He scratched at the scruff on his chin, then said, "Jake's kid...she ain't Lorna, Rye."

Ryler controlled his surprise, only blinked his eyes a couple of times. His mind raced to piece together what might have caused Chief to say something like that. Had AJ talked with Chief? If so, when? And why? Slowly, he said, "Yeah, Chief, I know that."

"Just thought you needed to hear it."

"And why is that?" Anger was beginning to burn in his chest.

"Because you're running scared."

"Stay out of it, Chief." Ryler caught himself from saying anything further, though the anger sparked at Vic's words.

"Rye, you know I respect you; you know I've got your back, and I always will. But you need to face this and see that AJ isn't Lorna. Don't judge her by the mistakes that woman made."

"I'm not," he growled.

"So how did AJ react when you told her about your leg?" Ryler glared at him in silence; his jaw clenched tight. "Yeah," Chief sighed and shook his head. "That's what I figured."

"You think she'll want this?" Ryler snarled, jerking his hand downward toward said leg. "You think she'll look at me and see a man?"

"I'd stake my life AJ wouldn't see you as anything less."

"I don't want her pity either." Ryler stared at the table, not meeting Vic's gaze.

"You won't even give her a chance?" Chief challenged. "You've written her off as a lost cause?" Ryler'd jaw worked, but he still refused to look up. "How do you know Jake hadn't planned this out, for you two to meet?"

"What did you say?" Ryler jerked his head up, now. "The heck are you saying?"

"He talked about it." Chief shrugged. "Hoped you and AJ could meet, that you two might work out."

Ryler laughed under his breath; his voice cracked in painful disbelief. "You've got to be kidding me. Jake told you that?"

"Not in so many words, Rye. But I could hear the hope in his voice. He loved you and he loved her; is it so hard to imagine he'd want the two of you to meet and hopefully fall for each other? That he'd hope you two could be happy together."

"And why would he think that? What would possess him to think that a girl like AJ would want a guy like me?"

"Ryler, why do people call you when they need something done? You think they call out of pity? You think it's no more than an offering to poor, broken Rye?" Ryler shook his head, rolling his eyes as he worked through these thoughts. Chief stabbed a finger at him, anger sparking in his eyes. "If that's what you think, Rye, then get the heck out of my bar. I offered you friendship and respect. Don't throw that back at me."

"I'm not, Chief." Ryler breathed in defeat. "You know I'm not. I just...I can't go through it again. It gutted me the first time. AJ will be worse. Far worse. I won't survive it."

"You can't run from it either, Rye. Once you start to run, you'll never stop."

"I'm not running, Chief."

"Good. You had me worried for a minute there. I thought that little girl had you scared to death."

"She does scare me to death. Everything about her is potent and terrifying."

Chief chuckled at that. "Yeah, I can see that as well."

"Thanks." Ryler nodded. "For talking…and for everything. I gotta run. I gotta figure out a way to talk with her, with AJ. Try to explain."

"Well, you've got some time. She's gone."

Ryler's heart slammed against his ribcage. "What do you mean, 'she's gone'?"

"Her landlady died unexpectedly. She left a couple days ago. Asked me to look after her cat."

Ryler felt his heart plummet again as he recalled AJ telling him about some crazy fan that had broken into her house. A strong sense of panic began to settle in his chest. "Her landlady? What? Did she say what happened, Chief?"

"No, she didn't. What's the matter?"

"She said she had a fan, one that had broken into her house, trashed the place. She'd been worried about something like this. Have you heard from her?"

"Nah, not since she left."

"I gotta go, Chief. I gotta call her. See if she's all right."

"All right. Keep me updated."

Ryler nodded, rising to his feet, even as he pulled his phone out. He'd dialed AJ's number before he'd even reached the Bronco. It rang several times before going to voicemail. Ryler slammed his fists against the steering wheel and tried the number again, with the same results. On the third attempt it went directly to voicemail. "*Dangit*! Come on, AJ, answer your phone!" Ryler took a breath and held it as he pinched the bridge of his nose. This time he left a message. "AJ, I just need to know you're all right. Please call or text. Heck, call Chief and check in with him; I just need to hear from you."

Driving home, Ryler tried not to stew too hard over the matter. But his mind refused to shut off. AJ'd been worried over this fan of hers, that they'd broken into her house, worried they'd harm someone, specifically her landlady. And now Mrs. Carson was dead. And AJ herself might be in danger. Anxiety boiled inside Ryler. Dread seeped into his bones, coating him from the inside out. He needed to know she was okay.

AJ

Sitting in the Coronado Police Department's waiting room, I tried to gather my thoughts before my meeting with Detective Whitaker. The mantra *This is my fault, this is my fault, this is my fault* seemed to play on endless repeat inside my skull, refusing to be silenced no matter what I did. And if that wasn't consuming my thoughts, then I continuously questioned what I might have done differently.

When the detective called yesterday, to schedule a time to come in to discuss the case, I was both relieved and anxious at the same time. I wanted this to be over with but was somewhat frightened by what I might learn. What if all of this was indeed my fault? *What if I truly was to blame?*

I'd been sitting here now for ten minutes; the detective was five minutes late. Feeling antsy, I paced the room, glancing out the windows onto the street, taking in the portraits of various officers, news articles, and awards on the walls. One portrait caught my attention. My heart clenched in remembrance—Officer Wade Irwin, of the San Diego Police Department and his partner had been ambushed on what should have been a routine stop. Irwin survived; his partner hadn't. The news had hit our community hard. The cold-heartedness of the senseless act that shattered so many lives had shocked us all. My heart had broken for the fallen officer's wife and children and could only be thankful Officer Irwin had survived. That his wife and children had been spared the pain his partner's family had gone through.

My phone buzzed, jerking me from my painful thoughts. Glancing at it through misting eyes, I saw it was Ryler. I blinked, staring at his name for several moments unsure what I wanted to do. The ringing stopped as the call went to voicemail. Seconds later the phone began buzzing again. Ryler was calling back. Again, I hesitated. I just wasn't ready to speak with him. It wasn't that I was mad. I just wasn't ready to talk, not after all I'd gone through these last several days.

Between what had happened between the two of us, and the revelations I'd learned from Chief to Mrs. Carson's death, I just didn't have anything left to address whatever he was after. I assumed he'd learned I'd left town and was trying to check up on me. And while I was able to acknowledge the kind gesture on his part, I just wasn't up to talking about it with him right then. I needed time to properly process everything.

My phone went silent once more, before notifying me I had a voicemail waiting.

"Ms. McAdams?"

Turning at the sound of the male voice, I took in the detective. He was close to six feet tall, clean-shaven, and bald; you could tell he stayed fit. His skin was so dark his eyes seemed to pop out of his face. And when he smiled, his teeth flashed, white and even. He wore plain street clothes, jeans and a blue polo-style shirt. His badge hung on a chain around his neck, his gun on display in its holster. "Yes," I said. "Are you Detective Whitaker?"

"I am; come on back." Detective Whitaker held a door for me, his demeanor friendly and open. I followed him down a long hallway to a cluster of desks in a large, spacious room. Indicating one of the two chairs in front of his metal desk, the detective sat down, drew a file out of the drawer, and flipped it open. He slid a yellow legal pad towards himself and pulled a pen from the top drawer. Before I could stop myself, my eyes had landed on the documents contained in that file, the pictures.

Even upside down I was able to ascertain that Mrs. Carson hadn't just been murdered. She'd been brutalized. This wasn't just a desperate act by someone trying to rob her and things had gotten out of hand, this was hatred. Malice. This was evil. Whoever had done this was evil. My heart clenched tightly, making me dizzy and glad I was already seated.

"Ms. McAdams, I know you've been out of town, and I'm sorry you've had to come back to something like this. We've been monitoring your blog, but so far, Amber hasn't responded to any of your recent posts."

"Are you sure my fan was involved then?" The lump in my throat made the words burn on their way out.

"We aren't ruling anything out as of yet. And while it may not have been that particular fan who broke in last week, we do think it has to do with you."

"And why is that?" If it was possible to feel even more lightheaded without passing out, I was there. The edges of my vision were dimming and black spots sprinkled across the view in front of me.

"In addition to what was done to your landlady, we found your books in a pile under her body. They'd been destroyed. Pages were ripped out, cut, and torn. And a message had been left for you."

"What was the message?" I whispered, desperate to calm myself, even as shivers skated over my body.

"She didn't have to die—but you had to be selfish, didn't you. No more games—this time I'm coming for you," he quoted, as he read the note. "It'd been written in her own blood."

Tears I wasn't able to hold back, slid from my eyes. This was all *my* fault. I'd done this. I'd brought this on poor Mrs. Carson. Those words boomed through my head, *my fault, this was my fault, my fault, my fault....*

"I'm sure this is a shock, Ms. McAdams." His voice was gentle as he slid a box of tissues my way. "But I need to ask if you have any idea, any at all, as to who might have done this."

I took a moment to collect myself, to clean myself up, and wipe away my tears. "I don't know...I can't even fathom why this might have happened, or who might have done this." *This is my fault, my fault, my fault.* "The only thing that strikes me is the use of the word *selfish*. Amber has called me that several times in her comments. And I hate to say it was her, as she just may be a reader with a strong opinion and have nothing to do with this at all. Honestly, I just don't know. I'm sorry."

"That's all right. Just take your time. Have you noticed anyone at any of your events that may have given off a weird vibe? Or noticed anyone hanging around the house? How many people outside your residence knew where you lived, Ms. McAdams?"

That question gave me a start. I hadn't considered that before. My address was not available to the public. I kept that private, using a post office box in San Diego, not here on Coronado Island. How had this person known where I lived?

"Detective Whitaker? My address, where I live, is private. I've never shared that with the public." I told him about my post office box, explaining I'd done that to ensure my privacy.

"This indicates the perpetrator may know you personally, Ms. McAdams. Does that thought bring anyone to mind?"

"*No.* No one. I...I mean, this is all just a bit crazy, you know. I don't know anyone who would want to do something like this."

"We've interviewed your housemates. Everyone checks out, at least at face-value. Can you think of anything about one of them that might have any bearing on this? Anyone come across that makes you uncomfortable?"

I considered them, trying to determine if anyone might have ever given off an odd vibe. Briefly, I considered Paul and his awkward comments, but then dismissed him, unwilling to bring such a quiet and private man into such intense scrutiny. I supposed that any one of my housemates might have told someone that they lived with me, but that was such a broad spectrum, I couldn't fathom how we could find that needle in the haystack.

Then I had another thought. It was farfetched, I knew, but still, it was at least something. "Um, Kat...Kat tends to bring men home. She's a bit of a cougar, if you know what I mean. Classy lady, but still. Maybe one of her dates...? I don't know. This is all just wild speculation."

Detective Whitaker wrote some notes in his binder, nodding to himself. "We've taken prints from the crime scene and photographed the entire area. So far, the only ones we've identified are of those who live there."

"Okay. Um, do you know when I'll be able to get in to move my things out?"

"I believe you should be able to get your things squared away today, or tomorrow at the latest. Our crime scene investigators should be finished processing the area soon."

"Thank you."

"How long are you planning to be in town?"

"Just long enough to get my things together. I've canceled a previously planned event that would have taken place next week. I just couldn't...not right now. I'm still staying in Sequim and am unsure just how long I'll be there. I may just stay there, as I have my dad's house now."

"Just be careful. We don't know who is behind this. You need to be on your guard."

"I will." *This is my fault, this is MY fault,* "Detective, I'm thinking about something...about doing something."

"Such as?"

"I'm thinking about using my blog to call out this person, challenging them maybe, getting them to respond, and hopefully slip up so we can catch them."

"I understand your feelings, Ms. McAdams, however, I'd advise against it at this point as we don't really know who, or what we're dealing with. The perpetrator could be anyone. You wouldn't know who to watch out for."

"I can't just sit around and do nothing. Mrs. Carson was killed. Murdered because of *me*. I *have* to do something."

"Again, I'd advise against doing anything at this point. Let us investigate."

"I don't want anyone else to be hurt on my account. I can't deal with that."

"I understand. But again, let us do our work. Maybe post about your heartbreak for Mrs. Carson and see if anyone responds…start there and let's see what happens."

I nodded as I stood to leave. "I'll see. Right now, I just want to get my things and get back home."

Detective Whitaker walked me back to the waiting room and saw me off. He shook my hand and again advised not to act rashly and let him and his team do their jobs.

CHAPTER NINE
Suspicions

AJ

The following day, Harley drove me to the house on Ocean Drive after she got off work. My stomach was in knots as we pulled into the driveway. The CPD were still there, removing crime scene tape. The moving truck I'd hired to haul my things to storage sat on the street, awaiting my arrival.

Kat was coming down the front walk as we got out of the car. Her face was streaked with tears, her eyes smudged and swollen. Despite this, she still looked good. Enough so, that she had not one, but two gentlemen assisting her as she moved her things out of the house. When she saw me, Kat lost it, breaking down as sobs shook her. Harley hung back, I knew, to give us privacy and to avoid the emotional displays that made her so uncomfortable. She'd always been like that. Holding everyone at arm's length; I was the only one she allowed to get close emotionally. I reached Kat's side and let her hug me close. "I'm so sorry, Kat." I whispered as she continued to cry. "I'm so sorry."

"Wasn't your fault, AJ," she hiccuped.

"Still." I swallowed the lump in my throat. "I'm sorry you found her. Did you see anything, hear anything?"

"No, she was...she was cold when I found her. I'd been away that night, stayed with a friend, ya know? When I came home, the front door was opened, just a little, like maybe it hadn't closed entirely, and the breeze blew it open. And then...then I found her in the study. It was awful. So awful. I still have nightmares...."

"I'm so sorry. Where are you going now?"

"I'm staying with, with a friend, and then, later, when I'm ready, I'll find myself a place. How about you, kid? What are your plans?"

It was on the tip of my tongue to tell her I was going back to Washington, but Detective Whitaker's warning rang in my skull, cautioning me. "I'm...not sure yet. I'm still trying to decide. You take care, all right?"

"You do the same, AJ."

We moved past each other and as I stepped over the threshold, my eyes were drawn to Mrs. Carson's study. The doors were closed and crime scene tape was still up. Harley maintained a silent, but steady presence. There if I needed her, but in no need of attention or acknowledgment. Swallowing, I turned to the staircase, pain and dread pooling in my middle. As I reached the landing, my phone buzzed. Ryler, again trying to reach me. I still hadn't responded to him. Still didn't know what to say. He wasn't, by his own words, ready for a relationship. And I wasn't sure how to remain his friend, keeping him at a distance, yet still allowing him close enough to comfort, or check on me.

I knew he meant well, I just didn't know how to keep my heart uninvolved—and it *always* wanted to get involved—while he worked through whatever he was trying to. So once again I sent Ryler's call to voicemail. And told myself I'd speak with him after I got back. Right now, I needed to take care of my things here.

Pausing on the landing, I caught the scent of fresh paint still in the air. Mrs. Carson hadn't waited to get the repairs done. I couldn't help but wonder if that might have had anything to do with the nature of her death. Taking a deep breath, I continued to my room.

Harley and I finished packing my things, getting them sealed and labeled. It didn't take too long, thankfully. And as we looked back over my old room, making sure we hadn't missed anything, I called down to the movers, letting them know I was ready. Most of this was going to storage, but I was going to ship some things to Sequim. Harley would take me to the airport in the morning. Tonight, I would stay at her place instead of the hotel where I'd had a room, where I'd stayed, holed up avoiding people.

I knew eventually I'd have to come back, if just to finish deciding what I was going to do with my things. But for right now they'd be safe enough in storage. We were just coming down the stairs when Paul came through the front door. He looked jittery and more uncomfortable than I could remember seeing him.

He stopped as he saw me, his brown eyes widening. He must have been miserable, being a man who enjoyed his privacy and routine. I caught that mild scent of cloves that always clung to him. "Hey, Paul." I smiled, hoping to comfort him.

"AJ." He seemed almost distant.

"You all right?" I could only imagine what this was doing to the normally private man.

He hesitated, then nodded. "As all right as one can be under the circumstances."

"You take it easy, okay?" I softly gripped his forearm as I passed.

"You do the same, AJ." He moved towards the stairs, then stopped, turning to face me. "Are you sticking around, then? Do the police need you to stay?"

Again, Detective Whitaker's warning echoed in my head. I hated this feeling of mistrust his warning gave. "No, the police don't need me, and I haven't decided yet what I'm doing. There are still things, I still have decisions to make. So," I shrugged, unhelpfully. "I just don't know."

It looked like he might say something further, but then he just nodded and continued to his room. Harley and I passed the police that were still stationed at the front door. They were there to lock up after the others had packed and moved out. I hoped Paul wasn't blaming me for Mrs. Carson's death; I was doing enough of that on my own. I also hoped he found another suitable living arrangement and was happy and able to continue his travel writing.

AJ

Blog Post

Hello Beach Bums,

Tonight, I'm writing to you in a state of heartache and shock. This is difficult to even talk about, but I need to share this with you. Earlier this week, my landlady, Mrs. Carson, was found by one of my housemates, murdered in our home. We still don't know what the motive could have been, but needless to say, we are, all of us, devastated by this news.

I'll be taking some time to deal with this but will try to be in touch with you soon. Thank you for understanding. Take care and stay safe. Hug someone close to you.

Your Siren of the Surf, AJ

AJ

Harley and I woke early. I had to be at the airport by seven, which meant I had to be up at the ungodly hour of four. Yesterday, on the way back to Harley's we'd stopped and I was able to mail my packages to Washington. So, this morning, all I needed to do was dress for the flight and grab my one carry-on bag. We made a stop at the Sun and Surf Café for a coffee and pastry before we headed to the airport. By chance, Kevin was working the early shift, so I was able to see him before I left.

"Hey, shorty!" Kevin fairly shouted as I stepped inside the Café. He came around the counter and scooped me up in a giant hug. "Long time, no see."

"Hello, tall man. What's new?"

"Same old, same old." He gave me a long look. "I read what happened, AJ, on your blog. I'm sorry; how're you really doing?"

"It's hard, Kev. She didn't deserve that. And I feel guilty about it."

"Ah, hey, that wasn't your fault. The fault lies squarely on the one who committed the crime, not you, hon."

"Yeah, I guess. Hey, I gotta get going though. My flight leaves early."

Kevin moved back behind the bar. "Same drink?" He looked at me and Harley, knowing our regular orders by heart.

I nodded.

"You coming back soon, or are you moving?"

My shoulders tightened as I considered my answer. Who could I trust? If I wasn't careful, I'd be suspicious of everyone. "Not sure yet, Kev; still working on some things, I guess."

"Fair enough; just don't be a stranger, shorty."

Less than five minutes later, he was handing us our coffee. I gave him a twenty and told him to keep the change, then we were out the door and walking back to Harley's car.

We'd agreed that Harley would just drop me off rather than try to fight terminal parking, so we said our goodbyes in the car at the curb. She promised me she'd see me soon, intending to see my fairy tale house before Christmas. Taking a deep breath, I waved at her as I carried my bag inside, getting into line for check-in. My flight was scheduled to land in Seattle at eleven this morning. I'd let Chief know the plans, and when I'd be home.

I'd left my car in long-term parking, so when I landed, I didn't have any extra wait time, other than just dealing with basic traffic. Glancing at the clock on the dash, I decided to do a little shopping and maybe some sightseeing. As my route would take me on the Edmonds-Kingston Ferry,

I decided to stop in Edmonds. The quaint little waterfront town had a historic old-town feel to it.

It was nice just walking along the shops, sipping from my coffee, or eating at one of the little cafes, and not thinking about Ryler, or Mrs. Carson, or my crazy fan. I found a wrought iron bench beneath a tall maple tree and sat, just watching the ferries as they loaded and unloaded passengers. It was a clear day. The sun was bright in the blue sky, the wind mild. Seagulls flew about, calling and looking for an easy meal.

Finally, after a couple hours, I got back in my car and boarded the Ferry. The crossing to Kingston wasn't long, just a half hour or so, and then I was on my way. On a whim, I decided to head to the Dungeness River Bridge at the Railroad Bridge Park. The historic bridge was a part of the Olympic Discovery Trail; the trees were beginning to change colors, just a hint of coral, pink, orange, and red. It was beautiful and I realized, as I walked along the bridge, taking in my surroundings, that I really missed hiking. Missed the long walks I used to take around Coronado, and along the beach.

I decided right then and there I was going to start hiking again. I had boots, I'd bought them a while ago, just had never used them. And there was no reason not to go. Besides, it'd probably do me some good—both physically and mentally. I knew there were trails on Jake's property, Kerry had highlighted them for me. So, when I got back to the house, I'd pull that map out and check out those trails. Finishing my walk, at a leisurely pace, I headed for home.

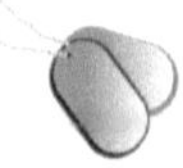

Ryler

Ryler's phone chirped, making him jump. He'd been clearing brush on the ridge behind his place. Even though everything was still pretty lush and green, Ryler tried to keep a fire barrier cleared just in case. Lightening could strike at any time, and when it did, it could have horrific results. When the text came in, he'd quickly pulled his gloves off with his teeth. "She'll be back sometime after noon, today," Chief's text read.

Shiv stretched as he climbed to his feet and arched his back. Then he lumbered in the direction of Jake's place. "Yeah, buddy, she'll be back today."

Shiv trotted a few paces away, rumbling deep in his throat, before turning back to Ryler. "She's not back yet. Later. We'll go see her later," Ryler told the dog. "And I'll find out just why she's been ignoring me and didn't bother to let me know she was all right."

Shiv whined, then with a sigh returned to his place in the shade he'd found. Ryler stared into the distance, looking towards Jake's place, imagining AJ there. Imagining what he would say when he saw her.

His phone buzzed again. "Give her space, Rye. She'll talk to you when she's good and ready."

"The heck?" he growled as he read Chief's text.

"Trust me." Chief texted again.

Ryler muttered under his breath before shoving the phone back in his pocket. He'd give her a day, a whole twenty-four hours before he sought her out. But that was it.

AJ

I found Kerry's maps. There were two trails. One that wound down below the house and off towards the west, and the other that went eastward, winding up the mountain behind Ryler's place. I checked in with Chief, letting him know I was back and thanked him again for watching over Josephine for me. And speaking of my cat, she'd been winding herself around my legs nearly nonstop, making it difficult to move about the house.

Rather than trip over her, I decided to just carry her around with me as I put things away and did laundry. That lasted for an hour or so until Josephine wanted her space once again. I decided to take today to just relax and hang out at home, especially as it was already in the afternoon, and I definitely didn't want a repeat of the last time I'd tried walking home after dark.

Tomorrow I'd need to go into town and pick up some groceries, but for tonight I was fine. Digging through the freezer, I found a personal sized gourmet frozen pizza that I know I didn't buy. I assumed Chief had bought it and placed it there for me. That was really thoughtful and appreciated, so I texted, thanking him for it.

"Sure thing." Chief replied. "Just a heads up, Rye's chomping at the bit."

"Yeah," I breathed to myself. "Yeah, I'm sure." Then texted back, "Got it. Thanks, Chief. For everything."

It occurred to me in the morning as I walked around the house with my new hiking boots on, that I might not want to attempt a long trail to start with. That maybe it'd be better to break in these boots before I took on any serious trails. With that thought in mind I pulled the boots off again and set them aside. I'd run to town and get my groceries, locate other easier trails, bring the groceries back, then head out for some mild hiking. Walking. Basically, I'd do some serious walking. I'd build up to actual hiking, making sure these boots were good and broke-in first.

I swung into *Charlie's* and gave Chief a hug. While there, I asked about any trails he might know of in the area. Chief grabbed a scratch piece of paper and jotted down about a half-dozen locations he thought might interest me. "You seen Rye yet?"

"No, not yet. I'm not sure what to say to him. I guess I don't know how to maintain a distance with him, ya know?"

Chief nodded. "You'll figure things out. Being a romance writer, you're bound to have some idea as to how to handle things."

I chuckled. "Yeah, you'd think so, wouldn't you?"

"How'd things go down there? Anything get solved?"

I sighed and shook my head. "I wish they had, but no. The police aren't any closer to knowing who murdered Mrs. Carson. The only thing they seem pretty sure of is that the murder was directed at me."

Chief became still; his eyes grew colder. "What does that mean? Are you in some kind of danger, kid?"

"I don't know, Chief." I swallowed. "I could be, I guess."

"What are the police doing about that?"

"Not much they can do. The detective encouraged me to be cautious and to let him know if I could think of anyone who might want to hurt me."

"Ryler needs to know this. Don't screw around, AJ. You make sure he knows."

"What can he do, Chief? I mean, yeah, I'll tell him, but there isn't much he can do. Not really."

"You'd be surprised. Just make sure you tell him."

"All right, I will. I promise." I left shortly after that, list of locations in hand, and headed to the grocery store.

CHAPTER TEN
Long Live the Rebel

AJ

It occurred to me the following morning that Ryler was not the only rebel I knew. Because as I sent another of his calls to voicemail, I grabbed my hiking boots and keys and quickly slunk out of my house like some sort of deviant trying to avoid authority and detection. *Long Live the Rebel*, I silently derided as I climbed into my car and headed down the driveway.

More like, long live the coward. Because after the fourth day of being home and avoiding Ryler, that was how I was feeling. That was what I was. A coward. Instead of just talking with him, like an adult, I avoided him. I had literally hidden in the house when he came to the door and knocked last night. Yes, I was still ignoring his phone calls. And I knew my actions were idiotic and borderline insane, but once I'd started down this path, I was completely unsure as to how to alter it.

I'd, understandably, been on edge this week. So far, Amber had not responded to my blog post. And her lack of response was grating. I'd been toying, again, with the idea of challenging the killer, whether it was truly her, or someone else, and calling them out. Maybe after my hike today, I'd call Detective Whitaker and see if he'd learned anything new. And maybe I'd run my idea by him again, see if he'd had a change of heart.

I'd hiked, so far, three of the six locations Chief had given me. The first two were rather easy. Each about three miles round trip, and the trails themselves were well-cared for and maintained. The third was a little harder, including more hills, and several creek-crossings. It had been longer also, being closer to five miles in length.

Today, I'd decided to hike that same trail, but I took it in reverse, starting from where I'd ended yesterday, just to offer a different perspective on it. I didn't rush it, just took my time, stopping to take pictures of the lush scenery. By the time I'd finished, I was good and tired. My body ached as I climbed back into my car. I sat there for several minutes, allowing my heartrate to drop back to normal. My clothes were damp with sweat and I wanted a shower, so I started the car and headed for home.

As I came back into cell service, my phone buzzed, indicating a missed call and a message. Assuming it was from Ryler again, I ignored it. You know what they say about assuming, right? Yeah. I should have answered the call or at least checked the voicemail. Because after I'd gone inside the house, I got the surprise of my life.

I tossed the keys on the counter and stumbled to the fridge for a bottle of water. Just as I pulled one out, I heard a deep *whine* come from behind me. Shrieking, I spun around to see Shiv ambling toward me, his big tail swinging back and forth in excitement. Ryler stood from where he'd been sitting half in the shadows of the living room. The look in his eye said murder and it wouldn't be pretty.

You'd think, especially after all I'd been through, that I'd have been more frightened. Instead, my heart pounded in my chest; emotion, strong and potent, entangling me in its grasp. Heat pooled and boiled inside me as I looked at him. And I could have sworn the earth shifted beneath my feet.

I wanted to go to him; I wanted him to come to me. I wanted the distance between us gone. I just didn't know how to get there, how to bridge the divide. Ryler was simmering. I could almost see the heatwaves coming off him. But what I wondered was if it was anger, or something warmer, something far more dangerous to me. Whatever it was, I wanted to answer it.

With trembling lips, I took a breath, about to speak, to break the deep silence, when my phone rang again. The noise startled me, bringing with it much-needed clarity.

"Your phone seems to be working." Ryler's voice was gravelly and low. "I'd wondered."

Flushing, not knowing what to say, I jerked my gaze from him to see who was calling. Recognizing the detective's number, I quickly answered. "Hello?"

"Ms. McAdams?"

"Hello, Detective. Do you have any more news?"

"I just might. Amber responded to your post. We're trying to get a trace on her."

My heart thudded. "What did she say?"

"You haven't read it yet?"

"No, I've...no." Dimly, I noted Ryler drifting closer. His presence both comforted and disturbed me.

"Here, I'll read it to you, then. She said, 'You shouldn't have pushed me; this is all your fault. And you can't hide from me. You should have stayed put.' End quote."

"So...oh my gosh...that means she did it, then. Doesn't it?" My heart clenched tightly.

"It certainly sounds that way. Now we just need to find her."

"Can you? I mean, can't you trace her IP address, or something?"

"It's a bit more complicated than that, Ms. McAdams. But we are working on it. Please keep your phone close in case I need to reach you."

"Okay." I nodded. "I will. And thank you for letting me know, Detective."

"Yeah. Of course." I heard papers ruffling in the background, like maybe he was shuffling and stacking them, then almost as an afterthought, he added, "Hey, are you with anyone up there?"

I looked at Ryler. "What do you mean?"

"Is there someone there you can trust? That you *know* you can trust? Just in case?"

"Do you...do you think she could come here? To Washington?" I rubbed at my chest.

"I hope not but think you should be careful. She definitely knows more about you than a stranger might. I just want you to be cautious."

Ryler held out his hand, indicating I give him the phone. The look he gave me was commanding. "Detective? Hold on, someone...someone wants to talk with you."

"Are you authorizing me to speak with this person about your case, Ms. McAdams?"

"Yes, yes, I am." I handed Ryler the phone.

"Detective?" Ryler's voice was cold and sure. Sharp, like ice, like the edge of a blade. "This is Ryler Dean. I'm...a friend of AJ's." His eyes seemed to dare me to contradict him. "Just to let you know, I'm Ranger trained, so I'm fully prepared, now what's going on?"

As the detective filled him in, Ryler held my gaze and I watched the fire in his eyes build, making a lie of his own words. What raged behind his eyes said this was so much more than friendship and I found it hard to breathe. He asked one or two questions in that low, controlled voice, nodding his head as he listened to the reply. His gaze never shifted from mine. "Here's my number, you take this down, and if anything, and I mean anything comes up, and you can't reach AJ, you call me. I'll give you Chief's number as well; he's also former military. You can consider us AJ's first and last line of defense. No one is getting to her. That's a promise."

After several more moments, Ryler handed the phone back to me. "Ms. McAdams?" the detective said, "It sounds like you're in good hands there. Just keep me posted if anything happens at your end, and I'll do the same here."

"All right." My breath stuck and I had to clear my throat. "Should I...should I respond to her, to Amber?"

"Yeah, see if you can get her to slip up in some way to indicate who she is, or where she is, for that matter."

"Okay, I will."

The call ended and I set the phone on the counter. In silence, Ryler held the bottle of water out. The one I'd dropped when Shiv had startled me. He must have picked it up at some point. "Thanks."

The silence lengthened and his gaze shifted, leaving my face and traveling in slow movements over me. Each spot his icy eyes skimmed over was like a physical touch. I'd cooled down somewhat from my hike, but now with his caressing eyes, I felt heated again, flushed.

After a moment or two, his tone now measured, he said, "Go shower, AJ."

"What?" That wasn't at all what I'd expected from him.

"Go take a shower." Nothing forceful about his words, but still, I found my hackles rising at the instruction, the order I heard there.

"I'm good, thanks."

"AJ," he shook his head slowly. "I'm trying to be courteous."

"Well, thanks, but I think I can decide for myself whether I need a shower or not."

"Fair enough." His eyes were focused on my mouth. "But you should know that I plan to kiss you in a moment."

"Oh." I swallowed.

"I'm going to kiss you, AJ." His gaze shot to mine and somehow intensified, like he was making sure I'd heard him clearly.

"Um, what...why...I mean, what?" While my ears heard him just fine, and my mouth wanted to get on with the kissing, my mind kept going back to his declaration that he just couldn't do this now. So, I hoped he could forgive my confusion. "What are you trying to say?"

"It means I'm going to spend some time kissing you and I figure you'd prefer to be showered. It doesn't matter to me really, but I thought maybe it might matter to you."

It occurred to me then that if this was a Regency novel, I'd be the innocent, but not so innocent miss, and he'd be the rake who knew precisely which lines he could cross, and which lines could be blurred. I'd be entirely under his thrall, clay in his capable hands. Because that's how I felt right now. Just hearing him speak those words had my knees so weak I honestly wasn't sure how I was still standing.

"Last chance, AJ," he growled.

Something clicked inside my brain then, maybe it was the tone of his voice, maybe it was the look in his eye, but I moved. Not towards him, but towards the stairs. He was right, I did want that shower. And I took my time with it, too. Letting the heat ease me. I washed my hair twice, and while I shaved, I let a deep conditioner soak into each follicle.

When I was done, the bathroom was full of steam. I toweled off and grabbed my favorite body lotion, one that smelled of coconuts and tropical islands. After I worked that into my skin, I pulled on a pair of knit lounge pants and an oversized, off-the-shoulder sweatshirt. I ran a brush through my hair, took a deep breath, and headed back downstairs.

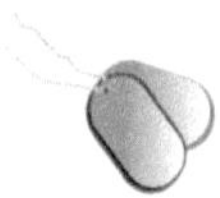

Ryler

Ryler leaned against the open door frame at the back patio, watching Shiv as the dog moved around the yard, snuffing at various scents he discovered. Ryler's eyes were on the hound, but his thoughts were elsewhere. Upstairs, in the bedroom, in that shower. And he was fighting with himself. One half of him was curled up, rocking back and forth in the corner of his mind, unwilling to open that door to relationship, to emotional closeness again. The other half was raging against that door, demanding to be let inside.

He wanted to go upstairs and he wanted to leave. He wanted her under him, against him, beside him. He wanted to taste her, but he also wanted to run from her. Ryler didn't want to go *too* far down that dangerous road but, he argued back, he'd already gone too far. Too far to turn back now. He was already involved. His heart was already open, already claimed. And he wanted her, needed her. He'd just have to ride this one out and see where it went. See what would happen.

Ryler heard the stairs creak as AJ came back down and prepared himself, taking a calming breath before turning to face her.

Her hair was damp, her skin flushed, and there was a warmth in her eyes. Her clothes were nondescript, sweats of some kind, but they, *she* inflamed him. Her shoulder was bare where the neckline had slipped, revealing her rose tattoo. Ryler drew in another long, slow breath. How did she do it? How did this little person turn him so inside out? He wanted every last part of her. And as he took her in, he saw something flicker in her gaze. Something unsure, uncertain, wary. She worried her lower lip for a moment, and he felt his breath catch.

Pain flashed in her eyes, and Ryler remembered why she'd been gone, what had happened. He recalled the last time they'd been together, what he'd said to her. And chastised himself for forgetting, but she did that to him. AJ had him twisted and tangled, and he wondered if she even knew it. As that pain flared again, he promised himself he'd take it away, that he'd keep her safe, and that no one would hurt her again.

He'd have to be cautious, careful with her. And if he was being honest, careful with himself as well. This couldn't be rushed. He'd have to take his time. And that eager part of himself, the part that wanted to breech the walls of her heart, rebelled at the idea. Slow? Careful? *Cautious*? That part howled in frustration. Ever the rebel, he chided himself. But as she stood there, waiting, and as he moved towards her, Shiv and the open door forgotten, he felt the absolute rightness of what he was doing now. And that other part of him relaxed, knowing he was going to succeed. Knowing he was going to get what he wanted. *Long live the Rebel*, Ryler thought as he reached her side.

CHAPTER ELEVEN
Caution Tape

AJ

A cautious light lingered in Ryler's gaze as he approached me. And as I studied him, studied his eyes closely, I realized the heat, that fire was still there, but it was tempered, controlled. This was a far cry from the murder I'd seen there earlier and wondered at the change. Caution tape, I suddenly thought. Our relationship seemed wreathed in caution tape.

His eyes searched mine intently, as if he was looking for some indication of what I wanted, of how I wanted him to proceed. Problem was, *I* didn't know what I wanted. Not exactly. Like, I wanted him to kiss me; I wanted his mouth on mine. I wanted him to take me in his arms. I wanted him to hold me. But, more than those things, I wanted him to stay. To not run away again and simply *stay*. With me. I wanted that safety, that assurance in him, in *us*.

But Ryler was still being *cautious*. And I didn't know what that meant. What *he* wanted. Would this be another embrace, full of fire and passion, only to have him retreat, leaving me cold, alone, and in need? Because I didn't want that. Definitely not. No, what I wanted was to rip through that tape, stride right in, and take charge.

But caution tape had its uses.

"Ryler." I stopped, needing to clear my throat. My voice sounded rough, almost clogged, to my own ears. I figured I should start with an apology. Try to explain *why* I hadn't told him I was leaving, *why* I hadn't answered any of his calls and texts while I was gone. "Hey…I'm sorry I didn't answer your calls. I…I just—"

His finger over my mouth cut me off. "Shhh." His voice rumbled low as he shook his head slowly, stepping closer. "We can talk about that later." He traced my mouth with his thumb, lingering a moment, before cupping my cheek. He stroked heatwaves across my skin. Leaning into him, his touch, I felt rather like a cat, wanting to purr, craving every sensation he conjured. My eyes flickered, then shut as tension I hadn't even known I'd been feeling began to fade. Welcoming that release, I simply held still, letting him do as he willed. Ryler slid one hand around to the back of my neck, massaging for moment before reaching up to cradle my head, still massaging. With eyes still closed, I felt him lean in. His mouth skimmed along my jaw, my neck where he inhaled long and slow. My breath shuddered as I absorbed him, letting my body experience every sensation.

Each and every little detail of him became a clear vision in my mind's eye. Ryler's fingers are long, but not slender. They're thick, and blunt-tipped. His palms are broad; the skin work-worn, and warm. There's an understated strength. Even in his fingers there is power and yet, he's gentle. His touch is gentle. His hands were like skin over steel, so much strength, and yet they held me with such tenderness. His scent was like a breeze through pine trees, like leather, and something spicier, warmer. It wrapped around, intoxicating me.

He leaned into me, over me, his body a solid warm wall as he pulled me closer. I couldn't have controlled the way my body arched, trying to be closer, to climb into his heat. His lips trailed fire up my neck, his teeth grazing, taking hold. Mint and something sharper, caressed my already heated skin as he slowly rolled my head to the side.

My hands, of their own accord, had risen, gripped his hips, his waist, holding myself steady, to keep from swaying, to keep our contact. And now I slid my arms around him, pulling him closer, needing that contact. The growl that sounded deep inside him at my touch, made my stomach clench in response, made an answering sound echo from my own throat.

His mouth found mine then, no more deviation. This was a claiming. Taking his time, in controlled movements, he placed his mouth against mine. Once. Twice. Three times. Then he settled there, tasting, moving. So deliberate, so intentional as he pulled at my lower lip, seeking entrance.

It felt like I'd barely got a taste of him before he moved on. Exploring once more. "When you were gone." He spoke against my neck; his teeth gently grazing the skin there. "When you'd left, it near stopped my heart, AJ." My brain wasn't working right; I struggled to form actual thoughts. Nothing registered but the sensations he created. There was only him. Only his mouth, only his hands on me. "Never again." His teeth gripped tighter, held on a moment, before releasing, his lips now soothing.

Something about his words took effect. Bringing clarity, as my brain began firing again. "You said," I swallowed, trying to find my breath. "You said you needed space, that you weren't ready."

He pulled back to meet my eyes. "I don't think I want space anymore."

"What *do* you want?" My voice was barely more than a breathy whisper.

"You," he rumbled against my mouth. "I think I just want you."

My heart galloped at those words, making the room tilt. I sucked in a deep breath, and as oxygen hit my brain, a much-needed dose of reality came with it. "I...Ryler, I think that sounds amazing, but...but there's this thing...with Mrs. Carson. With identifying her killer. And, and I'm not sure what I'm doing yet, and—"

Ryler kissed me quickly, cutting off my ramble. "We'll figure it out." He pulled me closer, held me tighter.

"Why?" I needed to know; it was important. "What changed your mind?"

He leaned back and silently studied me again before clenching his jaw and muttering, "You were gone. And I couldn't reach you, couldn't talk with you. And...I didn't like it."

My brows shot up. "*That's* what changed your mind? Me being gone?"

"Does it really matter? Isn't it enough to know that I don't want to lose you again?"

"I don't know." I pulled back, trying for a little space so I could think better. "I just don't know, and right now I'm not sure I'm in an emotionally stable place to figure it out. I need to solve Mrs. Carson's death. Find out who is responsible and why."

"Fair enough." He nodded, then leaned down so we were at eye level. "But I'll be right here. I meant what I said to that detective. No one is getting close to you. *I've* got you covered."

"Thanks." Stepping back, I took a deep breath and looked around the room, just trying to gather my thoughts.

Ryler let me go only so far, before moving, backing me into the wall. Having no means of escape, I held still. Waiting. One hand landed on the wall on either side of me, caging me in. When I finally met his gaze, his blue-grey eyes were molten. Such emotion in their depths. "We'll figure this out, AJ. I promise."

Testing his resolve, and mine, I ducked beneath his arm, knowing full-well he was letting me get away. "Okay." I nodded, then moved towards my staircase. "But I've got some work to do now, so...I guess I'll see you later, then."

The look in Ryler's eyes had shifted. Still heated, but with amusement flickering in them now. His lip curled before he turned, now heading towards the chair he'd been sitting in when I first got here.

I blinked. "Um, what are you doing?"

He settled in, taking the magazine from the side table and making himself comfortable. "You said you needed to work." His mental shrug came across loud and clear.

"Yes, I did." I spoke slowly. "And I will. But what are *you* doing?"

He looked at me, then down at himself, then back up to me. "I think it's pretty obvious. I'm sitting down. Now you can go work."

My hands fisted as I fought for calm. "I...I can't work with you *here*, Ryler!"

"Why not?" He opened the magazine. "You won't even know I'm here."

"You cannot be serious." My hands were now at my hips. Those blue-greys tracked my movements, lingering. Making my pulse race. Again. "I *will* know you're here."

"Are you about done? I'm trying to read here."

A frustrated, strangled sound erupted from between my clenched teeth as I spun away before I did something drastic, like, I don't know, maiming him somehow, and stomped my way back upstairs. Slamming my bedroom door, I continued stomping, just to get my point across, all the way to my desk, and flipped open my laptop. *Ugh!* Like I had time for this.

I needed to calm down. An eye-twitch was coming on; I just knew it. Irritating, asinine, aggravating man. I blew out a breath. Then did some breathing exercises. Whatever. He could stay down there. Fine. *I hope he gets a cramp in his butt.*

Opening my email, I skimmed through it. Not seeing anything needing my immediate attention, I opened my blog and read the comment from Amber. It certainly sounded like she'd had something to do with Mrs. Carson's death.

You shouldn't have pushed me; this is all your fault. And you can't hide from me. You should have stayed put. Pain and anger mixed in my chest, and I worked to hold back the moisture in my eyes. I hated that someone had done this to Mrs. Carson. That guilt washed over me again, making it difficult to breathe. Making a split decision, I quickly typed a reply to Amber. Maybe I'd get lucky and she'd slip up and give herself away.

Amber, are you saying you had something to do with this? I hit send. Now it was just a waiting game.

Leaving my email, I quickly opened my Word document with my current WIP. *Midnight Marine* was in its first round of edits, and I needed to get those to my editor by the end of the week. I got that completed and sent off, then began work on a new untitled project. Several hours later, I paused, stretched, and rose from my chair. Shockingly, the knowledge that Ryler was downstairs hadn't bothered me. Equally surprising was that he hadn't come upstairs to check on me. In fact, I wasn't even sure he was still down there, it was so quiet. Maybe he'd gotten bored and went home.

Tiptoeing to my door, I listened, then hearing nothing, opened it as quietly as possible. Feeling like an absolute idiot, I peered down the stairs. Not seeing anything, I figured he'd probably left. A scent hit me then. Something delicious. Mouthwatering. Something very much like food that was making my empty stomach complain noisily.

Coming down the stairs, my nose carrying me forward one careful step at a time, I found Ryler in the kitchen. I hadn't realized just how hungry I'd become and suddenly was ravenous, like I hadn't eaten for a lifetime. The table was set; a candle was lit and placed as the centerpiece. Ryler's back was to me, so when he turned away from the stove, in my direction, he paused. "Hey," he grinned hesitantly.

I looked around at all the pots and pans. "What's all this?"

He shrugged. "Just figured you'd be hungry."

"I am. Very." My stomach roared again, bearing witness to my hungry state.

"Sit down," he motioned to the table. "It's about ready; I'll get you a plate."

Mainly because I was just so hungry I couldn't think straight, I did as I was told. Moments later, Ryler brought me a steak, seared to perfection, with a shrimp scampi on the side. Then he brought me a knife, fork, and a napkin. Not hesitating at all, I cut into that steak. The inside was juicy and pink. And the *taste*, "MMmmmgosh, this is so good." My eyes rolled back in my head as I chewed.

Ryler sat opposite me, chuckling under his breath at my obvious enjoyment of his offering. When I was able to stop eating, to breathe for half a second, I tried one of the butter and garlic-soaked shrimp. Another hit. It was amazing. *Everything* was amazing. If I wasn't careful, I was going to lick this plate when I was done. I hadn't known food could taste this good.

I'd like to say I took my time and ate like a lady. With manners. But that would be a big fat lie. I *inhaled* this meal. Finally finished, I pushed back from the table, mainly so I wouldn't be tempted to lick that plate after all. When I looked up, Ryler was watching me, a look of near astonishment, with maybe a side of admiration mixed in was on his face.

I grinned sheepishly. "Guess I was hungry." Ryler just nodded, eyebrows raised at my understatement. I offered a half-hearted shrug. "You can cook for me any time, just saying."

At that, Ryler chuckled. "Good to know."

Feeling the heat of his gaze, I fought my blush and looked around the room. Dishes were piled, needing to be washed, yet he was a clean cook. No splatters or spills; his workstation was orderly. Continuing my perusal, my eyes landed on the magazine he'd picked up earlier. I'd snagged it at the airport for the return flight. It'd been one of those entertainment ones and had an exclusive interview with former Hollywood heartthrob, Asher Fitzpatrick and his wife Kate. It was one of those 'A Day in the Life' pieces.

I'd found their story so romantic. How he'd met her by chance at a coffee shop, and how, for him at least, it seemed to have been love at first sight. Nodding at it now, I turned back to face him. "Read anything interesting, Ryler?"

"Maybe." He snorted, grinned, then sobered again. "Nah, that...that dude on the cover looks a lot like a guy I met on a mission a few years back, though." He shook his head, seemingly lost in thought. "We were doing recon...then everything went to hell. There was...was this guy...I can't be certain. Everything was crazy for a hot minute. But this dude reminded me of him."

I laughed, more under my breath, than aloud, shock getting the better of me. "Wait. You're saying Asher Fitzpatrick, *Movie Star*, was on a recon mission with you? *How*? When?"

"I'm not saying it was him." He scratched his jaw. "I'm sure it wasn't. He just *looks* like that guy."

I was quiet for a moment, wanting to ask more about this mission, but sensed Ryler would clam up and pull away. His mood had already shifted, I could see it, feel it. My mind sought some way to lighten the load. "Could you imagine, though? He'd probably crap his pants." Ryler snorted again, a relieved look now in his eyes, then rose to begin cleaning up.

He stood at the sink, his back to me, and I found myself thoroughly engrossed in the play of muscle under his shirt as he moved. And just like that, my mind was wrapped up in him, in this attraction again.

My pulse beat faster as I rose to assist him, remembering the heat from earlier. Feeling it curl in my middle, stealing my breath. My hands held my plate, now forgotten as the echo of his touch, his taste flashed across my memory.

Ryler turned and paused, no doubt at the look on my face. That tension between us sizzled, then after a moment in which he seemed to reel himself back in, he slowly reached for the plate. Taking it, he turned back to the sink. "How'd your afternoon go?" he asked over his shoulder. "Did you get much work done?"

"Yeah. Yeah, I did." Did he hear the tremor in my voice? Did he know he was the cause of it?

"What did you work on?"

I wondered at his calm demeanor and fought for my own control, breathing deeply before slowly letting it out again. "I finished my edits for *Midnight Marine*. Got those sent off. Started a new project. And, I might have responded to the possible murderer stalking my blog page."

He turned the water off, reached for the towel, and dried his hands as he slowly turned to face me. "Might have?"

I nodded.

"Was that wise?"

"I think so." My shoulder shifted in a halfhearted shrug. "She mentioned that I'd forced her to act, that her actions were my fault." Taking a deep breath, I held it a moment as I considered my next words. "I needed to know if it was her, or if she's simply looking for attention."

"She?" His gaze ghosted over me before turning back to the sink. "Your problem fan is a woman?"

"Seems to be." I moved beside him, picking up the towel. "Her online name is Amber, at any rate."

"You know," he handed me the pan he'd washed and rinsed. "People become whoever they want online. Man, woman, young, or old."

"Yeah, I know." I gently nudged his shoulder with mine.

After several minutes of silent work, Ryler shut the water off. "Just...just be careful; be cautious. If your crazy fan is the one to blame, then you need to take this seriously."

"It's the *not knowing* and the *guilt*...that's the hardest part."

Ryler finished wiping down the counters and the table, my kitchen now looking spotless once more. He turned then, leaned against the counter and crossed his arms over his chest. "I just want you safe. I know nothing about this is easy, but I need you to trust me and rest assured I'll do whatever is needed to keep you safe."

I nodded. I'd heard his declaration to the detective. I knew he meant it in whatever capacity he was able. And I'd seen him practicing, so I knew he at least had some training, not to mention, he'd been a Ranger for crying out loud. Still, this not knowing *who* was behind all of this had my nerves a bit frazzled.

"AJ." I looked at him and Ryler held out his hand, inviting me closer. "You're safe with me; I promise." My hand slid into his, allowing him to pull me to him. Fitting me between his outspread legs, he cradled me against his chest. His heart beat under my ear, both soothing and stirring. My breathing regulated as my hands rose to slide around him. Burrowing into his warmth, I reveled in his scent, his strength. I pressed a kiss against his chest, my hands now gripping his shirt. I slid them downward, enjoying the feel of his solid frame, the ridges and dips under my palms. Ryler caught my hands, lifting them to his mouth. He nipped at my knuckles, before following that up with his lips. "Just relax, woman. I'm not after, or offering, anything other than comfort right now. We're taking things slow and easy."

I chuckled, then sighed as he pulled my head against his chest again, resting his cheek at my crown. We stayed that way for a while, and the beat of his heart under my ear was the only sound I heard, the only sound I wanted to hear.

CHAPTER TWELVE

Moose

Ryler

Ryler sat at his kitchen table, images flashing through his head as he wished AJ could somehow be here with him now. She calmed him. Centered him. But he hadn't shared this darkness with her yet. Didn't know *how* to share it with her. Was still too shaken by the whole thing, still trying to find his footing. After everything.

This week marked five years since it had happened, and normally Ryler would have headed into the wild, nothing but his ruck and Shiv to keep him company. But Ryler had promised AJ she'd be safe, that he wouldn't leave her alone. Especially with all that had happened with her landlady and psycho fan. Situations like this always had a strong potential to jump tracks and he wouldn't leave her unprotected. So instead of the isolation he needed, he forced himself to sit. To be still. To let the waves of memory strike.

Ryler's hands trembled as he reached for the bottle in front of him. He took a long, deep drink and ground his jaw. It was just supposed to have been a recon mission. Just information. Moose shouldn't have died. None of them should have...but betrayal carried a high price.

The mountain air near Paktia in eastern Afghanistan held a bite of the coming fall. Especially in the shadows. Most people imagine Afghanistan to be a hot, dry desert. And some parts were. With dust storms right out of a movie, the sand fine, like flour, tearing through, and getting into everything.

But snow would fill these passes in just three months, which was why Ryler and his small company were covering these mountains now. Intel indicated an insurgent stronghold somewhere along here. Attempts had been made to smoke them out, to no avail. Tension was high in the unit. They could feel the enemy, knew they were close. The Rangers just needed to pinpoint their exact location for the airstrike.

They were out on patrol; their mission, to conduct zone reconnaissance and report enemy movement and location to the rest of the unit. Ryler and Moose were on point, scouting the narrow trail in front. Casey, Colby, Jamison, Mitchell, and Simpson brought up the rear. The rest of their platoon were little more than a klick behind them, waiting back at the rally point. Ryler held his M4 close, loose and at the ready. They all did.

They'd followed a barely noticeable trail through several switchbacks into a deep ravine. It was slow going as they maneuvered the terrain in single-file formation. Each step, each move well thought-out and calculated, nothing wasted.

The cicadas were singing, and Ryler and his company moved silently so as not to disturb them. A mild breeze drifted through the trees, bringing with it a small relief from the heat, and a fleeting pungent scent, like burning rubber. Always there seemed to be the smell of burning rubber and refuse, at least when close to base or civilization. That, and the ever-present smell of body odor and septic—the Afghan water treatment method left much to be desired.

But once you were away, out in the open, the air tended to clear. So, getting that burnt-rubber smell immediately put them all on edge.

Moose glanced back over his shoulder, towards Ryler, warning him to be cautious. The two had become best friends at Basic. Their friendship had only deepened as they'd gone through Ranger training. It was an unspoken, deep-rooted knowledge the two of them shared, far above the closeness that comes simply from training together; Ryler and Moose always had each other's back. It was instinctive. In any and every situation. And today was no different.

Ryler blinked, remembering several things about that day, that moment. The sun had been sitting warmly at two o'clock. The dust barely stirred, despite the light breeze. Cedar and pine had teased his nostrils, offering a somewhat familiar and comforting scent. Birds had chattered happily from the branches overhead.

Then Moose had done that thing he always did. That knowing or sensing something just before it happened.

The sound, the very air, seemed to have been sucked directly into the atmosphere in a deafening roar. Ryler's eyes had been on Moose, had seen his eyes widen, seen his mouth move, screaming for him to get down. Seen, but hadn't responded fast enough. The explosion shook the ground, the rock walls, upending trees, strewing bodies and debris everywhere. Sound returned in spurts. Pops and snaps. Silence. Then more popping sounds, some sharp, some dull. The birds had stopped their chatter. In their place, were the sounds of yelling and screaming.

The smoke was thick; trees were on fire. Someone was on the radio, calling for support. The rest of A Company had caught up by then and were fully engaged. The Insurgents had been in well-prepared fighting positions, and they were putting up one hell of a fight. Ryler had been in and out of consciousness. He remembered the huge, dark shadow over him. The big man, so like that actor he'd seen in the magazine—uncanny, that—telling him to hold on, help was coming. He remembered the cold, shaky feeling as the man gripped his leg, trying to staunch the flow of blood. He never heard the helicopters. Had no memory of arriving at the hospital. Hadn't remembered what had happened until he'd asked for Moose.

Through the effects of Morphine, he'd learned what had happened. Who'd survived. Who hadn't. The Brass were calling it a success, despite the betrayal and the bad intel that led them into an ambush, that cost those six lives. Ryler understood warfare. Understood the necessity. Understood that those six lives, when weighed against the nearly four hundred enemy fighters that had been taken out, not to mention the training camp they'd demolished, were considered, if not acceptable, then at least not a complete loss.

His leg, his injury...learning about Moose and the others had overshadowed that. Ryler could accept what had happened to himself; it was those deaths he'd been unable to swallow.

Ryler rubbed a hand over his chest, over those marks tattooed there and took another swig from the bottle. His heart pounded and he inhaled slow and deep through his nose. He clenched his jaw, waiting for the grief, the guilt, the pain to strike. And it did. It always did. But this time, there was something different. Something changed. It was more subdued, had less bite. Ryler considered the difference, wondering about the cause. Attributing the shift to AJ. To what he felt for her. His cellphone vibrated with an incoming text.

Ryler checked the message, seeing it was from AJ. Rather than texting her back, simply needing to hear her voice, he called.

AJ

"Ryler?" my breath rushed his name.

"Hey, what's up?"

He sounded off somehow; I briefly wondered about it, before returning to my reason for calling. "I need you. There's something huge...some kind of...I don't know...a huge deer...or *something* in my backyard. Like, it's as big as an elephant. It's HUGE."

"All right..." I could hear the humor in his voice.

"Don't you *dare* laugh at me, Ryler James Dean." I growled as I stared out my window at the monstrosity eating away at my trees. At that, my use of his full name, like he was some small child, he burst out laughing.

"I'm not," he laughed. "I'm not laughing *at* you; I'm laughing *with* you."

"Funny, but *I'm* not laughing." That should have been obvious.

"Ah, c'mon. What are you freaked about? So, there's a deer in your yard." His mental shrug came through loud and clear. "We have tons of those here."

"Yeah, but this one is on steroids or something! What if it breaks into my house? What then, huh?"

Ryler chuckled. "Why would it do that?"

"Because...because I don't know, Ryler. It's an animal, why do animals do anything?"

He chuckled again. "Tell you what, I'll come down there and see about saving you from this Godzilla deer. How's that sound?"

"Yes, please." I was a little ashamed to hear the whiny tremor in my voice. "Just *hurry*. It's moving closer to the house...."

"Stay inside; I'll be there shortly."

Hanging up, I watched in slowly dawning horror as the large, antlered beast meandered in my direction. Quickly, I locked the patio door, then backed away. The concept that the animal literally had zero capability of opening the door not even registering. My heart thundered as I raced up the stairs to my room. As silently as possible, I opened the balcony door. And at first, I didn't see it and hoped it had run off. Afraid to breathe a sigh of relief just yet, I stepped quietly outside to see if I could spot it. And as I reached the railing, movement directly beneath me had my breath lodging in my throat.

The animal was *right* there. If I stretched, I was sure I could have touched it. And it was...eating my Wisteria. "*No!*" I screeched, slapping my hand against the wooden railing. The deer jerked violently, like it had been shot, before trotting off several feet, pieces of my plant still in its maw. "Get away!" I yelled, forgetting my fear for myself, as I now feared for the vine.

The animal stared at me with black eyes, then snorted. It shook its large head, and stomped a foot, before gingerly stepping toward my bush once more. Desperately, I looked around, trying to find some kind of weapon, something to drive the beast off. The deer had already begun nibbling at the Wisteria again. My heart clenched tightly with each *munch, munch* sound it made. I darted into my closet, hoping for something, anything, a baseball bat even, to materialize for my usage. But there was nothing. At all.

A cry of sheer frustration came from my throat as I headed back towards the balcony and my now shredded plant. Just then I heard the slamming of a door and my name called from down the stairs.

"I'm up here! Hurry!" I hollered back.

Seconds later, Ryler appeared beside me, just a tad short of breath. "Look!" I grabbed his hand, practically dragging him out the door, to the scene of the crime. "Look what it's doing! Ryler, you have to stop it!"

Ryler took one look at the deer and began laughing. He laughed until tears poured from his eyes, until his breath hitched in his chest. Laughed until his knees became weak and he had to hold the railing to keep from falling.

"This is. *Not.* Funny!" Panic took a firmer grip as the deer ate more of my favored vine.

Ryler coughed as he stood upright finally and wiped his tears with the back of his hand. "AJ." He coughed again. "AJ, that isn't a deer. That is a moose."

"A...A *moose?*"

"Yeah. We don't get too many around here, but every so often one or two will pop up."

"Well, can you stop it?" I gripped the railing, wishing I was somehow bigger and more formidable. "Ryler, it's eating my Wisteria!"

Shaking his head and quietly chuckling, no doubt over my mistake, Ryler pulled a handgun from under his shirt.

"No!" I cringed. "Don't shoot it!"

"Relax." He tossed me a long-suffering look. "I'm not going to shoot it. Just scare it off and hopefully save your vine."

"Oh." I nodded, biting my lip. "Okay. Just...just don't hurt it."

He arched a brow. "A second ago, you were considering going to war with it, now you don't want me to hurt it?"

"Yeah." I shrugged.

Ryler chuckled under his breath again. "You might want to plug your ears." Taking careful aim, he fired his gun twice, in rapid succession, into the ground near the moose. The sound spooked the animal, causing it to run off and into the trees at the back of the property. Ryler holstered his weapon and turned to me, a wide smile forming on lips.

His audacity to laugh at my mistake, at the situation, had me gritting my teeth and taking a swing at him. Ryler easily, *darn him anyway*, avoided my poor aim. He quickly stepped inside my limited reach, his left arm coming above my right, bringing it down, trapping mine against his side. He then closed on me, chest to chest. Struggling, I tried to free myself, only to be held tighter. After a brief moment of holding me in place, Ryler changed tactics, swinging me up into his arms. He kicked the door shut behind him, and moved towards the bed, depositing me unceremoniously on it.

Still chuckling, Ryler followed me onto the mattress, pinning me beneath him. He took a firm, but gentle grip on my wrists, holding them easily in place above my head. "This isn't the least bit funny, Ryler." I seethed, straining against him. "Now get *off* me."

I'd known he was strong, but just how strong had somehow eluded me. Until now. Ryler was a brick wall, a fortress. Immovable. And maybe it was all muscle, or maybe it was will, or maybe it was some combination of both. Whatever it was, the result was lethal. Because as I struggled against that strength, finding it to be impossible, it dawned on me that he'd become still. Motionless, except for the rise and fall of his chest.

He didn't strain trying to hold me. That seemed effortless. Still, Ryler was locked down, locked tight. A storm was brewing in those blue-grey eyes, like writhing, heavy clouds. Those eyes flickered to my mouth, lingering for a moment, warming them with his gaze, before returning to mine. He shifted his body, a tiny adjustment, that had my breath catching. Ryler leaned down, nuzzling his nose, his mouth along my temple. Down past my ear, to my neck, my throat. And there, against my skin, he growled low. "This wasn't supposed to happen, AJ." He nipped gently where his lips had been, before once more kissing the skin there. "None of this was supposed to happen. And now, what do I do...?"

I wasn't sure if he was speaking of me personally, or this situation, or what. But as my brain tried to reconcile his comments with his actions, my mind eventually gave up and just let my body take over. Ryler loosed my hands, which had still been demanding their release. His hands now slid under me, curving around my shoulder blades, lifting me. Bringing my neck closer. Burying his face there, his mouth made that place his own. Fingers scraped my scalp now, sending a rush of pleasure through me. Then they scalded as they traveled down my side, over my hips, to my thighs, pulling me closer to him.

I clung to him, demanding more, needing more. Ryler's mouth eventually found mine and I tasted him. Tasted the strong drink on his breath. Tasted his desire. And this, this was, consuming. Body and soul, I was consumed. And regretted nothing.

Ryler

She was killing him. Slowly, exquisitely, AJ was killing him. Her scent, that coconut, and cream, and ocean air scent of her, drove him insane. Her mouth, her taste. The feel of her hands as she raked her nails on his back, as she dragged him closer, demanding more. Those sounds she was making. That hitch in her breath. All of it. Everything. This was heaven. This was hell. He wanted more. He wanted all of it. He wanted her and he wanted her right now.

But Ryler held himself back, and that was what was killing him. That was what was gutting him. His frame of mind was not the right one, not for this. He didn't want to take her out of a need to dispel the pain he was feeling. He didn't want her to be just another drug to numb the past. When they came together, *if* they came together, he wanted it to be because they were mutually ready for it. Because they both wanted it. And AJ didn't know where his head had been before he'd come here. She had no way of knowing and he wouldn't use her like this.

Ryler took her hands again, raising them above her head, holding them there. Holding her there. He kissed her slowly before pulling back. AJ tried reaching for him again, and at the sound of her frustration, he almost relented. Instead, he held himself still, held himself in place, and waited for her to see him. When AJ finally opened her eyes, when she took him in, he leaned down and whispered against her jaw, "I want you, AJ."

She growled in frustrated agreement and tried freeing herself once more, but he held her and continued. "But, not like this. Not for the reasons in my head right now. I want you, and soon—I promise you—soon. Then I'll have you. But not yet." Ryler waited for her to acknowledge his words, to indicate she understood. At her slight nod, he loosened his grip. "I'm going to let you go, just...just behave."

Then he rolled, coming to a stop on his back beside her. AJ took several deep breaths, seemingly trying to get control of herself. Whether of her desire, or temper, Ryler wasn't sure. Both, he figured. He lay still, let himself settle, let her simmer down. When AJ finally moved, she sat up, her back to him. Slowly she scooted to the edge of the bed and stood.

The late morning sun dappled the floor where she stood, and with her back still to him, she spoke in a low, controlled voice. "I understand that you're fighting demons, Ryler. But I hate it when you do this; I hate it when you push me away." With those words she walked to her bathroom, closing the door quietly, and locking it behind her.

Had she slapped him, it couldn't have burned worse. Couldn't have left a deeper mark.

CHAPTER THIRTEEN
Coming Storm

AJ

I took my time in the bathroom. Running the bath water, pouring in the fragranced Epsom salts, and soaking for well over half an hour. Giving Ryler enough time to gather himself and leave. He was silent when he left, because I never heard a sound. Thoughts and fears ran rampant through my mind, bringing with it a throbbing inside my skull. Would we ever align correctly? Would every encounter with him end like this? The pulling closer, the pushing away, and never really together.

After my bath, I continued my slow process, toweling off, rubbing on my favorite body lotion. Running a brush through my hair. Wrapped in a towel, I opened my bathroom door and my body jerked to a stop, even as my heart lurched into motion. Ryler reclined on my bed against my headboard, arms crossed over his chest. His eyes were calm and focused on mine.

"I couldn't leave. Not like that." His shoulders lifted slightly, stiffly before settling once more.

"I see that." Fighting to calm my heart, which was still racing, I made my way to my dresser. I pulled out a pair of sweatpants and a T-shirt. "Be right back."

Ryler

Ryler had fought with himself as AJ left. Wanting to go to her, wanting to bring her back. Knowing he'd hurt her. But he knew if he did, they'd continue where they'd left off. Continue until they were finished.

He'd made a snap-decision before, when he'd pushed her away. But the purpose behind that decision had begun to firm up in his head now. He was turning over a new leaf so to speak. He wasn't too old to make changes, nor too young to ignore the need for them.

They'd both been hurt in the past. And maybe a part of that hurt was from rushing in too soon. Giving everything too fast. Treating something that should have held deep meaning, like it casually didn't matter. Lying to themselves each time that it was unimportant, maybe even meaningless and no big deal. Refusing to acknowledge the bruises inflicted on their own souls.

So, even though AJ had misunderstood his intentions and had been hurt by them, he'd let her go. Ryler needed to think. Think about what to say to her. How to say it when she came back out. He needed not to think about what she was doing, just a few feet away, behind that closed door.

He'd heard the water, heard the sound of the tub filling. He'd locked himself in place. Rigid. Immovable. He'd closed his eyes and just tried to breathe.

Then she opened the door, stepping out in a towel, scented steam billowing out around her. And he had to fight the groan that threatened to sound. Breathing shallowly, he held himself in place, striving to maintain control.

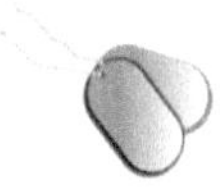

AJ

Ryler was where I'd left him. I wasn't sure what to do, where to go. Joining him on my bed didn't seem like a good idea, all things considered. So, I curled my frame into the chair near the window and waited for him to speak. Josephine slunk out from under the bed, her feline body stretching slowly, before ambling over, and jumping into my lap.

The silence stretched several minutes as I scratched behind her ears and listened to her purr, but I was determined to wait Ryler out. My patience was rewarded as he finally spoke. "We've been here before, haven't we?"

"Mmm," I mumbled, noncommittally.

He took a slow, deep breath. Held it, then let it out in a rush, his voice a little rough now. "You're right, AJ—I am fighting demons. Every day I'm fighting them. And for the most part, I'm able to successfully silence them. But there are days, times, when they roar louder than I'm able to combat. Hurting you is not something I want to do. Ever. And I'm sorry that I have."

"We all have demons, Ryler. We all have something we battle from our past."

"I know." He shook his head. "I'm not making excuses. I just wanted you to know. Today wasn't about the battle, not really. Today was me trying to show you respect. And I'm guessing it didn't come across the way I'd meant, and for that I'm sorry."

"So...what was today, then?"

"Today...was me trying not to use you like a pain killer."

I thought about that, about what that might have meant. I knew he'd been hurt, both physically and emotionally. I'd tasted the drink on his breath; what had he been facing before coming to my rescue? What had

I interrupted? "I don't pretend to understand what you faced, what you went through, or what you're dealing with, Ryler. But, if you want, I can listen."

He studied me closely, no doubt considering what I'd said. After several moments, he sat forward, pulling the hem of his shirt up to reveal those six marks across his heart. I tried to focus on what it was he was showing me and not the form, the ridges, the skin now bare before me.

"Moose, and Colby, Jamison, and Mitchell, Simpson, and Casey." He lightly touched each mark as he said their names. "Today marks five years since they...since we...we were in the same squad, and one moment we were all together and alive, and the next...the next, everything became a living hell, and they were gone." He paused briefly, then shook his head and continued. "Normally, on this date, I take off and spend time by myself, but this year I didn't."

"Why not?" I whispered, my heart clenching at his words, hurting over his hidden wounds. "Why did you stay?" Ryler just looked at me, his gaze focused, his silence deep and pointed. Realization dawned on me. "You stayed because of *me*? Why?"

"I meant what I said, AJ. I *will be* your first and last line of defense. There was no way I was leaving you unprotected."

I swallowed. "I don't know what to say. I...." I was at a loss, that's what I was. My earlier irritation had morphed into pained understanding. I didn't know how to feel about this revelation. Finally, I settled on the words, "Thank you. Ryler, thank you for, for thinking of me, for looking out for me first."

"Thanks aren't necessary. I'm glad to do it. I just wanted you to know why I'd...pushed you away today. It wouldn't have been right. I wouldn't have been right today."

We sat for several moments, then my stomach growled and Ryler's mouth quirked. I grinned and shook my head ruefully. "I'm hungry, obviously. How about you?"

"I wouldn't say no." Ryler stood, then offered a hand, lifting me to my feet. Josephine fussed as I rose but was happy enough to take my place on the chair I'd vacated. My nose was nearly pressed into his chest as I stood before him. His hand still held mine, and I remembered clearly what was beneath the black cotton of his shirt. His woodsy, spicy scent danced along my senses, teasing. Carefully, I slid my arms around him, needing him close. Just needing to hold him. And after a moment's hesitation, Ryler's arms came around me, pulling me closer still.

We ended up going out, once I remembered I'd needed to get groceries. After a couple minutes' worth of discussion, we headed to the Hiway 101 Diner where we each ordered a burger, fries, and shake.

As we ate, a thought kept tickling the back of my mind. Something I'd unintentionally put off for as long as I could. "I need to see Jake, where he's buried."

Ryler swallowed the bite in his mouth and took a sip from his vanilla shake. "All right. We can head over after we're done here if you want?"

"I do." I nodded. "Thank you. I know I should have asked sooner. I think I was just afraid to, but I can't keep putting it off, because time isn't always a guaranteed thing."

We finished eating and Ryler drove us to the Sequim View Cemetery. I'm not a fan of cemeteries. In fact, they sort of give me the creeps. Which is possibly why I'd avoided this activity until now. We drove about sixty yards in, the road veering to the right before Ryler slowed, then parked. He waited for me as I resolutely came around the front of his Bronco, trying to settle my nerves and stomach. He lifted his hand, offering something firm and solid and warm to hold onto. Gratefully, I accepted.

Ryler led us about twenty feet away from the road, towards a thick stand of trees. Jake's headstone was simple. Flat to the ground. An American flag was engraved on it, along with the words, "Jacob T. Daniels. Beloved. At ease, Soldier. Your watch is over."

As I stood there staring down at it, my eyes filled with tears. It took me a couple tries to swallow past the lump in my throat. Blinking, lips trembling, I whispered, "Who made these arrangements?"

"Jo did." He sighed, squeezing my hand gently. "She's your great aunt, you know? Jake's aunt. His mother's sister."

My breath rattled in my chest as I choked on a disbelieving chuckle. "Of course she is." With my free hand, I rubbed at my mouth, just fighting to remain calm. "Anyone else?"

"The elder Paige is a cousin of Jake's."

This news made me chuckle harder. "And they know, right? Who I am?"

"Yeah, AJ, they know. No one wanted to say anything...so you wouldn't feel uncomfortable, or pressured."

"What happened to them? Jake's parents? Are they still around?"

He shook his head. "About seven years ago now. She'd had cancer—I think that's partly why he'd refused treatment—he'd seen what it had done to her. And to his dad, watching the woman he loved just waste away. Less than a year after she'd gone, he'd had a stroke, and then a couple days later, he was gone as well. Ed and Ruthie. You would have liked them. Really good people."

I wiped the tears from my face and cleared my throat. "Are they buried here as well?"

Ryler nodded, then lead me four rows away. They were buried side by side, and as I looked around, I decided it really was a very nice and peaceful setting to lay a loved one to rest.

"Thank you." I turned to him. "For bringing me here, for allowing me to work through all this."

"No problem. I know this hasn't been easy for you; I know it's been hard, in fact, and I know I didn't make it any easier. But still, you're pretty tough and you've stuck it out, and I'm glad you did."

This made me laugh outright. I wiped my tears away with my sleeve and smiled at him.

"What?" he asked.

"*Now* you're glad I stayed, maybe. But you can't deny you didn't always feel this way about me."

Ryler chuckled darkly. "More or less. I think any negative feelings I harbored were more resentment over the way you made me feel. Against my will, I might add."

"And now?"

"Now? Now, I'm thinking I could get used to this."

His admission had me grinning, then my grin faded. "I'd like to make one more stop, if that's all right?"

"Jo's?" he guessed.

"Please."

As we pulled onto the highway, leaving the cemetery behind, my cell phone rang. It was Detective Whitaker. "Hello, Detective."

"I'll get right to it, Miss McAdams. Have you checked your blog? Amber responded."

"What did she say?" My heart dropped into my stomach.

"She said, and I quote, 'You think you're being so smart. But I'm smarter.' end quote."

"So," I swallowed. "Now what do I do? What does this mean? Can't you just arrest her?"

"It's not that simple, Miss McAdams. We don't even know who she is. We need you to try and keep her talking. Try to get her to reveal who she is or give some clue that might aid us."

"Okay." I nodded, my mind spinning. "I'm out right now, but I'll see what I can do when I get home."

"Good. And stay alert. You still have your friends with you, right?"

"Yes, I'm with Ryler right now."

"Good; make sure he's aware. And stay close to him."

"All right. I'll be in touch." Ryler had been silent as Detective Whitaker and I had talked, and as he shut off the Bronco, I realized we were outside Jo's.

He reached for my hand, gripping it firmly. "Storm's coming, isn't it?"

"Certainly, seems that way. Amber responded. She says she's smarter than me." I made air-quotations with my hands. "And now I think she's going to come after me or at least try to."

"Not gonna happen."

I took a slow, deep breath, and held it before letting it out again. "This thing with Amber…I just want it over with. If she's guilty, then I want her caught and locked away forever."

"We'll get her, AJ. She won't hurt you."

"I'm not worried about me, really. More those around me; I don't want anyone else hurt because of me."

"Why does that not surprise me?" He gave my hand a gentle squeeze. "Let's go see your aunt, then we'll deal with Amber, or whoever she is."

The word *aunt* caught me off-guard for just a moment. Then I realized he was speaking of Jo, my dad's aunt. *I had family here.* I had family period. I'd never really had one before. Mom hadn't been close to her relations, really, so the idea of having *family* was a new and surprising concept.

Jo was behind the counter; she looked up as the bell over the door jingled on our way in. Her bright blue eyes did a doubletake and she fumbled the change she was handing to the customer who'd just checked out. Ryler waved to her as he led us to an empty booth, where he could sit with his back against the wall, no doubt so he could view the room at large. I slid onto the seat first, then scooted over as he made to sit down beside me.

Silver glimmered at the edges of Jo's eyes, as she took a deep breath and headed our way. An emotional storm brewed there, but she quickly overcame it and was calm as she approached our table. She hesitated when she reached us, then Ryler nodded to the seat across from us. Jo's eyes flickered to me, then she sat down.

"She knows, Jo." Ryler rumbled in that deep voice of his.

Before I could say anything, before I was able to acknowledge what Ryler had said, Jo's eyes filled with tears again. Her lip trembled, and her breath caught. Then as her emotions got the best of her, she quickly stood, a trembling hand over her mouth and walked away. My heart tightened at her obvious upset. I nudged Ryler, wanting out of the booth, and waved him back as he made to follow me.

Ignoring the *Employees Only* sign, I quickly stepped behind the counter and trailed her through the swinging door into the kitchen. Jo stood near the sink, hunched and wrapped around herself, her shoulders shaking. Unsure how to proceed, I stood still for just a moment, before clearing my throat. "Um, Jo...I...I'm sorry I didn't...before. I didn't know. About you, about Jake. About anything. And I'm just so—"

Jo turned, faster than I could anticipate, and her strong arms were around me. She pulled me close, and wept. At a loss as to what to do, I simply held her. And tried to control my own emotions. After several moments, she quieted and pulled back. "Oh, I'm sorry, AJ. I shouldn't have...now you'll think...I'm just so happy, so thankful that you're here, that you know. I've waited. Trying to be patient. And now you're here."

"*I'm* sorry, Jo. I wish I'd known sooner. I'm sorry you've been hurting."

"No, child, don't apologize. I'm just glad you're here. Now we can talk and get to know each other." Jo searched my face, lighting on each and every feature. "You look like her, like my sister. Your grandmother. Same facial features, same smile."

Blinking back tears, I smiled. That she could see her family in me. That she recognized me. It gave me a sense of belonging. And that was something I'd been lacking for a long time.

The door into the kitchen opened and Ryler came in. "You guys all right now?"

Jo turned, her arm still around me. "Never better. Thank you, Rye."

Ryler smiled as his blue-grey eyes found mine and heat barreled through me. My mouth curved upwards in answer to him. My heart, despite all I'd gone through and all that had happened, my heart was happy.

We made plans for Jo to come to the house for dinner; she promised to bring Paige and Poppy with her.

CHAPTER FOURTEEN
The Light and The Tunnel

AJ

"AJ!" Leslie answered my call. "How are you? What's new?"

I wracked my brain for the exact words needed. "Lez...there are so many things. So. Many. Things. For starters...for starters things have sort of hit the proverbial fan with me personally." I took a deep breath. "You should probably sit down, if you're not already."

Leslie was silent a moment, no doubt trying to fathom what I was talking about. "What's going on, AJ? You've got me worried, now."

"I don't even know where to begin. I guess it all started when I posted on my blog about leaving Coronado for a while. You know I've got that blog, right?"

"Yeah."

"Well, I've also got this fan. Her name is Amber, or at least that's what she goes by. She wasn't happy with my announcement and began posting negative and derogatory comments. Expressing her anger at my leaving, saying I was being irresponsible towards my fans. And at first, I thought she was simply trolling and tried ignoring it, you know? But then...then someone broke into my house on Coronado and vandalized the place."

"Are you all right? Was anything stolen? What happened?"

"No, nothing was stolen, but messages were spray-painted on my door. But it gets worse. Someone...someone broke in again. And this time...this time, my landlady..." I cleared my throat and took a deep breath. "Mrs. Carson was murdered."

"Oh, AJ…I'm so sorry. Has the person been caught? Do they know who did it?"

"They're pretty sure it's my fan, and no, they haven't been caught yet. And there's more. The fan, Amber, is now, *possibly,* making threats against me."

"What?" Her voice turned brittle.

"That's what I needed to tell you. I'm not moving back to Coronado. I'm staying here. At least for the time being. I need you to cancel my appearance at the Authors Unlimited thing. I'm working with a detective with the CPD. We're trying to resolve this and get Mrs. Carson's murderer brought to justice."

"Yeah, I'll take care of that; of course. Do you have protection up there, AJ? Are the police doing everything they can to keep you safe?" Concern was evident in her voice.

"Yeah, they are." I nodded even though she couldn't see me. "And I've got someone, some people, friends that are looking out for me."

"I hope you know you are more than welcome to stay here in New York with me. You just keep that in mind, all right?" Conviction threaded through, giving her words an edge.

"Thanks, Leslie. I think I'm good here. And there seems to possibly be a light at the end of the tunnel, because we're trying to smoke Amber out and get her to take the bait so to speak. And if she does, hopefully they'll catch her and then this will all be over with."

"What do you mean, '*Take the bait*'?" she demanded.

"Well, I'm trying to communicate with her, trying to get her to reveal more about herself, who she is, where she is, etc.…."

"Why are *you* doing this?" Leslie was becoming agitated; I could hear it in her tone. "I thought the police were involved. Why aren't they the ones trying to communicate with her?"

"They're monitoring my account and as I want to help catch this person, I volunteered. Besides, she seems to be having these issues with me, so chances are greater that she'll be more willing to talk with me."

"But is that safe, AJ?"

I certainly hoped I'd be safe. As it was, I did what I could to offer assurances. "Like I said, I've got people here to protect me."

"I feel that, as your friend and as your agent, I should just say that I don't like this. Just, just be careful. And are you sure...about staying there I mean?"

"I am." I answered on both topics. "I'm being careful and, I am sure. Jake, my real dad, he...he made some great provisions for me here. And I just met family I never knew I had, and I just think staying here would be for the best right now."

"Well, stay in touch. And promise you'll keep me posted."

"Will do. You take it easy."

We hung up and I took a deep breath, because the harder phone call was the one I was about to make. Harley. She was *not* going to take this well. I'd promised her earlier that I wouldn't make this move a permanent one. Here I was going back on my word, doing just that.

I hoped she could understand—I hadn't planned this. It just sort of happened. And besides, I needed to deal with this Amber business, anyway. And it wasn't like we had lived together. I wasn't leaving her high and dry and in need of a roommate. After silently procrastinating for another couple of minutes, I picked up my phone again and dialed.

"Harley is hustling and can't answer the phone right now. If you want a call back, you better leave me your name and number," her voicemail said. And I couldn't contain my sigh of relief. I left her a quick message, ever thankful for my slight reprieve. Then, as I needed to confirm with Jo and the Paiges about dinner this weekend, I grabbed my purse and keys and headed into town.

My first stop was to see Jo. Her smile could have lit up the entire block when I walked in. The sight of it did funny things to my heart. I felt lighter. Freer. And couldn't help but return it. Jo came from behind the counter to give me a squeeze.

"Hi, Jo," I breathed as she held me tight.

"I'm so glad you came in."

"Me, too." I pulled back, offering my own little smile. "Hey, I just wanted to make sure we're still on for this Friday."

"I wouldn't miss it for the world."

"Good. Seven still a good time?"

"It's perfect." Jo smiled.

"Okay." I nodded, feeling both accomplished and nervous. "I'm cooking, so there isn't anything you need to do. Just come."

"Can't wait. The Paiges are planning to ride out with me. They're excited as well. Poppy was near to coming out of her skin when I told them you finally knew."

That made my smile bigger. "I wish I'd have known sooner. I'm heading there next. I just wanted to check in with you, and to give you my number."

I handed her my business card, and told her she could call at any time, for any reason. Then we said our goodbyes, and I headed back out. But not before she insisted I take a slice of her strudel with me.

On the way to *Turning Paiges,* I stopped in to see Kerry and let him know my plans. He congratulated me and said Jake would have been pleased. Hearing that made my heart clench; I smiled, nodded, then headed out.

Paige was behind the counter as I entered her store; I didn't see Poppy, though. She smiled and it seemed a little hesitant to me. But as I smiled back, hers blossomed. "Hello Paige. Jo says you guys know who I am."

She blinked back tears. "We're thrilled, just thrilled to have all this out in the open. It's been so hard trying not to spill the beans. Especially for Poppy."

"I'm sorry I made things so difficult." I wished there was something I could do or have done to ease their discomfort in some measure.

"No, no, please, do not apologize. None of this is your fault. We understand. We just didn't want to overwhelm you."

"I know." I shrugged. "Still, I feel bad this has been so hard on everyone."

"None of this has been your doing." She shook her head. "Decisions were made that have affected us all. Now, we forgive and we move forward." She smiled again, softer now. "We're really looking forward to dinner on Friday."

"That's what I came by for. Just wanted to make sure we were still on, and to give you this." I handed her my business card. "You can reach me anytime if you need to."

"Thank you. Poppy should be back any minute—she went to get coffee—I know she'll want to see you."

"I'll wait then, just look around."

Close to five minutes later, as I was perusing a row of used books, Poppy strolled in, paper cup in hand. She stopped when she saw me. The smile spreading across her face flashed like fireworks. "AJ!" Cup still in hand, she enthusiastically wrapped her arms around me and squeezed. "I've been waiting since like *forever* to do that! You have no idea."

Warmth trickled through me and I tried not to be overwhelmed by her exuberance. "Hello, Poppy."

"My tongue is literally black and blue from the amount of biting I've had to do to keep from spilling the beans that I knew who you were." She set her cup down and clutched her chest. "Oh my stars, it's such a weight off!"

Her goodwill and nature were soothing to the soul. "So, I came by for a couple reasons. I gave your mom my number, so you can get ahold of me if you need to. And I'm needing your advice on something. See, you have amazing hair and I need a good stylist...so I was hoping you could point me in the right direction."

Poppy squealed excitedly. "Yes! Tessa at *The Cut Corner*. She's amazing with hair. We can go over there now if you want?"

My phone buzzed and I saw it was Harley. "Uh, hey, another time, huh? I need to take this call. But I'll see you this Friday, all right?" I said a quick goodbye, then headed out to my car. The call had gone to my voicemail, so I waited a moment or two, then dialed her back.

"Hey, babe!" Harley sounded abnormally cheery, making me feel guilty for the news I was about to share.

"Whatcha doin'?" My heart thudded in my chest.

"Calling you back, obviously. I'm on break."

I chuckled, missing her and her humor. "Hey, so I've got something to tell you. And...I need you to listen...all right?"

She was silent a moment, then softly said, "You're not coming back, are you?"

She hit it on the head. "No. At least, I'm not moving back there. I'll come visit, but I think I'm going to stay here. Jake built a home here for me. And I just met family that I didn't know I'd had. And, I just think, all things considered, with everything that is going on, that staying here is best for right now."

Emotion tinged her voice. "I was afraid this was going to happen. I just had this feeling, you know? And I've been wanting to share something with you. But now you're not coming back...."

"I'm sorry; I don't mean to let you down. That was never my intent. And you can share anything with me. Anytime."

"I know." She whined a little now. "It's just not the same when you're not here. You were my wingman, AJ! I depended on you." Harley took a deep breath, then let it out in a rush. "Okay, here goes; I'm seeing Kevin."

I blinked a couple of times and waited for her to continue. When she remained silent, I said, "Kevin...?"

"You know...Kevin. Big, hunky, good-looking guy that always smells like coffee and yum?"

My mind was trying to put together what she was saying. When my silence continued to drag, she burst out, "Kevin! From the Sun and Surf Café?? Kevin Keith Rhoades."

"You and Kevin?" I finally asked. *His name is Kevin Keith Rhoades?* Huh.

"Yes, AJ. Me and Kevin."

"Wow. When did this happen?"

"Sort of right after you'd left this last time. I'd needed a pick-me-up and stopped in the next day, looking glum, apparently. Because you were gone again and I was worried. And he bought my drink and as he was just getting off work...we talked. And it was nice. And I like him."

"That's awesome, Harley!"

"You're not mad?"

"Psht, no! Why would I be?"

"I dunno...I kind of thought you'd liked him."

"I mean, I think he's a cutie and all—who wouldn't—but no, I don't like him like that. Actually," I smiled, feeling warm and happy over this news. "I think it's perfect."

"You do? Truly?"

"Truly." This was an honest to goodness weight off my shoulders. I didn't feel so horrible, like I'd abandoned her, so much now. "Kevin's great."

"You're not just saying that, to make me feel better, because you feel guilty for not coming back, right?"

"Oh. My. Word. Harley, I am happy for you. And for Kevin. And besides, I'm sort of interested in someone here, though I'm not sure just where that is going...."

"Ryler, right? I'm right, aren't I? I knew it! Your voice changes when you talk about him."

"It does not."

She snorted. "Yes, it does."

"Whatever."

She chuckled. "Thanks for calling, babe, but my break is up and I really gotta get back in there. I'll see you in a little over four weeks, though, right?"

"Definitely. Can't wait to see you and show you around. You'll love Sequim! Love you, Harley. Give my best to Kevin."

Relief over this phone call radiated through me. Losing Harley wasn't something I'd have been able to handle. I was so thankful she'd understood. But her and Kevin? It was shocking, that's for sure, but honestly, Kevin was really great. I'd just never thought of the two of them together. But now that I consider it, he really was a perfect fit for her.

Marking two items off my mental to-do list, I headed for home, knowing I'd need to prepare for dealing with Amber and any possible new developments with her.

I checked my email first, answering the ones that needed my attention, deleting ones I didn't care to acknowledge. Next, I checked my social media. Then finally, I went to my blog page.

Sure enough, a comment from Amber waited for me. "You think everything is about you and don't care who you hurt. But AJ, you will care. And soon."

The threat was there. Subtle, but there. What I needed was for her to get really angry at me. Get her to flip out and hopefully slip up. Give something away. Or even just to come after me and leave everyone else alone. I needed to find a way to push her buttons and rile her.

"Amber, you're a joke. A troll. You're the one making this about me. I don't even know you. And if you weren't such a coward, you'd either get a life and leave me alone, or you'd stop hiding behind your keyboard just playing games. Go away. I'm done."

At the very least, I hoped my response showed her I wasn't intimidated.

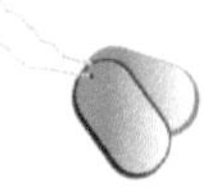

Ryler

Ryler had begun following AJ's blog a week or more back. Something he never thought he'd *ever* do. But he and Chief had agreed they needed to do it to keep an eye on the Amber situation. He happened to be online when AJ posted her latest reply and nearly choked on the coffee he'd been trying to swallow. Staring in disbelief, not sure if he should be impressed or worried about her, he heard his phone buzz. Ryler answered without even looking at who was calling. "Yeah?"

"You see her latest reply to Amber?" Chief asked without preamble.

"Looking at it right now."

"Is she looking for a fight with this woman?"

Ryler blew out a breath. "I think she's just looking for a reaction." He hoped that was all it was.

"This should do it."

Ryler nodded to himself. "Agreed."

"Head on a swivel."

"I'm on it." Ryler rose to his feet as they hung up. He whistled for Shiv as he grabbed his keys and headed out the door.

Minutes later he parked at Jake's; Shiv headed off, sniffing after something in the brush. Ryler knocked, waited, knocked again. Then let himself in. The house was quiet. "AJ?" No answer. Her car was parked out front, so he knew she was here. "AJ?" he called out louder. Still no answer. Telling himself he was being ridiculous, Ryler tried to calm his pulse. He was probably blowing his concerns out of proportion, but he couldn't seem to help himself.

Still, he thoroughly checked downstairs with no sign of her, before heading to the second floor. He hoped maybe she was just out on the balcony and hadn't heard him come in, or call. Maybe she had headphones in or something. Or, he supposed, she could be in the shower. That made his pulse pick up for an entirely different reason.

Ryler's heart tripped over itself as he entered her bedroom. Late afternoon sunshine, peaking beneath the low clouds, was spilling through the open balcony doors, bringing a mild breeze in with it. Somewhere off in the distance he heard the rumble of thunder and could smell rain on the air. AJ was asleep on her bed, facing the coming storm, a small throw blanket was pulled partially over her. She lay on her side; her hands tucked under her chin.

Walking softly, Ryler approached the bed, watching her intently. AJ shifted, one leg sliding down, out from beneath her blanket. A small patch of sunlight caught the sun tattoo on her thigh, and he took a slow, deep breath. He hadn't wanted this. This need, this attraction. And yet, here it was. Here she was.

Ryler had been in an endless tunnel since the explosion, since Lorna had left. And now, somewhere in the here and now and the future, he could see a light. AJ was the light. She'd streaked across his sky like a comet, lighting everything up. Lighting him up. She'd changed him. Sparking something deep within. And now he didn't know that he'd ever be able to let her go.

Ryler was still processing all that AJ had awoken inside him. And the thought of that light somehow being in danger, made him livid. His jaw clenched as he tried to control the flash of anger. Whoever this person was, man, or woman, they would never touch her. Ryler would see to that.

AJ shifted again, as if she'd sensed his presence, and rolled onto her back. She startled as her eyes landed on him, no doubt surprised by his sudden presence. She slid to a sitting position, her brows raised.

"You threw down the gauntlet with Amber." Ryler shrugged, settling himself. "I just came to make sure you're all right."

"How...who told you that?" She traced her finger along the edge of the blanket, not meeting his gaze.

"I saw it, read it."

Her eyes snapped up to his. "You were on my blog?"

Ryler gave one slow nod. "I've been following it for the last week or so."

"You're kidding." Her tone was dry with maybe a hint of humor.

Ryler pinned her to the bed with a look, contemplating the various ways this could all play out. Waring with himself over what he wanted versus what was right. Finally, he decided to address the humor he'd picked up on earlier. "What?" he lifted his chin and crossed his arms over his chest, determined to keep from reaching for her.

"Nothing." She snorted under her breath, tempting him even more. "I'm just having a hard time picturing *you* reading a romance author's blog is all."

He muttered under his breath, making a growling, frustrated sort of sound. "You trying to give me a heart attack, or something?" Her blank look had him continuing, "You *challenged* her, AJ. What were you thinking?"

"That I want her behind bars, like yesterday."

He sighed. "I get that and agree, but you've got to be careful. Challenging someone who may be a murderer is *not* being safe, or smart."

AJ shrugged, letting her gaze move around the room, obviously unwilling to admit anything he'd said might be correct. Ryler tried not to be distracted by the sight of her legs, her skin, but somehow, he found himself caught up by her. Somewhere in the back of his mind, he knew he should be trying to convince her to be just a tad more cautious and take this all a little more serious. But really all he wanted to do was get his hands on her. He wanted to explore, and taste, and see.

Instead, using superhuman strength, Ryler stayed where he was. Then, flexing that strength just a bit more, he said, "I gotta get going, gotta get some things done tonight before it gets dark. I'll let myself out. Just wanted to check on you."

Quickly, before AJ could really respond, he forced himself back down the stairs and out the door, locking it firmly behind himself. On her doorstep, he took a deep breath. Then another. He knew he'd basically just run like a coward, but with her looking all sleepy, and so much skin bare to him... He'd been terrified she'd indicate he stay. He'd have joined her on that bed and given in to all he'd been dreaming about. But Ryler was determined not to crush that new leaf he'd turned over.

AJ

Dinner with my newly discovered family was everything my soul needed. It was everything I'd hoped it would be and more. Though, it had started off a little awkward. We were, all of us, trying to feel out the dynamics of this new venture. But, after a little while, the four of us—me, Jo, Paige, and Poppy—relaxed into each other. Initially, I'd thought about inviting Ryler, then decided I really just wanted to get to know my family on my own. There'd be time with them and Ryler later. This first dinner, this was just the ladies of my family.

We'd talked, and laughed, and cried. Jo told stories about my grandparents, tales of them growing up together. She told me about Jake and some of the things he'd done as a rebellious teen. And what giving me up had done to him. Every time I thought about it, the anger towards my mother grew. I knew what had happened wasn't entirely her fault; Jake had agreed to her plan, but still, I was angry.

CHAPTER FIFTEEN
Deadly Curves

AJ

I picked Harley up in Seattle on a Sunday morning in early September. She looked different. Good, but different. Attempting to study her casually, so as not to seem like I was studying her, I tried to determine what the exact difference was. We'd taken our time getting home. Meandering along, doing some shopping and sightseeing in Edmonds and Kingston. Harley asked to stop several times, wanting to snap a picture. It wasn't until the seventh or eighth time that I figured out what the difference was.

It was Kevin. She was sending him pictures. Sharing her trip with him. It was this new relationship. I'd seen Harley in several relationships, but she was never one to stick around for long or even share her life with the person. She'd always held them at arm's length and found some reason to abandon the relationship and move on. But this, this thing with Kevin was different. Now, I saw happiness and dare I say peace.

Harley caught me looking. "What?" A faint tinge of pink crept onto her face.

"You're happy." I told her.

"Mmm, yeah." She smiled, indicating the two of us, like it should have been obvious. We were standing on the open deck of the ferry as it carried us across the Puget Sound from Edmonds to Kingston. The wind was cool, brisk and refreshing. I loved it.

"No." I shook my head, turning my back on the amazing view. "It's not me. Or, at least, it's not *only* me." I grinned. "I think it's Kevin. I think *he's* making you happy."

Harley took a deep breath, then shook her head and shrugged. "He does." She looked off into the distance, silent for a moment, before continuing softly, barely loud enough to hear above the wind. "He really does. I've never...never felt anything like this. I've never had anyone treat me the way he treats me. Like *I'm* special. Like I'm *worthwhile*. He cherishes me. It's amazing. I'm in love with him, AJ."

My heart thudded at her revelation. Wondering at how she'd ever doubted her worth, wondering if I'd done something to cause her to feel this way. Simultaneously, I was immensely grateful that Kevin had been wise enough to see her for who she truly is. To see her big heart. That he hadn't wasted his opportunity. That she had been receptive. I reached for her hand, squeezing it gently, yet firmly. "Then I'm very happy for you. For both of you." And I was. I wouldn't say Harley and I were joined at the hip or anything, but we were *close*. Always had been. My move to Washington had worried me on her account. But as I studied her and found light and warmth in her eyes—something I'd never seen there before—I was happy. Content. And I prayed this would never end for the two of them.

The sun was just beginning to set when we drove through Sequim. Harley *oooohed* and *ahhhhed* many times as she'd looked around. "This place is so amazing, AJ. Not like Coronado, with the warmth and soft colors, not like that. Sequim is...rugged, moody. The colors are deeper, stronger. I see why you like it."

I smiled. "Wait until you see the house; Jake and Ryler did an amazing job."

The day after tomorrow Jo and the Paiges, along with Chief and Ryler, were coming over for dinner. I wanted them all to meet Harley. But tonight, tonight was mine with my best friend. I wasn't ready to share her just yet. Not even with Ryler. I simply needed some serious Harley and me time. In my new house. I needed her to be okay with my decision to stay. And, while she'd said she understood, I got the impression she was still somewhat reserving judgement.

As the house came into view, Harley sat up straighter in her seat. "You've got to be kidding me...AJ, this is a *freaking castle!*"

She was exaggerating. A little. It wasn't quite that big or luxurious. But it was lovely and breathtaking. Chuckling, I parked the car. "That was kind of my reaction when I first saw it as well."

We carried her bags inside and I took her up to the guest chamber down the hall from my door. Once her luggage was deposited, I gave her the grand tour. Later that night, as we sat before the fire, warmed by the flame and each other's company, I said, "Thank you, Harley."

"For what?" She rotated her head in my direction. We were both wrapped in blankets, legs tucked under us, as we sunk into the fluffy sofa.

"For being here. For loving me and being understanding."

Harley slid her hand from under the blanket and reached for mine. "I love you, AJ. You're my best friend and I'll always love you. I'll admit I wasn't happy to hear you were staying, but I get it. I totally get it now. And, in some ways, I think this has been good for both of us." My questioning look had her explain, "I think we both needed to grow. You were definitely my crutch. My wingman for sure; my partner in crime, but also my crutch. And I think you held yourself back to some extent, because I wasn't ready to spread my wings, you know?"

"Harley...I don't." I squeezed her hand. "I *never* felt like that. You must believe that."

"I know. I know, AJ. It's just something I came to realize lately. It's not your fault, or my fault. It just is. Or was. I guess what I'm trying to say is...I'm happy for you and I'm happy for me, too."

We stayed there for a few more hours, letting the fire burn to embers, just talking, before finally calling it a night. The next morning, Harley and I had our coffee on the back patio and made plans to show her around more.

Two hours later, I parked along the curb in downtown Sequim. We wanted to spend the day walking through the little city, doing more shopping, showing her the sights, introducing her to a few people before they came over for dinner the following evening.

The first place we stopped was *Jo's*. Jo made sure we had our coffee and some warm-from-the-oven apple fritters. Hugs and pleasantries were exchanged, then we were off to see the Paiges. Just as I anticipated, Harley was head over heels for the store. From there we went to *Charlie's* so she could meet Chief. We had lunch there. Harley swooned over it. She said the place reminded her of something from the OG Top Gun. Then we headed to the grocery store so I could stock up for the week. I sent a text to Ryler, reminding him about the time for dinner tomorrow night.

Harley and I unloaded our purchases and decided to explore and do a little hiking around the house.

We were gone for no longer than two hours, but when we returned to the house, a box was sitting on the front porch. I mentally scratched my head trying to remember what I'd ordered and wondered how I'd missed the UPS truck, impressed they'd been able to find the place. Usually, I get a slip notifying me I had a package to pick up at the nearest facility. The box wasn't big, only about fifteen by twelve by six inches, and was fairly light as well. It reminded me of something flowers would come in, though the label didn't mention anything live inside.

Checking the return label, I saw that the sender was Readers Anonymous. I hadn't ordered anything from them, had never even heard of them before, but that didn't always mean anything. I received free gifts from different reading and writing houses all the time. I debated what to do with it for a moment, then decided to put it off until Harley was gone—I wanted my time with her and would just consider myself on vacation while she was here. Setting it on the shelf in the hall closet, I promised myself I'd open it and respond to the sender after she left.

Once we were all cleaned up and relaxed from our hike and time in town, I began work on dinner. I kept it light, broiling some chicken breasts and making a salad. Then Harley and I popped the latest Thor movie in and settled in before the TV to eat and relax. After the movie we called it a night.

Harley said she'd wanted to call Kevin before bed, and I told her to tell him hello for me.

The next morning, we had our coffee on the back patio. It was chilly, so I'd lit the outdoor fireplace. Neither of us were morning people, so we'd sipped in silence. Until she'd gasped as three deer entered my backyard. Then, I'd had to tell her about the moose and calling Ryler for help. We'd chuckled quietly over that, not wanting to disturb my backyard guests. On our second cup, Harley gave me a direct look. "So, tell me about Ryler. What's his story? And why aren't you sure of him?"

I looked at her over the rim of my mug. "Why do you assume I'm not sure of him?"

Her brow lifted. "If you were, you'd have told me all about him by now."

Considering her statement, I shrugged then took another sip, delaying. "I dunno; it's complicated, I guess."

"Complicated how?" She gave me a hard look, then. "He's not married or anything, is he?"

"No! Definitely not. What kind of girl do you think I am?" Harley grinned and I knew she was just kidding. "Truth be told, he wasn't all that impressed with me when I first came here. Ryler was pretty protective of Jake and felt I'd been unfair and unkind to him."

She was quick to defend me. "But you hadn't even known about Jake."

"I know that, and you know that, but Ryler hadn't known that."

Harley took another sip of coffee, then indicated the direction of Ryler's house with her cup. "But he knows now, right?"

"Yes, he knows now."

"So, what's the hold up?"

I chuckled. "No hold up. Not really. Ryler has a lot he's working through. Past things. And to be honest, I wasn't quite sure I wanted to dive into a relationship. Especially when I wasn't sure if I was even staying here or not."

"And now?"

"Now...now I'd say we're just taking it one day at a time. I don't even want to think about a relationship when this thing with Amber is hanging over my head. I need that resolved, first."

"Fair enough," she mused. "Will I meet him tonight?"

"You will." I assured.

Ryler

Ryler hated crowds even when they consisted of those he knew well and was strongly considering backing out of this evening's events. By no means would he consider himself a people-person. Tension always seemed to seep in, making him feel closed-in, tight, and restless.

He knew AJ wanted him to meet her best friend. And really, she would be the only one there he didn't know. And further, it was just a small group. Only a handful of people.

So, what was his problem then? Ryler couldn't very well claim this was a large gathering. The number of people didn't even quite make up a crowd. No, this was something else. Something different.

It was the friend. The *best* friend. Harley. Harley would be the first of AJ's acquaintances from her old life that he'd meet. He felt as if he might be on trial, somehow. Part of him argued the feeling was all in his head. Another part argued back, what if he didn't measure up? What if Harley found him lacking? Would AJ be easily swayed by Harley's opinion? Did Harley hold that much clout?

As these thoughts chased each other in his head, Ryler stayed busy. He dragged branches and logs, clearing a section of the forest around his cabin. The air held a mild bite of the coming winter, reminding him firewood needed to be stocked.

The season was changing. He could see it. Feel it. Hear it. The cry of geese overhead as they made their way south. The color shift in the trees and foliage. Change; there was another word Ryler didn't care for. He'd had a lot of changes to adjust to over these last few years. AJ had brought many more with her.

But, Ryler considered, he liked AJ. Liked *that* change. Liked pretty much all of her. Like a curveball, she'd entered his life and turned it upside down. Ryler paused, wiping the sweat from his brow as he thought of the petite brunette. He liked *her* curves. Deadly as they might be, he wanted to take those curves at high speed. He also wanted to savor them. Take his time. Lean into each one. He really needed to stop thinking about that. He had a lot to finish before this evening.

If he continued down this road, he'd be useless to himself for the rest of the day. Aj said she liked him. So, what was he worried about then? With Harley? AJ'd said they weren't through. Said she wanted more from him. Ryler considered that as he dragged the dead tree. And decided he was an idiot. After all, he'd faced worse and lived to tell about it. Besides, AJ wasn't Lorna.

An hour or so later, Ryler glanced at his watch, then tossed the tree to the pile he'd been making and whistled for Shiv. He needed to shower before heading to AJ's.

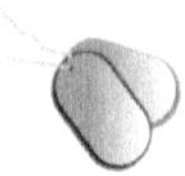

AJ

At first, I'd intended to make my chicken enchiladas, the ones I knew Harley liked so much, but then, I thought maybe she'd want to have that when it was just me and her. And besides, Ryler had already had that dish. So instead, I made a seafood Alfredo dish with garlic bread and a Caesar salad. My stomach grumbled a little as I cooked, reminding me I hadn't eaten since breakfast. Glancing at the clock, I saw my guests should begin arriving at any time.

No sooner had that realization hit, than I heard a knock at the door. Harley was out on the patio, enjoying the evening air. She's been falling in love with Sequim, just like I hoped she would. Answering the door, I found Ryler standing there. He seemed almost solemn tonight. And hesitant. Like he wasn't sure if he should be here. His eyes were clouded, like an overcast day.

He searched my gaze, seemingly looking for something. What, I wasn't sure. But something. My heart picked up as I watched the questions in his eyes, that almost hesitancy faded and a heat began to build in its place. Attempting to offer him a welcoming smile I'm sure came out all sorts of wrong, I opened the door wider. "Hi," my voice sounded breathy to my own ears. And again, I wondered if he would always do that to me, or if, years down the road maybe, this reaction would begin to wear off. Ryler brushed his lips across my cheek as he stepped into the foyer. His scent, that woodsy, spicy, scent of his tickled my nose. And I couldn't help the slow, drawn-in breath that I took. Nor the way my eyes fluttered as I let that intoxicating scent invade me. Did he always have to smell this delicious?

Taking a moment to collect myself, I made sure the front door was closed properly. Because, you know, that required all my concentration. His scent was still there, warming me, teasing me. When I turned around, intending to follow him into the kitchen, so he wouldn't think I was an idiot or something, I found Ryler standing there. Right there. My nose nearly bumped into him. Before I could recover from that shock, he stepped closer. His hands, those amazing, strong hands, slid up my arms, over my shoulders, thumbs brushing my collarbone as he tilted my head back. And then he kissed me.

It wasn't the onslaught of passion that had this kiss igniting something inside me. No, it was more the control he exhibited. That taste of feral just out of reach. Of something deeper, something more to come that had my breath catching and my pulse racing. He was slow, but thorough.

So *incredibly* thorough. His mouth on mine. His lips, taking his time, savoring, relishing. The whiskers on his jaw a soft abrasion as his fingers branded my skin. I swayed and he leaned in, pressing me against the door, holding me steady.

My arms were around him, pulling that hard, unrelenting body closer. This wasn't a fevered meeting. But a slow build of need. A gentle stoking of the fire. Gentle, and all encompassing. All engrossing. All consuming.

When Ryler lifted his head, it took a moment or two to come back down, to open my eyes. When I did, his eyes surveyed me again, lighting on my face, my mouth. He seemed to like what he saw there, and the clouds were gone from his eyes now. The hesitancy erased. Something stronger, deeper, and more secure, was there now.

After a moment, Ryler stepped back and I shivered as the sudden cool rush of air hit me from the loss of his body warmth. That coolness was fast replaced with heat of a different nature when I spied Harley standing there.

"AJ...I've read your books." She fanned herself. "They can be steamy, but *dang*, those books have nothing on what I just witnessed." Then she tossed me a cheeky grin and waved at Ryler as she continued. "Hi. You must be Ryler. I'm Harley, AJ's best friend. It's nice to finally meet you."

Ryler recovered from whatever shock he might have felt in the moment, stepping forward to shake Harley's hand, before reaching back for mine, pulling me close to him. "Nice to meet you as well, Harley. I've heard a lot about you."

"Just the good stuff, I hope." She grinned again. "The oven was beeping, AJ—guess you were a tad distracted. I pulled it out, no worries."

My blush deepened. Shaking my head, I exhaled and headed back to the kitchen. Before I could go more than three steps, there was another knock at the front door. Ryler placed a hand on my arm as I paused, then pressed a soft kiss at my temple. "I've got the door, go on ahead."

"Thanks." Grateful, I headed back to the kitchen. Ryler had distracted me and I had a couple more things to finish before we could eat.

Dinner couldn't have gone any better than it had. The food was plentiful and delicious. The conversation peaceful and diverting. I'd wondered how Harley would take to everyone. Being from Coronado, I wasn't sure how she'd react to my small-town crowd. But I'd had nothing to worry about. She thoroughly enjoyed them, and they, her. Harley managed to describe some of our crazier shenanigans when we were growing up in Florida, and later in Coronado.

In between the stories being swapped back and forth, Paige asked if I'd be willing to do a book signing at her store. And of course, I agreed. We decided on a date a few weeks away, and I promised to do whatever I could to make it the best signing they'd ever had.

Over dessert, a lovely, warm coffee cake with a dollop of ice-cold whipped cream on top, Chief asked me, "Ryler tell you about the shindig I have going on at *Charlie's* in a couple weeks?"

"No, not yet." I glanced at Ryler. "Why, what's going on?"

"Every year I host a stopping point for several motorcycle clubs in a Veteran's charity ride. We BBQ, play some music, and the riders swing in and out all day. Thought maybe you'd like to attend."

Before I could ponder too far as to why Ryler hadn't mentioned it yet, he nudged me. "We've both just been pretty busy and you've had a lot on your mind with everything; I was simply waiting until a more appropriate time. But now that the cat's out of the bag, what do you say? Want to go?"

"Yeah." I smiled, feeling less concerned and more excited about us going out together. Like an actual date. "That sounds like fun. Wait. Will I have to ride a bike?" That thought had my happy feeling dimming just a bit.

Chief chuckled. "No. You can just come hang out and enjoy yourself. How's that sound?"

"Perfect."

Ryler caught my eye, a spark flashing in their blue grey depths. "You're more than welcome to wear leathers and ride a bike; I certainly wouldn't stop you."

His comment, the heat in his look, had me blushing. "We'll see."

We spoke a little longer, about the upcoming event and book news. Then, as the evening seemed to be winding down, Ryler caught my eye and indicated the others with a nod and a lifted brow. Guessing his intent, I gave him a slight dip of my chin and looked to those at the table. "Hey," I caught their attention. "I need to share something with you guys. Chief and Ryler, and Harley already know about this, but I think everyone needs to know. Just to be safe."

"What's the matter, AJ?" Jo sat a little straighter, concern clearly stamped on her face. Poppy cast a sharp look at her mom, but Paige shook her head—no, she didn't know what was going on either.

I inhaled, then slowly exhaled as I collected my thoughts. "I've got a bit of a problem, so to speak." Ryler snorted softly. "It seems I've got a crazy stalker, or possibly a murdering fan, or both." Jo slowly covered her mouth with her hand, her eyes going wide, looking from me to Ryler, then Chief and back. I shrugged, trying to seem unworried. "Amber is the name she goes by online, but I suppose she could be any-one. However, a few weeks back, my landlady, Mrs. Carson," pausing, I took another deep breath. "She was found murdered in her home." Poppy gasped, a stricken look now on her face. "Amber has indicated on my blog page that she's responsible. And she's threatening me now as well."

There was silence around the table for a moment or two. Then Paige said, "I'm so sorry, AJ. This is horrible. I'm assuming the police are involved...what are they saying?"

"They are involved." I nodded. "They're trying to figure out who she is and where she is."

"What does she want?" Poppy asked. "Why is she doing this?"

"I don't know. She was angry when I came up here, said she felt I was letting my fans down. Then she was furious when I said I was staying."

"Are you in danger?" Jo's face had paled noticeably.

I started to respond, but Ryler spoke first. "Chief and I are keeping an eye on things."

"AJ, maybe we shouldn't do the signing?" Paige suggested, worry in her eyes. "I mean, if it's not safe...."

"No." I shook my head, offering a reassuring smile. "No, it should be fine. I'm not worried. Of course, I'll do it."

"We'll be there to keep watch." Chief assured us. "She'll be fine."

Harley's phone rang then, bringing the conversation to an abrupt end. When Harley rose, excusing herself, I said, "Tell Kevin I said hello." She blushed, tossing me a grin as she left the table.

Harley's exodus seemed to indicate an end to the evening's activities. By silent agreement, we stood and began cleaning up. I kissed Jo goodbye, and gave a hug to the Paiges, and told Chief I'd see him soon. He'd pulled me close for a quick bearhug before heading out. Ryler stayed to help me finish drying and putting the dishes away. Then we settled onto the couch, a fire kindled in the fireplace.

"Thank you for coming." I kept my voice low, not wanting to disturb the ambiance, the crackle of the flames a soothing backdrop. I snuggled deeper into Ryler, enjoying his warmth and pressed my mouth against his chest. "I'd wondered if you would, you know." Ryler had been absentmindedly rubbing the back of my neck, his fingers trailing their own fire. When he heard that, he gripped me, tilting my head in his direction, a question in his eyes. "Well. I know you're not exactly a big fan of crowds and things...so, yeah...I wondered."

"Hmm." His grunted sound somehow exiting in a noncommittal sort of way. His gaze shifted south, landing on my mouth. Focusing there. Intently. Maybe he hadn't been so absentminded after all.

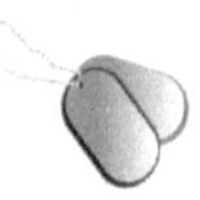

Ryler

Ryler knew he probably had a lot of other things to be considering right now. Anything other than AJ's mouth. Her lips. Her heat pressed against him and those sounds he knew she'd make. But his mind wasn't on anything but her. Desire was a feral animal at present. One he was struggling to contain.

Sure, dinner was amazing. Harley was an incredible friend for AJ; the two clicking together like puzzle pieces. The conversation had flowed with ease. Any concerns he'd arrived with, regarding Harley, had completely dissipated by the evening's end.

Heck, he might have even spared a thought or two about Amber and the possible threat she posed to AJ.

But no. No, his thoughts were focused on something much more pressing. More primal. Because desire was quickly morphing into need. Ryler needed AJ. He needed to tell her the truth about himself. He needed to give her that chance, that choice. He needed to face this fear and conquer it.

And there were other needs. Deep, writhing ones. Ryler needed to get ahold of himself, control the flame. Leash the animal and stay calm. But she was right there. That mouth was right there.

_AJ_

With an almost predatory focus, he leaned toward me, his blue-grey eyes somehow turning molten. "Your mouth is driving me crazy. _You're_ driving me crazy." And then his mouth was on mine. Pressure, warmth, a sliding of texture. Slow. Deliberate. So much restrained intent in his kiss. I wanted. Needed. A sound, full of desperation threaded its way up my throat. At the sound, he lifted his mouth from mine. His thumb traced along my jaw, over my lower lip. "I know we started off a bit rocky, and I know there are still things to work out, things you're trying to figure out. Things I'm still trying to figure out. But, AJ, I want to be here. With you. And we'll get through them."

I heard the *together* in his words, even though he hadn't spoken it aloud. My heart swelled at the sentiment even as my eyes misted. Blinking, I buried my head against his chest, simply breathing in his earthy-pine scent and let myself believe in us. Time would tell whether Ryler and I went the distance. But right now, at this time, it seemed things were looking brighter. I was pretty sure the road ahead held curves, maybe even painful or deadly ones, but sitting here with Ryler, I felt confidence bloom, knowing we'd face them together.

CHAPTER SIXTEEN
Rolling Thunder

AJ

Those women you always see in movies, the ones wearing leather like a second skin, like there was nothing to it—all lies. It had to be. Because I'd only been able to keep the leather pants on for a half hour tops before I was melting into a sweaty puddle on the floor.

For authenticity purposes, Harley'd convinced me to give them a shot. And I had, but no more. I'd stick with a pair of jeans, my ice-pink long sleeve t-shirt, my black combat-style boots, and that leather vest, or cut—as real bikers called them—I'd found at the thrift store.

Three days ago, I'd driven Harley back to the airport. We said our teary goodbyes and admonished each other to be safe and to stay in touch. "Next time, bring Kevin with you." I hugged her one more time.

"Next time; I promise." Harley grinned as she got in the long line at the security check point. I waited, watching until she was through and beyond my viewpoint. Then I'd headed home, reminding myself we'd see each other again soon.

Now, as I stood in front of my mirror, I felt I looked, if not like an actual biker-chick, then at least like I wouldn't stick out like a sore thumb for the event. Ryler would be here shortly. He was picking me up. Like a real date and I was beyond thrilled. And I know we've been out together before, but this was the first time that *he'd* asked *me*.

Kissing Josephine goodbye, where she was sprawled on my bed, I headed downstairs to wait for Ryler. I didn't have long to wait, just enough time to wash my coffee mug, dry it, and put it away. At the sound of his knock, I grabbed my small purse and headed for the door.

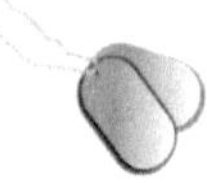

Ryler

After knocking on AJ's front door, Ryler stepped back, not wanting to crowd her. And who was he kidding, he wanted the space to be able to study her. AJ required a careful study, and Ryler didn't want to miss a moment of it. He was facing away from the door, staring off into the trees, reflecting on the last couple of months, when the door opened. He took a moment to settle himself before turning.

Ryler let his eyes travel her slowly. Taking in each and every detail. He started at her feet. At those wannabe combat boots she was wearing. He marveled at the length of her legs, showcased to perfection in those soft, well-fitted jeans. The way her shirt seemed to hug her shape without being vulgar. And where she'd found that unadorned cut, he had no idea. A grin slowly grew on his mouth, lighting his eyes. He planned to get her on a bike today. Wanted her wrapped around him, the wind in their faces.

Ryler took a slow, deep breath, willing the animal inside him to settle.

AJ

For the first time, since I'd been coming to *Charlie's* at least, the parking lot was filled to overflowing. A band was set up on the west side of the establishment, some kind of rock group. They sounded good. There were several food trucks parked around, offering anything from Mexican, to burgers, to ice cream. Families strode around, talking and chatting with each other. And row, upon row of motorcycles. Every kind you could imagine. Some obviously made for show and probably saw very little use. Others seemed more like an extension of the person riding them.

Ryler parked across the street, and we made our way slowly and carefully through the bikes and riders. Several stopped Ryler to say hello. They eyed me curiously, no doubt wondering who I was. As we moved through the throng, I kept an eye on Ryler. Wondering if the sheer mass of people and noise would stress him out. He surprised me, though. His demeanor was almost friendly, not quite open, still somewhat reserved, but not aggressive either. I'd wondered...but Ryler seemed fine, even though he'd left Shiv back at the cabin—too much noise for the hound, he'd said. The creative side of me studied the scene, taking in all the colors, the smudges of blacks, chrome, and grey. If I was a painter, I'd title this piece as *Rolling Thunder*.

It was just as packed inside as it was out when we went in to see Chief. Every spot at the bar was filled as were each booth and table. Three new helpers were behind the bar with him, all hard at work slinging orders. Ryler took my hand, leading me through the crowd, clearing a path for me. Chief smiled as he saw us, then came around the bar to give me a hug. I liked that we were on those terms. We chatted over the volume of the crowd for a minute, then ordered a drink. "Full house, huh?" I said to Chief over the dull roar.

He nodded, his eyes taking in the crowd before returning to me. "Not all are military. Some are just along for the ride. There'll be some idiots in the crowd, so stay close to Rye."

"Will do." I smiled as Ryler slid his arm around me, pulling me closer.

Chief got to work on our drinks and told us to make sure we checked out the burgers being grilled to perfection just outside. As we waited, I felt Ryler still beside me. My eyes lifted, but his gaze was locked on a small group of people standing near the other side of the bar. Three men and two women. Two of the men and one woman were in riding leathers, obviously a party to the ride taking place today. The other man seemed somewhat out of place here. Not a biker at least. He was tall, slim, but not skinny. Well-proportioned I'd say. He had strength but wasn't as built as Ryler. He was darker though, dark hair and eyes, maybe of Italian descent, I mused. He was dressed simply, in dark jeans, boots, and shirt. The woman with him was petite, nearly childlike next to his tall frame. Her hair was a beautiful shade of red.

Ryler had a thoughtful, calculating look in his eyes now. I turned more fully to him, my arms tightening some. "What's up?" I asked. "Do you know them?"

"Maybe." He spoke so quietly, I almost had to strain to hear him over the din. Ryler shook his head, then took my hand and led me over to the group. Again, I trailed behind him as he moved through the crowd, liking the feeling that Ryler was looking out for me. The three in riding leathers were walking away as we approached, moving on to greet another set of people. Ryler didn't spare them a glance. His focus was on the dark man.

As we drew closer, the man suddenly turned toward us, almost as if he'd felt Ryler's regard. Something about the man told me he probably did. His eyes, as they landed on us, held something sharp, discerning, and calculating, much like a predator. His focus had shifted swiftly to Ryler as soon as he'd seen us. His quick assessment seemed to determine we weren't a threat. The woman's grey eyes were calm as they took us in. Her small baby bump evident through the soft green dress she wore. Freckles were sprinkled endearingly across her face.

"Darrante." Ryler extended his hand. The man took it offering a firm grip. "It's been a long time."

"Ryler Dean, how the heck are you?" The man's voice was deep, yet even.

"I'm still kicking," Ryler replied. He pulled me forward, a hand settling on my back. "Samuel, this is AJ McAdams. AJ, this is Samuel Darrante." Ryler offered me a quick look before focusing once more on the man before us. Almost like he was having a hard time believing his eyes. "We met...a few years ago." Samuel shook my hand, then Ryler told him, "Jake Daniels was her father."

Dark brows rose at this. "I'd heard the news." His gaze shifted back to me. "Sorry for your loss." At my nod of appreciation, he turned to the woman beside him, his arm going around her shoulders. "This is my wife, Tiffy."

Tiffy was beautiful, her pregnancy glow only adding to her beauty. And standing beside her, I realized I was only an inch or so taller than she was. She'd seemed so small next to Samuel. Then again, I'm not really known for my height either. I took her offered hand and smiled. "It's nice to meet you. When are you due?"

"February." She smiled back. "It's nice to meet you as well."

Ryler blew out a soft breath, then pressed a kiss to my temple. "Samuel and I served together a few years back. And he'd known your dad from before then." He turned back to Samuel. "So, what's new? You still in?"

"Got out just after I last saw you." He glanced at Tiffy. "It was time."

"What are you doing in this neck of the woods?"

"Just passing through. Happened to see the event, thought we'd stop in and see what's up, lend our support."

"It's appreciated. Where're you guys heading?"

"Some friends of ours suggested a cabin over near the Forks area. It's near the beach, supposed to be really nice. We're going to stay for a few days, just relax."

"Yeah, it's pretty over there. Lots of green. Real nice. You still in California then?"

Samuel shook his head. "We bought a place in Wyoming a few years back. Tiffy loves the country life. And I love Tiffy, so now I'm a rancher."

The blush that touched her face was soft and sweet. She looked up at him with eyes full of love. And I wondered if I'd ever look at someone that way. If that someone would be Ryler.

Ryler chuckled. "You? A *rancher*? Never thought I'd hear that coming from your mouth, Samuel."

"Oh, I know. But times change. A friend of mine got into the dude ranch business up near Cody. Tiff and I met there. She liked it so much we decided to stay, start our own place."

"You're working a dude ranch?"

"No," Tiffy said now. "Just a small place, a little under fifteen acres. We have a few horses, some chickens, a couple cows and pigs. Enough to keep us busy and happy."

"How about you guys?" Samuel asked, his eyes moving between the two of us, having already glanced at my ring finger. "You guys...?"

"We're thinking about it, Samuel. AJ just moved here, just heard about Jake, so...we're taking things slow."

"Good idea. No rush." Samuel's seemed gaze drawn to Tiffy. He pulled her close, kissing her forehead. "Well, we're going to head out. If you're ever in Wyoming, look us up."

"Will do. You guys take care." Ryler shook Samuel's hand once more.

After watching them go, we waded through the crowd back to the bar. "It's a bit tight in here," Ryler intoned, close to my ear after we got our drinks, causing a delicious shiver to skim over me. "You want to head back outside?"

Somewhat breathless, I nodded my agreement and we waved goodbye to Chief. As I was blinking against the glare of the sun and reaching for the sunglasses on my head, I caught a whiff of cloves. Looking around, I tried to find its source. The scent was so familiar, like those cigarettes Paul would smoke. But he wasn't the only person who smoked that particular brand, and this was a large crowd after all. Just a familiar scent that made me think of Coronado.

Ryler ordered our meals: a bacon cheeseburger each and plate of cheesy fries. We took them to the Bronco to eat, lowering the tailgate. We enjoyed our meal and just listened to the music, watching the various groups ride in and out. We'd been sitting there maybe forty-five minutes or so when I again, caught that scent of cloves. Carefully, I searched, scanning the faces, trying to locate its source.

Of course, Ryler noticed. "Looking for someone?"

"No...not really...do you smell cloves?"

"A little, why?" His eyes scanned the parking lot.

"Can you tell where it's coming from?"

"It's pretty faint. And with this crowd, it could be from anywhere."

"One of the roommates I'd lived with on Coronado used to smoke clove cigarettes. This just reminds me of those, I guess."

Ryler seemed to tighten, his eyes doing a more careful look now. "You think they'd be here?"

"No...well, I mean maybe. He writes for a travel magazine; it would be a pretty big coincidence if he was. Like I said, the smell just made me think of him."

"Were you guys close?" Steel coated his voice, mild but still present.

I laughed at that idea. "No, definitely not. He was just a quiet, sometimes awkward guy that lived in the same house I did."

Ryler continued to covertly study the throng of people milling about, taking the measure of each one of them. Evaluating. A couple minutes later, he looked at me. "Nine o'clock. Tan jacket. Against the building." Ryler flicked his gaze in the direction he meant. Taking a moment to swallow my last french fry, I casually turned, just stretching from sitting too long in one position. And then I saw him.

Paul stood in the shadows, leaning against the wall of *Charlies*. A couple of different cameras hung around his neck. The clove cigarette was between his lips. He saw me, had been looking in my direction. Paul raised his hand, just a shy, casual, two-fingered wave, before lowering it once more. Then he shifted, adjusting his position, as if he was embarrassed to be caught staring. I waved back and smiled. And now was faced with the dilemma of deciding whether or not I was going to walk over and say hello. I guess it would be rude to stay over here and ignore him now that we'd already acknowledged each other. Besides, I'd take Ryler with me and then I wouldn't be obligated to stay and chat.

"That's Paul." I told Ryler, chuckling. "My former roommate."

"What's he doing here?"

"Working, I guess." I shrugged. Ryler rumbled something noncommittal under his breath. "I should probably go say hello."

"All right." Ryler stood to his feet.

"You wanna come with?" He seemed almost eager.

He shot me an amused look. "Oh, I'm definitely coming."

I chuckled at the tone in his voice. "He's harmless."

"Still coming." He lifted me down from the tailgate, his hands lingering just a moment longer than necessary around my waist. I tried to control the flutter in my stomach at his touch. Wanting his hands back on me. We gathered our trash, then he led me towards *Charlies*. At our approach, Paul began fidgeting, crossing, then uncrossing his arms. Hooking his thumbs in his belt loops. Shifting. I felt bad; obviously his nerves were getting the better of him. And Ryler wasn't exactly what I'd call unintimidating.

Ryler tossed our trash in the container and took my hand, lacing his fingers with mine. His thumb rubbed across my skin and whether he intended it or not, the butterflies in my stomach took flight, swirling and dipping. Causing my breath to hitch in my throat. He shot me a flashing grin, then turned his gaze back to Paul. I watched the steel in his eyes harden and hoped he didn't give poor Paul a heart attack. The guy had already been through enough.

"Hi, Paul." I smiled as we reached him.

"Hi, AJ." He replied a little hesitantly as his eyes shifted between me and Ryler. "Surprised to see me here, huh?"

"Yeah, I guess I am. Paul, this is...my friend Ryler. Ryler, this is Paul."

"Paul." Ryler extended his hand.

Paul hesitated just a fraction of a moment, then shook Ryler's hand. "Hi, Ryler."

"AJ tells me you write for a travel magazine. Are you doing a piece on Sequim, then?"

"Yes. I am. Well, not just Sequim, but several other cities in the area. It'll cover quite a bit of the Olympic National Park, really."

Ryler was still studying him, and I could tell something about Paul was raising his hackles. "How long will you be in the area, Paul?" I squeezed Ryler's hand, trying to get him to relax.

Paul shrugged, clearly uncomfortable with the attention. Color touched his light skin. "Dunno. It's nice here...different from Coronado. I'll probably stay a week or so, then check out some other areas. Oak Harbor, Port Angeles, maybe even over near Forks, then maybe swing back in."

"What's your last name, Paul?" Ryler asked. "I'd like to look up some of your work."

Paul was quiet for a moment, then said softly, "Ashland. It's Paul Ashland."

"Well, Paul Ashland, see you around. Hope you write something nice about our place, and this event." Ryler gently tugged my hand, pulling me along with him, keeping between me and Paul as we moved to the entrance. Tension poured off Ryler in a steady wave.

"What's the matter?" I asked as we neared the bar.

He shrugged stiffly. "I don't like him."

"Yeah, I can see that. But why?"

His lips pressed and he shook his head. "Something about him rubs me the wrong way."

"Well." I didn't know what to say, knowing Paul gave off an odd vibe. I'd always chalked it up to him just being so overtly shy and socially awkward, but he didn't mean any harm. I just let it drop, doubting I'd see Paul any more anyway. Though, I was relieved that he seemed recovered from the last time I'd seen him, when Mrs. Carson had died.

The crowd had thinned somewhat, and Chief was taking a break, sitting with a group of four men, working through a mountain of nachos.

"You guys eat?" Chief asked as we approached.

"We did." I smiled. "I can't eat another bite."

Chief introduced me to those he was talking with. More Veterans supporting Veterans. We chatted for a couple minutes. Just friendly, curious talk. As we talked, I noted Ryler saying something to Chief. Chief looked briefly in my direction, then nodded to Ryler. It wouldn't have caught my notice if they hadn't made such an attempt to be so subtle about it. Now, I was wondering. My eyes flitted back and forth between the two, trying to solve the mystery.

Ryler caught my look, and something flashed in his blue-grey eyes. Then he did something I wasn't expecting. Expecting or prepared for. Right in front of those men I'd been talking with, in front of Chief, in front of the entire bar crowd, he kissed me. Not passion. Just presence. Like he was staking a claim. Calmly, gently, and unequivocally. Then he released my mouth and nuzzled the side of my neck. "You about ready to go?" Still reeling from that kiss, from the tone of his voice, the heat from his touch, I simply nodded. "We'll see you all later."

Chief grinned at us, offering a small two-finger salute as we left.

Ryler climbed into the Bronco after seeing me in first. A spark was in his eyes now. "I've got a surprise for you."

"Oh, yeah?"

He looked me over, letting his eyes linger, then grinned. "You trust me?"

That look in his eye was giving me pause. "Trust you with what? And why?"

Ryler chuckled and I waited for him to explain, but he remained silent as we drove back to Jake's. He parked in front of Jake's house and turned to me. "Take a moment if you need to, freshen up. I'll be back in about fifteen minutes." He helped me down, then kissed my forehead and nodded toward the house. I knew he was waiting for me to go inside before leaving. As I reached my door, he called, "Don't forget your sunglasses!" Ryler wasn't gone long; no more than ten or fifteen minutes. I'd had enough time to use the bathroom, spritz on some perfume, and brush my teeth. As I came back down the stairs, I heard a loud rumble. It vibrated through the house and brought me to the front door. Stepping outside, I saw Ryler perched casually on the seat of a large black motorcycle. There wasn't much in the way of chrome on it. Most of the finish was in a matte black shade.

I watched in surprised consternation as he put the kickstand down and swung off. Looking pretty dang hot while doing it. In fact, my temperature was climbing rapidly. Ryler shut the bike off, removed his helmet and sunglasses and placed them on the seat before walking up to meet me. "You wanna be a real biker chick? Put those boots and that cut to good use?"

"You never told me you had a bike. Why weren't you riding today?"

"Because I was with you."

"You could have gone." I searched his face. "You didn't have to stay with me."

"I know that." He lowered his head so we were at eye level. "Besides, I can go now. I just want you to go with me."

"On *that*?" My brows rose as my heart thudded in my chest.

"On this. Behind me. You're not scared, are you?"

I blew out a breath. "Maybe just a little."

"There's nothing to it. You just need to hang on to me. I'll do the rest."

"Have you ever wrecked?" I stared at the bike, trying to talk myself into not being a chicken.

"I have. But I won't now. Not with you on board."

My mouth dried out. "How do you know?"

Ryler stalked closer. "You'll be safe with me, AJ. I promise."

My heart thudded even harder in my chest as I nodded. "All right. Just don't kill me, Ryler. I have edits due, and a book coming out, and Harley would be upset, and Josephine, too, and—"

Ryler cut off my ramble, his mouth on mine. This wasn't a passionate kiss, but more a continuation of that claiming sort of kiss from earlier. I tasted the promise, the assurance on his tongue. Felt them in his touch as his hands coursed up my arms, traveled over my shoulders, cupping my face, positioning it just so. Holding me steady. He would keep me safe. As that realization struck, I lunged for him, deepening the kiss, trying to set fire to it. Ryler made a deep sound low in his throat, the vibration doing all sorts of things to me. Then he pulled back. "If we don't stop now," he growled again. "I won't be held responsible for what happens next."

Those words nearly had my knees giving out. Ryler made sure I could stand on my own before stepping back. His gaze tracked my movements as I took a steadying breath, simply trying to clear my head. Calm my racing pulse. Ryler made sure the door was locked then led me down to the bike. Which looked way bigger and more menacing the closer I got. From a side bag he pulled another helmet and placed it on my head, adjusting the straps to fit properly. Then he put his back on.

"We're all set." Ryler turned towards the bike. "I'm going to get on first, get it started, then you'll climb on behind me. All you have to do is hold tight to me. I'll take care of everything else."

I inhaled slow and deep, then exhaled the same. "All right. Let's do this."

Ryler swung his leg over and settled into the seat. That simple action caused a rush of heat to flood my body. He righted the bike, then started it. The rumble was loud, but not overly so. I wasn't trying to cover my ears at least. One hand on the bike, keeping it upright, he motioned for me to climb on. Just when I'd thought I'd have to make a jump for it, Ryler indicated a metal peg sticking out from the side. He offered a hand as I stepped on it and swung my leg over.

It felt a bit like being on horse. That vibrated. I wondered if I'd be sore after this ride like I typically was after horseback riding. Ryler waited for me to wrap my arms around him before taking off. It didn't take much incentive. Even through the leather he was warm. So warm. Addicting.

Though I'd never ridden a motorcycle before, I was seriously glad I'd done so now. Was it scary? Maybe at first, but then...then the wind was in my face. And suddenly I was free as we were flying down the road and it was nothing short of exhilarating. Holding onto Ryler might have helped with this feeling, but still. He and the machine were one and I was one with them. We moved with the road, effortless, powerful. We were thunder. Wild, rolling thunder.

CHAPTER SEVENTEEN
Burnt Amber

Ryler

Ryler lay awake long into the night. The windows were open, letting in the cool evening air. A fire still crackled in the hearth. On one side of him lay Shiv, the hound snoring softly. On the other, on the nightstand, stood an untouched glass of amber liquid. Condensation dripped down the sides from the slowly melting ice cubes inside it. The flames danced through the grate, catching the glass, making the liquid in the cup seem to burn.

Ryler thought of AJ. Thought of their ride today. Thought about the way she'd felt, her arms and legs wrapped around him.

She'd trusted him. Had faith in him. Ryler'd seen her hesitation, that uncertainty about the bike ride. Still, she'd allowed him to strap the helmet on, still she'd climbed on that bike behind him. She'd melded her body to his. It was hard to put into thoughts, much less words, what that had done to him. How much her belief in him had affected him.

Was this love? This feeling, this emotion? He didn't know. Once he'd thought he'd loved Lorna. And maybe he had. Certainly, he'd felt more for her than she'd felt for him. But this seemed different. Deeper. Stronger. This made him feel whole. As if those pieces missing from himself, those pieces that left him feeling like half a man, as if those were repaired and made new. Unseen, but no longer absent. So, was this love? Maybe. Maybe it was. Ryler reached for the glass and downed it in one swallow. All he knew was that he didn't want to give this up.

AJ

I think I'm falling in love with Ryler. I hadn't meant to. It just kind of happened. Things were complicated at first. *He* was complicated. But then, who wasn't really? Everyone carried around some kind of baggage. Things from their past that tended to snag and snarl their present or future. Underneath that gruff exterior, I sensed a deep well of emotion. So deep that I wanted to drown in it. Drown in him. The bike ride today...it had awoken something inside me. Being with him on that machine, our bodies in tandem, moving together as we followed the path in front of us—it had sparked something. Ignited a flame I didn't know how to extinguish, or if I even wanted to. No matter the curve or the bend in the road, that flame told me we'd go through it all together. And somehow, that road began to look an awful lot like the future. Unknown. New possibilities around every bend. And yet, I wanted to take them all with Ryler. Side by side, together, I wanted to walk into our future.

But what did he want? Would he want that? Want me? A future? That I didn't know but wanted to find out.

After he dropped me off, after Ryler had kissed me, slow and tortuous, on the porch, and said he should definitely *not* come in tonight, I'd taken a long bath. I appreciated the fact that he was aware of his limits. That he took my limits into account and wasn't inclined to just roll with it and see what happened. Even that had me longing for that future with him.

I'd lit all my favorite candles, poured my favorite bath salts, and soaked in all the warmth, all the heat that had been missing since he'd left. I wanted Ryler. Wanted him more than I'd ever wanted anyone before. But I wanted this time to be right. This time to be true, and forever. To be real. So, I'd wait. Hold these feelings close to my chest, let him work through what he needed to. Then hopefully, we'd get that opportunity. And while I soaked, I did something I hadn't done in a long while. I prayed. I talked to God, asking for guidance, for peace, for assurance. Not just with Ryler. With Amber, too. And as I did, a deep, soul-touching peace settled over me.

The bathwater was tepid by the time I climbed out. Taking my time toweling off, I attempted to clear my mind, think about something other than Ryler for the time being. So, I reached for my favorite amber body lotion. And thought, amber is an interesting thing. As is musk, another favorite scent of mine And, just like that, my mind jumped the tracks and was now considering that my favorite scents were derived from fossilized trees and male musk deer. And that maybe that made me an odd person for loving those smells so much. But I reminded myself as I blew out the candles, many people love those fragrances, so I was in good company, or at least just company.

After slipping on a pair of knit pajama bottoms and a tank top, I brewed some of my favorite chamomile tea, then decided to share my biker chick experience on my blog. Amber had been strangely silent these last couple of weeks. I didn't know whether to be relieved or concerned. I'd talked with Detective Whitaker, and he'd said the police were no closer to identifying who Amber was, or who the killer was, if they were different.

After logging on, I checked the comments. Nothing from Amber. Maybe she had gone away. Maybe I'd burned her enough and she'd decided to back off and leave me alone. Of course, that also put us back to square one in finding Mrs. Carson's murderer. After posting about the ride, I went to bed, sleep claiming me swiftly.

Over coffee the next morning, the sun not even up yet, wrapped in my robe, I began work on a new story. One that had been floating around in my head over the last several months. *Rebel Ranger*, I was calling it. I worked on that for several hours, just fleshing out my characters and exploring the plot. Building the storyline. Once I figured that I'd had a pretty solid handle on it, I took a break and checked the blog to see how my readers liked my motorcycle experience.

A comment from Amber waited. "Did you get my package?" Just that. Nothing more.

Package? What package?

Rising from my desk, I headed downstairs to the small mountain of fan mail that still needed sorting. A total of six packages, ranging from small boxes, to large envelopes in size were in the mix. I took each one of them and checked the shipping and return label, looking for anything, any clue that one of these might be from Amber. Not seeing anything to indicate one way or another, I picked up the first one and opened it. It was a scarf. From a kind and generous fan. She'd seen it and thought I'd like the colors, so bought it for me. It wasn't from Amber. I moved to the next, and the next. Opening each package. Nothing from Amber. Nothing out of the ordinary.

My phone rang, making me jump. I hadn't realized how fast my heart had been pounding. With shaking hands, I hit the answer button. "Don't open anything until I get there!" Ryler fairly shouted at me.

"There isn't anything from her," I said quietly. "I've already opened them."

"Just sit still. I'll be there in a couple moments."

"All right." I sank into the chair next to me, figuring Ryler must have been monitoring my blog page again and seen Amber's comment. I don't remember hanging up or really anything between talking with Ryler and seeing him kneeling in front of me. He must have used his key. Ryler pulled me into his arms, just holding me. He held me until the shaking subsided, then pressed his lips against my temple, lingering for a moment before pulling back. "Where are the packages?"

I jerked my chin to the table behind him, indicating the ones I'd opened. "These are all of them?" He looked through everything thoroughly, with a careful eye.

"Yeah, I think so." I whispered. "No, wait." I'd forgotten. "There is one more." When Harley was here. One was left on the front step. "I'd...I'd forgotten about it."

"Where is it, AJ?"

"In the closet by the front door. I...I forgot I'd put it there. I'd meant to deal with it after Harley left but just forgot about it."

"Stay here." I heard him open the closet door, then heard the sounds of the box being opened. Then, "Son of a...."

"What?" I rose to my feet, moving fearfully towards him. "What is it?"

"Stay there, AJ. Do NOT come over here. Just...stay there."

"Ryler, what is it?" Fear gripped me, making it difficult to breathe. "Is it from her? Is it from Amber?"

"Just stay there. *Dang it*! Sick, son of a—" Ryler moved back to me. "I need you to do me a favor. I need you to go upstairs. Make sure your cat is there and that she's all right. Okay? Can you do that?"

My heart clenched so tightly I was seeing spots. "What...what does that mean? What are you saying?"

He gripped my arms, taking a firm hold. "Just do what I asked, please. *Go.* I need to take care of a few things."

Turning swiftly, I raced up the stairs, calling for Josephine. Panic made me uncoordinated and I stumbled on the landing, nearly falling into the wall. Righting myself, I made my way into my bedroom. My eyes roved all around, searching. I found Josephine curled up under my desk and wept with relief. Picking her up carefully, I held her as the tears poured down. After several minutes, she began struggling, wanting down. Sniffing, wiping at my cheeks, I let her go and put her back where I'd found her.

I went into the bathroom and splashed cold water on my face. Just needing a couple of moments to calm down, I ran a brush through my hair, then brushed my teeth as well. Before heading back downstairs, I quickly threw on some clothes, knowing I needed to address whatever it was Amber had sent. Ryler was on the phone when I came back down. He stood near the stairs watching for me. As I reached the bottom step, my eyes went to the front hall, where that closet was, and, I assumed, the box. Ryler stepped to me, his arm going around me, pulling me close. Then he led me over to the couch where we sat down. I didn't have long to wonder who he was on the phone with. "Yeah, Detective. I will. I'll call right now. Just wanted you to know. Yeah. Bye."

"What's in the box, Ryler?" My voice was low, choked with emotion.

He took a deep breath, his arm tightening around me. "A note, and...and the remains of a dead cat. The carcass was well wrapped in plastic. The coat is similar to Josephine's, so I just wanted to be sure. This one has been dead a long, long while."

I wanted to throw up. My hand covered my mouth as I tried to control the urge to heave. "This...this...this is sick."

"It is sick. In every way this is sick." Ryler squeezed my hand gently, letting me know he was there, that he had me. "I need to call the police, all right?"

I just nodded, too spent to do much of anything else. How had Amber known about my cat? How did she know my address here? Had I ever mentioned Josephine on the blog page? I tried to remember. The box had arrived while Harley was here. And nothing else had happened since she'd left. What if she was somehow involved? *Oh, my gosh,* I stuttered over this thought. *What if* Harley *was Amber*? No. No, she couldn't be. Why would she do something like that? Harley would never hurt me.

"Both Chief and the police are on their way over."

"Okay," I whispered. "What, what did the note say?"

Ryler sighed, shaking his head, his agitation under control, yet on display. "It just said, 'Who will be next?'"

Five minutes later, a knock sounded at the door and Ryler moved to answer it. Chief looked angry. Cold. His eyes went to me. I stood as he approached and Chief wrapped me in his arms. "You all right?" he rumbled. Nodding, I tried remain calm. "No, you're not." He held me tighter as my body trembled. "You're frightened." He held me until the tremors stopped, then pulled back to look me in the eye. "This sicko will not hurt you, AJ."

"What about others?" I whispered past the knot in my throat. "What if she hurts someone else? What if it's you guys?"

"You don't need to worry about us. Rye and I can take care of ourselves."

"But what about the others? She's already proven she'll hurt them. I just wish I knew what she wanted."

"And what if you knew, AJ?" Ryler asked. "Would you comply with her demands?"

"No…I don't know—I just want to *know*. Maybe it'll make sense if I knew."

"Evil never makes sense. It's just evil. And we have to stand against it," Chief said.

He was right. I knew he was right. Still, it was the not knowing that was the hardest. I worried over *who* this person was. What they wanted. And *why*. Why make these choices? Why take these actions? Why come after me? How had I offended them?

Another knock at the door had Ryler going back to answer it. Moments later, he led the officer into the room. "Miss McAdams? I'm Detective Andrews with the Sequim Police Department. I've already spoken with Detective Whitaker with the CPD. He's filled me in on what's been happening. May I see the box?"

"It's here, Caleb." Ryler pointed to it. Detective Andrews squatted down to look at the contents. He set down a small bag, almost like a briefcase, before opening it and withdrawing a pair of rubber gloves. He then pulled a pencil from inside and began to search through the box, lifting or moving around the contents. He worked quietly, but swiftly. Several minutes later, having taken numerous photos, dusting for fingerprints, then bagging and labeling the contents, he pulled the gloves off and shoved them in his pants pocket as he stood to his feet.

"Miss McAdams." He approached me again. "When did you receive this package?"

I thought for a moment, then said, "It was Monday, September the tenth."

"You sound very certain of the date." Chief rose while we spoke and went to the kitchen where I heard water running and some clanking noises.

"I am. The day before, I'd just picked my best friend up at the airport in Seattle. The package arrived the day after she got here. We'd been out hiking when it was dropped off."

"Why wait until now to open it?"

"I thought...I thought it was from a book publisher, wanting me to read a book for them. They do that sometimes. I was having company over that night, so put it in the front closet there. I rarely use that closet and just forgot it was there. I only looked for it because she—"

"Amber, you mean?" he interrupted.

"Yes, Amber." I exhaled, my breath rattling. "She'd asked if I'd received her package."

The detective gave me sharp look. "Asked when, how?"

"Early this morning. It was posted to my blog page."

He wrote something on his legal pad, then asked, "She posted, asking if you had received her package?"

"Yes." I nodded. Chief returned then with a steaming mug of tea, handing it to me, nodding, indicating I should drink up. The tea was dark, just a hint of sweetness, and a splash of something spicier. Something to calm my nerves. It really hit the spot and my eyes pricked from his thoughtfulness.

More writing. "And you don't have any idea who this Amber person is?"

I shook my head. "No, no I don't."

"Miss McAdams," he looked at me. "Is there anywhere you can go? Anyone you feel safe with?"

"AJ's coming to stay with me, Caleb." Ryler faced me, the look in his eye warning me not to go against him. "Don't argue. Amber, or whoever the heck she is, knows your address. You're not staying here."

"But, what about Josephine?" I heard the whine in my own voice but couldn't seem to help it. "And won't she just find me at your house anyway?"

"Bring the cat with you." Ryler took my hand, smoothing his thumb over the back, no doubt trying to calm me. And, by golly, it did. "Shiv won't mind. And if Amber brings the fight to us, to *my* doorstep, I'll unleash hell on her."

"Go with him, kid." Chief chimed in. "Trust us on this."

Unable to come up with any other excuses, I finally nodded in agreement. "I need to pack some things."

"Go ahead." Ryler nodded. "I'll wait here. Then I'm taking you to my place."

Nodding again, I set my cup down, then headed upstairs.

Ryler

It was like the light inside AJ had been snuffed out. Ryler watched her trudge up the staircase and wanted to kill someone. Break something. Once she was out of sight, he turned to Caleb Andrews. "What do you think?"

"I think this has strong potential to be a disaster if not handled correctly," he replied. "I'll take this back to the office, send it off to be processed. It'll go to Seattle; that's the closet lab. Might take several weeks to get any results back. So, you guys need to keep a close eye on things."

Ryler and Chief nodded and saw him out. "Thanks, Caleb. Keep me posted."

"Speaking of things found out," Chief said once the door was shut. "You asked me to look into Paul Ashland."

"Yeah." Ryler's gaze sharpened.

"There's not much and we had to dig deep, but we did learn a couple things. He's former military. Served in Iraq, a few years after Jake, and before you arrived on the scene. He was a sharp-shooter until he was court-martialed and dishonorably discharged for conduct unbecoming."

"Interesting." Ryler scratched thoughtfully at his jaw. "I wonder if AJ knows that about her former roommate?"

Chief shrugged. "You asked me to check, so I did."

"Who was your source on this?"

"You met him at the ride. Him and his new wife. Samuel Darrante. That man has more connections than you could imagine."

Ryler raised a brow. "I'm indebted. Thank you."

"He said to tell you, if you asked who supplied that information, that his debt is now paid to you."

Something flashed in Ryler's eyes as he thought back to that mission, to what had happened. Words wanted to spill out, but he bit them all back, forcing them down. Then he jerked his chin in acknowledgement as they settled back to wait for AJ to finish packing.

CHAPTER EIGHTEEN
Witch Hunt

Ryler unlocked the door to his cabin and swung it wide to let me in. Shiv greeted us as we stepped over the threshold, tail wagging, nose sniffing. Josephine grumbled at the hound's curiosity from inside her crate. "This way." Ryler patted Shiv and nudged him aside as he led me to the second floor. "Stay, Shiv." The scruffy black dog heaved a sigh as he settled obediently to wait. "My room is there on the first floor. You'll have the upstairs to yourself. There's a small, private living room—it's more of a study, I guess—with a fireplace down the hall here, at the end." He nodded to his left, before turning right. "And your room is here. There's an attached bathroom."

The room Ryler led me into wasn't as big as the one I currently resided in at Jake's house. But it was still a lovely room. There was a queen-sized bed, a matching dresser, two nightstands, and a wingback chair. The walls were white-washed split logs, the floors stained a dark color. The bedding, chair, and curtains were all in varying, yet complimenting shades of green. Ryler set my bag on the bed and all the cat necessities on the floor beside it. "I'll leave you to it. Get her settled in," he nodded at Josephine's crate. "Then, if you want, come on back downstairs and I'll make breakfast."

I thanked him and with a soft kiss to my temple, Ryler silently left, closing the door behind himself. The bathroom was larger than I'd expected. That was a bonus. I put Josephine's litter box and bowls there, rather than in the bedroom. While Josephine inspected her new surroundings, I filled her food and water bowls.

Taking a few moments to simply breathe and settle myself, I stood before the mirror in the bathroom and studied my reflection. My hair was longer, needing a trim once more. Stress and worry were taking their toll; pale, almost bruise-like stains now resided under my eyes. And my skin seemed sallow. I needed sunshine. Heat. The sound of the ocean waves. I needed Amber, or whoever had killed Mrs. Carson, and was now threatening me, behind bars. And sleep. I could probably use a good amount of sleep as well.

My belly rumbled then, reminding me I'd also need food. So, I told Josephine to stay and closed the door behind me. From below I smelled coffee and bacon, causing my stomach to complain loudly. Following my nose, I found Ryler standing at the stove, tending to the bacon, as well as a pan of eggs he was scrambling.

Hearing some silent sound, he turned as I entered the room. His blue-grey eyes flared with some emotion that flashed in and out before I could read it properly. Then he nodded to the steaming coffee mug sitting on the table.

"Thank you." Shiv waited until I was seated before coming to greet me. And as he stood beside me, tail again wagging, I marveled at how massive he was. His back was taller than the table. He put his large head into my lap, just letting it rest there, like he was trying to comfort me. I let my fingers comb through his thick, wavy fur and felt a little of the tension begin to ease.

Ryler brought me a plate and fork, setting it on the table in front of me. Then he brought a small glass of orange juice and a napkin. I waited to begin eating until he'd sat down as well. Shiv sighed deeply then stretched out under the table, hoping, I'm sure, for any wayward pieces. "You're not afraid of the kitchen, are you?" I asked Ryler as I took my first bite. Everything was cooked to perfection.

"Not afraid of much, really," he replied, also eating.

"Thank you." I said after a moment or two. "For...for everything. For...the coffee, bacon, the eggs, letting me and Josephine crash at your bachelor pad."

Ryler chuckled. "Well, you don't exactly make it a hardship." There was a heat in his tone. An implication. One I wanted to explore. He looked up then. Those blue-grey eyes turning a liquid silver as my breath stuttered in my chest. I felt jittery, like I needed to move. Wanted to move. Toward him. I wanted to climb into his lap, curl up there, and breathe him in. I wondered if this was how Josephine felt. When she'd head for that patch of sunlight, stretching, and curling into it, just absorbing its heat. At this point, I doubted I'd be shocked if I began purring.

"So..." I cleared my throat. "What do we do now?" My voice still came out low with an unintended, almost sultry quality. Clearing my throat again, I continued, "About Amber, I mean?"

Ryler studied me quietly over the rim of his cup. "About Amber...we wait. And hopefully flush her out. There's no sense in rushing into a witch hunt when we don't even know who all the players are. So, we'll wait it out." I nodded, seeing the wisdom in his words. "You can set up your workstation wherever. Here, on the porch, upstairs. Whatever works for you."

"Thank you."

"I'll be in and out all day. Not far—in case you need me. But you won't be tripping over me either."

I shook my head. "You don't have to...don't leave because of me, Ryler. I don't want to run you out of your house."

He leaned forward. "You're not. Trust me. I have work to do. And I figure you probably want to work as well." He sighed deeply. "Besides, if I stay away, you'll have more opportunity to accomplish that work. Because if I stay here...if I stay, I'm going to spend a fair amount of time doing all the things taking place in my head right now."

Heat stabbed through me. "Okay," I breathed, not sure just which *okay* I'd been agreeing to. Okay, he should go? Or, okay, he should stay.

Ryler stood, taking his plate with him. "I'll do the dishes," I said as he reached the sink. He nodded, not meeting my eyes, like maybe he didn't trust himself. I finished the last bite of bacon and carried my plate to the sink as well.

Ryler stepped back, giving me room. "The soap is here in the dispenser. Towels are in the drawer there, third from the bottom."

Nodding at his instruction, I picked up the sponge. Turning the hot water on, I got the sink filling with soapy water. When I turned to wipe off the table, Ryler was already gone. Making quick work of the table, I washed and dried it before the sink was even full. Next, I took several paper towels and laid them in the frying pan to soak up the grease from the bacon. Then I scraped the plates clean into the trash.

I washed quietly, lost in my thoughts, and was just setting the last dish onto the drying rack when Ryler was suddenly at my back. Leaning in, carefully pressing me into the counter. His arms made a cage, holding me in place, one on either side of me. His breath on my skin gave the slightest of warnings, just before his mouth touched against the side of my neck. A deep rumbling noise came from his throat as he dragged his mouth across my skin, making goosebumps rise. "I told myself I'd stay away. Give you space. That I wouldn't do...this. And yet...here I am." His nose traced the shell of my ear, breathing me in, continuing his thoughts. "Why is that do you think?"

Answers were impossible as Ryler's hands loosened their grip on the counter and smoothed themselves over and around me. One spread flat across my middle, tugging me closer. The other moved northward, to cup around my throat, angling me for better access. This was heaven and hell. Torment, and pure bliss. His mouth, his teeth, as they nipped, made my knees weak. Made my blood boil. If he hadn't been holding me up, I'd have been a puddle on the floor. How he made me feel this, want this, with everything going on...I hadn't a clue. I just knew I wanted him. Needed him.

Ryler spun me around then, his mouth finding mine. Hot hands lifted me until I was on the lip of the sink. My choices were to sink into what remained of the wash water or glue myself to him. There was no choice, really—I glued myself to him. Plastered and wrapped myself around him. This wasn't gentle. Wasn't sweet. It was pure need. Need brought on by too much...too much longing, too much pent-up emotion and tension. So much tension. Feeling like I was on the verge of an explosion, I said his name, whimpered it more like. Maybe it was the sound of my voice, maybe it was something else, but Ryler locked down.

He didn't pull away. No, my legs were still around him, arms still clinging to him. My breath still ragged. His hands, one was gripping my thigh, hitching it, holding it to him, the other held the back of my neck. His mouth had stilled just below my ear. One kiss. Two. Slowly, ever so slowly he moved until his mouth was over mine. Forehead against forehead, we let our breath calm. That explosion morphed into an implosion, as reality returned. As my lungs tried to swallow down air.

Against my mouth, he breathed, his voice hoarse. "One day...one day, this won't be for the wrong reasons. One day, everything will align properly. But, as much as I want you, right *here*, and right *now*." He growled low in his throat, sending a tremor through me. "I won't take you out desperation, or fear, or pain. It'll be for the right reasons, or it won't be at all, AJ."

My heart and my mind accepted what he was saying, appreciated the respect, the sentiment in his words, even as my body cursed him in seven languages. As my body whimpered and cried in near agony. By slow degrees, Ryler released me, until we were no longer touching. His eyes searched mine. He must have seen what was still burning in my gaze, because Ryler backed away several steps, until he came up against the table, bumping into it. "Don't look at me like that." His nostrils flared, his jaw clenched. "Don't make this harder than it already is. I'm trying to do the right thing, here." I opened my mouth to respond, but he cut me off, "Just...let me do the right thing."

There was such desperation in his voice that I simply nodded. Nodded, knowing things could jump the track easily. That all I had to do to reignite this already highly-combustible flame, was to look at him with the heat still burning me from the inside. Let him see that need, that desire. And there'd be no stopping us this time. We'd be lucky if there was furniture left standing.

Sliding from the counter, I turned from him, reached into the sink to drain the water, then squeezed out the sponge to dry. "Thank you," Ryler said. And I understood what he was thanking me for. Taking a deep breath, I faced him again. Hoping my emotions were well in check and not written all over my sometimes too-expressive face. Nodding, I dried my hands on the towel, then wiped the counter down with it.

Ryler left without another word, closing the door softly, but firmly behind himself. I watched him from the window as he stomped into the trees, the big black hound trailing after him. I wasn't sure just how long I stood there, watching out that window. Long enough for my breath to have completely calmed. Long enough to develop a cramp in my back from standing so still for so long. Long enough for my legs to be trustworthy enough to carry me back up the stairs to get my laptop.

Ryler's kitchen table was nicely situated, centered in a large bay window. From this vantage point, I had a great view of a fair portion of Ryler's property where it sloped away from the house. I set my laptop up at the table, then got to work. Ryler stayed away all day, not even returning for lunch. It wasn't until the sun was setting, filling his clearing with long shadows, that Shiv came trotting through the trees to the west, Ryler just minutes later. I'd taken it upon myself to go through his freezer and refrigerator, trying to see what I'd have to work with for dinner. It didn't take long to see that we'd need to go to the store. I'd found just a half-dozen eggs, another slab of bacon, several steaks, and four roasts. Clearly, he'd not been expecting company. A slow cooker sat on the counter, so I made a mental note to put one of the roasts in for tomorrow's meal. But for tonight, I'd made a couple steaks. And buried beneath one of the roasts, I'd found some frozen broccoli. I fried that in butter, adding some seasonings and Parmesan cheese, to spruce the dish up.

By the time Ryler had returned to the house, dinner was ready. He'd commented on how things smelled when he came inside, then he'd gone to wash up. We ate in silence, each lost in our own thoughts. The silence wasn't so much from unease, or tension, as much as it was from awareness. Such an awareness. Of each other. Of those unanswered needs. It wasn't quite like walking on eggshells, but close enough. We were careful. Cautious. Speaking in soft tones. No fast movements.

"How...Ryler, how long do think I'll need to be here?" I asked as we finished eating.

"As long as it takes." His tone was definitive, the subject clearly not up for discussion.

I blew out a breath. "Can you give me a little more to go on? Like, if it's going to be for several days, then we're going to need more food."

"Already taken care of." At my questioning look he continued, "Paige is going shopping for us tomorrow, enough to last the week. Then Chief will run it out here."

"I...they don't have to do that, Ryler. We can go to town. We'll just be careful."

"We don't know who your crazy fan is. AJ, they know about Jake's place. That means they've been there. That package wasn't delivered by any service. It was brought by the person themselves. They're playing with you. You need to be safe."

I hadn't considered that. That they'd been to Jake's house. To my house. Now I felt violated.

"Have you heard from Amber?" Ryler asked after a moment of silence.

"I haven't checked since this morning." Rising from my chair, I moved to the couch for my laptop. It took me a couple minutes to log in, then to scan the comments. "She says, 'You can't hide from me, so come out and play.'"

Ryler moved to my side, his hand on my shoulder. "Don't respond to her."

I rubbed my forehead and continued. "She...she also asked, 'Who should be next?'"

His hand tightened gently, no doubt offering comfort, or at least attempting to. "She's just pushing your buttons, trying to get a rise out of you."

"You think?" Exasperation was strong in my voice, though I'd tried to tone it down.

"Don't let her get to you."

"That's easier said than done, Ryler. She's already proven she's willing to kill just to get a rise out of me. That's hard to ignore."

Ryler began clearing the table. "I know it is." His voice was decidedly calm, measured. "Still, rising to her bait...that just gives her a weapon against you. She has enough of those. Don't give her anything else. That's all I'm saying."

Frustration over everything suddenly boiled up inside me, spilling out. "What do you know about it, Ryler? You've been in this position before?"

The look he gave was hard, shuttered. "I've been close enough to know, AJ. Close enough to know."

I swallowed and stood to my feet. "I'm sorry. I shouldn't have snapped. I...I'm sorry."

"Don't apologize. I get it."

Harley called then and I remembered we'd planned to talk this evening. Ryler turned back to the kitchen to clean up. I stared at him for a moment, then answered. "Hey."

"AJ." Harley's voice was trembling. "I'm at the hospital—I'm okay, but it's Kevin. He...he was hit by a car...it never even stopped. He's in the OR right now. There was some internal damage, the doctors said. I'm so worried, AJ."

"Oh...Harley, I'm so sorry. It was a hit and run? Did they get a license plate number?"

"No, I don't know. I...I just don't know. We never even saw the car coming."

"Were you there with him?" My heart clenched at the thought.

"Yes, we'd been walking along Ocean Boulevard, when the car swerved in our direction. He, Kevin shoved me out of the way."

"You were almost hit?" Panic struck hard and fast. Ryler came back around the corner, now on high alert. His face was grave, focused. An angry flint sparked his eyes.

"I just heard the sound of the engine as it gunned towards us. I looked over my shoulder...and then Kevin shoved me. The sound...the sound of him...hitting the windshield...I'll never forget that as long as I live."

"Harley." Nausea threatened and I tried to swallow it back. "Are the police saying this was an accident? Or...or do they think it was Amber?"

She sniffed. "They think someone tried to run us over today."

"You remember that package we found on my doorstep? When you were here?"

"Yeah...?"

"It was her. She'd been here. At my house."

"Oh my...what...what was in the package?"

"A...a dead cat. One that looked like Josephine."

Harley choked on a sob. "AJ, this is getting really scary. This person is insane. Are you thinking that your fan tried to run us over?"

"I, I don't...know. If it was intentional, then I doubt they were trying for Kevin. I think you may have been the target."

"What should I do?" Fear was thick in her voice. But before I could respond, she said, "AJ, I need to go. Kevin's sister just arrived."

"Okay, keep me posted. And stay safe."

We ended the call and Ryler said, "You need to let that detective know what happened."

Nodding, I put a call in to Detective Whitaker's number. He didn't answer, but I hadn't really expected him to. He was busy, I was sure.

So, I left a message, explaining what had happened to Harley and Kevin. Stressing that we needed to find Amber. Before she could hurt anyone else.

CHAPTER NINETEEN
Eye of the Storm

AJ

For six days I didn't leave the cabin and now have a very clear, very precise understanding of what the phrase, 'going stir-crazy' means. Chief brought us groceries, and I stayed away from the doors and windows. Fear taunted me as Amber continued to hound me. She posted a photo of Kevin and Harley walking hand in hand along the street. She'd post her comments, "Where are you. Come out, come out and play."

The detectives had been able to ping her IP but felt she must have been using a VPN for all the good the pinging had done them. I couldn't focus on anything as thoughts raced around my brain. Worry over everyone I held dear and the strain of it all had me jumping at odd noises. Sleep seemed like a distant memory. Food was unpalatable. Shiv seemed torn, wanting to comfort me, but needing to calm Ryler as well. Which only added a new layer to the guilt I'd been feeling at dragging everyone into my mess.

Chief had some of his...he called them his 'boys,' but I assumed they were all former military he'd served with, watching Jo and the Paiges. Despite the weight, the pressure of it all, I tried not to dwell on any of it. Ryler had a workout room toward the back of the house where I'd go to try and sweat my stress away. Or I'd retreat to my room for a long, hot soak, letting Josephine keep me company. She liked to curl on the mat, or sometimes even perch on the side of the tub, no doubt my strain was registering with her, as well. Ryler was a constant, steady presence through all of it. Sometimes he simply held me, let me breathe through my anxiety, just letting me know he was there. Sometimes he'd catch my hand as I passed, then lean down for a soft kiss. He didn't go far from the cabin either, other than to let Shiv out, or to bring in more firewood, he stayed fairly close, doing what he'd call perimeter sweeps. I think he was being ultra cautious and didn't want to leave me alone and I didn't have the words to express how much that meant to me.

This morning Detective Whitaker called. They'd been able to get a trace on Amber's IP address. Good news was they'd been able to do it. Bad news was that it looked as though she was on the move, heading north. Possibly coming here. The address was originally located in San Diego, with one brief transmission from Seattle, the same week Harley had been here—I refused to give that any deeper consideration. The address, they'd learned, was registered to an A.P. Ericson, though they'd been unable to find any more information on this person.

After hanging up with the detective, I took a deep breath and tried to focus. Ryler was out with Shiv doing another sweep; I'd have to tell him the news when he returned. Amber had been strangely silent these last two days. I didn't bother hoping she'd gone away or been captured. Instead, it felt like the eye of the proverbial storm. I waited for the other shoe to drop. Waited for things to hit the fan. Waited.

And when the waiting became too much, when I felt like I would claw my skin off, when I couldn't take these same four walls any longer, I went out. Not far. I didn't leave Ryler's property. But I went outside. I breathed in the fresh air, taking it deep into my lungs. Held it, then let it out once more. Ryler was around somewhere. He'd said he wanted to make sure the dead brush was cleared while doing his sweep. Not sure just where he was at, I followed a dim trail into the trees, carefully stepping around or over heavy brush, or fallen limbs. Soon the sunshine faded as the trees became thicker. The terrain became rockier, more rugged. It didn't take long for me to be out of breath. Ryler's property was much hillier than mine. The trail I followed led down, then up, twisting and turning, as it went. I wasn't sure just how long I'd been walking, no more than an hour, surely. My lungs were definitely getting a workout, though. As were my butt and thighs. In fact, I felt old and worn out, even though I was only twenty-three.

Resting, I leaned against a tree which stood near an overhang. Far below, way off in the distance, I could see the glimmer of the setting sun on the Strait and knew I should be heading back soon. I didn't want to become lost in these trees. As I stood there, letting my heartbeat slow down, before turning around, just trying to breathe rather than wheeze, I heard, from somewhere in the distance, a loud pop, followed by an echoing crack. It reminded me of a car backfiring, or maybe a lightning strike. I glanced upward to said sky, fearful of being stuck in these trees in a lightning storm. Simultaneously, the tree I'd been leaning against seemed to explode.

Bark splintered and shot out of the pine, cutting into my face, neck, shoulder, and arm. The force of it toppled me, and I lost my balance, just as the trail I'd been on gave way and fell from under me. My ears were full of the sound of buckling trees and soil. My breath was knocked from me. Dirt was in my eyes and mouth. In my ears. I tried to stop my forward momentum as I tumbled head over heels. Clawing, scraping, trying to cling to anything to stop myself. My right hand snagged around a small sapling, jerking me off course and to the side. A scream ripped from my throat as my body slammed into a large tree somewhere near the bottom. Then everything went black.

Ryler

Ryler knew that sound. Gunfire. From a high-powered rifle. His heart slammed in his chest as he hit the ground. It took him a moment to realize he was home. Not across the world. Not under enemy attack, watching his men be butchered. Nausea rolled through him and he fought to keep his stomach intact.

Hunters shouldn't be anywhere near this area. It's been fenced off and posted for years now. And Ryler walked that fence each year to make sure it was still in good shape. He lay still for several moments, trying to ascertain where that shot had come from. If he was in any more danger. Because the idea was beginning to dawn on him that the shot had been deliberate. Then he slowly inched his way into the shadows, careful to keep his movements minimal, careful to stay out of sight.

When several minutes passed and no other shots were fired, another thought occurred to him, *AJ—was she all right?* Suddenly, Shiv's booming bark rent the air as the hound tried to locate him. "Here, Shiv." He kept his voice low. Whining and growling, the Wolfhound approached on his belly. But he was antsy and wouldn't stay, kept trying to lead Ryler off, away. Back toward the cabin.

Whether from the dog's need to get him to safety, or because AJ was in trouble, Ryler didn't know. But he scrambled fast over the rough ground, needing to get to her, to make sure she was all right.

"AJ!" Ryler yelled as he cleared the porch in a leap, barely stopping to open the door. The house was empty. Silent. Shiv whined and scratched at the door.

Ryler checked his cell phone, but there was nothing from her. On a whim he sent a 911 to Chief. Told him what had happened, and just to be on the safe side, to check in with Jo, Paige, and Poppy. Then he told the sailor he was going to look for AJ. Ryler was about to open the cabin door, when something white caught his notice from the corner of his eye. There, on the floor, under the kitchen table, was a piece of paper. Hoping against hope, that it was a note from her, Ryler picked it up. His hope was well-founded. AJ'd said she was going for a walk, not far, just down the trail and she'd be back before it got dark. The sun wasn't completely down, but the shadows were deep and long. He needed to find her and soon.

"Come on, Shiv." He stepped off the porch. "Find her."

AJ

When consciousness returned, it rolled in with the force of a crashing wave. My eyes opened, stinging and watering, to darkness. It took several long moments to piece together where I was and what had happened. And as the events leading to my current predicament came crashing in, the pain came with it. Unbidden, the whimper came from my lips. I tried holding still, to not tremble, because the movement sent pain radiating through me again. But being motionless hurt as well. Each breath caused that pain to lance through me. I wondered if I had broken ribs. Bruised ones at the very least.

Turning my head, gritting my teeth against the throbbing, I tried to ascertain my position, to identify my surroundings. Nothing was visible from this angle, I couldn't see anything. And it was so dark. My head throbbed anew as my eyes strained to see through the gloom. The trees surrounding me took on the shapes of feral beasts and monsters and I fought against a shudder of fear. Telling myself it was a trick of the light, or rather a trick from the lack of light. Carefully as I could, I took inventory of myself. I'd come to a stop on my stomach. My right arm was twisted at an odd angle and when I tried to move it, I nearly blacked out again. A part of me wished I had, because right now I just wanted to scream.

Biting my lip, I fought against the panic and pain. Ryler would come for me. I knew he would; I just needed to remain calm until he arrived. But the minutes seemed more like hours. Like days. And in the darkness, noises heralded the arrival of monstrous, wicked things. I couldn't stop the trembling, the shaking. With my left hand, I tried to push myself up. But my legs were stuck under something. I tried shifting them, but an excruciating pain stabbed through me, and I bit back another scream.

Panic again sunk its talons into me, and I gritted my teeth to stave off the sobs I could feel were coming. I couldn't move. I was trapped and every muscle ached. Every nerve screamed in agony. Tears clouded my vision and I couldn't stop the tremors, couldn't stop the fear.

Cold from the air, from the ground, seeped into every pore on my body. A part of me wondered if this wasn't shock settling in, but I could see my breath. See the puffs of frosty air as I labored to get breath in my lungs. From somewhere above me, I couldn't tell what direction it was coming from, came the sharp sounds of branches snapping. Something moved through the trees, through the underbrush, in my direction. Something big.

My terror took on epic proportions as I imagined the large, carnivorous beast planning to make me its evening meal. I imagined the teeth and claws as they tore through me. Frantically, I scratched at the soil, trying to dig myself out. Unwilling to die on my face, unwilling to be eaten alive. My breath was a sob in my chest. *No, no, no...please, no.* Then I heard it. The whine. The blessedly familiar whine from Shiv. My relief nearly choked me. "Sh-sh-Shiv." I panted through my tears. The hound let out a series of loud barks, alerting Ryler to my position. Moments later, my name was called.

"Here!" I tried to yell. But it came out hoarse and too low. "I'm here, Ryler!"

Still, he must have heard, because he called, "I'm coming, AJ. Stay still. Don't move. Shiv! Where is she, Shiv?"

The black dog barked again, and again, drawing Ryler to us. And then I could hear him, through the brush. The beam from his flashlight lit up the tree I was under. "I'm here, Ryler. Under, under the tree. I can't move."

"AJ, hang on. Just hold still. I'm going to try and approach you from downhill. You've managed to land between two trees growing between two boulders. So, hang tight."

"Okay," I breathed. I heard him as he moved around. Snapping branches and more soil falling away. It seemed to take forever, but then I saw him.

Ryler studied the area, making sure of where he'd need to step, what he'd need to move to get me safely out.

"Hey." His voice was gentle as he crawled towards me, then leaned down to press his lips against my temple. "You're doing good, all right? Do you know if anything is broken? Can you tell?"

"Um, my shoulder, my right shoulder...I think it's broken, maybe. I can't use it."

"All right. All right. Nothing else? How about your legs?"

The tears wouldn't stop. I think it was just nerves, certainly crazy emotions, but I choked through them. "I think, I think my leg might be broken. I can't move it; it hurts, and I'm st-stuck under this tree."

"All right. Good. Can you take a deep breath for me? Anything hurt, or feel off, or different there when you breathe?"

I did as he asked. "No, I mean, I'm sore. But nothing feels...off."

"Good, good. Well, it's a good thing this is not a huge tree. I should be able to get it off you. I'm going to try and dig some of the soil away under you, then I'll lift the tree, and you're going to need to slide yourself out. It's going to hurt like hell, AJ, but can you do that?"

"Yeah, I think so."

"Shiv, come boy. Help me dig." Ryler began to claw the dirt from under me and Shiv soon joined in. Between the two of them they made quick work of it. "All right, boy. Let's get her out. Pull!"

Ryler grunted at the weight of the tree as he strained to lift it from me. Shiv grabbed my jacket in his teeth and pulled, jerking me. Ryler had to set the tree down again to get a better grip on it. Then we continued our efforts. And slowly, but surely, I made it out. Ryler helped me roll to my back, then gently looked me over, no doubt just making sure I wasn't about to pass out or even bleed out on him. When he seemed satisfied I wasn't dying, he said, "There's a little clearing about ten yards uphill and to the west. We'll head there and then I can take a better look at you, all right?"

Tears hadn't stopped falling since he'd found me. I wasn't sure if I could climb or move. But I wasn't going to be left behind. So, I just nodded.

"We'll take it slow." He pulled my left arm over his shoulder and wrapped his right arm around my waist. "There's no rush."

His calm assurance was like a shot of adrenaline, but even with Ryler bearing most of my weight, it took us nearly a half hour to reach that clearing. Every step brought a flash of burning, searing heat through my battered body. When we finally stopped, I just wanted to cry. I did whimper as he slid me gently to the ground. Ryler knelt beside me and had me lay on my back. He had to cut away my zippered hoodie to get a better look.

Now that he had more room to work, he gently, painstakingly, examined me. After a minute or two, he said, "I'm pretty sure your leg is broken. And your shoulder is dislocated. I'll need to set them." He looked around, for what, I wasn't sure. Then he rose to his feet. "Sit tight; I'll be right back. Shiv stay." He moved out of my line of sight, and I tried not to panic at his going. More snapping noises, then he was back with two sticks, each around two feet in length.

"I'm going to try to stabilize your leg until we can get you to the hospital, but your shoulder I can do here."

I nodded and watched as he worked in careful, swift motions. Soon my leg felt a little more secure, though the swelling was killing me. My only compensation was knowing that the brace he'd made was temporary and that I'd get a proper cast once we got to the hospital. Once my leg was done, Ryler knelt beside me. The look he gave me had my stomach clenching, though I couldn't say why exactly.

When those eyes shifted to my shoulder and back, I tensed. "Is this where you do the countdown thing, making me think you're going to move it on three, but instead you move it on two?"

"Please." Ryler rolled his eyes. His thumbs tenderly stroked my skin, where his hands rested on me, trying to calm me for what we both knew was coming. "That wouldn't work on you. Besides, you already know about it, and you'd tense up and that would make things worse. No, I'm just going to have to do it the—" Without warning, he moved, jerking my arm back into place. "...old-fashioned way."

The pain flared sharply, then was gone, and only a dull throbbing was left behind. "I am going to kill you, Ryler." I gasped and clutched at my shoulder.

He just chuckled. "I think you mean kiss. You're going to kiss me, right? I did just fix your shoulder and made it as painless as I possibly could. And rescued you. So...."

"Whatever."

"Ah, c'mon, Banana."

Despite the pain, I couldn't help the chuckle. "I'm laying here practically dying, and you're mocking me."

"You're not dying, Banana." He tenderly cupped my cheek. His thumb brushed over my lip. "Trust me."

"It sure feels like it." My voice came out small, fragile. I hated it.

"Yeah, I know...all joking aside...we need to get you out of here." The light in his eyes shifted, solidifying. "And...I don't want you to panic, but I'm pretty sure someone took a shot at you today."

Dread coated me. "What?"

"I heard a gunshot...and then found you like this. It adds up."

My breath left me in a rush, making my ribs throb. "The tree...the tree beside me exploded."

Ryler nodded, confirming what he already suspected, his jaw tight. "Let's get you out of here."

He helped me upright, moving slow and sure. "You're going to be sore and you'll need to be careful as we go. We'll get back to the cabin, then get you down to the hospital for x-rays."

"I hate hospitals," I groaned.

He chuckled. "I'm not a fan either, but we need to make sure nothing internal is damaged."

That thought brought on a whole new round of panic that I tried to overcome. And slowly we trudged up the mountain.

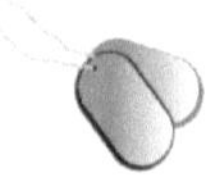

Ryler

Seeing AJ's bloody, torn body was one of the scariest things Ryler had ever experienced. And it was only through the grace of God Almighty and the training the Army had given him, that allowed him to stay calm and focused. That held him together when he wanted to vomit and tremble. Hearing her voice, pained and shaky as it was, had been one of the most beautiful sounds he'd ever heard. He'd had to touch her, feel her at that point.

Ryler had allowed all his field training to come to the fore as he'd assessed her. To compartmentalize and devise a plan to get her out, all while wondering if another shot was coming. If the shooter was still out there. If they'd moved to a better position. If he was even now in the crosshairs. Training had allowed Ryler to ignore those possibilities and just get the job done.

Truth be told, he'd been anticipating *something* happening. Things were too silent—too much calm layered with too much tension. Too many things lining up, indicating AJ's attacker was closing in. It had felt a bit like they'd been standing in the eye of a massive storm bearing down on them. So, he'd braced himself to ride it out.

CHAPTER TWENTY
No Safe Haven

AJ

It seemed like it had taken days rather than an hour to hike up that mountain. Ryler had angled us to follow the path of my near destruction as we ascended. Several times he'd had me sit and rest, while he scouted around. What he was looking for exactly, I wasn't sure. We found where I'd been standing when I'd heard that shot. The trail and the soil were gone, having slid down the mountain, though the tree was still there, somehow clinging to the side of the hill.

Ryler sat me several feet away as he carefully inspected the tree and the surrounding area. Using his phone's flashlight, he took out his knife and dug around in the wood, then put whatever it was he'd found, the bullet maybe, into his pocket. He took pictures, lots of pictures. He also studied the angle of the impact, seeming almost lost in thought.

Once back at the cabin, I'd needed a minute or two to catch my breath, so with me resting on the couch and hydrating, he called Chief to update him. Shiv stayed glued to my side, seemingly more concerned with me at this point than Ryler. After Ryler ended that call, he dialed Detective Whitaker and left a message. He also called the Sequim PD and left a message there for Caleb as well.

Ten minutes after arriving back at the cabin, Ryler led me through his bedroom, and out the patio door there. Whether due to the pain, or the darkness, I barely registered what his room looked like. The bed—I noticed that—mainly because we had to walk right past it. But it was large, definitely a king. The back of the house was really dark; I could barely see. "Careful now." He intoned quietly after locking Shiv inside, telling him to 'guard.' We shuffled around the cabin to where his Bronco was parked. There, he silently, carefully lifted me inside. It was a little nerve-wracking, all this cloak and dagger stuff.

He got it started, but instead of backing it up to head down the driveway to the main highway, Ryler drove forward across the backyard. He didn't use headlights, just the running lights. Not until we were well into the trees did he turn the lights on. The road we followed was barely cleared, no more than an overgrown trail. Grass swished against the bottom of the vehicle as we went.

"Where are we going?" My lips were tight as I regulated my breathing to get through the pain.

He shot an apologetic look before turning once more to the road. "One should always have a secondary means of escape. Never allow yourself to be bottled in and trapped."

I raised my brow. "Oh. Okay."

Ryler tried to go slow, to not bump along the ground, so I wouldn't be in too much discomfort. But that made it seem like we were barely crawling. Towards the bottom of the mountain, we crossed over a swift moving stream. About twenty feet on the other side of it were two smaller trees lying across the road. It didn't take him long to move the trees, then he climbed back inside and we were off again. About five minutes later we came to a locked gate. Again, he climbed out, this time to unlock the gate.

I must have fallen asleep, exhaustion finally getting the better of me. I remembered the gate, going through it, but everything else became murky after that. Next thing I knew he was carrying me into the ER at the Olympic Medical Center in Port Angeles. Chief was already there waiting for us, along with Caleb Andrews. Ryler took me to the triage station, and I caught a glimpse of myself in the glass from the window. Blood and dirt warred for dominance across my face and down my neck. A cut above my right eye, near my hairline had bled quite profusely. My lips and cheek were scraped raw and swelling. I hadn't realized how bad I'd looked, all that had happened to me, until this moment. I couldn't stop the tears from welling up or spilling over.

Ryler tenderly hugged me closer, even as the nurses brought a wheelchair. They wanted to get me into imaging to see what, if any, damage had been done internally. I didn't want to let him go and clung to him. "Hey." His grip was warm and comforting and everything I needed in that moment. "I'm right here. You're safe. You just need to get checked out, all right?"

"Stay with me," I begged; too tired, too scared to worry about the fact that I was begging.

"I will." He looked to the nurses, his voice firming. "I'm staying."

They agreed, then let him push me toward the imaging department. Over the next several hours, I was poked and prodded. Photographed. Questioned. Questioned some more. From everyone. The nursing staff, the technicians, the doctors, the police. I'd kept my eyes glued to Ryler the entire time. And while that kept me calm, allowing me to deal with everything, he seemed off somehow. Distant and withdrawn. Like he was being ratcheted down. I didn't know what to make of it. My head hurt too much to try and solve that mystery right now. At one point he'd pulled Detective Andrews aside and gave him something from his pocket. Then showed him the pictures he'd taken earlier. The detective looked everything over, had Ryler send him the photos, and said he'd send whatever Ryler had given him off to be evaluated.

At the end of it, I had what they were calling a closed, fibular, shaft-fracture. I was assured this was actually a good break, as those were quite easy to set. Ryler was praised by the doctor for having done such a good job stabilizing my leg earlier. My right shoulder was all right thanks to Ryler having set it, though it still ached some. My right ankle was sprained, and I'd bruised some ribs as well. Basically, my right side had taken the most abuse, but at least I'd be able to use my right arm which meant I would be able to continue writing. My leg would be out of commission for a while, though, and in a cast. The cut near my hairline had to be stitched—four in total. Last, but not least, it was believed I had a mild concussion, in addition to the myriad scrapes and bruises covering my body. I was still alive, I reminded myself.

We didn't leave until close to four in the morning. Exhaustion was weighing heavy on me by this point. I was told I'd need to keep my leg elevated and still as much as possible, even though it was in a bulky cast, so they'd rolled me out in a wheelchair. Chief pulled Ryler aside while I was filling out paperwork, and they had a short, yet tense discussion. As I was finishing up, Chief patted Ryler on the shoulder. It looked like he might have been about to say something more, then he turned and headed in my direction. "Well, kid, you've looked better."

Wincing, I grimaced. "No doubt, and thanks."

"You just rest. We've got this, all right?"

I nodded, not sure exactly what it was that he had, but still, he was so confident about it, I simply agreed with him. As Ryler drove us back to Sequim, I angled my head in his direction. At first, I just stared at his profile, tracing each contour with my eyes. And even with the pain throbbing mildly, I felt a warmth stirring in my middle, and a pang in my heart.

"What's up?" Ryler shot me a look before turning his gaze back to the highway.

"I'm sorry." To my shame, my voice trembled.

"For what?" Disbelief coated his words.

"For dragging you into this whole mess. It's not fair to you...and...I'm sorry." I'd been thinking about that look in his eyes at the hospital, that distant, locked-down look. Wondering if he'd reached overcapacity with all the stress I seemed to bring. Wondering if he was now regretting involving himself with me.

"Why are *you* apologizing?" His voice held a growling quality now. Almost savage in its intensity. "You didn't do this. Don't you *dare* apologize, AJ. This isn't your fault." Unsure how to respond to his statement, I remained quiet. "Is that what you think?" The tone of his voice, the emotion there sent a shiver of warmth skating over me. "That I'm somehow mad at you or something?"

"I don't know. You seemed…off. Distant. I thought maybe…maybe you were regretting…things."

"No." He gently took my hand in his, raising it to his mouth. Against my skin he said, "I don't regret anything, other than that I haven't nailed this guy yet."

My heart thudded and I had to swallow. "Something was bothering you at the hospital. I could see it."

Ryler inhaled, long and slow. He pressed a kiss against the back of my hand. "I don't like hospitals. Too many bad memories."

"Because of your injuries?"

"That. And other things."

"Those men…Moose, and them?"

He nodded silently. "And your dad. Just a lot of bad memories."

"I'm sorry." I whispered. "That you had to deal with all that again. That those memories came up."

"It's not your fault. *None* of this was your fault."

"Is there anything else? Bothering you, I mean?"

He shot me another look, and something flashed in his eyes, turning the blue-grey to cold steel. "Someone took a shot at you today. That wasn't lightning, wasn't an accident. This person is dead serious. And I want *them* dead. Not caught, just dead."

"Oh." I nodded. "Yeah, me, too."

We pulled into Jake's long driveway, and it occurred to me that we weren't going the back way. "No back way this time?"

"Chief had a couple of his boys clear the woods along the drive and around my place. It's safe now."

"You mean…?"

"They did a sweep, making sure the shooter was no longer in the area."

"I take it they were gone?"

"Yep. But they left a burnout mark in the gravel a quarter mile or so from Jake's drive."

I swallowed at that news and looked around us. It was dark; I couldn't see beyond the headlights and tried not to be fearful but couldn't help the worry. Couldn't help the way my eyes darted between the shadows, looking for those things that go bump in the night. The realization that someone had taken a shot at me today was...terrifying. And even though I'd experienced the event, I was still having a difficult time processing that truth in my brain. Ryler's haven suddenly didn't seem as safe as it had before.

After parking and turning the Bronco off, Ryler helped me out, then carefully carried me inside. They'd cleaned me up some at the hospital and had given me a clean hospital gown to come home in, but there was still blood and dirt and grime. In my hair and on my skin. So, as we moved to the couch, I stopped him. "I'm dirty...I need to clean up, somehow."

Ryler paused, considering my request. He glanced to the staircase and back. "All right." He nodded, then, without further comment, gently readjusted me in his arms and carried me through his room and into the bathroom. He looked towards the shower, then the tub, then back to me. "Uh, which one? Can you stand all right? Or do you need to be sitting?"

He carefully set me on my feet, keeping one hand at my waist to steady me. "I need to wash my hair...."

His eyes studied my hair, my shoulder. "Can you lift your arm to do that? Try." Tears pricked my eyes at the sheer frustration of the situation as I tried lifting it. My left arm didn't hurt too bad, but my ribs screamed in protest, my body trembling with the attempt. "No." Ryler shook his head. "You can't. Look, I can...I'll help you. If you want." I nodded, tears still streaming down my face. "Sit here for a sec. Don't move; I'll be right back." He maneuvered me to his toilet and sat me down there. A minute later, he was back, rolling a meshed-back office chair into the room. "This reclines and I'm not worried about it getting wet. Should make it easier to wash your hair. How's that?"

"All right." I whispered past the lump in my throat. After getting me into the chair, he stepped back. "What, uh, what are you planning to wear? After you're clean, I mean? Did you need something to change into?"

Nonplussed, I blinked my eyes in slow movements, unable to form thoughts and probably looking pathetic even trying. Ryler's face softened as he studied me. He leaned down and kissed my forehead. "How about you stay in that for right now, then after your hair is clean, we can get you out of that and you can finish cleaning up."

I hadn't thought about that. The getting undressed part. The changing of clothes part. I'd only been thinking about being clean. Now, I couldn't think of any way to do this other than how Ryler was suggesting. "Um...I think my robe might be best. That'd be easiest at any rate. It's hanging on a hook in the bathroom."

Ryler left to get it, and I tried to relax as I waited. He wasn't gone for more than a couple minutes, but I began wondering if he'd be able to find it. If I'd need to help him, and *how* I'd accomplish that. But then he returned, robe over his shoulder, towels in his arms, along with my shampoo, conditioner, and body scrub.

He surveyed all he'd retrieved, no doubt checking to make sure he had all he'd need. His gaze landed on my walking boot, and he thoughtfully scratched his chin. "That's not a cast; still, it shouldn't get wet. Hang on a sec—I've got an idea."

He quickly left the bathroom once more, soon returning with a black plastic trash bag along with a roll of medical tape. "I'm going to put this on your leg, then tape it thoroughly. That should keep the water out long enough to accomplish your shower."

"Thank you, Ryler." I took as deep a breath as my sore ribs allowed. "I feel like I say that a lot to you. But I really do mean it. Thank you."

"Thanks aren't needed." Ryler worked quickly and efficiently. "But you're welcome, all the same."

Surreal—I've always wondered what exactly that word would look and feel like. I've certainly read the definition before but hadn't truly experienced it. Until now. The water was warm, relaxing. The spray soothing. The thin cotton of the hospital gown clung like a second skin where the water and fabric met. And Ryler's hands as they held my head, as they gently rinsed the water over my hair, as they scrubbed my scalp, cleansing me from all the dirt and blood—it was all just very *surreal*. I couldn't help but think of that scene from *Out of Africa*, where Robert Redford washed Meryl Streep's hair. Yeah, it was like that. Surreal and somehow still swoony.

When he finished, Ryler helped me lean forward in the chair so he could reach the ties at the back of my gown. After a moment, he asked if I was attached to it. "No," I told him on a breathy chuckle. Using his knife, he carefully sliced through the back of the gown from top to as far as he could reach at the bottom. Then gently, wordlessly, he washed my back in soft, circular motions. We were silent, and though there was pain and the stress from everything, there was also tension. A sweetly, coiling tension. What Ryler did was not meant to be stirring, yet somehow it was.

Finally, Ryler helped me stand, making sure I wasn't in danger of falling. He took my hand, placing a kiss on my palm, before setting it on the rail. He kissed my shoulder, then stepped back. "Can you get it from here?" His voice was low, almost guttural, barely more than a whisper. It brushed across my skin, causing me to shiver. Unable to speak, I simply nodded. "I'll step out. Give you some privacy to finish. Holler when you're done and I'll help you out of here. Sit on the bench there if you need to; I'll be right outside the door."

I nodded silently and he left, somehow leaving the room colder at his going. Breathing in through my nose, then out my mouth, I tried to calm my racing heart. After a few moments, I carefully peeled off what was left of the wet gown, dropping it on the shower floor. Feeling shaky and a little unsteady, I washed as quickly as I was able. Then, clearing my throat, I called Ryler back. Already, just this little bit of time on my own, I was exhausted, fighting against fatigue.

"AJ?" Ryler called softly from outside the bathroom door. "I'm going to turn the lights off...to give you...so that...I'm just going to turn them off, all right?"

"Okay," I whispered. My back was to the door. I heard it open, then the lights went out. He'd left the bedroom light on, though, so we weren't in complete darkness. There was the rustle of fabric from behind me. Then he wrapped the towel around my shoulders and carefully patted my skin down. "I'm going to lift you now."

I tried not to brace myself as Ryler gently gathered me into his arms, lifting, then setting me on the rug outside the shower. In silence he finished drying me, starting at my feet and working upwards. Again, that tension returned. That heaviness in the air. The tingling along my skin as if each and every nerve ending were firing in undulating waves.

"Here's your robe, you can let that towel drop."

He settled the robe across my shoulders and I did as instructed, letting go of the towel. Cool air touched along my front before Ryler helped me. Standing at my back, he slid my arms into the sleeves. First the right, then the left. I tied the belt as securely as I could and just hoped it stayed together.

"Do you need anything else?" His voice gravely, his body a solid warm mass behind me, lending me comfort, lending me strength.

"I don't want to be alone, Ryler." I breathed.

I felt him tense up, lock down. Keeping one hand on my waist, he moved to stand before me. Whatever look was upon my face must have answered those questions I'd seen in his because he simply nodded. "Finish what you need to do, then we'll figure it out. I'll wait outside."

He turned to go, leaving me there, wrapped in my robe. I heard the click as the door closed softly, yet firmly between us, but not before Ryler had flicked the light on, keeping his back to me the entire time.

Blinking, I glanced around me. On the counter beside his sink was my toothbrush and toothpaste. Beside the shower was my crutch. I hadn't realized he'd brought these in. The thoughtfulness nearly brought me to tears. Again. I needed to get this watery mess under control. Reaching for the crutch, I got it under my arm, then carefully hobbled to the sink. The mirror stated plainly that I wasn't even registering as a hot mess. Nope. This was a mess, plain and simple. My face was full of scratches and bruises. And stitches.

After a moment, I sniffed, exhaled, and reached for my toothbrush. Ryler must have been listening at the door, because just as the water shut off, he knocked, asking if I was ready. "Yeah," I called.

"I figured we'd take the couch. I can prop your leg up on pillows...there's room for me beside you. If that's what you want."

I nodded and he ran a quick, assessing eye over me before carrying me out to the sofa, where he gently set me down. After I was settled, he returned to his room for a couple blankets. Not long after, he was beside me, tenderly curling me into his right side. Silence settled between us and my muscles twitched, jerking, as I tried to relax. After a several minutes, in a somewhat sleepy voice, I said, "You're a safe haven, you know that, Ryler? You're my safe haven."

His lips pressed against my temple, held there as his arm around me tightened the slightest. Then sleep claimed me.

CHAPTER TWENTY-ONE
I See You

AJ

The sun was already well up by the time I woke the next morning curled into Ryler. Shiv lay to my other side on the couch, lightly snoring with his massive head in my lap. Ryler's heart steadily drummed under my ear. From my vantage point, Ryler's boots were visible where he'd propped them on the coffee table beside my feet. Last night, he'd covered us with the blanket but at some point, during the evening, it had shifted. Slipping off to the side. Ryler's right pant leg had ridden up. Confusion clouded my head as I tried to comprehend what I was seeing.

Where his skin, or even a sock, should have been, a black metal rod poked from the top of Ryler's boot. My head lifted slowly, my gaze focused on Ryler's feet. I tried to remember a time when I'd seen him without shoes on, or in shorts. I'd seen him without his shirt on. But that was it. That faint squeak I'd heard...all this time I'd thought he'd worn a leg brace. Not a prosthetic.

Without looking, I knew the moment Ryler awoke. When he saw what I was seeing. His body went from relaxed to rigid in less than a heartbeat. Moving tenderly, I sat up and turned. Horror and panic raced across his features, then faster than a bullet he shot off the couch. My ribs protested with his sudden movement. Shiv jumped, growling from being startled awake. He stood between Ryler and me, growling still, no doubt trying to figure out what was happening, what had alerted him.

Ryler's chest was heaving as he raked his hands through his hair, leaving it in disarray.

"Ryler," I began.

"No, no, no, no...," he whispered. My mouth opened, my lungs drawing in breath. "No!" he fairly growled, eyes bright with unspent emotion.

"Ryler, just talk to me!" Heated anxiety laced my own words.

He shot me a hard look, then spun for his room, slamming his door behind him.

Shock left me cold, then hot. *This.* This is what has been between us all this time. This is what has sent him running from me each and every time we'd get close. Chief had said Lorna, Ryler's wife, had left him, unable to handle the wounds and scars he'd earned as a Ranger. She'd left while he'd still been in the hospital. Left before he'd even begun to heal. His wounds must go deep. Soul deep. I needed to see him, talk with him, get him to understand. His wounds and scars didn't matter to me—didn't scare me. I didn't see him as anything other than a beautiful, powerful man. As my rescuer, my hero. My safe haven.

"Ryler!" I fairly shouted from the couch. Of course, he didn't respond. Shiv had laid down near Ryler's closed door, head on his paws. He whined, obviously sensing his owner's distress. Gritting my teeth, feeling obstinately determined, I inched my way to my feet. Swaying for a moment, I considered my course of action. The hallway was about twelve feet from where I currently stood; I just needed to get there. My crutch must have still been in Ryler's bathroom because I didn't see it anywhere. Clenching my jaw against the pain, I took a steadying breath and moved. Hobbling, balanced on my left foot, I worked my way to the edge of the sofa, then lurched to the chair, cursing his stubbornness under my breath the entire way.

My next stop was the wall, then one slow, soft, aching hop at a time, I worked my way down the hall. Trembling and out of breath, I made it to his door. Which he'd locked. *Stubborn idiot.* After several long moments, trying to catch my breath, I knocked, starting to feel desperate. "Dang it,

Ryler!" I slapped my palm against the wood, bringing a new throbbing to my limbs. "Open the door and talk with me! *Please!*"

I didn't know how upset he was, whether he was stable or not. Fear made it difficult to think clearly.

"Ryler, *please!*" My forehead thumped against the door, as I fought against fatigue, panic, and pain. "Talk with me. Please."

Without warning, the door jerked open and I fell forward. Had Ryler not been standing right there, had he not been fast enough and strong enough, I'd have hit the floor. As it was, my ribs smarted, bringing fresh tears to my eyes. A sharp moan escaped, and I tried to control my breathing. Ryler cursed under his breath. "Stubborn woman!" His words were laced with so much emotion; I couldn't identify any of it. His fingers dug lightly into my waist, his frustration evident. "Why didn't you just stay put."

"Why'd you run away from me?" I groaned, the throbbing making itself distinctly known.

"You know why." His voice was low now, almost empty.

"Because you're ashamed of your leg, or because you think I'll feel differently now that I know?"

Ryler jerked his gaze down to mine, those blue-grey eyes of his turbulent like storm-tossed waves. After what seemed like hours, but was in reality only seconds, he blinked. "You need to get off your feet. Doc said that leg needs to stay elevated."

"Well, I'm too tired to hop back down the hallway. And I can barely breathe right now, my ribs are hurting so bad. And it's all your fault."

Ryler chuckled under his breath and shook his head. "I'm sorry."

In what was soon becoming habit for the two of us, he carefully, tenderly lifted me in his arms. But this time, instead of taking me back to the couch, he carried me to his bed. Holding me with one arm, he pulled back the quilts and the slate-grey top sheet then set me down. Ryler helped position me against the headboard, then placed pillows under my knee to elevate my leg. He disappeared into the bathroom but returned momentarily with a glass of water. He held out his hand, placing two Ibuprofen in my palm when I'd held mine out in return. Then, he came around the bed, climbing up beside me.

My body and mind registered the shock of being in his bed. Enjoying the feel of the cotton beneath me, his scent all around me. I could have stayed here forever. Could have just closed my eyes and dropped off. But I knew this was a pivotal moment for us and I needed to stay here, stay alert. Still, we sat quietly for several long moments, then finally, Ryler spoke. His voice held little emotion now, almost dull. "You wanted to talk, AJ. So, talk."

I breathed steadily as I gathered my thoughts. "Ryler, I'm sorry. I'm sorry you didn't feel you could trust me, that you ever doubted my affection. You must know this doesn't make any difference to me. At all."

Ryler grunted under his breath and folded his arms over his chest. "It's not that I didn't trust you, AJ. I do. Maybe I just didn't...trust myself to be good enough for you."

"Is that what she told you? Your ex?" I knew I had to tread carefully here, but he needed to know where I stood. How I felt.

Ryler ground his jaw, seemingly struggling with his emotions, with his words. "I've got...a lot of...scarring. Extensive. More than just the leg. It all, it frightened her. It was way more than she could handle."

Shaking my head, I reached for his hand. "I see you, Ryler James Dean. I see *you*. And I'm not afraid. I'm not disgusted. I'm not turned off. In fact, it's quite the opposite."

That caught him. Ryler held still. Hope warred with fear in his eyes as he gazed at me. He cleared his throat and shook his head. "All she could see was the scarring. The wound. She only saw the missing leg. Never me."

"Come here." I tried tugging him closer. "It hurts too darn much to come to you, thanks to my hopping down your stupid hallway." He chuckled under his breath, then rolled onto his side toward me. "I'm not afraid. Not of your wounds, not of your scars, not of you."

He lifted a hand, resting it on mine, gently squeezing before sliding it up my arm, trailing fingers along my throat. He stopped at my lips, thumb tracing along their curves. He raised himself up and leaned over, pressing a soft kiss against the corner of my mouth.

"I see you, Ryler," I breathed against him. "And I want *you*."

He kissed me, gently, his mouth on mine, so very careful with me. "I want you, too, AJ." His voice was no more than a mutter as he trailed heat down my neck to my collarbone. My shivery reaction caused my breath to catch as my ribs complained. "But I think we'll wait for all that. You need to heal and you need to rest. And I need to hunt."

"Hunt?" My eyes snapped open. "What do you mean by *hunt*, Ryler? You mean, like, go after Amber?"

"I mean, go after, find, and destroy the person who took a shot at you on my property."

"Oh, so if it had occurred on my property, that would be just fine, then?"

"You know what I meant."

"Okay, but why do *you* need to hunt? Isn't that for the police to do?"

"This is what I do." He kissed me again, his lips pressed to mine. "What I've been trained and conditioned for."

"Ryler," I exhaled. "I don't...just...just be careful. All right?"

"I will." He assured as he kissed the tip of my nose, then pulled back. "Now, are you hungry? How about I bring you breakfast in bed?"

I'd never had someone bring me breakfast in bed before; I smiled. "That sounds wonderful, actually."

Ryler got to his knees, then leaned over me. My heart lurched in my chest. Carefully, he planted one hand on either side of me, then lowered his lips to mine. Just a light touch. A promise of more to come. And a thought occurred to me, but I wasn't sure how to ask it. Ryler must have seen the question in my eyes because he nuzzled the skin below my ear and said, "What?"

I cleared my throat. "I, uh...I was just wondering...."

"Wondering what?" His mouth moved along shoulder now, making me breathless.

Trying to take a deep breath and failing, I stumbled over my words. "Can you...I mean...does everything still...what I mean to say is, can you, uh," I shrugged as he lifted his head to stare at me. "Are you still able to...you know?"

"Am I able to...?" A gleam was in his eye now.

"You *know.*" My face flushed; I could feel the heat.

That gleam in his eyes shifted, becoming heat, which shifted again, deepening, turning them to molten liquid. "Yes, AJ." His tone was decisive now. "Yes, I am *fully* able to."

"Oh, good," I breathed.

Ryler chuckled darkly under his breath, shook his head, then climbed carefully off the bed. "Relax. We've got time for that. I promise." He nodded over his shoulder towards the door. "I'm going to get you that breakfast."

I offered him a grateful smile and closed my eyes, trying to calm my breathing. Trying to settle my nerves. To think of something else. And, let's face it, there was plenty for me to think about. Like Harley. I should check on her, check to see how Kevin was doing. I'd need my cell for that. I couldn't remember when I'd last had it. Certainly, before the incident. But where?

Thinking back, I tried to remember what I'd been doing before I'd stepped out to go walking that day. *That day*—it had only been yesterday. Yesterday, yet it seemed forever ago. I probably needed to call my mom and Dave as well, let them know what had happened. And Leslie, too. *I really need my phone.*

Just when I'd reached the end of my limited patience, intending to go find said phone, Ryler returned with a tray of food. "What do you think you're doing?"

His sudden reappearance and question startled me. Jumping, then flinching, I pulled the covers back over me. "I just...needed my phone."

Ryler set the tray down on the bed. "Then you ask me to get it. You don't get up."

Still startled from being caught, I snapped as irritation sparked. "I'm not staying here. Like here in this bed, Ryler."

He surveyed me, his gaze somehow heavy, like a touch. "I like you there. In my bed."

I ignored the emphasis he'd placed on 'in my bed.' "Still, you've already set me up in the bedroom upstairs. I don't need to take up your personal space as well. I'm sure you want your privacy."

His blue-grey eyes studied me carefully now. "What brought all this on? Before I left, you were asking if I was able to st—"

"I know what I was asking." I cut him off. "I just don't want to invade your space. Neither of us planned for this, for me to be foisted upon you, and I don't want to, to become a burden that you have no escape from."

He leaned over me, into me, forcing me to meet his gaze. "I don't want to escape, AJ. Far from it. You're not a burden. I don't think you've been foisted upon me. And I *like* you in my bed. A lot." His eyes ghosted across my body, trailing heat as they went. There was a growling tone to his voice as he took a slow, deep breath. "That is a sight I could get used to."

"Oh." I inhaled, wincing as I did. "Okay."

"Glad we got that cleared up." He placed the tray on my lap. "You eat. I'll find your phone."

Ten minutes later he was back, phone in hand. "Found it under the sofa."

"Oh, yeah...I'd been sitting there, then decided I'd needed some fresh air."

"We probably knocked it to the floor last night." Ryler handed me the phone. It was dead. I was just getting ready to ask him to grab my cord from upstairs, when I found it dangling in my face. He plugged that in, then handed me the end. "Thanks," I smiled as I connected the cord.

Ten seconds after I turned it on, the phone buzzed with an incoming text. Thinking it was most likely from Harley, I quickly opened it. The air left my chest in a rush as the blood drained from my face. The text came from an unknown number. "Peek-a-Boo—I see you." With it was a picture. From last night. At the ER. Of me.

"AJ?" Ryler asked. Wordlessly, with trembling hands, I extended my phone. Taking it, he swore under his breath. "She was there." Fear choked me, my lungs didn't want to work.

Ryler sat beside me, taking my hand in his, offering comfort. He dialed his phone and we waited for someone to pick up. "Caleb Andrews, please," he said when the phone was answered. "Tell him it's Ryler—I'll hold." A few moments later, Caleb was on the line. "The bastard was at the hospital last night, Caleb. AJ just got a text from an unknown number, with a picture of her from the hospital." He was a quiet a moment, then said, "Get the hospital surveillance. I want to know who and what we're dealing with." He was quiet again, then nodded. "Let me know as soon as you get something. Yeah, I got it. I know the drill, Caleb."

Ryler ended the call and looked down at me. "AJ, I *will* find this person. And I will end them." He made sure I heard him, that I understood, then rose to his feet, careful not to shake the bed. "Chief is going to get your prescription filled and drop it off later. Are you good for now, or do you need some Tylenol?"

Blinking, coming out from wherever I'd mentally retreated to, I quickly shook my head. I was fine for now and could wait on my prescription. Though fear thrummed through me, exhaustion began to settle in my limbs. I tried to fight it, but Ryler saw. "You can sleep. I'll be right here. You're safe."

Reaching for his hand, I tugged him down, wanting him beside me. Ryler resisted, only to come around the bed and crawl up next to me. He lay down and wrapped his arms around me, tenderly holding me. His breath tickled my neck, just a light caress. His heat soothed me, and before I realized it, I was out.

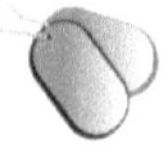

Ryler

AJ's breathing had settled. And while it wasn't deep, it seemed restful. Ryler watched the rise and fall of her chest. And felt his own stir in response. There was so much she brought out in him. So much she made him feel. Things he hadn't thought he'd ever feel again. Now, he needed this threat ended. Needed her safe. Needed her period. The very idea that this was being threatened, that she was in danger, made him see red.

Caleb had reminded him that he wasn't the police and couldn't just take the law into his hands. Couldn't just hunt this person down and kill them. "This is not your mission, Rye," he'd cautioned.

Well, Ryler thought. *The Army may not have sent me out, but this is definitely my mission.* And when he found the one responsible, he'd end them. Painfully. Ryler's phone buzzed. Glancing at it, he saw it was Chief calling.

"'Lo," he answered, keeping his voice soft so as not to wake AJ. She mumbled a little under her breath and turned into him more fully. And he couldn't help the way his mouth hitched to the side, nor the way his body reacted to her. The way his heart had lurched in his chest just now.

"I'll be heading your way in about an hour. Keep an eye out and don't shoot me," Chief replied.

"The bastard was at the hospital last night." Ryler growled, his voice barely more than a whisper.

"Come again."

"He was there."

"You know this how?"

"She got a text this morning with a picture. Of her. At the hospital."

Chief swore in full color, long and loud. "This piece of crap needs to be dead."

"He will be. Caleb's checking the hospital surveillance."

"You know you can't let Caleb be involved, right?"

"I do."

"All right. Stay low. I'll see you in a bit."

Ryler hung up and looked down at AJ. Carefully, he slid down next to her. Shiv would wake him if there was a problem. Right now, he just wanted to hold her. Needed to hold her. He let his eyes trace her features, noting the stitches in her hairline. The faint bruises, and the brighter scratches. Her arm, where it rested in the sling. Her leg, propped on several pillows, in the walking boot. The curve of her hip. The shape of her mouth.

He reflected on the fact that AJ was here. In his bed. Beside him. He'd dreamed of it. Often. And while this was not the way he'd pictured her when she was here, it still brought him a sense of wellbeing. And he wondered if he wasn't the biggest jerk on the planet. For feeling that wellbeing when she was in such pain. Upon further and deeper reflection, he decided the wellbeing was justified. Mostly because she was here beside him where he could keep her safe. Where she was literally within arm's reach. Less, even; and that was an immense relief.

For now, he'd stay here. Just soaking her in. Breathing her in. Keeping watch over her.

CHAPTER TWENTY-TWO
Of Predator and Prey

AJ

Three weeks had gone by, and the police were no closer to finding the person responsible for the attacks on me and Mrs. Carson. They had confirmed, however, that it truly had been an attack. I'd been shot at. And not by accident.

At first, every little sound had me jumping and looking over my shoulder. But eventually, those responses lessened. I chalked it up to being here with Ryler and Shiv. They calmed me. Shiv had taken to following me around the house, his presence a soothing balm. The big hound just had that kind of effect. His fuzzy, warm body, soft sighs, and deep gruff noises, not to mention his entirely expressive facial expressions reduced my inner turmoil. For that alone I'd be forever thankful.

A couple weeks back, maybe a week or so after the attack, Caleb Andrews, the detective assigned to my case here in Sequim, had shown us the surveillance video from the hospital. Everything indicated the person we were looking for was a middle-aged woman with deep red, shoulder-length hair who favored wide-brimmed straw hats, cardigans, and below-the-knee floral dresses.

As I watched the woman walk down the hospital halls, I tried to note anything about her that maybe I recognized. But there was nothing. Was *this* Amber? Surveillance video captured her taking my picture, so it had to be. But this seemingly unremarkable woman was my attacker? The one who'd most likely brutally murdered Mrs. Carson? I couldn't wrap my mind around it. She seemed so...so...entirely not dangerous. Someone I might run into at the grocery store, or the library. Harmless.

Ryler argued that the wide brim of the hat effectively covered her face, so we really didn't know what she looked like. That it might have been anybody. Weirdly enough, Amber had been silent on my blog lately. Her silence made my fans happy, cheering each other on that they'd run her off. The silence made *me* queasy, because I didn't think for a second she'd given up and decided to leave me alone. Or that she'd somehow been stopped already. My head wouldn't accept that either. I knew she was still out there. Biding her time. Waiting.

Amber aside, my wounds were healing. I don't know if I'd say that *I* was healing, though. My mind and heart still hurt, struggling with the truth that someone wanted me dead. But my body was healing at least. Slowly, painfully even, but still, I was on the mend. Deep breathing was no longer terribly painful. My cuts and bruises had mostly faded. The stitches near my hairline had been removed. Though it was still a bit early, I'd removed the sling and now had good function of my arm. I'd been able to upgrade to one of those rolling knee scooters and was happy to see the crutches go.

Josephine had made herself at home in the three weeks since the accident, somehow managing to take over the entire house. She acted like she owned the place, strutting around, fluffy tail curling with an almost seductive flair around every seeming surface she could wrap it. Completely unconcerned with anyone else living under the roof. She slept on Shiv's bed. Ate and drank from Shiv's bowls. Slept on Ryler's bed, even after he'd repeatedly pushed her off. She'd finally worn even him out. Shiv shot many longsuffering looks my way, begging me to get control of her. Though Shiv eventually gave up the fight as well.

My mother had been beside herself, insisting I needed to come back to Florida. That none of this would have happened if I'd chosen a real vocation. Needless to say, I made that conversation short. Dave took the news better, said he was worried, that I needed to be more careful, and that he hoped the attacker was caught. He also offered me a place to stay if I needed one. Harley didn't take it so well. Her voice hit notes I hadn't been aware she was capable of. On a side note, Kevin was doing much better. I tried to get her to focus on that, reminding her, when that failed, that I had Ryler and Chief and was well protected.

Leslie was the one who surprised me. Everyone else pretty much took the news the way I'd anticipated. But Leslie said words I hadn't known *she'd* known. She was normally a calm, gentle person. *This* Leslie was a vicious, raging beast. She ranted and screeched for several minutes, and I'd had to just let her run her course and wait for her to finish. Eventually, she quieted, then calmed down and I assured her the police were doing all they could to keep me safe. And that Ryler was as well.

"Then why hasn't she been caught yet?" Leslie demanded.

"We don't even know who we're looking for, Lez." I tried reasoning.

"You can't just be a sitting duck—something needs to be done!" Her voice was rising again.

"Ryler's working on it." I placated, willing her to remain calm.

"Yeah? What's he doing?"

"He's...he's hunting. Trying to find this person."

"At least that's something," she conceded begrudgingly.

"It is. I'm all right, Leslie. I promise."

Her voice choked and she had to clear her throat a couple times. "I *hate* this, AJ. I hate what you're going through and that you even must go through it. Just promise that if anything else happens, you'll let me know. And don't forget my offer—my place is always open. Always."

Her genuine concern and emotions on my behalf were touching, making me emotional as well. I really had scored the best agent when I'd landed her. "Thanks, Lez. I appreciate it. I'll talk with you soon; promise."

I hadn't lied to her about Ryler. He was out hunting. He and Chief and some of the boys Chief had rounded up. All military trained. They were out nearly every day hunting for this person. They had teams watching Sequim, watching over Jo and the Paiges. Teams monitoring online. And teams covering Jake's mountain. Ryler assured me I was never alone. That someone was always here guarding. A tiny, idiotic part of me wondered if Ryler was really trying to find my attacker, or if he was simply escaping the house. Because I was here and underfoot. But then he'd smile at me, or kiss me, or just hold me, and in his touch, I felt his regard and it helped to dispel my fears and worries.

This morning I'd put a roast in the slow cooker. A feat I was incredibly proud of considering my injuries. In place of potatoes, I'd added several radishes. When cooked like this, you really couldn't tell they're radishes and not potatoes and I was eager for Ryler to try it. I didn't plan to tell him what they were until after he'd eaten. Devious, I know. But I'd learned it's sometimes better to spring things like this on a person after the fact.

Shiv was asleep on the sofa beside me, his head in my lap. Josephine had climbed up about an hour ago, weaseling her way under the book I was reading, managing to take up most of my lap space. Shiv had sighed in exasperation, shifting the tiniest bit to make room for her. Just as I glanced at the clock, Shiv raised his head and looked expectantly at the door.

Not even a minute later, Ryler stepped inside. His eyes found me instantly, and heat poured through my veins. The way those blue-greys turned to liquid silver, the way his face seemed to indicate he'd missed me and was just as glad to see me, I really couldn't help the stupid grin that hit my face.

"Something smells good." He leaned down to kiss my forehead, then ruffled Shiv's head and even scratched Josephine. "You look comfortable. How's the pain today?"

I've come to the recent conclusion that forehead kisses are the best. There's just something incredibly satisfying and comforting about them. And Ryler did them so well. The way he lingered, prolonging the moment. My skin still tingled from where his lips had touched. "Thanks." I smiled, entirely breathless. "That's dinner you're smelling. And I'm pretty comfortable; the pain hasn't been too bad today."

"I hadn't noticed a dinner smell—I was talking about you." He leaned back down, lifting my chin. "You always smell of coconut. And cream." That last was slightly smeared as he kissed me deeply.

He raised his head and I breathed, "I see." His chuckle had me opening my eyes again, unaware I'd even closed them.

"Do I have time to shower? Or is dinner ready now?"

"No, you're fine." I blinked, trying to form thoughts. "You've got time."

One more light forehead kiss and he was gone. Fifteen minutes later, Ryler was back, smelling wet and clean, and *male* and heaven help me....

We ate at the table, and I grinned as he scraped his spoon in his bowl, trying to get every last drop. Ryler caught me grinning. "What?"

Soup dripped down his chin. "Nothing." I smiled bigger. "Just glad you liked it."

"You be glad; I'm going back for more. You want some?"

"I'm full, thanks. You eat up."

"Not going to argue that."

Once our dinner was eaten, and Ryler had washed, then dried the dishes and put them away, we headed to the couch and settled there. Soon both Shiv and Josephine joined us.

"So, how'd things go today?" I scratched Josephine, loving her deep, throaty purr.

"We're still looking." Ryler put his arm around my shoulders, his fingers playing in my hair.

"Do you think she's moved on?" Anxiety had my heart pounding in my chest.

"No." His finger grazed my ear, then he began a slow massage of the muscles at the back of my neck, almost like he knew my fear was spiking. "I don't. This person isn't going to give up. They're smart and they're waiting."

"How do you hunt someone when you don't even know who that someone is?" I couldn't contain the shiver that ran through me.

"Very carefully." His lips found my temple, lingering there. Whiskers scratched against the shell of my ear and my eyes fluttered.

"But...who is the predator, and who is the prey?"

Teeth took hold on my throat. Firm, yet gentle. "*I* am the protector, the defender. He is the prey."

I swallowed, my head feeling light and heavy at the same time. "You're still convinced this is a man and not a woman. How do you know?"

"Gut instinct."

"But what if you're wrong?" Worry had me pulling away to face him more easily.

Ryler held my gaze, seemingly allowing his assurance to settle into my head, my heart. He took my hand in his, threading his fingers through mine. "Regardless of their gender, I *will* stop them. *I* am hunting *them*. And I always get what I hunt." Ryler gently squeezed my hand, just a reassuring touch. And I felt his lips in my hairline again, felt his breath on my neck, and closed my eyes and simply tried to relax.

I hadn't meant to fall asleep; I hadn't told him yet about the radishes. But with Ryler being so warm, and me being full from our meal, my eyes became heavier and soon I was out.

Ryler

Ryler came instantly awake without moving. His ears took in the room around him before he opened his eyes. He scanned the shadows then the woman sleeping beside him. He hadn't meant to fall asleep, but they'd both had a long couple of weeks. Now, something had alerted him, had brought him out of a dead sleep. Some sound. He tried to pinpoint the direction it was coming from. Tried to discern if it was a threat, or harmless.

Shiv was on his feet facing the front door with hackles raised. A low growl emitted from deep within the dog. Ryler carefully shifted AJ off his shoulder, settling her back against the cushions of the couch.

Firearm in hand, he rose, moving silently to the door, his weapon at the ready. Without actually touching anything, he moved to the window beside the door and peered through the slit in the blinds, studying the porch. He saw nothing. Farther out it was too dark, but he wanted a closer look. "Come on, Shiv," he whispered to the hound. "Let's check it out." Dog and man moved quietly through the bedroom to the back patio door.

Before exiting the house, or even touching the door, he did a thorough check there as well. As he reached for the doorknob, his phone buzzed. Seeing it was Chief, he answered, voice low as to not wake AJ. "Whatcha got?"

"Ian was hit."

"Bad?"

"Glancing blow. He'll pull through and pay better attention next time. Whoever they are, they're headed in your direction. Be alert."

"Shiv heard something."

"Stay put, we're headed your way." The call ended abruptly. Ryler made sure the backdoor was still locked and told Shiv to get back to AJ. The hound immediately loped back to the couch with Ryler just behind him. All was quiet. While Shiv guarded AJ, Ryler moved from window to window, never putting himself in the line of fire, scanning, always scanning.

AJ mumbled in her sleep, restless and reaching for him. Ryler quickly, but carefully, sat beside her, easing her back against him. Ten minutes later, Shiv focused intently on the door, head cocked. Moments later a soft knock sounded. Once more, Ryler carefully got to his feet. Gun at the ready, he peered through the side window and saw Chief standing there.

Opening the door, with a finger raised for silence, he motioned the other man inside. Chief nodded as he stepped over the threshold, spying AJ. Ryler jerked his thumb towards the kitchen and the men moved in there.

Ryler pulled a couple bottles of Guinness from the fridge. "What'd you find? Anything?"

Chief took a swallow and shook his head. "Your place is clean. No unfriendlies. I'll keep a couple guys posted for extra eyes and ears, though."

Ryler nodded, taking his own swallow. "Any idea yet who we're dealing with?"

Chief squinted, his gaze somewhere in the distance. "I'd be willing to wager heavy whoever this is they're military trained. Or they've just done a lot of prepping and practicing on their own."

"Why's that?" Ryler's eyes hardened, hearing what he'd long suspected.

"They're too good." Chief finished his drink, silently setting the empty bottle on the counter. "They know exactly what they're doing. It's ticking me off."

"That makes two of us." Ryler finished his own drink, setting his bottle beside Chief's to dispose of tomorrow.

"I'm going to put another call into Darrante, see what he can come up with."

"Let me know as soon as you hear anything."

"Will do." Chief offered a two fingered salute as he moved to the front door. "See you. Stay low."

"Likewise." Ryler locked the door after him, then walked the inside perimeter of the house once more before carefully carrying AJ to bed. He settled beside her, wrapping himself around her, knowing Shiv would alert him if anyone got close.

AJ

I had no recollection of going to bed, but that was where I woke up the next morning. In Ryler's bed with him snoring softly beside me. This had been our arrangement since my attack. Getting up and down the stairs had been impossible and Ryler had refused to let me sleep on the couch. He'd insisted I take the bed; I'd agreed, but only if he too was not relegated to the couch. I'd told him his bed was plenty big enough for the two of us. He'd just have to be a gentleman and keep his hands to himself.

At least his groaning had been of the good-natured sort.

Watching him now as he slept, I told myself it wasn't creepy at all. He was beautiful. A veritable feast for the eyes. Stubble covered his jaw, surrounding those incredible lips. Just the thought of their texture and how they felt on me had a sizzling warmth dance its way through my body. Igniting needs I did my best to stamp down.

My eyes moved over him again. He looked so peaceful as he slept and for that I was grateful. I contemplated what he'd said last night. About being the predator. And Amber being the prey.

Amber is the name cemented in my brain. The name of my tormentor. The name of the faceless, red-haired woman from the hospital. And while Ryler insisted the one he hunted was a man, I just couldn't help but wonder if he was wrong. Or, what if there are *two* people? Both a man *and* a woman? But again, why? Why target me? Whatever the outcome to these questions, I did know one thing. Ryler might be the predator between him and my attacker, but *I* was still the prey. The one being hunted.

That knowledge left me entirely unsettled. I didn't want to be the prey any longer and was heartedly sick and tired of it.

Ryler mumbled in his sleep, bringing my gaze back to him. I let my eyes travel over his sleeping form. Taking in the darkly tanned and toned skin. The tattoos. The sheer animalistic power sheathed in the man beside me. Hunter. Predator. Protector. He possessed that confidence. That instinct. That drive.

I wondered how one acquired those attributes. Was it something born in him that was simply honed over the years? Or was it something he'd needed to learn for survival?

"What're you thinking about?" he rumbled, his voice low and gravelly. My eyes shot to his, but they were still closed. "You've been staring a hole in me for some time now, AJ."

Heat stained my face. "Just thinking, I guess. Sorry to disturb you."

"Don't be sorry. Waking with you next to me...*I'm* not sorry." Ryler cracked an eye open and gave me one of his crooked grins. "Now, what's eating you?"

Taking a deep breath, I let it out in a rush as I formed my words. "Just contemplating the differences between a predator and its prey."

Ryler cocked a brow and studied me silently for a moment before rolling, angling his body, bringing his face into better alignment with mine. "Predator and prey, huh?" He rubbed at his bottom lip. A thoroughly enticing action.

Several moments later, I realized I'd been staring at his mouth and that he'd caught me looking. Heat stained my cheeks and I shook myself out of that train of thought. I jerked my chin at him. "You're obviously a predator. And I'm obviously the prey. Amber, or whoever is after me, is, I suppose, both. And...I'm just wondering how one becomes one or the other."

He played with a stray strand of my hair, wrapping and unwrapping it from his finger. "A predator is one who hunts others, typically for consumption, though some just seem to enjoy killing. The prey is almost always the victim. *I* am not a predator."

"You're hunting Amber, though."

"*That* is an act of self-defense." He gave a gentle tug on that strand. "I'm not hunting because I'm hungry or I just enjoy it. I'm hunting to protect one I care about. I'm more of what you'd call a sheepdog. I guard *against* the predator."

His self-description had my lip curling. "I can't picture you as a sheepdog. Have you ever seen one? They're fluffy. And cute. You're more like a wolf."

"I'm a sheepdog crossed with a wolf. How's that?" His brow lifted again.

"With a lot of that wolf inside." I conceded.

"Lots." Something sparked and heated in Ryler's gaze, turning those blue-grey eyes to liquid silver. Making my stomach flutter. Carefully, he leaned closer, his hand cradling the back of my head. Warm lips covered mine, moved, opened, and for a moment the kiss was primed to explode. I was primed to explode. Then Ryler pulled back, his eyes searching mine for a brief moment. It was like a shutter opened. His eyes had shifted, had become solid steel, and against my mouth he growled low and menacing as his fingers tightened in my hair. "I *will* find this person. And I will *end* them."

A chill crept down my spine at the promise in his voice, the words he used. Ryler meant it. Every word of it. He planned to kill Amber. And while I could see his point about self-defense, could see that Amber may make this a necessary move, the idea still filled me with no small amount of trepidation.

Even knowing what Amber was capable of, if she truly was the one who'd killed Mrs. Carson and had made the attempt on my life, I was still having a hard time reconciling the image of the woman from the hospital with some vile predator. Maybe that was what made this so difficult. When I thought of a predator, it was something evil, almost demonic maybe.

A cardigan-wearing woman does *not* come to mind.

Unless she was demon possessed.

And now I feel like I've entered an episode of *Supernatural*. Where are the Winchesters when I need them?

Ryler cupped my cheek, his thumb grazing my lip. "Hey, you all right? You just got a little pale."

A breathless laugh escaped as I nodded. "So...how does one *not* be a victim, or prey?"

That thumb swiped over my lip again. "By learning to defend yourself. By not waiting on the police to do it for you."

"You make it sound so simple."

"It is."

"What does that even mean? Not waiting on the police? Isn't that what they're there for?"

"No, actually. Think about it—there aren't enough police to provide protection for each person. The police are there to catch the bad guys after the fact. And only occasionally beforehand, or in the process of."

"So, how does one learn to defend oneself?"

He pressed his lips against my temple. "Self-defense begins in the mind. It's a mind frame. Whether you decide to use your hand, a knife, a rock, whatever, you make up your mind to defend yourself, even if it means hurting the other person."

"Okay." I tried to picture it in my head. Me defending myself. Hurting another person. And I struggled with the image. Ryler must have noticed where my mind was wandering, because he reached for my hand again, gently squeezing it.

When I met his gaze, he said, "Hey, you don't have to worry about that right now. *I've* got you covered. And when you're feeling better and out of this brace, I'll teach you a few things."

"Okay."

Ryler watched me quietly for a few moments, then kissed me quickly before rolling to his feet. Well, foot. He wasn't wearing his prosthetic yet. He was still somewhat shy about letting me see more of him and his wounds, but I didn't want to pressure him. "I'm going to shower real quick, then we can eat something, and then I'm going to teach you how to use a gun. Your brace doesn't need to be off for that."

"Um, what? Like, now?"

"No, not now. After my shower, and after we eat."

"But like with a real gun?" I think my brows were in my hairline at this point.

He chuckled softly. "Well, I suppose we could try a fake one, but I don't know how much good that'd do ya."

Rolling my eyes, I threw one of the pillows at him. "Go shower. I'll figure out something for breakfast."

CHAPTER TWENTY-THREE
Not Your Damsel

AJ

So, it turns out guns are really not that scary. Well, not after you learn to handle one at least. After breakfast, Ryler pulled out his weapon, ejected the magazine, removed the round from the chamber, and placed all of it on the kitchen table where I was still seated. My eyebrows rose as he reached behind the fridge and pulled out a second gun. "Insurance," he said indicating the weapon in his hand.

Ryler put this gun down next to the first one. "This one," he said, tapping the one he normally carried. "Is a Sig P220 in a .45. And this one," he tapped the other, "is a Springfield XD.40. Now, don't let any of that confuse you. Look at it like the difference between a Ford and a Chevy. Just different makes, but both do basically the same thing."

"Okay." I nodded, ignoring the way my stomach fluttered.

"Now, before we head out back to the range, let's just go over a few things first. Gun Anatomy 101, if you will."

"All right."

"First rule about using a firearm," Ryler said, standing beside me, one warm hand on my shoulder, one leaning on the table. "Is to remember it's not a toy. Nor is it something to be feared. A gun is a tool. And a tool can be used for both good and evil depending on the intentions of the one using it. Respect a gun, but don't fear it. Next, always assume a firearm is loaded unless you yourself have personally just unloaded it. Third, never point a gun at something or someone you're not willing to destroy. I mean that."

He squeezed my shoulder gently. "When you point that gun at something, or someone, it had better be because you intend to destroy them."

He let that information soak in before moving on, tapping a finger against the handle of the gun. "This is the grip and this is the barrel—bullet comes out here. This is the trigger guard...," Ryler indicated each part of the firearm one piece at a time. Then he showed me how to put everything back together, including racking the slide. And had me take them apart, meaning ejecting the magazine and the round in the chamber. He had me do this several times in a row until I felt confident in what I was doing. He even had me do it with my eyes closed, telling me I may need to use a gun in the dark, when light wasn't possible.

Once we were out at the range behind his house and I was standing in front of the target, my stomach knotted and I wondered if eating had been a good idea. I was pretty sure I had the basics. I knew the parts and the mechanisms. Did I really need to train, or whatever it was he had in store for me? "Can't I just fire like a warning shot or something?"

Ryler snorted. "No. When you shoot, you shoot to kill. Not to scare. Not to maim. Not to wound. When you're being attacked and have to use your weapon, the time for manners and politeness is gone. This is kill or be killed. And by you shooting to kill, *you* didn't put your attacker's life in jeopardy. They did. When they made the choice to attack, they put their own life in danger. Not you. Are we clear?"

I exhaled in a rush and tried to ignore the feeling of lightheadedness the thought of killing someone brought on. "Yeah." I blinked. "We're clear."

"Good. Now, another thing to remember is to keep your finger off the trigger until you're ready to fire." I nodded, swallowed, then inhaled, still trying to banish my nerves. "Another consideration is to know, or at least be aware of, what's *behind* your target. Know the path your bullet will take. What, or who you might hit. Now, I know that's a lot to take in, and it'll make more sense once you're actually firing, but any questions so far?"

I shook my head.

"All right. Let's get you shooting."

Ryler showed me where and how to stand and made sure my eye and ear protection fit properly. Then he handed me the Springfield and as I took it from him, I reminded myself to keep my finger off the trigger and that this was a loaded gun. "Now, extend your arm out, not quite that far." He stood to my left and adjusted my grip, bringing my left hand up to support my right, aligning my thumbs. "Point the end of the barrel, sort of like you'd point your finger at the target, aiming where you want to hit and pull the trigger. We'll figure out what needs to be adjusted as we go."

I nodded, not quite able to speak. Ryler stood directly behind me now, his hands resting lightly on my hips. His grip was reassuring and surprisingly, only mildly distracting. Taking a deep breath, I looked at the dark silhouette of the target in front of me. Noting the outline of the human figure, the circles showing which areas were most likely to stop an attack and pulled the trigger. My bullet hit the target! Just over the right elbow of my assailant. In the white.

While I hadn't been expecting a dead-center hit, I'd been hoping I'd do better than a complete miss. Ryler wasn't fazed, however. He just had me readjust and continue shooting. I don't know how many boxes of ammo we went through, but I did a lot of shooting. Ryler had me shoot with both hands, then one, then the other. He had me shoot while seated. While laying down. On my back, my stomach, and on both sides. He had me take my time and aim, correcting my index finger placement and my grip. He had me fire rapidly until I'd emptied the entire magazine. Then he had me fire my shots in a pattern. Three shots, one, two more, then three more, and so on until I was empty. And every so often he'd have me disassemble my weapon, then reassemble and continue firing.

Two or more hours later, when I was beginning to feel all the shooting, he called it a day. And though I was sore and tired and my mouth was dry, a sense of pride coursed through me. I'd done it. I'd shot a gun. And I'd improved and had been hitting my target. Slowly tightening my grouping had been Ryler's words. And as we made our way back to the house, I thought rather smugly, *I'm no one's damsel.*

A certain kind of invincibility, a sense of power almost settled over me with the knowledge and ability to wield a weapon with confidence. I wasn't contemplating going vigilante and taking on the underworld, nor should anyone really, but I did feel pretty good about being able to defend myself if the need arose. And hopefully, if it did—and it very well could—I wouldn't be the one cowering in the corner, trying to find cover, and praying the police arrived in time.

Ryler

Ryler monitored AJ as they walked along the path to the front door. She was tired and a little slow in her movements, but there was a difference in her walk back to the house. Her shoulders, though weighted with fatigue, were pulled back. There was a spark in her eye. She was proud. As she should be. AJ handled today well. Really well. She was an apt student and showed a lot of promise. Ryler reached for the door, opening it for her. "How about you hit the shower first, and when you're done, I'll shower, then let's go to town and have dinner."

"That sounds *amazing*. Could we? I haven't been to town in forever!"

He grinned. "Go on; go shower."

Forty-five minutes later, Ryler'd helped AJ into the Bronco, and they were headed to town. He'd already called Chief, informing him of their plans. He drove them to the Dockside Grill where they'd enjoyed a leisurely meal of fresh seafood while the sun set in radiant display across the John Wayne Marina. Afterwards, they headed to *Charlie's*. Chief greeted them as they came in. He shook Ryler's hand, then carefully pulled AJ in for a hug. "Missed you, kid"

"Missed you, too, Chief." AJ returned the hug.

As they sat and talked, just catching up, Ryler began to feel...well, he wasn't sure just what he was feeling. But it was something. Pressure seemed to accumulate in his chest. Circling and making itself known. There was a strength behind it. Tension building. And it wasn't entirely unpleasant. He watched AJ as she laughed with a couple of regulars; men well into their sixties. The age difference didn't seem to bother them in the least. They pestered her with questions and flirted shamelessly. Ryler let his eyes ghost over the graceful curve of her neck, where it met her shoulder. And needed to touch and taste.

He watched as she threw her head back and laughed. Laughed until moisture spilled from her eyes. He shook his head slightly, feeling his own lip curl. It had been like this right from the start, the energy around her, the contagion. Ryler wasn't jealous. In fact, he was enjoying her enjoyment. Her pleasure was his pleasure. And as he watched her smile and laugh, he had a strong desire to hold her in his arms. To feel her body pressed to his. It'd been a while since he'd tasted her, and his mouth missed her, missed that flavor that was all AJ. His hands itched, and he longed to soothe them on her skin.

Rising from where he'd been seated, Ryler made his way to her side. AJ smiled at his approach, and something in his look caught her, had her breath visibly catching. And suddenly it was too noisy, too crowded, and he was ready to be alone with her. She rose to meet him, her gaze locking with his. They said quick goodbyes and Ryler led her out the door to the Bronco.

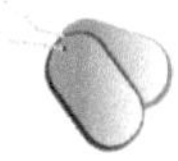

AJ

Ryler's hand in mine was warm and comforting, and yet still somehow managed to bring a level of excitement as well. Each brush of his thumb across my skin, sent heat through me as we drove home. The Bronco was filled with the scent of him, tickling my senses as Bob Seger growled and crooned softly from the speakers. I breathed slow and deep. But rather than ease the pressure, it seemed to only build it. Adding new layers with each breath I took. In an effort to relax, to bring a much-needed level of calm, I thanked him. My voice came out low and throaty, revealing my tension. "That was...tonight, getting out, was so very needed."

Ryler squeezed my hand, whether in response to my words, or to what I was feeling, I didn't know. After a moment or two he said as his eyes traveled leisurely over me before returning to the street, "I was glad to do it. You know, you're beautiful when you laugh. Well, you're beautiful regardless, but tonight...." He squeezed my hand again, then lifted it to kiss along my knuckles.

"You're not half-bad yourself." I shrugged.

Ryler chuckled, his eyes crinkling. Then swore under his breath. His voice held just enough violence that I jerked my gaze from our enjoined hands to his face. But he was staring through the windshield at something ahead of us. Following his gaze, I took in the sight of the car parked in the driveway, dangerously close to Jake's house, completely engulfed in flames.

The Bronco slid to a stop and Ryler snarled. "Keep the doors locked. Dial 911, get the fire department up here, STAT. I'm going to see if I can put it out. Stay here. If something happens...," he trailed off as he looked down at the walking boot on my still-healing leg. And slammed his hand against the steering wheel. "Son of a...you can't drive. I never should have taken you out tonight."

"Ryler?" My voice trembled, as I tried keeping up with his train of thought.

"You're in danger. This is most likely a setup, or trap. I need to get you out of here." Ryler slammed the Bronco into reverse and got on the line to Chief as he sped down the driveway. He reached over and gently pulled me as far down as the seatbelt and my ribs allowed. "Keep down, just stay there."

"Chief!" he cried as the other man answered. "Get a fire truck to Jake's, STAT. There's a car on fire in the driveway. I've gotta get AJ out of here. Have your boys check out the area, make sure it's secure."

The call ended as suddenly as it had begun. "Where are we going?" Panic was taking hold. "What about Shiv? And Josephine? And the house! We need to go back!"

"No!" Ryler kept one hand on me, holding me down, one hand on the steering wheel. "Chief and the boys will take care it. I just need to get you to safety."

"But, but we could go the back way. We can't leave them there!"

His hand caressed now, no doubt attempting to soothe. "AJ, it'll be all right. Just let me get you somewhere safe."

The euphoria from earlier, over having learned to handle a weapon and with proficiency, faded fast under this new assault. *Would this nightmare never end?* Ryler drove long into the night, repeatedly checking the rearview, making sure no one followed us. After what seemed like hours, but was probably much less, he pulled the Bronco off the road, killing the engine and lights. Then we waited. For what, I didn't know. Several minutes went by as my heart pounded out a steady rhythm. "You can sit up now. Just...sit still and...stay here. I'll be right back."

He was out of the Bronco before I could respond and I tried to ascertain what he was doing, but it was too dark to see. He'd walked towards the rear of the vehicle, disappearing into the gloom. The minutes ticked by agonizingly slow as I waited for him to return. When he did, he climbed in and started the engine once more, then pulled back onto the highway.

"What's going on?" I cleared my throat and continued. "What were you doing?"

"Making sure no one followed us, even with their headlights off."

"What...who's car do you think that was?"

Ryler scratched at his head, his movements indicating irritation. "I don't know...could be any number of possibilities."

"Such as?"

He glanced at me, then back to the road. His hand reached for mine. "AJ, you need to try and relax. And trust me. I won't know anything, *we* won't know anything until Chief, and the Fire Marshal and the police are finished with their investigation."

"I understand that, Ryler. But I'd still like to know what you think. Who, or what do you think that was?"

"Obviously the car didn't end up there by mistake. Someone drove that car there and set it on fire. Now, my money is on your attacker. Whoever they are. What the purpose was for this act, I don't know."

I faced the front again. "Where are we going?"

"Chief has a hunting cabin. There're only a handful of people that know of it. We're headed there. It's the safest place I could think of until we know more."

Ryler squeezed my hand again, no doubt offering reassurance. I gave him a small smile and leaned back in my seat. The headlights illuminated a sign indicating we were entering the Olympic National Forest. Ten minutes later, we turned right off the highway onto a dirt track. We followed that for maybe a mile then the cabin came into view. It was single story and square-shaped.

Ryler shut the engine off and we sat quietly for a moment or two. Then, wordlessly, he got out and came around to my side. Helping me down from the Bronco, he led me to the cabin door. A couple minutes later, we were inside and he'd closed the door and hit the lights.

The cabin was simple with a strong sense of mancave. Two mismatched and well-loved couches, a wood stove, a kitchen, and a bathroom. The color scheme was varied shades of green and brown. Ryler shook out and swept off the cushions of one couch, then turned to me. "Not sure when the last time this place was used, but it should be free of spiders."

Instead of sitting on the couch—the word spiders cured me of any desire to sit on the couches—I headed for the table in the little kitchen. A shiver skated down my spine as everything hit. Seeing me tremble, Ryler headed to the wood stove. First came the crackle of the flames, then heat began to permeate the small room. As I began to warm up, exhaustion settled over me like a heavy blanket.

Ryler wrapped his arms around me, tugging me close. His hands trailed up and down my spine, seemingly trying to get the blood flowing. We stood like that for several minutes and gradually the tremors stopped. "I'm going to check in with Chief, then I'll see what he has in the way of provisions. He generally keeps this place well-stocked."

"How long do you think we'll have to stay here?"

"Hopefully no longer than tonight."

I nodded and he pulled his cellphone out. "Hey," he said when Chief answered. "We're here. No one followed—I made sure of it. What've you heard so far?" He was quiet for a moment, listening to whatever Chief had to say. Then, "A body? Man, or woman?"

My heart skipped. A body? *What?*

"All right," Ryler continued. "Keep me posted."

"Ryler, was...what was that about a body? Who died?"

"They found a body in that car. They can't tell who they were, if they were male or female. The coroner will be doing some tests, trying to identify the person. Meanwhile, the police are running the plates."

"There was a body in the car." I needed to verify that piece of information. "That's what you're saying, right?"

"Yes. That's what Chief said."

"But...who could it have been? Do you think it was Amber? Do you think she killed herself in my driveway?"

"I think there was a body. That's it. I don't like to speculate."

"But, maybe...maybe this is all over with...maybe...."

Ryler took my face in his hands and gently kissed my mouth. "AJ, shhhh...don't think about it. Don't...just relax. Speculation does nothing to help."

I couldn't help the tears that formed and fell from my eyes. Today was filled with such highs and lows. My mind seemed broken, somewhere beyond exhaustion. Thoughts refused to formulate into any sort of action.

My limbs were heavy, useless. Ryler caught me as I sagged. He lifted and carried me to the couch. Then he sat with me in his lap and just held me. His hands stroked my back. His mouth pressed against my temple. Every touch brought comfort and kept me sealed in reality. Still, I was exhausted. My eyes drooped, and I let the exhaustion take me.

CHAPTER TWENTY-FOUR
Find Me

AJ

The sun was just brightening the blinds when I woke and tried to place where I was. Then, as my eyes traveled the unfamiliar room, as everything came crashing back, I jerked upright. Ryler was instantly awake, his arms tightening around me where I'd been resting, still on his lap, still in his arms. "It's all right. I've got you."

I cleared my throat. "What time is it?"

Ryler glanced at his watch. "Just after seven. You hungry?"

"Not really."

"Come on...you should eat something."

Sighing deeply, I agreed, knowing he'd have his way regardless. Ryler stood with me still in his arms, then set me on my feet. He took my hand and led me to the table. Before sitting, I stretched, trying to loosen up. "Have you heard anything else?" I asked as I sat down.

Ryler pulled a canister of coffee out of the cupboard, then ran the water in the sink for a moment or two, before he filled the coffee pot. As he placed the filter in the maker, and measured out the proper amount, he said, "No. Chief checked in to see how we were doing, but there's been no news. We'll eat, freshen up as best we can, then we need to get to the police station for a statement."

Nodding, I just sat quietly, listening to the coffee as it percolated. Two birds chirped happily, fluttering around outside the kitchen window. I watched them, lost in thought. We left about an hour later and headed back to Sequim. The sun shone brightly through the trees as we turned onto Jake's drive. My heart was in my throat, wondering how that beautiful house had fared. If the fire had destroyed it. As the trees gave way and the house came into view, I had to choke back a sob. It was still standing, though the side nearest to the garage was blackened and somewhat damaged. We got out and looked around. Ryler held my hand, keeping me grounded, keeping me secure. The car was gone. Only a damp, blackened area remained to mark it had been there.

The fire marshal was still there. He walked toward us, clipboard in hand. As he reached us, he shook Ryler's hand in greeting. "Rod," Ryler said.

"Ryler. It's been a while. How are you?"

"I'll be a lot better when you give me the status on this place."

Rod looked in my direction. "You must be Jake's kid. I've heard a lot about you." He extended his hand to greet me as well.

I tried to keep the emotion out of my voice. "AJ. How's my house?"

Rod turned to the structure. "It's basically fine. Only has some superficial damage, though the wall there near the kitchen will need to be replaced. Could've been much worse. Glad you're all right."

Ryler squeezed my hand. "We'll get it fixed, AJ. It'll be good as new. No worries."

Nodding, I turned back to the house. Tuning out the conversation between the two men, I just let my eyes travel over Jake's house. The idea of losing this house somehow seemed equivalent to losing Jake all over again. And even though I have no real memory of him, being here, in his house, had felt like I knew him. Or, at least, that I'd been getting to know him. And the thought of losing that made me want to vomit. It cracked my heart right down the middle. I had to take several deep breaths. Arms wrapped around me from behind. Ryler pulled me into his chest, one arm around my waist, the other across my collarbone. And he just held me. He let me work through my emotions. Occasionally, he'd kiss me. At my temple, behind my ear, on my neck. And all the while, he just held me.

After several minutes, I pulled away and nodded. Ryler hollered to Rod that we were leaving. The drive to his cabin was a silent one. I knew we'd need to drive back into town; there was still our statement for the police.

When we arrived back at Ryler's cabin, Chief and his boys were waiting for us. They'd thoroughly searched it and made sure the animals were all right. Now, they sat on the porch, watching as we pulled up. Shiv charged toward us, nearly barreling Ryler over in his greeting. His deep-throated bark booming, tail wagging. Ryler knelt and affectionately grappled with him. My eyes pricked with fresh tears. I'd been so worried about the animals. Shiv came to me next, whining in his excitement to see me. He rubbed against me like a huge, vibrating feline.

Chief pulled me in for a hug, then gently patted my back. "Go on in, AJ. It's safe. I've made sure of it."

Nodding, I thanked those standing there, then headed inside. I needed to see Josephine. And then, I wanted a long, hot shower.

Ryler

Ryler watched her walk away, saw her close the door, then turned to Chief. "What do we know?"

"The body is male."

Ryler's eyes tightened. "And the car?"

"Still working on that."

Ryler thought for a moment, then asked, "Darrante come up with anything else?"

"Not as yet, but he's still digging."

"All right." Ryler nodded his gratitude.

Chief glanced towards the house. "How is she?"

Ryler ran his hands over his head in agitation. "She's freaked. Though she's trying not to show it. I want that bastard yesterday. He should have been dead already."

"What are we missing?" Chief leaned against the railing, arms crossed.

"That's the question now, isn't it?" Ryler sat on the step, and as he did, the others settled down around him, waiting to hear what new direction this mission would take. They were all former military. Highly trained. And no stranger to violence. Franklin, or Red as he was known by, due to his deep red hair, had been with the Seals and served three tours. Then there was Alvin, an old-school Marine. And lastly, there was Laars; he'd been with the Army, and then the Washington National Guard.

Alvin leaned a broad shoulder against the side of the cabin. His dark eyes were always scanning the area. He crossed his arms over his chest, the tats barely discernible on his dark skin. "Lay it out for us, Rye," he rumbled in his deep voice.

Ryler looked them all over, then launched into a short, yet detailed description of the situation. They talked for several minutes. Discussing and debating various options and possibilities. At the end of it, the only thing that had been settled was that the utmost caution would need to be taken and that this person be stopped quickly.

AJ

It was two weeks before we heard anything more from the police. Ryler and I had gone to the station and given our statements the day after the fire. Afterwards, the detective had just advised we go home and wait. To stay safe. It had been a quiet two weeks. I read and wrote a lot, and finished the first draft of my latest piece, *Rebel Ranger*. I'd sent it off to a few Beta Readers, along with a handful of questions for them to answer.

And now, as I sat on the couch and watched as Ryler opened the door for Detective Andrews, I tried to calm my pulse. After greetings were made, Caleb sat across from me on one of the armchairs. "We received the preliminary forensics report back this morning. Thought you'd like to know. The vehicle was a Toyota Camry; it was registered to a Paul Ashland."

"*What*?" I gasped, my heart clenching painfully. "Paul's *dead?* Oh no, no, no." Ryler pulled me into his shoulder, and I buried my head for a moment.

"Ms. McAdams, how did you know Mr. Ashland?"

Facing forward once more, I swallowed. "He...he was a housemate of mine back on Coronado."

"Was he here visiting you?"

"No." I shook my head, fighting tears. "No, he wasn't."

"Do you know what he was doing in this area?"

"Um, yes." I took a breath and Ryler gently squeezed my shoulder, pressing me closer. "We, we saw him a few weeks back."

"At the benefit ride." Ryler added.

"Paul is, was," I stumbled over the word, "a travel writer and pho-tographer. He was here doing a piece on the Olympic National Forest."

"When did you see him last? Be as specific as possible, if you can."

"At the ride." I told him. "It was mid to late afternoon. Maybe around three?" A shiver shook me and I was glad for Ryler's presence. I hadn't wanted Paul to get involved in any of this. I hadn't wanted anyone hurt. Now Mrs. Carson and Paul were dead. Because of me. He'd always been so private and quiet. And now...now he was dead. "Are you certain that the body in the car was Paul?" Maybe they'd made a mistake. Maybe it was someone else.

"The car was registered to him. We found photography equipment and a suitcase with his clothing inside. And the victim was the right height, age, and gender."

"When will you know for certain?" Ryler asked.

"We're waiting on dental records right now. Depending on how back-logged it is…it shouldn't take more than a month at the most."

The detective stayed another ten minutes, then left with a promise to be in touch when he received more information. Ryler walked him out, and while he was gone, I went to my laptop. I wondered if Amber had anything else to say. She'd been quiet, no new comments, though I hadn't checked since the day before yesterday.

Sure enough, early yesterday morning, she'd posted a new message. "How many more before you pay attention?"

My breath lodged in my throat, and I felt equal parts fear, anger, and anguish course through me. "Find. *Me*," I whispered to the screen, past the lump in my throat. "You stupid, sorry excuse for a human being." My voice shook with emotion, and tears ran down my face. "You come after *me*! You find me!"

"AJ?" Ryler asked from behind me. "Hey now…talk with me. What's going on?"

I hadn't even heard him return. My mind had been consumed with Amber and the destruction she was causing. "I'm done running, Ryler. If Amber wants me, she can have me. I'm done with others being hurt because of me. I'm just done. I won't go through it any longer."

Ryler pulled me to my feet; his hands grasped my face, holding me carefully. "Now, what kind of crazy talk is this? Are you quitting? Giving up? You're going to let her win?"

"I won't have anyone else hurt because of me, Ryler. No one else."

"No one else will be hurt. We'll get this person. We'll stop them."

"You don't know that!" I screamed. Ryler pulled me against him, his arms locking like vices around me. I struggled, trying to free myself. But he just held me. Held me together as I fell apart. As I shattered.

"Shhh…," he whispered against my ear. "It's all right, AJ. We'll figure this out. I promise you."

"I can't go through this any longer. I'm just so tired. I can't…." And then the sobs started. They shook me, tore me apart, and drained me.

"I know." He pressed his lips to me again and again. "I know and I'm sorry. Let me take care of you. I'll take care of this."

Eventually my tears ran their course and I was dry. Hollow. Like I was simply a shell. My heart and my throat ached. This time when I pulled back, Ryler let me. Though he didn't let me get far. Only about an arm's distance. He took one look at me and pulled me close again, let his mouth linger at my forehead. "Come on."

He led me into the bathroom and shut the lid of the toilet, then settled me on it. He ran the water in the sink until it was ice cold, then soaked a washcloth in the icy stream, before wringing the cloth out lightly and gently wiping my face. He rinsed the cloth once more, wrung it again, then handed it to me. Taking it gratefully, I held the cool cloth to my hot face, savoring the way it felt, the way it refreshed.

When I was done, he gave me two Ibuprofen and a glass of water. I wondered if he could read the headache pounding inside my skull on my face. Then he lifted and carried me to bed. Only he settled onto it first, then simply held me. His heartbeat soothed, calmed, and restored. My eyes became heavy, drifting downward, until I finally gave in and let go.

Amber

Amber sat before her computer screen and fingered her red hair. She looked through the numerous photographs she'd collected of the object of her desire. Her heart swelled with emotion and longing. If only AJ would be sensible. None of this needed to happen. But AJ was being childish and selfish. And now Amber had to be firm with her. And people were going to get hurt. *You are mine, AJ.* You belong with me. I will find you and then you will know me. And love me.

"And," she spoke into the silence of her room, "if that boy is keeping you away from me, then I'll have to stop him. I'll have to hurt him, too."

CHAPTER TWENTY-FIVE
Crosshairs

Ryler

Ryler stood beside the bed, his gaze on the woman asleep there. AJ was in the crosshairs, and he would give anything to keep her safe. How, was the question. His one lead had unraveled last week. Now he was back to square one. And AJ was still in danger. Silently, he checked the locks at the back door, then made his way to the front room. He brewed a pot of coffee and watched as a doe with two fawns made their way across his lawn.

It was just after seven on a Thursday morning. The last week or so had been stressful and Ryler was feeling it. His body was stiff and sore, and despite lying beside AJ, her warmth pressed against him, he'd needed to get up and move, stretch, and flex. Amanda's IP address had pinged a half dozen times this last week. Once, here in Sequim, then in Port Angeles, Seattle, Forks, Quinault, and Whidby Island. Chief had sent teams out on recon and told us to stay close. What this sudden flurry of activity from her meant was anyone's guess, but it couldn't be good. Everyone was stressed and stretched thin. Something had to give and soon.

Ryler refilled his mug, then returned to the window. He took in the exterior, studied the trees and shadows, looking for anything out of place. The mounting tension, the pressure in the air, felt like a storm bearing down on them. He just wanted to control when, where, and how it landed.

Soft arms came around him from the back. AJ's hands crept upwards, splaying across his chest. Her front to his back. He closed his eyes and exhaled as his hand slid to cover hers. This was heaven and he wouldn't let it be destroyed.

AJ

Ryler was strength. He was purpose and energy. I held all of that in my arms and it was a heady feeling. As I listened to his breath, I soaked in the warmth and safety he radiated. Briefly, I closed my eyes and simply held onto that safety. Let it engulf and consume me. Then, as he drew me around to the front of him, and as my head nestled against his chest, and his hand came up to cradle the back of my skull, I let the tension go.

My breath came easier than it had these last couple of weeks. Fear no longer suffocated me. I believed in him. Believed that things would be all right. That he would take care of me. That Amber would be stopped.

"Coffee's hot. You want a cup?" he rumbled quietly.

"Yeah, that sounds good." I blinked through a yawn. "Then maybe we can sip it on the porch?"

"It's a bit frosty out there this morning. Only in the upper-thirties...are you sure?"

"The sun is out. How cold can it be with the sun out?"

"Plenty. But, yeah, we'll go out there."

Ten minutes later, I was rethinking my beliefs on the sun and the cold. Shivering, I leaned closer to Ryler and sipped my coffee.

"Cold?" he teased.

"No," I shivered. "I'm fr-freezing. How is it possible to be this cold in this much sunlight? Where is the warmth?"

Ryler chuckled. "We're in the north, you know? It gets cold here."

Sighing, I sipped more of my coffee and leaned even closer. "You know what I miss?"

"What's that?" He rubbed his nose along the back of my ear.

"Heat. The sun. The kind that bakes your skin. I miss the hot sand and the sound of the waves crashing."

Ryler became still. I hadn't thought about what I was saying until after I'd said it. Or that my desires might not be taken as enthusiastically as I'd hoped. "You'd go with me, right? Just for a little bit, just to visit, to feel that warmth?"

He shrugged. "I don't know...I'm not really a hot sun, beach kind of guy, you know?"

"You wouldn't go?" I turned to face him.

"AJ, come on." He tapped his prosthetic. "Remember? This isn't exactly a beach-fit sort of body."

"I think your body is great. Like, really great." I might have rubbed a hand across his chest to make my point. Just enjoying the muscle there. "And who cares what anyone else thinks. You're not going to be with them; you're going to be with me."

"I get that. I just...the beach isn't for me." He shrugged again.

I opened my mouth to respond, when Ryler's phone buzzed with an incoming call. He checked the caller ID. "Caleb." He answered the call. "Oh, yeah? Whatcha got? Uh-huh. Yeah. Yeah, I got it. I'll let her know. Thanks."

"What is it?" My heart thudded loudly.

"They got the results back on that body. It wasn't Paul. It was a guy that'd gone missing from Port Townsend last month."

"So...so, I'm confused. Does that mean Paul could still be alive? He could still be alive! Are they looking for him?"

"Yeah, they're looking for him."

Hope filled me. Just maybe I wasn't responsible for two murders. My eyes filled with tears. Ryler cupped my face. "Hey, none of that. We don't know what this means."

"I know, but he could still be aliv—" Ryler jerked and something sticky, warm, and wet sprayed up my neck. His hands were dragged from my face as he fell backward down the steps, and I stumbled from his sudden absence. My leg gave way, unable to hold my weight, and I pitched over. Then, as my face neared the wooden planks of the porch, I heard the sharp report echo off the surrounding trees. I knew that sound. Knew what it meant. Had heard it before.

Trying to break my fall, I put my hands out in front of me. My shoulder wrenched with the impact, sending pain through me. And my cheek slammed into the deck. My ears were ringing. My heart pounded. Something was wrong. Something had happened. Ryler. Where was Ryler, what had happened?

"Ryler!" I coughed.

A groan came from somewhere out of sight. Then I heard a rough, whispered cough. "AJ, get inside." Ryler was panting heavy. Blinking, I tried to clear my head. I needed to get to my feet. Ryler needed help. Crawling, dragging myself with one arm, I reached the steps and saw Ryler sprawled there, face down. Deep red stained the back of his grey shirt.

"Ryler!" I reached for him with a sob.

"AJ, listen to me. You need to get inside. Now. Lock the doors."

"Not without you!" Gritting my teeth, I clawed my way to him. Ryler's face was pale. And there was so much blood. He tried to turn over, but his arms gave way. His legs were tangled, so I helped him get them situated, then helped him turn over. "Now, come on. Help me. We need to get inside. Help me, Ryler."

His right arm hung limp at his side, blood pulsing down it. Ryler pushed with his legs, trying to get up those steps. And as he pushed, I pulled. Inch by inch we made slow progress. Four steps had never seemed remotely like a challenge before. Now, they were more like Everest. With much panting and cursing we somehow made it up those steps and into the house. The blood was coming faster now, and Ryler collapsed just over the threshold. Shiv was barking, frantic and in the way. I got the door closed behind us, then hobbled down the hallway and into the bathroom for towels, calling for Shiv as I went.

Blessedly, the big hound came with me, and I was able to shut him in the bedroom. I gathered the supplies I'd need. Towels, bandages, and on a whim, grabbed my box of tampons. I was sure I'd read or heard somewhere that soldiers would use them in the field to stop the bleeding from a bullet hole. I made my way back down the hallway and was halfway there when I jerked to a stop.

Ryler's eyes were on me. Rage and fear warring in his look. The front door stood open. And standing just to the right of Ryler, near the sofa, was a figure. The woman wore a light brown flowy dress with large yellow and white roses printed on it. A cream cardigan sat on her shoulders and nylons were on her legs. Her hair was deep red and hung unadorned, straight past her wide shoulders. I couldn't see her face, angled the way it was.

She held a handgun trained right on Ryler. "Come in, AJ." The voice was high-pitched, and girly, almost sounding put on, or fake. And the tone, the attitude behind it, like she was happy to see me, like she and I were friends. Nausea curled in my stomach and my vision clouded. Still Ryler stared at me.

"Come in and join us." Her singsong voice hardened when I still hadn't moved. "Sit, AJ. Or I'll kill him right now."

Fear had me moving, desperate to keep Ryler safe. "Okay."

Slowly, I made my way to the couch, sitting nearest to Ryler, keeping my eyes on him. The woman moved, pivoting around Ryler, keeping us both in her sights. She closed and locked the door, then walked towards me. Her gait was almost swaying, like she was executing a dance, as opposed to just taking a step. I kept my eyes down, on Ryler, trying to garner whatever his eyes were trying to tell me. The woman cleared her throat expectantly, no doubt wanting my attention. Ryler nodded ever so slightly. So, taking a slow, deep breath, I looked up into familiar plain brown eyes.

"Paul?" I gasped, shocked and even more lightheaded. His palm slapped across my face, bringing tears.

"My name is Amber, AJ." Paul spoke in that girly voice. "Say it. Say hello, Amber." Tears fell as fear choked me and I couldn't get the words past my lips. "Say it!" Paul yelled, a note of hysteria in his voice.

"H-hello, Amber."

"There." He smiled through lips painted a deep red. "Now, you be a good girl, AJ. We're going to spend some time together. You're going to love me, just you wait and see."

Shiv had been barking and snarling at the bedroom door, and I cursed myself soundly for locking him inside. The barking stopped suddenly and we heard the shatter of breaking glass, then a high-pitched yelp. Seconds later, everything went silent. We sat there quietly for several moments, our eyes darting around the room, from window to window. Ryler lay still, though his eyes were bright with pain. "Um, Pa-Amber, may I please help him?" I indicated Ryler, who shook his head. "He's bleeding."

"He's going to be a problem, isn't he?" Paul asked.

"No. No, he isn't." I quickly assured, sniffing back tears.

"Don't *lie* to me, AJ. I won't abide a liar."

"I'm not. Please, I'm sorry."

"I forgive you. Now, I think I'd like a drink—I'm a little thirsty. Would you, please, get me a drink?"

Ryler again nodded. His eyes darted to Paul's gun then back to me. And I remembered the "insurance" gun Ryler kept behind the fridge. Rising to my feet, I turned away and moved toward the kitchen.

"What would you like, Amber?" My voice trembled and I tried to calm it. "I can see what's in the fridge."

As I reached the kitchen, I glanced over my shoulder and froze. Paul stood there—I hadn't even heard him move. Close enough to keep me in sight and his gun trained on Ryler. Swallowing, I opened the fridge and peered inside. "We have, um, iced tea, water, and Guinness."

"Water, please. With ice. And thank you." All politeness, like I was truly being a gracious host. Like he hadn't just shot the man I loved and was holding us against our will.

Pulling a bottle out, I turned back to him, offering it with an outstretched hand.

"I said with ice, AJ. Did you forget? Please take out a glass, add some ice, then pour the water in. Thank you."

I did as he said and once again offered it to him.

"Let's take it to the living room, please." Paul's graciousness was grating. Nauseating. I wanted to hit him. My mind raced, trying to figure out how to stop him. How to get help. How to aid Ryler before he bled out.

After I was settled back on the couch, again as close to Ryler as I could get, he slid his hand ever so slowly, lightly gripping my ankle. Barely keeping from jerking at the unexpected touch, I glanced down. His eyes shifted to the easy chair near the fireplace, then back to me again. He did this several times, until I finally caught on.

He must have another gun somewhere near the chair. How to get it? I needed Paul to relax. To trust me. I needed him to talk. "Um, Amber," I turned to Paul. "Have, have we ever met before? Like, how do you know me?"

"Oh, AJ...I'm your biggest fan. I've read all your books. And I've followed you faithfully, but then you left. You left me, and that wasn't very nice."

"I'm sorry, Amber. I didn't know."

"Don't *lie* to me! You did know, AJ. I told you. We talked."

"When?"

"On your webpage. You talked with me. I told you it was selfish for you to leave. But you wouldn't listen."

"I-I'm sorry."

"It's all right. I don't blame you. I blame *him*. He took you away from me."

I needed to get Paul's attention off Ryler. "Amber, do you know Paul? I used to know him. We lived in the same house."

"Paul?" He seemed momentarily confused, blinking several times.

"Yes, Amber. Paul. He lived with me in the big house on Coronado. With Mrs. Carson. Do you remember her?"

"She was mean." Paul sounded petulant, like a spoiled child. "She wouldn't tell me where you'd gone. And she screamed...a lot. It was all very annoying. I was glad when she finally shut up."

Bile surged, and I had to swallow to clear my throat. I blinked back tears and took a fortifying breath. "How do you know Paul, Amber? I'm...I'm worried about him. I haven't been able to reach him. Is he all right?"

Amber, or rather Paul, stared at me silently. Something flashed in his eyes and a thrill of fear shot through me. His hand, the one holding the gun, trembled ever so slightly. "Are you cold, Amber? You're shivering. Would you like me to stoke the fire? Make it a little warmer in here?"

He smiled. Nothing warm or friendly in it. "I've had you both in my crosshairs so many times." He giggled girlishly. "But killing you from afar wouldn't have been very satisfying. I wanted you to see and know me first. You're going to love me before the end, AJ. I just know it."

I swallowed my fear. "Amber, would you like the fire stoked? I don't want you to catch cold."

Ryler

Good girl, thought Ryler. Keep him talking. Keep him distracted. Ryler needed time...he needed....

Ryler blinked, trying to stay focused. If he didn't get the blood stopped, he'd be dead soon. But AJ needed him. He'd made her a promise. Told her he'd end the threat and nothing and no one would hurt her. He'd failed.

Anger scorched him, bringing some much-needed clarity. He hoped AJ found a way to get to the armchair by the fireplace. To the firearm tucked inside it. Another insurance gun. AJ stood then, drawing his attention. He tried to follow her movements, but the strain was getting to him. He had to focus. Had to...

AJ

Carefully, with no sudden movements, I made my way to the fireplace. Kneeling as best I was able, I placed my hand on the seat of the chair, using it to brace myself. My fingertips felt something beneath the cushions, towards the back, against the spine of the chair, and my pulse leaped. That must be the other insurance gun. Keeping my hands and eyes away from its location, I went about my business, opening the grate, gathering more wood, raking the coals. Soon, I had a blazing fire.

Feigning the need to catch my breath before I stood, I sat in the chair for a minute, angling myself in Amber's direction. The gun was now behind my left hip still under the cushion. "Sorry." I apologized as I took a slow deep breath. "I slipped and fell a few weeks back. I hurt myself pretty badly and am still a bit unsteady on my feet. You were telling me about Paul...?"

The look in his eyes was hard as flint. "I don't want to talk about Paul. He has nothing to do with this. I know you never liked him."

"I didn't really know him." I placated, trying to shift my position. "Though we talked a few times."

"Remember what I said about lying, AJ." His tone became stern, before relaxing once more into the girlish sounds he'd been uttering previously. "Now, that's enough resting. You can come back over here now."

Surreptitiously, I slid my left hand behind me, fingers searching. Getting a grip on the pistol, I stood, keeping it hidden against my side, trying to remain calm. My mind ran through all that Ryler had taught me. And I knew I'd have no problem harming another person. Because I was going to kill Paul.

My heart pounded, making me dizzy. Swaying for a moment, I touched my forehead and took a deep breath. Ryler needed me. I could do this. Just like he taught me. My eyes focused on Paul, trying to make my face calm and friendly, and offered him a small smile. Several things seemed to happen at once, then. As I walked through each step in my head, Ryler suddenly coughed, drawing Paul's attention. From one moment to the next, I was moving. The gun lifted and my finger squeezed the trigger; we were no more than two yards apart—I couldn't miss. As I moved, his eyes darted back to me, his gun realigning. Then Ryler rolled and was somehow firing. Paul's body jerked with the impact and flew backward into the couch then lay still. His grasp loosened and the gun toppled to the floor with a thud.

My heart pounded as Ryler reached, drawing Paul's weapon to himself. His movements were slow, measured; he was so pale. I couldn't fathom how he was even moving. When I'd mastered myself and was in no danger of passing out, I stumbled forward. Dropping to my knees at his side, I reached for him as his eyes closed. "Ryler!" He didn't respond and my heart hammered as I felt for a pulse. It was there, but faint.

Sobbing, I dialed the paramedics and waited for what seemed an eternity before the ambulance arrived. During that long wait, I talked with Ryler, told him how much I loved him. That we were safe now. That I needed him. That he couldn't die. I kissed him and lay beside him, trying to keep him warm.

And, just as I heard the sirens, Ryler gripped my hand, my name a whisper on his lips.

CHAPTER TWENTY-SIX
Worth It

AJ

The conference room at the *Hotel del Coronado* was packed. Not quite standing room only, but pretty close. The line from just my table stretched all the way to the doors. The noise from the various vendors, authors, and fellow book fanatics, was close to a dull roar. It was a little overwhelming, but fun, too. I smiled, shook hands, posed for and took pictures with fans, and of course signed each book, poster, t-shirt, bag, or bookmark presented to me. And though there was plenty to keep my mind busy, all the while, my thoughts wandered. Hopefully, no one noticed. My mind was just so full.

Yesterday, when I'd arrived back on Coronado, Harley'd had to work, but we'd made plans to get together for dinner. Then, at dinner...Harley. And Kevin. *Engaged.* Boy, that had been a shock. Not an unpleasant one, just...just one I hadn't been expecting at the time. We'd done a lot of laughing, crying, and squealing.

The noise had only become louder as Harley flashed her ring finger at me. "Whaaaaaat? Are you for real?" The setting was stunning. "It's so beautiful! Why didn't I hear about this sooner?"

"Told you she'd be angry." Harley had elbowed Kevin.

"Forgive me, shorty?" Kevin's face had been radiant as he'd looked towards his future bride.

"Of course!" My heart was still so full of happiness for them. Even now, it still brought a tear to my eye just thinking about it. My girl Harley was engaged. My heart swelled at the thought, at the memory.

And now, today, at the event. The sheer size of the crowds. It was, all of it, a lot to process. I, and the other authors, had been at it for the last three hours at least. I was hoping for a break soon, at least just to pee and freshen up. I'd have to ask Leslie when she returned with another box of T-shirts—one of many I'd shipped down last week before the conference. Leslie had contacted me close to a month ago about doing a signing for the Southern California Book Fest. As it was the middle of January, and Sequim was cold and wet, I'd jumped at the opportunity, nearly crying over the thought of warm sand and sunshine. Not that January was particularly warm and sunny on Coronado, but it was a lot easier to imagine here than up north.

Checking my phone for the time, I saw Ryler's image and smiled. Then had to keep my laughter silent as I remembered my autocorrect faux pas from the night before. Stupid, *stupid* autocorrect.

Ryler was mostly healed now. We both were. My ribs ached occasionally, but not horribly. Ryler's shoulder was still sore, but he did his best not to show it. The bullet had shattered his collarbone and had required surgery. Thankfully, no major internal damage had been done. Just blood loss and torn muscle tissue. Though he was healed for the most part, he'd still opted to stay behind in Sequim. And while I was disappointed, because I missed him so terribly, I understood. I didn't push the point—the man had more than earned his privacy and rest.

Not that he rested much, despite what the doctors instructed. Still, I missed him. I missed the sound of his voice, the way he smelled. I missed his arms around me. I just missed *him*.

And the sad thing? I'd only been gone for two days. I'd be gone for a total of seven days, though. Ah, well. But last night, last night I'd been *attempting* to send him a text, just trying to tell him that I loved him. This morning however, I awoke to Ryler's reply. "I like every you?" he'd asked.

Confused, I'd texted back, "What are you talking about?"

"That's what you sent to me."

What? Then I'd looked at my text. Sure enough, autocorrect struck again. Somehow, as I'd typed the words, "I love you" into my phone, it had corrected itself to say, "I like every you." *What does that even mean?* I'd texted Ryler back, laughing to myself the entire time and explained what had happened. I still hadn't heard back from him, but knew he liked to stay busy. Still, I missed him.

Several more people came through my line. All of them kind, wonderful, generous people. I really did have some of the best readers on the face of the planet. Blessed was putting it mildly. I won't deny that my shoulders would tighten every so often; apprehension making itself known. I tried not to think about it. Tried not to let it get to me. But I couldn't seem to keep Paul off my mind.

What a sick and twisted man. He'd been a twin. His twin sister—*Amber*—had died just after childbirth. The family had never received counseling for their grief, and as Paul grew up, his mind had basically splintered. Especially as his mother had lamented long through his childhood that she'd wished her daughter had been the one who'd lived. Wished that he had died instead. *Who says that to their own child?* And his dad had been useless. Had drunk away his pain and eventually his family as well.

I learned all this well after the shooting, from the detectives handling the case. And while I felt sorry for what he'd gone through, I refused to allow myself to feel guilt over the fact that I'd shot and killed him. Well, Ryler and I had. My bullet had gone through the chest; Ryler's had drilled Paul's temple. How he'd been able to make that shot...it boggled the mind. I could only be thankful.

And Paul, he'd made those choices, not me. Besides, there was nothing I could do about it now anyway. Paul had set everything in motion, bringing us to the point we had reached. He'd chosen to make it a kill or be killed kind of situation. And I'd wanted to live.

Thinking about Paul, wondering at the possible signs that might have been missed and the messed-up life he'd been forced to live, brought to mind my issues with my own mother. She'd never done anything like what Paul's mother had done, but I had to acknowledge the pain she'd inflicted. Not just on Jake, but on myself, too. Part of me was honest enough to understand where she may have been coming from, what her desire had been. As angry as I am over it, as hurt, I couldn't convince myself what she'd done had been out of a malicious heart and mind.

Three weeks ago, I'd tried to make amends, to at least begin to try and repair what was left of our relationship. She'd wanted no part of it. Mom felt I'd chosen Jake over her. She even refused to accept that I was staying in Sequim now. And, in the course of our conversation, somehow, I'd ended up the bad guy and she the victim. It blew my mind how she managed to do that. I'd like to say that we eventually worked things out, but that would be a lie.

Mom refused to listen. Refused to apologize for her part in what had happened. Other than a flippant, "Well, I'm sorry! But he did things, too!" She'd offered no other words to indicate she regretted her decisions. She blamed me for the attack from Paul. Said none of this would have happened had I just stayed in Florida with her. Had I just had a real job instead of writing make-believe all the time. It was at that point it really hit that we may never have a healthy mother-daughter relationship. I couldn't fathom what her fears were, what she wanted from me, but there was something there. Something about me that just ruffled her feathers.

I no longer wanted to ride that emotional roller coaster. It wasn't healthy. Not for her. Not for me. So, I said goodbye. I told her I loved her and said goodbye. Ryler had held me as I grieved over the loss. The realization. Maybe someday in the future, if she got some help, maybe we could try again. But not the way things were right now. Not like this.

Bringing my focus back to the event at hand, I had to give Leslie all the credit. She had given the event staff specific directions about how I liked my display, so there really hadn't been anything for me to do other than greet the readers. She was just good like that and knew me so well. Really, this had to be one of the best events I'd been to in a long while.

Leslie had sat beside me, acting as my assistant basically the whole time. And as she sat back down beside me, the box of t-shirts I was giving away in hand, I said, "Wow, this is insane! I've never seen a crowd like this one. Have you?"

"No." She shook her head. "But I think a lot are here because of what happened, you know. You were in the news quite a lot over the whole thing. People can be morbidly curious."

Thirty or so minutes later, as I was posing for a picture with two sisters, a small commotion came from the back of the line. The crowd was too thick to really see what had happened, but several people began turning, gasping, and craning their necks. My heart skipped a beat, and I had to remind myself it was over. Paul was dead. I breathed deeply, trying to calm my racing heart. People were still turning away, some gasping, mouths covered. Cellphones were now out. I had to fight my desire to stand, wanting to alleviate my building anxiety. Needing to see what the problem was. It took all of my formidable will to remain seated, reminding myself once more that Paul was dead and I was safe.

But then the crowds parted and I saw him.

Shiv trotted towards me, all healed from his injuries when he crashed through the patio door in Ryler's room, trying to get to Ryler, or alert someone of our need. He'd had three large gashes from the glass and had needed surgery. It had been touch-and-go with the big hound, but thankfully, he'd pulled through. My heart and mind had refused to even consider what it might have done to Ryler if Shiv hadn't made it. The vet said, if we hadn't found him when we did, he'd have lost too much blood. I thanked God repeatedly, that I'd had the mind-frame to remember Shiv, alerting Chief to find him as the ambulance rushed us to the hospital.

And now, as he moved towards me, tail wagging and a giant white bow around his neck, I felt tears prick my eyes. What was he even doing here?

Looking beyond the hound, I saw my soldier. My heart stopped completely before coming back to life.

Ryler was in uniform, cleaned and pressed, and he made my mouth water. My goodness the man was good looking. His right pant leg was rolled and pinned up, his prosthetic fully exposed. It had taken some time, but he'd finally shown me his injury. His wounded shoulder had placed him in need of my care, a pill that had been difficult for him to swallow. He'd let me ask my questions, then had instructed me on how to prepare his limb for the prosthetic, how to attach it. And while, yes, there was scarring and much of it, there was beauty there as well. Rugged, masculine beauty. He was beautiful both inside and out and I was fervently thankful he was mine.

Having no recollection of rising, I found myself on my feet. My hands trembled as they covered my mouth and tears leaked from my eyes. Shiv came right to me, his whole body wagging, whining, happy to see me. Trying to give myself time to calm down, I wrapped my arms around the hound's neck and felt a papery something tied with the bow.

It was a note. "I like every you, too."

A sob caught me, even as I laughed. I looked up in time to see Ryler come behind the table and drop to one knee before me. Those blue-greys were liquid heat as they touched me. He took a deep breath, then exhaled. I caught just a hint of something spicy, something minty on his breath. The entire room had quieted, the focus entirely on us. Cameras clicked and flashed all around us. "AJ." His voice broke just a little and my heart clenched. Ryler cleared his throat and continued. "I'm not perfect—I'm going to mess up. But I love you and promise to keep loving you, no matter what. I'll spend every day proving it. Just say you'll marry me." His hand trembled as he lifted his palm, where a beautiful, yet simple, solitaire teardrop diamond ring lay. "Marry me. Please."

My breath shuddered as I tried to master my emotions and it was difficult to form the words, to get them past the knot in my throat. "I love you! Yes, Ryler, I'll marry you."

The words had barely left my mouth and Ryler was on his feet. Then I was in his arms, and his mouth was on mine and the crowd erupted in cheers.

"Thank you, AJ." He growled against my neck. "You won't regret it."

"Never." Ryler slipped that ring on my finger, and I couldn't help but think just how worth it the last six months had been. I'd found family and had fallen in love. I stared at the ring for a moment, as a watery smile split my face. Never would I regret him. Never. This man, this warrior, this rebel, he was mine and I was his. And nothing and no one would ever come between us.

The End

Read on for a never seen before bonus chapter.

BONUS CHAPTER

Jake's Place

Ten Months Later

AJ

My eyes drifted over my sleeping husband. *Husband.* It still sent a thrill through me. Still made me giddy and I fell in love with him more and more each day. Last night, he'd loved me so thoroughly, so deeply...just the thought sent a warmth moving through me. Made my heart rate kick up. Waking beside him every morning was a blessing I hadn't known I'd needed. Lately, I'd found myself praying a lot more. Just thankful. So thankful for this life I was privileged to live. For this life I got to share with the man lying beside me.

Ryler was on his stomach, one arm thrown over me, holding me close. As if, even in sleep, he couldn't bear to part with me. It made my heart tremble, the amount of emotion it contained on his behalf.

We'd been home from our honeymoon for nearly two weeks now. As a surprise, he'd taken me to Hawaii; a place he'd been confident would provide enough sun, sand, ocean, and heat to last me through winter in the Pacific Northwest. Knowing his aversion to all those things, it had touched deeply that he'd done that. For me. Sometimes, I didn't know what to do with all the love he gave to me. To be loved so thoroughly and succinctly...my cup runneth over.

As I studied his sleeping form, my eyes mapping, enjoying every dip, valley, and plain of his physique, I thought back to our wedding day.

We should be getting at least some of the proofs any day now.

As a wedding gift, Leslie had arranged for a reputable photographer for our special day. In appreciation, I'd offered the photographer an exclusive on the event.

We'd kept it small and private. Just family and close friends. *Fox-Bell Weddings and Events* in Port Angeles had worked out beautifully for our needs.

I was dying to see those pictures.

Jo and Paige had purchased my wedding dress. I'd tried to talk them out of it, but they'd insisted. And there'd been no arguing with them. Leading up to the day, my heart had been a little tender, thinking of Jake. Of all that could have been. I was simply tender. And in lieu of my actual father walking me down the aisle, I'd asked both Chief and Dave to do the honors. Teary-eyed, they'd both agreed.

Of course, Harley had been my maid of honor and Poppy had been my only bridesmaid. For Ryler, he'd asked Chief to be his best man and Kevin was his only groomsman. With Chief pulling double duty in the ceremony, we'd made some adjustments. After Chief had escorted Harley to her position at the front, he'd walked back to Dave and me where we'd waited out of sight. Then, after Kevin and Poppy had made their way down to join Harley, with Dave to my right and Chief to my left, we'd walked down to meet my soon-to-be husband. At the pastor's query, Chief and Dave had both intoned their intent to give me away. Then Chief had kissed my cheek before moving to his position beside Kevin. Dave had done the same then took his seat beside my mother.

Yes, my mother. I still couldn't believe we were actually talking now. She'd called about seven months ago, having seen a news article in some magazine or other about my engagement. At first, I'd been prepared for the worst. But it had been the first conversation we'd had where she hadn't attempted to play the victim and place blame. We'd simply *talked*. She'd told me she didn't want to miss any more of my life and could we, please, start again? Hesitantly, I'd agreed. She'd wanted to know all about Ryler. Asked how my writing was going. If I still liked it here. To be honest, it had all been just a little disconcerting. I'd been afraid to hope and hesitant to read anything into it. But then, after that initial conversation, we got into the habit of talking about once a week or so. And soon, I'd been sharing my wedding plans with her. I don't know what happened exactly that caused her to make peace with her past, but I had found myself offering heartfelt appreciation to God. Thanking Him for whatever this was. Praying it continued and we never experienced another falling out.

And everything had worked out beautifully. I couldn't have imagined a more magical, emotional, and fulfilling moment in time as my wedding day.

And now, as Ryler and I lay in bed, Shiv snoring softly from the floor on Ryler's side, tears pricked my eyes as those overwhelmingly beautiful emotions once more overflowed. I blinked, then wiped my cheeks, trying not to shake the bed, not wanting to disturb my husband.

My husband, whose hand tightened on my hip.

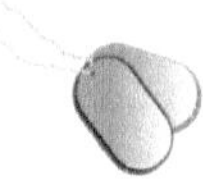

Ryler

Ryler smelled her first, that ever-present alluring scent that was all AJ. Coconut and Cream and *his*. Like a siren call it had pulled him from sleep. And though he'd thoroughly had her just hours before, he found he was in need again. He tightened his grip. His thumb made heavy, possessive strokes across her hip. Claiming that territory. Like a magnet pulled in her direction, he turned his face into her side, just above the curve of her hip and nuzzled. Did she have any idea what she did to him? Was she even remotely aware? His grip tightened even further, pulling her down beside him. Moving, he leaned up, kissing her belly, nipping at her. From there, he peeked up at her, letting his intent, his desire show through.

"Good morning, Wife." He didn't give her opportunity to reply. No, he pulled himself forward until his mouth found hers even as he settled over her. Even as he loved her completely once more.

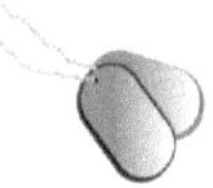

AJ

Some two hours later, wrapped in my 'The Mrs.' robe, I watched as my husband, wearing a matching set of pajama bottoms, with 'The Mr.' across his backside—a gift from Kevin and Harley—expertly flipped pancakes at the stove. I cradled my coffee and reflected that even though we'd literally *just,* I wouldn't be averse to going again. But then, Ryler did that to me. Throw in his mad kitchen skills and obscenely attractive maleness and it was a wonder we managed to dress ourselves at all.

He turned and caught me ogling him and I blushed under his regard. The corner of his mouth lifted. "Careful, Wife." He'd taken to calling me that rather than AJ now and I couldn't say I minded. That name caressed across my soul. I could listen to it on his mouth for eternity. "You keep looking at me like that and these pancakes will burn."

"It's a good thing we have more ingredients." I shrugged carefully.

Ryler moved from the stove, leaned down and gripped my chin, then kissed me most decisively. Kissed me until I was nearly begging for more. Then he kissed my nose and turned back to the stove. Moments later, he carried a plate of golden cakes to the table along with half a dozen sausage links. I could wait. I knew we'd get through breakfast and wash dishes later. Much later.

Ryler

"I've been thinking." Ryler said as he sipped his coffee.

"About?"

"The cabin." That's what they'd taken to calling his old place. They'd talked some over the last couple of months about what to do with their two houses. His cabin and Jake's house. Well, her house. *Their* house. But no decision had been made yet. With all the work Jake had done on this place, they definitely didn't want to sell it. There was too much of him in these walls. And they didn't want to sell the cabin either. They liked their privacy. But they also didn't want to let it fall into ruin. One idea had been to Airbnb it. But again, privacy.

Just before the wedding, Ryler'd boxed his stuff up and while they were gone, Chief and some of his boys had moved his stuff to AJ's place. They still had lots of unpacking to do and there were boxes everywhere. AJ hadn't even dealt with the stuff she'd left back in storage on Coronado yet. She'd mentioned thinking she might do something similar to what Mrs. Carson had done. Per her will, the older woman had liquidated everything, then split it between the nearest homeless shelter and animal shelter. Though, AJ had mentioned she'd been thinking of donating to a Veterans charity.

"I've been knocking this idea around for a while now." Ryler's gaze settled on his wife, hoping she'd be on board with his plan. It'd be a lot to take on, no doubt about that, but he felt in his gut, it was the right thing to do. "I think I want to turn it into a retreat...or rehab place for injured and traumatized Veterans."

AJ stared at Ryler, her eyes blinking. She took a shuddering breath then reached for his hand, lifting it to her mouth where she pressed a kiss to his knuckles. "I love you." She kissed him again. "So much."

He leaned forward, his hands cradling her face, pulling her closer, kissing her deeply. "And I you."

He tucked a strand of hair behind her ear, then she threaded their fingers together and whispered, "Tell me your ideas. How do you see this shaping up?"

"It'd have to be smaller." He rubbed at his chin with his free hand, then rapped a knuckle gently against the table. "Nothing big. The cabin isn't made for that. I could add on, or I suppose even build a second cabin there." Ryler stared in the distance, imagining all the possibilities. Both good and bad. "I'd need to talk with Chief, see if he has any knowledge about how to do something like this. Any connections. Maybe Kerry might know of any legal hoops we'd have to jump through." He lifted their enjoined hands and kissed her palm. He wasn't even aware he'd done it. He'd simply needed to kiss her. "Lots to consider, but one thing I do know. I know what I want to name it."

"Tell me."

Ryler felt his heart pound as he squeezed her hand. "Jake's Place." AJ was silent as tears filled her eyes, and spilled over, trailing down her cheeks. Ryler leaned forward and tenderly wiped those tears away. She wasn't sad. He could see that. Emotion has simply overwhelmed her. "If it wasn't for him," Ryler explained. "For his heart for *this* wounded Veteran...we wouldn't...*I* wouldn't be here. I want to carry that torch on. I want to encourage others like me who are struggling. I want them to know they're not alone."

AJ sat so still, he almost questioned if she was alright. Then suddenly she was moving, lunging forward, crawling into his lap and kissing him. From one heartbeat to the next, the flame between them had ignited once more and he was carrying her back upstairs.

AJ

My phone rang, Harley's ringtone sounding, pulling my thoughts from my husband and what he'd just done to me, what he'd just shared with me. The plans he had. My heart swelled with joy. With desire. Knowing he was healed enough, strong enough to contemplate helping others this way. How could I not love him? I had to swallow back my emotions as they threatened to boil over. But *man,* did I love him.

Ryler stood at the sink where he washed dishes from breakfast, insisting I sit and relax. Later, we intended to run to town for groceries at some point.

I answered Harley's call just before it went to voicemail. "Good morning, Mrs. Dean." Harley took pleasure in calling me that all the time now.

"Good morning." I chuckled as I put her on speakerphone.

"Morning, Harley!" Ryler called over his shoulder as he rinsed a plate.

"So...you two sound chipper." I inhaled to respond, but she cut me off. "I don't want to know."

I snorted as Ryler tossed me a heated look full of innuendo. "Then don't comment."

Harley's deep, throaty chuckle sounded now. "I actually have a reason for this call."

"Oh yeah, what's up? You guys finally set a date?" They'd had three so far.

"Yes, actually. Please, if you two wouldn't mind, and if you can pull yourselves out of the bedroom, mark your calendars for December 1st."

"Who says we need a bedroom!" Ryler hollered.

I shook my head and grinned. "December 1st? As in like two and a half months away?"

"Ew, Rye. And yes, AJ."

I chuckled. "For real this time?"

"One hundred percent positive."

"Okay, I'm marking it down." I put the date in my calendar.

"One more thing. Well, two more things. First, you and your hubs are our only attendants. Congratulations."

I chuckled again. "Thanks."

"Second, drum roll, please...we're moving. To. Sequim!"

I couldn't have heard her right. "Say that again."

"You heard me the first time. I'm going to need you guys to take us house shopping or find me a good realtor. Because we. Are moving. There!"

Once I'd stopped giddily screaming and dancing around the kitchen, Harley and I hung up and Ryler pulled me into his arms. How was this my life now? Married to the man of my dreams. Living out my dream vocation. Residing in this beautiful house in this beautiful location. Having the family I had here. And now, I got to have my best friend here, too.

I couldn't have written a better outcome. Again, I was struck at how my cup was quite literally running over. Everything was working out. No doubt, we'd face challenges. Especially as we tried to get Jake's Place up and going, but with Ryler at my side, and God at the helm, I knew we'd make it and nothing could stop us.

Nine Months Later

Ryler

With local camera crews present and at the ready and far more attention than Ryler was comfortable with, he pressed firmly on the step and dug the shovel blade into the soil. Cheers went up all around and AJ threw her arms around him, settling him. Jake's Place was officially in business. Well, Ryler reflected, they'd actually received their licensing last month, so he guessed that was their official start. But this groundbreaking was sure a great feeling.

After AJ and Ryler had spoken with Chief and Kerry, they'd had a crap ton of legal hoops to jump through. But eventually, they'd been approved for a second cabin and had even aligned with a couple licensed counselors. Ryler, AJ, Chief and some of his boys had all willingly gone through background checks, so they were now all approved staff for the facility. They'd even managed to acquire approval for medical and physical therapy services through the local hospital. With Chief and Kerry both deciding to partner with Jake's Place, and with the large, anonymous donations marked specifically for service dogs they'd received, everything was coming together. Ryler still choked up over that donation. Knowing the help those service dogs would be for these men and women.

The cabin was scheduled for completion by the end of August, with the first guests arriving shortly after. No more than four at a time. Two per cabin. An addition would be added, connecting the two cabins, for staff housing. Jake's Place would be a true refuge. A quiet place for those wounded souls to heal and reenter civilian life. To learn how to live and breathe again. To make decisions and face life as solitary men and women as opposed to being a cog in the well-greased military-life wheel.

With eyes and heart and mind wide open, Ryler embraced this gift that was his life now. Fervently thankful for it. For the beautiful, strong, and brave woman at his side who saw his scars and loved him anyway, loved him as the man he was. Ryler cleared his throat as he swallowed back his emotion, then leaned down to kiss his wife.

The End

Dear Reader, please, if you wouldn't mind, leave a review. Reviews are life to an author. Thank you.

Acknowledgements

I may be the one who sits and writes and sweats and bleeds these words, but I couldn't do it without a number of people.

First, to the Reader. Thank you. Thank you for giving my work a chance, for giving me a chance, for reviewing this book, for telling others about it. Truly, I appreciate you and you make this possible. You make it viable. You give me a reason to continue, so sincerely, from the bottom of my heart, thank you.

To my Beta Readers: Dawn, Morgan, Amanda, Mary, and Cortney. For being willing to read and share your thoughts. For helping me to shape this story and finding the spots that needed filling in. Ladies, I THANK YOU. Hero status right there.

To Kristin Vayden. Every time. Every time you see what I'm trying so desperately to say in my words. Thank you for helping me to shape and mold this story, to make it the best it can be. Thank you for your friendship, advice, and guidance. You make me a better writer. Also, Sammy, Dean, and Cas say hello.

To Jena Brignola. Yet again, you have done an amazing job at creating a cover image that speaks of this book, its tone, and its characters. It's absolutely beautiful and I love it. THANK YOU.

To my family. Thank you for allowing me time to write and for cheering me on. Your encouragement means the world to me. Especially to my husband, lover, and best friend, William, thank you for being my lifelong MMC.

Finally, to my Lord and Savior, Jesus Christ. I am truly nothing without You. Thank You, Lord, for loving me, forgiving me, guiding me, and for providing me with the capability to write these stories. Amen.

About the Author

A child of divorce and abuse, E. L. Irwin found escape in reading and writing. She's a self-described romantic-rebel who wears her heart on her sleeve and tends to shoot from the hip on subjects that matter. E.L. lives in the Pacific Northwest on a small farm with her husband, children, and four dogs. When not reading or writing romance, E.L. enjoys riding horses, going for drives, tattoos, antique shopping, starry nights, the smell and sound of rain, a deep red wine, a smooth whisk(e)y, camping, bonfires, and hanging out with her horses, cows, chickens,ducks, and goats.

Author Note

Well, if you've made it this far, you're truly dedicated and I appreciate that. I wanted to discuss a couple things.

First, Wade Irwin, mentioned in this book, is my brother-in-law. My husband's youngest brother. What was mentioned regarding him and his partner, was done so with Wade's permission because it was a true accounting. That really happened. Our LEOs face often-impossible split-second decisions with incredible courage. I will never forget that phone call for as long as I live.

Second, PTSD is real and nothing to be ashamed of. It is a part of healing. Healing isn't just physical. It's mental, psychological, and emotional, too. Let me say that again. PTSD IS A PART OF HEALING. If you or a loved one is struggling with it, please, *please,* seek help. Help does NOT make you weak. Help gives you the weapons to win this fight. Help lets you know that you are not alone. And you are NOT a mistake. There is purpose for your life. Trust me.

Here are some listed resources: Tunnels to Towers, Warriors and Quiet Waters, and The Gary Sinise Foundation.

Read on for Newsletter signup.

NEWSLETTER SIGNUP HERE: Scan the code and sign up for my newsletter to receive firsthand knowledge of upcoming projects, release news, and giveaways. When you sign up, you'll receive the prequel chapters for Out of the Blue, book 1 in the Blues Avenue series.

www.ingramcontent.com/pod-product-compliance
Lightning Source LLC
Chambersburg PA
CBHW061416160726
47995CB00003B/628